Critical Praise for Corporate Thrillers by Brian Lutterman

Downfall

"Downfall is an exhilarating, action-packed financial thriller . . ."
— *Harriet Klausner, Mystery Gazette*

". . . a fantastic read . . . an entertaining and engrossing book."
— *Charline Ratcliff Reviews*

"*Downfall* is a very intense thriller. Once I started reading, I couldn't put it down."
— *Mystery Sequels*

"*Downfall* by Brian Lutterman is a well-constructed thriller . . . an excellent read."
— *Larry Krantz, Readers' Favorite Reviews*

". . . replete with suspense made even more dramatic by the protagonist being confined to a wheelchair."
— *John A. Broussard, I Love a Mystery*

Bound to Die

Minnesota Book Award Runner-Up

"...a taut, swift-paced and well-plotted debut thriller by a Minnesota author."
— *St. Paul Pioneer Press*

"...a gripping, twisted, lethal saga, and one that quickly captures the reader's total attention and won't let go until the shocking climax..."
— *Midwest Book Review*

"An inexplicable quadruple murder, a duplicitous presidential adviser and a mysterious and deadly cult called the Bound bear mysterious connections to each other in lawyer Brian Lutterman's debut mystery, *Bound to Die*. Widow Tori McMillan wanders jungles, mountains and the nation's capital as she tries to find her best friend and a group of missing children, as well as to determine what actually happened to her husband."
—*Publishers Weekly*

"...bound to entertain...gets your interest from the get-go."
—Kristofer Upjohn, *Pine Bluff Commercial*

"With the help of an infatuated police officer and the hindrance of an FBI agent, Tori finds herself traveling from the Yucatan jungle into the mountains of Denver to the steps of the White House. Before it is over, Tori will question all that she believes to be good. Tori also puts her life on the line in order to solve the mystery that now threatens her sanity."
—Susan Johnson, *All About Murder*

Poised to Kill

"Author Brian Lutterman has proven himself to be a master storyteller in this masterfully woven tale of tycoons and terrorists. *Poised to Kill* is highly recommended reading, especially for enthusiasts of contemporary action/adventure thrillers."
—*Midwest Book Review*

"Lutterman keeps his readers on the edge of their chairs until the last page. The twists, chases, and shootings by professional terrorists keep occurring with increasing tension. Written in the first person, Lutterman draws his readers into the thriller. Lutterman is the author of **BOUND TO DIE**, another taut, top quality thriller. This is a suspenseful, must read book."

—Marion Cason, *I Love a Mystery*

"...a good, enjoyable read, with satisfying links to today's society. Lutterman should garner wide audiences for this story, and for those to come."

—Carl Brookins, *Reviewing the Evidence*

"Lawyer and author Brian P. Lutterman's latest novel, *Poised to Kill*, is an action-packed suspense thriller that's just simply enjoyable. Lutterman, who packed a punch with his debut novel, *Bound to Die*, proves that he is not just a flash in the pan or a one-book wonder with *Poised to Kill*... Highly recommended."

—*New Mystery Reader Review*

"...tightly plotted and has a fascinating take on an interesting scenario."

—*Books 'n' Bytes*

"Layers of betrayal is the name of the game in *Poised to Kill*. The plot ventures cross country and back around many twists and turns to uncover who might be behind the plan to cripple a nation, a major company, and ruin one man's life. *Poised to Kill* is very intriguing and full of unlikely suspects. It will keep you turning the pages and digging to find out which betrayal is the root, or are they all just pieces of one big plan."

—Joy Spear, *Murder and Mayhem Book Club*

Windfall

Brian Lutterman

Conquill Press

DOWNFALL

Cover Design: Rebecca Treadway

Library of Congress Control Number: 2015944628

Lutterman, Brian

Windfall: a novel / by Brian Lutterman – 1st edition

ISBN: 978-0-9908461-3-0

Conquill Press/September 2015

Printed in the United States of America

10 9 8 7 6 5 4 3 2 1

For Angela Schneeman, John Lutterman, and Kara Pratt.

The sibs behind the stories—and so much more.

Also by Brian Lutterman

Downfall

Bound to Die

Poised to Kill

Acknowledgments

The author gratefully acknowledges the assistance of Shawn Dean, President of the Minnesota Spinal Cord Injury Association, and Lizabeth A. Rhodes, assistant US attorney for the Central District of California, for their help in researching this book. Any errors contained herein are mine, not theirs. And, a special thanks to Christopher Valen and Jenifer LeClair, the founders of Conquill Press, for making the publication of this book possible.

Chapter 1

An hour had passed before she was able to flee the house. At least that's how long it seemed; she actually wasn't sure how much time had elapsed. In some ways it seemed like mere minutes; in other ways it seemed as though the terror had always been with her, that she'd had no life before it. That the man she fled from had long since left her house was utterly beside the point.

On the plus side, she hadn't yet committed suicide. That seemed the man's major concern; he had watched her for nearly an hour before leaving. The urge will subside, he'd said, even though that was hard to imagine now.

Subside, he'd added, but not disappear.

She'd avoided the mirror while hunting for her clothing, stopping to feel her hands, her face, her body. Yes, she was still here.

And it *had* really happened.

He'd talked a lot, probably just to fill the time. He'd told her his name, Terrence, which he said was his actual given name. He had been solicitous—apologetic even, assuring her that the ordeal was necessary and was not about her. He had said she'd be able to function again in a couple of days.

It had taken her forever to get dressed in the dim light; why hadn't she turned the damn lights on? He had removed her clothing—for her comfort, he'd said. She finally located her clothes, and with a supreme effort of concentration, hindered by jerky, uncoordinated motions as well as the sheer terror, she managed to get them on.

He'd apparently been serious when he had warned her against fleeing. "You won't be in much shape to drive," he'd said. And then he'd added, in the most accurate statement he had made during their time together: "You won't be able to run from this experience."

But she also could not have stopped herself from running.

She staggered out the door to the garage, got into her vehicle, and after several tries was able to start the engine. She took deep breaths, forcing herself to concentrate as she backed the car down the driveway. Then she shifted to drive and moved forward. Abruptly, waves of terror returned, and she floored the accelerator. The car careened wildly down the street, striking at least two other vehicles. But she pressed on, despite having no destination.

She stopped the car at an intersection after a while—perhaps ten minutes. She sat for several more minutes, taking big, heaving breaths, managing to calm herself down. Then she fumbled in her purse, managing to extract her phone and punch in a speed dial number.

"Yes?"

"It's me. I—I . . ."

"What's wrong?"

"A man. He—oh, God."

"What happened, for heaven's sake?"

"I—I can't . . ."

"Is he gone?"

"Yes."

"Did you call the police?"

"No! I can't!"

"I'll be right over."

"I'm not at home." She looked up at the street signs and read off the names.

"Don't move. I'll be right there. We'll get your car back home, and then you can tell me what happened, and we'll get you to a hospital, or—"

"No! I need to hide."

A pause. "Just hold on. I'll be right there."

She waited, looking out the car windows. The roads were nearly deserted, and she realized that it must be late—past midnight. She might live until help arrived, or even longer. But for her, it would always be the middle of the night.

Chapter 2

Monday, March 4
Los Angeles
Office of the US Attorney

I'm a lawyer, not an astronaut. But, like the spaceman who had to advise a large Texas city of a little problem, I was about to declare an in-flight emergency. Our mission at the US attorney's office—putting a crooked congressman in jail—was a tough one to begin with, in some ways facing longer odds than a moon landing. And failure, unfortunately, was definitely an option, especially if I didn't locate my star witness, and fast.

I hollered over to Cassandra, our section's intern, whose cubicle was across the corridor and slightly down from my open office door. "Anything on Lisa?"

"Nothing," she called back.

"She should be here in this office right now, working with us," I said. "What about the airline and the hotel?" We'd arranged for Lisa Darden to be put up at a downtown hotel for the entire week, which we planned to spend with her, preparing the case.

"She wasn't on the flight last night and never showed up at the hotel," Cassandra said.

I needed more detail than that. But unfortunately, that necessitated a trip to the Ice Box, otherwise known as Cassandra's cubicle. I could have asked her to come down to my office, of course, but that would have created an additional grievance for the Ice Box's occupant, who seemed to have a lot of them already. And Cassandra, being seven months' pregnant, wasn't much more mobile than I was at the moment. I backed my wheelchair away from my desk, rolled out the door, and proceeded down the aisle.

Cassandra Freeman was a graduate of the top-notch Boalt Hall law school at U-Cal-Berkeley and a licensed attorney. But thanks to the dismal job market for attorneys, she was working as an underpaid intern, hoping the gig might turn into a permanent position. She was a striking black woman, nearly six feet tall. I am actually six feet tall myself, though few people realize it. Now she sat awkwardly, her bulk preventing her from moving up close enough to her desk. Half a dozen bottles of vitamins and supplements sat in a neat line on the shelf above the desk, and classical music played softly from two speakers that had been aimed at her abdomen.

The drop in temperature as I rolled across the threshold was only imaginary, of course, but I shivered nonetheless. "Maybe you could expand a little bit on what you found out about Lisa," I said.

She gave me a look that reminded me of winter in Minnesota. "What is it you want to know?"

As usual, I was going to have to drag it out of her. "Maybe who you've checked with, and what their responses were."

She managed to avoid rolling her eyes, although she clearly disliked being questioned or ordered around by me. She seemed resentful about a lot of things, but I, for reasons unknown, appeared to be the resentee-in-chief.

She picked up a notepad and read from it. "I checked with Lisa's sister, her mother, and her boyfriend." She looked up. "Do you want to know their names?"

"How about the Minneapolis police?"

"They won't help, Pen."

"Why not?"

She ticked off the reasons. "Lisa Darden is an adult—twenty-eight. She's only been out of touch for a couple of days. No sign of foul play. No report filed by the parents, sister, or boyfriend. The Minneapolis police won't even take a missing person's report unless the person is considered a vulnerable adult or a danger to herself or others."

We needed to connect with Lisa today. We had only a week left until a critical status hearing before the cranky Judge Raymond T. Cooley, who inspired as much fear in unprepared prosecutors as he did in guilty defendants. "Adam is going to be pissed," I said. "Where is Adam, anyway?"

"I haven't seen him." Cassandra shrugged. That was one of the few advantages of being an underpaid, overqualified intern —it wasn't her problem.

"Try the police again," I said. "We're not just Joe Blow coming in off the street with a missing relative. We're fellow law enforcers, looking for cooperation."

I rolled over to the office of Adam Rosenthal, chief of the Public Corruption and Civil Rights section of the US attorney's office. I'd joined Adam's staff after half a year apprenticing in General Crimes. Adam was my boss, but we were close in age and worked well together. I looked forward to trying the upcoming case with him.

Adam's door was closed and the lights were off. I rolled back to my office and called his cell. No answer. I checked with reception. He hadn't checked in today.

Frustrated, I called John Gibson, the FBI agent we were working most closely with in the investigation and prosecution of Congressman Latham Shields.

"John, it's Pen Wilkinson."

"Yes?" Gibson, a former military lawyer, wasn't big on pleasantries. I had a feeling he also wasn't big on female prosecutors. Or maybe he just wasn't big on me.

"We've got a problem, John. Lisa Darden has sort of disappeared on us." I explained.

"Okay," he said when I finished. "And?"

"And, I was wondering if you could put out a trace on her," I said. "You know, check her cell phone records, or maybe light a fire under the police in Minnesota."

"Do you have any evidence of a threat to her well-being?"

"Other than what I've told you, no."

"Let's take it from the top." I ran down Lisa's flights and hotel, and the efforts we'd made to locate her.

"I'll see what I can do—maybe get back to you in a day or two."

"We've got a time problem, John. There's that status hearing a week from today. We need to be ready."

"I'll do what I can," he repeated.

"Thanks."

I hung up, wondering what it might have taken for Gibson to show some actual urgency. He wasn't, I reflected, the one who had to go unprepared before Judge Cooley.

I picked up the phone and checked again—still no Adam. I tried Lisa Darden's home and cell phones again, leaving more messages. I checked the hotel again. She hadn't checked in.

I pondered my next move. I didn't want to overreact or to appear panicky or not in control. On the other hand, the stakes were high. Congressman Latham "Larry" Shields had been indicted on charges of taking bribes from defense contractor Pacific Technology Group. The indictment alleged that PTG had funneled the money to Shields by paying a contractor who had done extensive work on Shields's vacation home on Lake Arrowhead. The value of the work was, we had calculated, nearly half a million dollars. In return, Shields had used his influence to help PTG secure a major Navy contract for completely overhauling and upgrading the electronics on a fleet of fighter planes. The FBI had received an anonymous tip about the corrupt transaction, which later turned out to have come from Lisa Darden, a young member of the congressman's staff in Washington.

The case, far from being a slam-dunk, was complicated by several factors. First, there was no smoking gun. The evidence of financial chicanery, using a building contractor as an intermediary, was complicated and circumstantial. Second, Lisa Darden's testimony was hearsay. She had no direct knowledge of the transaction; the congressman, in an unguarded, alcohol-fueled moment, had boasted of having been paid well for good work and invited her to visit him at his newly-renovated vacation home when it was completed. Finally, there was political awkwardness. The current US attorney, Dave O'Shea, was a member of the same party as Shields, but O'Shea and his superiors in Washington obviously felt they had no choice but to go ahead and prosecute Shields anyway. Shields and two co-defendants from PTG had proclaimed their innocence and defended the case vigorously.

I leaned back in my wheelchair and exhaled. Lisa Darden was not just our star witness; she was *the* witness. I picked up the phone and called Adam's boss.

Chapter 3

Rick Stouffer was not a loser, and he'd be damned if he would be treated like one. That's what Windfall was all about, really. Strolling off the golf course with two companions, he allowed himself to gloat a little. He'd beaten both of his friends handily, and he felt good about himself. Of course, his fellow players had made excuses, lamenting that they just couldn't find time to get out onto the course anymore. That was one of the attitudes separating Stouffer from the losers: he valued his own time. He valued himself. He valued feeling good about himself.

Stouffer was a senior vice president and felt good about that. He had a new wife who was thirty-two and had done some modeling. He lived in an oceanfront house in San Clemente. He worked with a trainer and a nutritionist—looked and felt great. But unfortunately, when you were one of life's winners, the losers were always resentful, always scheming to take you down. Winners never let that happen.

His cell phone buzzed in his pocket. He was about to let the call go to voicemail but realized that it might be about Windfall.

He recognized the number, excused himself, and walked away from the group to take the call. "Yes?"

"We're on track," the voice said without preamble. "She's been neutralized."

Stouffer allowed himself a small smile. He assumed that "neutralized" meant intimidated or bought off, but he wasn't sure and didn't really want to know. "Excellent," he said. "We also need her out of sight, at least until Windfall, or our partners won't cooperate."

"Shouldn't be a problem," said the man named Terrence. "The Treatment always works."

Stouffer frowned. "What if they try to proceed with the trial anyway, even if their witness isn't cooperating?"

"I'm told that's not feasible."

"But what if—"

"Look, you hired me to neutralize the witness and the prosecutor. Are you saying more is needed?"

"What you've done should be enough. If it isn't, we may need you to do more."

"That's not something we discussed," Terrence said.

"We may need to discuss it. Stand by."

"All right."

"And for God's sake, be subtle," Stouffer said. "We're taking enough risk already."

"Subtle is a high priority," Terrence assured him. Then he added: "Effective is higher."

Chapter 4

"Connie got your message and wants to see you," Cassandra told me as I rolled by her desk on the way to my office. "And no, I haven't found Lisa or heard from Adam."

Damn, I thought. Now I had to go alone to see my boss's boss with really bad news. I was getting seriously pissed at Adam; he'd picked a hell of a time to vanish.

I approached the office of Consuela Reyes Harper, chief of the Criminal Division of the US attorney's office, wondering how to break the news. Her first question would be one I couldn't answer: Where the hell was Adam?

Connie's assistant told me to wait in the outer office. I took deep breaths. Had I acted rashly in calling Connie? And if they asked me what to do, I would have to confess I didn't have a clue.

"Pen?"

I turned to see Connie's deputy, Vikram Tandon. Vik was a heavyset, smiling, reassuring presence. Everything, in other words, that Connie was not. He served as a necessary buffer between Connie and the rest of the office—maybe the rest of the world.

"Your message got our attention," he said.

The implication wasn't hard to discern: This had better be important. Vik walked with me into Connie's inner sanctum.

I doubted that too many people ever bothered Connie with trivial things, or stopped by her office to shoot the breeze. She was in her mid-forties, short, bronze-skinned, with expensive clothing and hairstyle. She was an intense, demanding workaholic who got up at 4:30 a.m. and put in a punishing hour in the gym before work. She was divorced with a teenaged son and had a long-suffering sort-of boyfriend whom she seldom actually saw. Her predecessor, Amy Connelly, had hired me, and Connie took me aside shortly after Amy had left for private practice. "I didn't approve of your hiring," she'd said. "You didn't come up through normal channels and pay your dues like everyone else here."

I had practiced law for seven years before becoming a prosecutor, and I thought I was doing a damned good job and had paid plenty of dues, but I didn't say anything.

"Obviously Amy saw something in you," she continued. "I will expect to see it, too."

After six months, I still wasn't sure what she was looking for, or if she saw it. I had asked Adam once where I stood with her, and he'd given me a thoughtful look. "I think she likes you," he said. "You're a good attorney, of course, and you're serious and professional. She appreciates all that, I'm sure. But you dress as well as she does, and she might have a problem with that." It was true that I spent too much money on clothes and took my appearance and image seriously. But I suspected that now, I might have a slightly bigger problem with her than that.

Connie looked up from her stand-up desk. A sit-down desk stood in the corner, but no one had ever seen her use it. Two visitors' chairs faced her, but both invariably held stacks of files, which forced visitors to stand before her like supplicants. That didn't apply to me, of course, but I figured that at least it made for short meetings.

Connie studied me, as if grudgingly forced to acknowledge my existence. "Got your message. How did you lose her?"

"She lost herself, Connie. I had everything set up for her to come down yesterday, and she confirmed it on Friday. She didn't show up."

Her look told me she wasn't buying it. "What are you doing to re-establish contact?"

I quickly ran down my efforts to track down Lisa Darden. "Gibson agreed to help, but it doesn't seem to be a priority for him," I concluded.

I expected her to pick up the phone and tell Gibson or his boss to get off their fat butts and get out there and find Lisa, pronto. Instead, I saw a momentary flash of doubt cross her face. "Fine, get the Bureau to help," she said. "But it's your responsibility to find her."

I said, "Look, if Adam could call her—"

"Adam quit."

For the second time in an hour, I found myself speechless.

"Last Friday, effective immediately," she said. "Via a faxed resignation letter."

"Holy—"

"Yes, it sucks, but we don't have time to stew about it. Right now, we have a trial to prepare for."

"Who's in charge of the case?" I asked.

"As of now, you're the only attorney up to speed on the case. Just run with it."

I sat back in my chair, flabbergasted. The idea of my handling a case of this magnitude, with this level of responsibility and public scrutiny—even temporarily—was unimaginable.

Vik spoke for the first time. "We're assigning Kathy to work with you for now." Kathy North was the second most junior attorney in the section. "We'll have to assign a senior attorney to take charge of the case soon," he said, "but we haven't had a chance to think about it."

"We'll need a trial postponement," I said, thinking fast. The trial date was now only three weeks away.

"File the motion immediately," Connie said. "The judge will bitch and moan, but with Adam's departure, we have a valid reason. He'll give us a new date at the status hearing on Monday."

"The defendants might jump on it," Vik warned.

"Yes, they might," I agreed. Congressman Shields and his co-defendants, who had tried to delay the proceedings as long as possible, might now reverse course and demand a speedy trial, hoping to take advantage of our disarray. And it went without saying that the Honorable Raymond T. Cooley would tear me a new one for screwing up his trial calendar.

"I'll talk to Dave," Connie said, referring to Dave O'Shea, the US attorney. "I'll tell him we plan to establish contact with Lisa Darden and have her fully back on board by the time of the hearing on Monday. Without fail."

No pressure, I thought.

Connie looked at me as if daring me to say anything more. I had a dozen questions but figured I'd better just go back and get at it. I wheeled out into the hallway, where Vik caught up with me, motioning me into his own office.

Vik's office was cluttered, the walls covered with photos of, and artwork produced by, his three young children. Behind his desk was a picture of Vik and his wife on their honeymoon in India, where their parents had been born. "Sorry to dump this on you," he said, sitting down heavily behind his desk.

"What on earth happened with Adam?"

"We're not sure. His letter said a great opportunity in private practice had just come up, but they wanted him right away, and how sorry he was, blah, blah, blah."

"So he took another job," I said. "He didn't quit to start campaigning?"

"Apparently not." Adam had a longstanding interest in politics and had his eye on a state assembly seat, but as a career employee of the Justice Department, he was prohibited from engaging in most political activities. He would have made a great politician.

"Will he at least be available for questions or consulting over the next few weeks?" I asked.

14

"I don't know." He toyed with a pencil. "What's your gut feeling about Lisa, Pen? Do you think this is just a case of her getting cold feet, or something more serious?"

"I can't answer that," I said. "Not without communicating with her."

Suddenly he looked at me, as if just remembering something. "You're from Minnesota, right?"

I had blonde hair and looked the part, I supposed. But I'd grown up in Florida, and my accent definitely wasn't Midwestern. "No, I just worked there, for less than a year."

Vik nodded but still looked a little curious. "We'll just have to see what the FBI comes up with."

I was starting to feel something akin to panic. It looked as if our meeting was winding down, and I was basically on my own. I said, "If we're going to impress the defense and the media of our seriousness, don't you think it might be a good idea to announce the assignment of a senior attorney to lead the case?"

He rubbed his eyes. "We're considering our options. We don't have any great ones right now."

Chapter 5

I sat at my desk in late afternoon and worked the phones, trying to connect with Lisa Darden. I had never actually met her—Adam had done the bulk of the work with her to date—but if she was a normal human being, she might well have had entirely rational second thoughts about testifying. She was about to implicate a powerful congressman and his equally formidable military and corporate allies. She would be put through hell on the stand; the defendants had undoubtedly investigated every detail of her background—who knew what skeletons they had unearthed?

Once again, I tried Lisa's sister, Stacy Ellis, who lived a few miles from Lisa in the Minneapolis area. No answer. I talked to Lisa's boyfriend, Nathan, who worked for a Senate committee in Washington, DC. He told me he hadn't heard from her and had been communicating with her less often since she resigned from Shields's staff and moved back to Minnesota several months ago. She hadn't mentioned any second thoughts about testifying, he said. I got him to send links for her Facebook and Twitter accounts to Cassandra. I called Lisa's parents, who now lived in Salt Lake City. They hadn't heard from her recently and lamented that she didn't call them nearly often enough.

I had Cassandra locate the neighbors on either side of Lisa's rented house in Minneapolis. She got hold of one of them, who had not seen any sign of Lisa for several days. I sat back in my chair and sighed in exasperation. I was nearing the end of what could be done over the phone, half a continent away. There was no employer to call; Lisa had decided not to look for a job until the Shields case was over.

My phone rang. I checked the number and rolled my eyes. I reached for the phone, then drew back. I knew I shouldn't take the call.

The phone rang again. I reached over to answer it. But . . . I picked up the call, knowing I would regret it. "What is it, Milt?"

"Hey, Pen. Rough day?" Milt Hammer's job title was assistant general counsel of Pacific Technology Group, the company charged with bribing Congressman Shields. He apparently did have a law degree, but in reality he was a fixer and sometimes bag man for his company's CEO, Wilson Lopez. Hammer and Lopez had both been present at the meeting in a Los Angeles hotel where Congressman Shields had agreed to take their money to get PTG a Pentagon contract.

"Milt, you know I'm not supposed to talk to you." It was bad form to talk directly to a defendant who was represented by counsel. Defendants were supposed to communicate through their attorneys, a fact I had reminded Hammer of when he'd called me on two other occasions to chat me up about the case. But Hammer was a lawyer himself, so he couldn't claim I was taking advantage of him. I had dutifully mentioned the calls to his attorney, who had thrown up his hands and told me not to worry about it. Milt was going to do whatever the hell he wanted. Even so, I had tried to end the calls as quickly as possible and carefully written up a memo summarizing each conversation, as I would for this one.

"But it's such an interesting day," Hammer persisted with his usual genial enthusiasm. "What's the story on Adam?"

"He quit," I said.

"And now you're in charge?"

"Just temporarily."

"I doubt that," he said. "They've found their attorney, Pen, and it's you."

For a fleeting moment I wondered whether Hammer might know something I didn't, but I just as quickly concluded that his observation was simply BS.

"So, is the trial going ahead?" he asked.

"Nice try, but yes, it's going ahead."

"On time?"

"Maybe not," I conceded.

"So we can expect a motion soon?"

"Talk to your lawyer about it."

"You know the defendants will be opposing that vigorously. We're entitled to a speedy trial."

"Which is why you've delayed the case at every juncture until now? We'll get the continuance."

"Grumpy today, Pen. Are we having witness problems?"

Now I was on full alert. Had he or his co-defendants been in touch with Lisa? "What are you talking about?" I demanded.

"Well, it might be understandable if Ms. Darden had some hesitation in going forward, especially as her testimony will be a cock-and-bull story."

"Milt, if you or anybody on the defense side has tampered with this witness, there's going to be trouble."

He chuckled. "Touchy, touchy. Yes, I'd say we're definitely having witness problems. Having said that, I categorically deny having communicated, directly or indirectly, with Ms. Darden." He shifted to a more serious tone. "Give it up, Pen. This trial isn't going to happen."

"Wishful thinking."

"You have a bright future. Don't hitch your wagon to this loser of a case."

"Goodbye, Milt." I slammed the phone down, knowing I would now have to make a memo of this conversation to cover myself. As usual, Hammer had pushed all of my buttons. Today, everybody had.

Chapter 6

Fog and light mist gradually shrouded the lights that twinkled across Newport Harbor as James Carter and I sat out on the deck of his boat, the *Alicia C.*, docked at a small marina on Bayside Drive. I sipped from a glass of white wine while James, a tall black man dressed in a windbreaker and jeans, nursed a Diet Coke. James exuded confidence and, as always, looked as if he'd stepped out of some magazine featuring ads with beautiful people and expensive cars and watches. At his last company he'd been nicknamed Dandy Jim.

"I shouldn't be here," I said. "I should be working."

James shook his head. "You need down time. You'll feel better and work more efficiently. Pulling all-nighters doesn't work."

"Come on, James. It's easy for you to say now that you run your own shop. When you ran big banks you were the worst workaholic."

"And it trashed my marriage, made me a lousy father, and generally magnified all my asshole tendencies."

"So how did you become the sensitive, introspective pussycat you are today?"

He smiled. "You know how."

I returned the smile. James was generous in attributing all kinds of positive things to my influence since we'd begun dating a little more than a year ago. Maybe he was partly right. But the James Carter I'd first met, the powerful, confident CEO of a large Minnesota bank holding company, would never have given a second look at a paraplegic woman eight years his junior. Adversity, in the form of a scandal manufactured by corporate saboteurs, had forced him to reach out for help to a junior attorney—me—who was likewise ostracized and fired. In a larger sense, the scandal had caused him to reexamine his assumptions, about people and life in general. He had been a hard-charging Type A in the corporate world. Now a gentler version of that former self, he ran his own venture capital firm, specializing in startups in the medical device industry.

When we met, James had been dating a woman closer to his own age—an elegant, accomplished corporate executive named Celia Sims. If James harbored any remorse over dropping her for me, he never showed it. In fact, he never gave me any reason to doubt him at all.

Despite that, we were proceeding cautiously. James had gone through a spectacularly unsuccessful marriage and probably wasn't eager to take the plunge again. For my part, I loved James, and I wasn't sure I would have made it through the last year without him. And yet, I also might not have made it without my stubborn independence. So I lived on my own, in a modest apartment in Long Beach, about halfway between his place in Laguna Beach and my office in downtown LA. And I pursued my fledgling career as a prosecutor, which now faced an uncertain future.

Over the last couple of months I'd begun to sense a bit of impatience on his part. I feared that I was taking my own caution too far, that I was holding back a part of myself, and that he knew it. But I couldn't seem to help it.

"Did you hear from Alicia today?" I asked, pulling my sweater more closely around my shoulders.

His face lit up. "Just a text. She scored ten points last night." James's thirteen-year-old daughter, Alicia, who lived with her mother and stepfather in Minnesota, was a mainstay of her middle-school basketball team. We talked for a while longer before picking up our earlier thread.

"Something is going on at work," I said. "Something weird."

James shrugged. "Your witness got cold feet. It must happen every once in a while."

"It's not just Lisa. Something is funny with Adam, Connie, and the FBI. Too many strange things happening all at once."

He considered it. "The thing with Adam does sound a little weird. You don't just up and quit like that, burning your bridges. Still, from what you've told me, he is ambitious. A politician."

"That's a contradiction," I pointed out. "Politicians don't burn their bridges. If he really wants that Assembly seat up in the Valley, he can't go around blowing people off, especially longtime employers."

"Maybe he's found new friends who are even more useful to him."

"Why can't he have both the old and the new?"

"Good question," James said. "Any chance he's just resigning to start his campaign?"

"Vik says not—he's already taken another job. And the election is nearly two years off, anyway."

"So, what's happening with Connie and the FBI?"

"It's nothing I can put my finger on. But Gibson didn't have any urgency about finding Lisa, and Connie didn't seem inclined to lean on him. On top of that, she knew about Adam's resignation on Friday and didn't tell me right away. I had to find out about it the hard way today."

James rotated the soda can in his hand. "Could this be political somehow?"

"I suppose—Shields is a congressman, and Dave O'Shea is a political appointee. But I don't pretend to understand all the political angles. And I don't see how people can vote for a sleaze like Shields."

James fell silent.

I looked over at him. "Don't tell me."

"Hey, I didn't know the guy was a crook," James protested.

21

I shouldn't have been surprised; James was more conservative than I and usually voted for Shields's party.

"Don't worry," he continued. "Voters will catch on. You
can't fool all the people all the time."

"But you can give it your best shot. And believe me, Larry
Shields isn't going quietly." I sipped from my glass. "Now I'm
afraid he's going to slip away."

"Don't let him. Look at all these strange developments as
an opportunity. Your big chance to step up to the plate."

"That's all I can do, I guess. But I still feel as though I'm a
pawn somehow. Bigger things are going on."

He stood up and wandered over next to me. "That's the
way of the world, Pen. Bigger things are always going on. We
need to just roll with the punches." He leaned down, kissed me,
and smiled. "But that's never been your way, has it?"

"Or yours," I retorted.

He stared out over the harbor, hands in his pockets, and
chuckled. "Yeah, I'm still a contrary SOB."

We finished our drinks. The barely-perceptible mist had
changed into a drizzle, and the fog was thick. I said I had to get
going, and James helped me into the sling chair attached to the
hoist he'd installed on the dock to lift me on and off the boat.
After I swung over to the dock, he lifted my wheelchair over
and helped me back into it. He walked me out to the parking
lot, where I pulled out my key ring and extended the ramp to
my hand-controlled van. After rolling on and locking my chair
into place in front of the steering wheel, I leaned through the
window and kissed him.

"'Night, James."

"Hang in there."

Chapter 7

I was in the office early, resuming the search for Lisa Darden. When I'd gotten home last night, I had once again tried Lisa, her sister Stacy, and Adam, getting voicemails each time. I'd checked again with Lisa's neighbors and put in a message to her parents. Sitting at my desk, I repeated all the calls with a similar lack of response.

I hung up and sat for a long moment, looking at my screen, ready to explode with frustration. What the *hell* was going on? Sometime, some way, before the case was tried or after it was over, I was going to get some damn answers.

After a quick cup of coffee, I pulled out my legal pad and began making notes on the steps that would be needed to prepare for the case. On a separate sheet, I made notes on what would have to be done to keep my other cases current, and on which of those items could be delegated to Cassandra or to Kathy North, the new attorney assigned to help me. I tried to delegate as much as possible; like all assistant US attorneys, I had a heavy caseload. I couldn't just drop everything to find Lisa Darden. I had to keep the balls in the air.

In making my to-do list, I was assuming there would be a trial, that we'd have a relatively short time to prepare for it, and that without Adam, it would be up to me to keep things going until a new lead attorney was assigned. A lot of time would have to be spent with the FBI forensic accountants, who would unravel Congressman Shields's finances and the funds that had been paid to the contractors working on his vacation home. There would be hundreds, if not thousands, of pages of exhibits to authenticate and explain to the jury. Other witnesses from the Department of the Navy and Capitol Hill would testify to the influence used by Shields on behalf of PTG, which had been awarded a massive $2.5 billion contract to retrofit all the electronics on the Navy's fleet of fighter planes. Then we would introduce surveillance footage to show that Shields and PTG, represented by Assistant General Counsel Milt Hammer and CEO Wilson Lopez, had arrived in close time proximity at a downtown hotel, suggesting a clandestine meeting. Finally, Darden would testify that after the meeting, Shields had boasted of receiving a large commitment of money from PTG in exchange for using his influence.

My phone buzzed. It was Lana, the receptionist. "You have visitors, Pen. Police officers."

I was puzzled; I couldn't think of a current case where I was working with a local police department. And no one had called to set up a meeting. "I'll be right over," I said.

When I rolled down to reception, two detectives, an older, distinguished-looking man and a younger woman, waited for me. The man stepped forward, and I rolled toward him, my hand extended. He responded not with a hand but with his badge, introducing himself as Lieutenant Dan Howard of the Newport Beach Police. He looked tense and vigilant. I turned toward the woman, who also had her credentials out, identifying her as Detective Mary Kozlowski. She, too, looked as though she might be preparing to draw down on me. I looked around the reception area, trying to figure out what was making them act strangely. At least one cause for their discomfort was obvious: they hadn't expected a paraplegic.

"What can I do for you?" I asked Howard.

"Is there somewhere we can talk?"

I had Lana locate a conference room for us. "Follow me," I said.

The detectives followed me down the hall into the windowless room, both still looking grim and tense as they closed the door behind us.

"Ms. Wilkinson," Howard announced, "we're investigating a homicide. We have some questions for you."

"Okay. Do you have a case number I can reference?" But I knew by now this wasn't about one of my cases.

"Uh, no. My first question is, are you carrying a weapon of any kind?"

My mouth dropped open. "Are you kidding me?"

He didn't respond.

"No," I said. "I mean, you can't carry weapons in here. There's a metal detector downstairs. But why—"

"I'm sorry, but we're going to have to search you. Just routine."

"Good Lord. What on earth is going on?"

"Just routine," he repeated.

"All right, if it makes you feel better. Wait—is James okay?"

"Is there some reason he shouldn't be?" Howard asked.

"You're from Newport Beach—that's near where he lives —James Carter, I mean. Is he okay?"

"He's fine," Kozlowski replied.

How did she know? She approached me, and I held my hands up. She patted me down and checked my purse.

"Thank you," she said.

"All right," I said. "I've been patient here. You come into my office and search me. Now how about telling me what's going on?"

Without answering, both detectives took chairs at the conference table. I pulled up between them.

Howard said, "Could we see some identification, please?"

I produced my US attorney ID and driver's license. Howard copied down the information, then looked up. "Your given name is Doris Penny Wilkinson?"

"Yes."

"But you go by 'Pen,' is that right?"

I nodded. Howard made a check in his notebook and said, "Would you please describe your whereabouts and movements last night?"

I felt cold all over. "You're sure James is okay?" I said.

They didn't respond, and I tried to pull myself together. "I left the office around six. Then I went straight home. Then I met James for dinner at Las Brisas, down in Laguna, at seven-forty-five. We left around nine and went down to his boat at the marina on Bayside. I left there at around ten-thirty and went directly home for the night."

"And your home is at this Long Beach address."

"Yes."

"Are you sure about the time you left the boat?"

"Pretty sure. It had to be within a few minutes of that."

"We'll need to go over that timeline in a lot more detail," Howard said. "Do you know Celia Sims?"

"Yes."

"When was the last time you saw her?"

I thought about it. "It was after Christmas. Probably a couple of weeks after. I'd say mid-January."

"Where did you see her?"

"At Fashion Island. James and I were shopping and we ran into her."

"What is the nature of her relationship with James Carter?"

"Right now? She doesn't have one. They broke up more than a year ago."

"Are you sure about that?"

"Very."

"What is your relationship with Carter?"

"We've been dating exclusively for a little over a year."

Howard and Kozlowski looked at each other, exchanging a complicated set of glances.

"We need you to come down to Newport for more questions," Howard said.

"Why? What's going on?"

"Celia Sims was murdered last night. On Carter's boat."

Chapter 8

I felt sick, my breathing shallow, as Detective Mary Kozlowski rode with me in my van down to Newport Beach. They had allowed me to retrieve my coat from my office and leave Cassandra a short voicemail saying I needed to go down to Newport. Kozlowski didn't say a word during the entire ride, which left me to try to sort things out. Someone, incredibly, had murdered Celia, and done it on James's boat. It obviously had occurred after I left. James had remained on the boat after I'd gone home at ten-thirty. Had Celia come to see him? If so, why? And then what had happened?

For whatever reason, the police obviously considered me a person of interest—maybe a suspect. Did I have a motive to kill Celia? Howard and Kozlowski obviously thought I might. I supposed I might have considered Celia a rival for James's affections, and in fact I had to fight off lingering feelings of jealousy. When the three of us had met at the shopping mall a couple of months ago, the brief encounter had been tense and awkward. But she and I had worked together to find the corporate saboteurs who'd taken down both James and me, and afterward, she and James had parted with little drama or animosity. The police had been deadly serious in their questioning of me at my office, so there had to be a lot more going on—things I didn't know.

That left me with the question of what I should do now. Talking to the police without an attorney was stupid, period. It was unwise for anyone, even if you were innocent, and even if, like me, you were familiar with criminal law and procedure. And I was about to go and do it anyway.

I told myself I just wasn't that worried about being investigated for Celia's murder. I wasn't naive enough to believe that mere innocence would be enough to get me out of trouble, but when it came down to it, what evidence did they have against me? There wouldn't be any physical evidence—no blood or gunshot residue, no weapon, no witnesses, and no video. I may have had a motive to dislike Celia, but certainly not one to kill her.

But there were other reasons to waive my rights. I wasn't even sure where I'd find an attorney to represent me, or how I'd pay one. I didn't want my bosses to believe I had anything to hide, and I wanted to show I was cooperating fully. It would be awkward and embarrassing enough just to explain why I was being questioned. Finally, I simply did not have time to lawyer up. I was in full emergency mode at work and needed to get through this as quickly as possible. I had to just tell the truth and hope the police would get it right. Usually, they did.

Usually.

I would have given anything to call James, but I obviously couldn't do it now.

We reached the Newport Beach police station, a white low-rise building just off Jamboree, and Kozlowski, a tall, slender woman in her late thirties with mousy brown shoulder-length hair, escorted me inside to an interview room, where Lieutenant Howard waited for us.

We sat down, and Howard asked me if I needed anything to drink or to use the bathroom. I declined. He turned on a recorder and recited the time, date and interviewee. He was about to ask his first question when I said, "Am I in custody, Lieutenant Howard?"

"That's really a legal question," he said with exaggerated patience. "You're probably better qualified to answer that than I am."

Now it was my turn to be exasperated. "Fine, then. Am I free to leave?"

It was a key moment. If they said yes, they didn't have to read me my Miranda rights, but they could still use my answers against me. If they said no, they'd have to Mirandize me, and at that point, I might decide to clam up or retain counsel. It was a little game of chicken. The two detectives looked at each other, engaging in non-verbal consultations.

"Yes, you're free to leave," Howard said at last. Of course, if I actually tried to leave, that might change. Probably would. Bottom line: I wasn't going anywhere, and they knew it.

"Okay," I said. I told them to go ahead and ask their questions.

They responded with relieved looks. They started the recorder and recited the time, date, and place for the record, and they got me to agree on the record that I was answering questions voluntarily and was free to leave. Then they resumed the questioning. They took me again through my evening, zeroing in on my time on the boat. Was I sure about my arrival and departure times? Had anyone seen us there? What was Carter's frame of mind? Did I make any calls?

Howard, who was asking most of the questions, looked up from his notes. "Ms. Wilkinson, are you able to walk at all?"

"No, I'm not. I'm a T-7 paraplegic."

He wrote it down. "You're completely paralyzed below the waist?"

"Yes."

"And how did that paralysis come about?"

"I was in a car accident four years ago in Florida."

"Was anyone else injured in the accident?"

"Yes. My six-year-old niece was killed."

"Was alcohol or drug use involved in the accident?"

"Not by me." They took down the date and location of the crash, which meant they'd check out the circumstances. They would find that an ex-felon with multiple citations for drunken and careless driving had forced me off I-75 and down an embankment. And he'd done it at a time when I'd unfastened my seat belt to help my niece, who had spilled soda in the back seat.

"Were you an attorney when you lived in Florida?"

"Yes," I said, knowing they'd check the records there for any disciplinary proceedings.

"What kind of law did you practice?"

"I was a plaintiff's personal injury lawyer with the firm of Harris and Dunleavy in Tampa."

"At some point you left that firm?"

"Yes."

"Before or after the accident?"

"After."

"Why did you leave?"

"I didn't make partner." In fact, the firm had let me go after my accident, believing, rightly or wrongly, that a paraplegic attorney would attract sympathy from juries that needed to be directed toward the injured client.

"Are you able to get onto the boat by yourself?" Howard asked.

"Yes, using the hoist on the dock. I think I could bring my chair over by disassembling it and carrying it over piece by piece, but I've never tried it."

"Have you ever been to the boat by yourself?"

"No."

"Has Celia Sims ever been to the boat?"

"I don't know." She almost certainly had, but I wasn't about to speculate.

"Do you own a weapon of any kind?"

I was about to say no but caught myself. "There is a knife in my van, which could be used as a weapon."

The detectives' poker faces gave way. Both reacted with startled expressions, and I knew then that the murder weapon had been a knife. For the first time, I felt real fear. But at the same time I felt a measure of relief; it would be far more difficult for me to stab someone to death than to commit murder with a gun.

"May we search your van?" Howard asked.

"We can get a warrant," Kozlowski added.

"No need for a warrant," I said. "You can search it. I'll want to be present, though."

Kozlowski rolled her eyes, but I couldn't see that they had much cause for complaint.

We adjourned the questioning and went out to the parking lot. The detectives asked for my keys but quickly realized they didn't know how to use the hand controls. At their request I drove it into the garage, under Kozlowski's watchful eye. For the next hour a crime-scene team went through everything in my specially-modified Chrysler minivan, photographing, videotaping, inventorying, swabbing, and taking samples. I was tempted to tape the proceedings on my cell phone, but I knew I'd be entitled to access the police video if necessary. These police officers seemed professional and reasonable enough; I doubted that they'd plant a murder weapon or commit a major screw-up. But the stakes were high, and I watched them every minute. They found the knife right away, where I told them it would be. They photographed it, tagged it, and took it away for tests. I found myself wondering again if I was physically capable of stabbing someone to death. How much strength would it take? Could it be done from a sitting position?

I decided that under the right conditions, it could.

The forensic team finished, and we went back in for more questioning. By now it was early afternoon, but lunch was the last thing on my mind. Now the questioning focused on my relationship with James Carter, and his with Celia, and any interactions between Celia and me. They appeared interested when I told them how Celia had helped us find the killers who had targeted Carter, me, and our company, a Minnesota bank. They asked how James and I had begun dating. And when they quizzed me about our relationship since then, I sensed their incredulity that a prominent man like James would date a paraplegic nobody like me. Or maybe I only thought I sensed it. Maybe I was only feeling my own latent doubts.

After another hour they got up and left the interview room. They left me waiting there for more than half an hour while I wondered what evidence they had and what James was doing.

When they returned, Howard said, "We're finished for now. Expect more questions in the next day or two. Do you have any travel plans?"

"No."

"Good."

I rolled out of the room and down the hallway.

"Ms. Wilkinson?" Howard called after me.

I stopped, and he could see I already had my cell out of my purse.

"If you're going to call Mr. Carter, don't bother. He's here." He stopped and gave me a thin smile. "And he's not free to leave."

Chapter 9

I rolled out into a cloudy, windy day and found my van, now back in the lot. With a shaking hand I hit the button on my keychain to lower the van's profile, open the door, and extend the ramp, then wheeled myself up into the vehicle. I clamped my chair into place behind the steering wheel while the ramp retracted and the door closed. I was starting the engine when the text notification on my cell phone chirped. I pulled the phone from my purse and saw that I had two texts. The first was from Rena Karros, a close friend. It said "Heard about Celia. Call me."

The second text said, "Don't leave. I'll be right there. Eric."

Half a minute later an Audi sedan pulled into the space next to me. A tall black man with graying, close-cropped hair and glasses got out, came over, and opened the van's passenger door. "Are you doing all right?" asked Eric Carter, James's older brother. He was a senior partner at a large LA law firm that specialized in corporate securities work. He grasped my hand.

"Eric, my God. What on earth is happening? James is really in jail?"

"Yes."

"For Celia's murder?"

He nodded.

"Is he all right?" I asked.

"He's doing okay. But it looks like they're going to charge him."

He paused to let that sink in.

"In the meantime," Eric continued, "I'm preparing to try to get him out if he's charged. A partner of mine is ready to represent him at the initial appearance. They may not be ready to file charges by tomorrow, but they'll have to either charge him or let him go by Thursday morning—that's when the forty-eight-hour period after his arrest will expire. I'm working with his financial advisors to round up enough assets to post a bond. It won't be easy, of course—there's no guarantee of bail at all in a murder case, and if the judge does grant it, the amount will be well into seven figures."

"Has any of this become public?"

"Celia's murder has. The media knows an arrest has been made, but James's identity hasn't been released yet."

"Why do they think he did it?"

"Well, obviously they're not a hundred percent sure—they appear interested in you, too. Celia's body was found on the *Alicia C*. James has had a prior relationship with Celia and owns the boat. They have to have some evidence other than that, but I don't know what it is."

"Are there any security videos?"

"None that are useful. I checked with the manager at the marina. One of the parking lot cameras, and the camera covering Dock D, aren't functioning, and the fog and drizzle has made the remaining footage pretty much useless."

"Who would want to kill Celia?"

"I don't know. She and James were still on good terms."

I said nothing. As far as I knew they weren't on any "terms" at all since their breakup. Now I wondered.

"Tell me what you know," he said.

I started with the previous night, describing our evening and our time on the boat. Then I skipped to the next morning, describing the arrival of Howard and Kozlowski, followed by questioning downtown and then in Newport. "They went over my van inch by inch," I said.

"They must not have found anything. But when you arrive home, you might find things in disarray."

I slammed the heel of my hand against the steering wheel. "Of course. By now they've pulled and executed a warrant for the apartment." I grabbed my phone and checked the missed calls—sure enough, my landlady had tried to call me an hour earlier.

"Looks like they've got two things to work with," Eric said. "First, the fact that you were there last night, and second, they're trying to set up a love triangle with you, Celia, and James."

"There wasn't any triangle," I said.

He nodded in agreement, but he wasn't as emphatic as I would have liked. "They can still create the inference, though. Somebody had a motive, and right now yours might look as good to them as any."

"So what should I do?" I asked.

"Can you take a few days off?"

"Not a chance." I described the problems I was having with the Shields case.

"I see. Normally, of course, you'd need representation. Maybe you should be talking to somebody."

"I can't, Eric, for a number of reasons." I explained.

"You should reconsider. The police let you go, but I wouldn't get too confident."

"I need to talk to James."

"No," he said firmly. "I understand why you want to, but you can't communicate with him. It will hurt his defense as well as yours if you have any opportunity to synchronize your stories."

Once again, I punched the steering wheel in frustration. I knew he was right. I had to stay away from James, at least until he was out of jail.

"And," he added, "James is not in a great frame of mind right now."

I studied his face, and I realized he meant that James was distraught over Celia's death. It didn't make me feel any better.

"Have you talked to Alicia?" I asked, suddenly realizing that James's daughter needed to be told.

"Not directly," Eric said.

"You talked to Anita."

"Yes. She was actually very reasonable. She said she knew James had to be innocent and that she would explain it to Alicia."

I was relieved; James's ex-wife rarely missed an opportunity to disparage him, and a murder charge represented a huge potential weapon.

"However," Eric added, "she asked that you give Alicia a call."

"I will." Alicia and I had developed a close relationship, and she would need all the support she could get.

"Try to avoid the media," Eric said. "Just do the best you can at work. In the meantime, we've got to get James out of jail and hope the police find the killer."

I nodded. It didn't sound like much of a plan, but I didn't have any better ideas.

Eric took my hand. "Take care of yourself," he said. He got out, went back to his car, and left.

Chapter 10

I dragged myself, shaking and exhausted, back to the office in late afternoon. I made my way back to my desk, knowing I had to focus on something else—even something as miserable as the Shields case—to take my mind off Celia's murder. Before leaving for LA I had called my landlady, Mrs. Tompkins, who lived in the unit upstairs. She had confirmed that she had provided a key to the police officers who had searched my apartment. On the radio in the van I caught a news report on the murder, which stated only that an arrest had been made; they didn't identify James.

I stopped by the Ice Box and checked with Cassandra. "Any word on Lisa?" I asked.

"No," came the predictably frosty reply.

I was too tired to drag the details out of her, so I said, "Do you have the updated exhibit list?"

"We were supposed to discuss that this afternoon," she said. "But you weren't here. And now I have to go. Anthony is meeting me for an appointment at the obstetrician's." I was impressed; Cassandra routinely portrayed her fiancé, Anthony, as a hapless chucklehead, but here he was, attending a doctor's appointment with her.

When Cassandra left, I figured I'd better take the initiative to explain my mysterious visitors and abrupt departure. I went down to see Vikram Tandon, who looked distracted but listened without comment as I told him about my encounter with the Newport Beach detectives.

"Are you a suspect?" he asked.

There was no use trying to downplay it, I thought. "I'd say not a strong one. They didn't Mirandize me."

"Continue to cooperate for now," he said. "I'll talk to Connie."

"Thanks, Vik. I'm really sorry about the disruption."

"What do you think about the message from Lisa?" he said.

"What message?"

"Cassandra didn't tell you?"

"No, she didn't." I wanted to slap her silly.

"We accessed Adam's office email, and there was a message from Lisa." He glanced at his watch. "We've got a meeting in twenty minutes to discuss it. Dave will be there."

Vik and Connie were already in the conference room when I arrived twenty minutes later. Both looked grim.

I moved a chair aside and took a spot at the table. We all looked at each other awkwardly. Vik said, "It's a video message. We'll all watch it when Dave gets here."

"At the risk of provoking a spoiler alert, I take it the news isn't good," I said. Vik shook his head. Connie looked like she wanted to slug somebody.

US Attorney Dave O'Shea bounded in after about five minutes, accompanied by his assistant, Susan Hecht, a smartly-dressed, middle-aged woman with stylish horn-rimmed glasses. O'Shea, a stocky, energetic figure with a fleshy face and hair as impressive as a televangelist's, was, like all US attorneys, a Presidential appointee. He oversaw the more than two hundred attorneys in the US attorney's office for the Central District of California. He nodded to Connie and Vik as he took the chair at the head of the table. He didn't even glance in my direction; I had shaken his hand once but never had a substantive conversation with him.

"When did we get this?" he asked Connie.

"It came on Sunday," Connie replied. "We accessed it this morning and sent it over to Susan right away."

"And nobody's actually talked to the witness?"

"That's correct."

"Well, let's watch the damn thing."

Susan Hecht, who was sitting at a computer terminal on a side table, reached over and dimmed the lights, then punched in some commands on her keyboard. A large screen on the wall flickered to life. I felt my pulse rate climb as I watched. My right foot, which I couldn't actually feel, did a furious phantom jiggle, as it had often done for real before I'd become a paraplegic.

The video that popped up on the screen was exceptionally grainy and jerky. "Was this recorded on a cell phone?" O'Shea asked.

"Yes," said Hecht. "You can see it more clearly on a smaller screen."

Lisa Darden, an attractive blonde with shoulder-length hair, looked hesitantly into the camera. She appeared older than her twenty-eight years, but it was hard to tell on the poor-quality video, which undoubtedly suffered from being shown on a big screen. "Adam," she said, "I'm really sorry to do this to you. I know how hard you've worked on the case. But I've thought about it, and worried about it, and when push came to shove, I just couldn't get onto that plane." She paused, gulped, and went on. "I just can't stand the thought of being put through hell on the stand, with all of them calling me a slut and a liar. I've got to move on with my life. I just can't go through with this. If I leave them alone now, maybe I'll have a shot at some kind of career."

Lisa turned away, her face quivering. Then she composed herself and looked back at the camera. "I know this is the coward's way out. I should have told you in person. But I'm just at the end of my rope, and I've made up my mind. I'm too tired to debate this or have anybody try to talk me out of it. I need to get away. So I'm going to go on vacation for a couple of weeks, and I won't be reachable. I'm so sorry to have started all this and put you through all this work. I thought I was strong enough. But I'm not. I'm sorry, Adam." The screen went blank.

The lights came up. "You sent this to the Bureau?" O'Shea asked Susan Hecht.

"Yes. The FBI says . . ." She consulted a sheet of paper. ". . . that the message came through her email account, that in their judgment the person in the video is in fact Lisa Darden, and that the video is genuine."

"Genuine," Connie said. "In other words, it's not spliced together or faked somehow?"

"Correct."

Vik looked troubled. "The big question is whether the statement was voluntary. In other words, was she under duress? Is somebody off camera holding a gun on her or holding her parents hostage or something?"

"She sounded pretty damn sincere and convincing to me," O'Shea said.

I thought so, too, but I didn't say anything.

Hecht said, "The FBI couldn't give a definitive answer on that. They did an analysis, using other video testimony from her as a baseline. They said she appeared to be under moderate stress, but with no definitive signs of coercion or deception."

"So," Connie said, "there is no evidence that this statement was involuntary."

"Right," Hecht said.

"But no definitive proof that it's voluntary, either," O'Shea added.

There was a long silence as we all looked at each other. "All right, get her on the phone," O'Shea said at last.

There were embarrassed looks around the table. "We've been trying for two days to reach her," Vik said. "She's not responding."

"Just get her on the phone," O'Shea repeated. "I'll talk to her."

I was startled; was O'Shea really that full of himself?

Susan Hecht dutifully dialed the number. "Voicemail," she said a moment later.

"Well, leave a message," O'Shea grumbled. He shook his head, more uncomprehending than angry. This witness had blown off *Dave O'Shea*. "Damnit, we deserve better than a second-hand, after-the-fact phone message," he said.

Nobody disagreed.

"So what is happening here?" he asked. "Did Shields or Lopez get to her somehow?"

No one responded. Without an investigation, the question was unanswerable.

O'Shea persisted. "Is there some skeleton in her closet they've dug up and threatened to use against her?"

"I doubt it," Vik said. "We vetted her very thoroughly. Of course, that wouldn't stop them from trashing her on the stand with innuendo."

"We can't just give up," O'Shea said. "We have to talk to her in person and try to re-recruit her. What have we been doing to establish contact with her?"

Eyes turned to me, and I brought the group up to date on our efforts. "I've asked the FBI to ping her cell phone and check databases for travel, credit card use, and ATM withdrawals. They say they will get to it soon."

There was an uncomfortable silence.

"They have their procedures, and sometimes they work on their own schedule," O'Shea said. I found this cavalier stance hard to take seriously. I was reasonably sure that if he felt like it, O'Shea could call up his buddy, the assistant director in charge of the FBI's LA field office, and ask him to get serious about finding Lisa right away.

"Do we have any evidence that somebody has gotten to her or that she's in danger?" he asked.

No one spoke.

"All right, then. I'll give the Bureau a call, tell them we're in a bind." He didn't sound enthusiastic or optimistic.

"What if we can't get her back on the reservation?" Vik asked. "What are our options for the trial?"

My pulse quickened as eyes turned to me. "Assuming she can be found, we should subpoena her," I said. "We should compel her testimony. If she tried to change her story, we could confront her with her prior sworn testimony to the grand jury."

Vik shook his head doubtfully. "That would be tough," he said.

"Tough" didn't begin to describe it, I thought. Compelling direct testimony from a hostile witness was tricky enough. But for a star witness, giving hearsay testimony, in a difficult, well-publicized case, it was risky as hell. The Shields case was difficult to begin with—maybe a fifty-fifty proposition. Without Lisa's willing, unambiguous testimony, the odds would shift against us, perhaps decisively. And that was assuming we could find her and serve her. If we couldn't, there would be no case at all.

O'Shea responded with a grim nod. "Just keep at it. Find her and get her back with the program."

"What about the status hearing on Monday?" Connie asked.

O'Shea leaned forward and clasped his hands together on the table. "Just keep her on the witness list. We're planning on having her testify—one way or the other."

"The defense knows she's missing," I said. "I don't know how they found out, unless of course they're responsible in some way. What if I'm asked point-blank on Monday?"

"Hopefully we'll have something to tell them by then," O'Shea said. He looked around the table; no one had anything to add. "Keep me informed," he said, and with that, he stood up abruptly and stalked out of the room, followed by Hecht.

Connie, Vik, and I looked at each other. Finally Vik stood up. "I guess we have our orders."

"Is there anything additional I should be doing?" I asked.

"Keep doing what you're doing," Connie answered. "Except get some results."

The meeting broke up, and I headed back to my office. My job was even harder now than it had been half an hour ago. And I had no idea what to do next.

I called John Gibson, but the FBI agent didn't answer his phone. Then I tried Stacy Ellis, Lisa's sister. More voicemail. Today, the whole world was avoiding me. I looked up Adam Rosenthal's home number. I figured Adam's girlfriend, Pam LaRue, a pediatrician, might be home.

For once, I was in luck. Pam was at home.

"Pen," she said. "I've been half-expecting you to call."

"So what's going on? Where is Adam?"

"It was all very abrupt," Pam said. "He told me last Wednesday he'd gotten a job offer from the LA office of a big multinational law firm based in London, and he was going to take it. He just announced it, like I had no say at all. We had a terrible fight."

"So where is he now?"

"Singapore. They made the offer last week and wanted a response right away because they wanted to send him to this week-long conference over there."

"Have you heard from him at all?" I asked.

"All I've gotten is a quick email telling me he got there okay and will call later. His cell phone doesn't work over there. I'm not happy."

"I'm not too wild about it myself. He left us high and dry. If you talk to him, will you tell him Lisa Darden has changed her mind and won't testify?"

"Uh-oh."

"I'm really in a bind, Pam."

"Sounds that way. I'm hoping he'll call soon, and I'll definitely pass along what you said. Along with a few choice thoughts of my own."

"Can you join us tomorrow night?" Wednesday was girls' night out for Rena and me, and Pam sometimes joined us.

"I think so. I might be a little late—probably around eight."

"Great. See you then. Thanks, Pam."

I hung up.

Adam was the key, I thought. If anybody could get through to Lisa and persuade her to cooperate, it would be him. I took a few minutes to compose an email to Adam, in the event he might be checking his messages. Then I forced myself to work on trial preparation, even though it seemed increasingly pointless. I worked on a number of motions that were due to be considered at the status hearing on Monday. Then I spent half an hour writing notes for Cassandra and Kathy on the exhibits to be presented by the forensic accountants.

I could prepare all I wanted, but it still all came down to Lisa Darden and her testimony about Shields's meeting at the Discovery Hotel in downtown Los Angeles. We could prove that two representatives of Pacific Technology Group, Assistant General Counsel Milt Hammer and CEO Wilson Lopez, had been there. The following evening, back in Washington, Lisa had been working late when Shields came into the office, feeling no pain after attending a reception given by a lobbyist. He hit on his attractive young aide, but she fended off his advances. Shields had boasted about the PTG meeting, how he'd delivered for them, and how much they owed him. And he'd said that PTG had come through with a big payoff. Then he invited Lisa to spend a weekend with him at his newly-renovated Lake Arrowhead home.

It was drunken talk, designed to impress a woman, but it was consistent with all the facts: the flow of money, shown by accounting and bank records; the surveillance tape showing the presence of the PTG representatives at a meeting not on Shields's calendar or schedule; the congressman's vigorous lobbying at the Pentagon on PTG's behalf; and PTG's successful procurement of the bid. A bigger potential problem with Lisa's testimony was that it was hearsay. But the hearsay rule is riddled with exceptions, and the judge had indicated he was going to allow the testimony. The case had two crucial components: the influence being applied by Shields, and the money being funneled to him by the beneficiaries of the influence. Lisa's testimony provided the critical link between the two.

When Lisa came forward, Shields and his fellow defendants had, predictably, lawyered up and refused to talk. When called to testify before the grand jury, they invoked their Fifth Amendment right to remain silent. After being indicted, they defended the case vigorously. At the same time, they waged a surreptitious media campaign to discredit Lisa Darden, portraying her as an opportunist, a head case, a slut, and more. Lisa resigned from Shields's staff and moved to the Minneapolis area, where she'd grown up and where her sister lived. Until now, Lisa had remained determined to testify, insisting that she was personally offended by Shields's conduct. What, I wondered now, had caused her to change her mind?

Shields, a cocky, folksy ex-Navy fighter pilot, had hardly been chastened by the scandal. He ran for re-election and won handily in his conservative district, although a conviction would probably produce a different result next time; it's hard to campaign from a jail cell. He had at least backed off on his lobbying for PTG, which might have implications for upcoming bids. Within weeks, PTG would be bidding against archcompetitors Benning, Inc. and Horrey Technologies for a huge contract to supply the avionics for the Pentagon's F-35 fighter jets.

A little before seven, I finally called it quits. Before leaving, I tried calling my friend Rena, who was still at the office and in a meeting. I left and drove home. But as I drove, the thoughts of James and Celia and my interrogation by the police came flooding back, and I longed for further distraction.

Instead of going directly home, I drove past my neighborhood in Belmont Shore and down to the supermarket on Pacific Coast Highway. I didn't really need anything there, but it was something to do. After picking up a few items, I rolled out to the parking lot, put my groceries into the van, and pondered my options for dinner.

I decided on a French bakery-type restaurant, next door to the supermarket, that didn't have waiter service but was a nice step up from a fast-food place. I bought my dinner and took it to my table. The tray balanced precariously on my lap, but my long legs caused my knees to stick up, making the tray slope toward my body, reducing the hazard. I pulled a chair away and rolled up to a table.

"Pen?"

Startled, I looked up. It was Milt Hammer, assistant general counsel of Pacific Technology Group.

"Well, hello there," he said. "What a coincidence."

I didn't believe for a moment that his presence here was a coincidence, and it creeped me out.

"Someone who didn't know better might conclude that you're stalking me," I said.

He just laughed and shook his head.

He was right, of course—who'd want to stalk me? Still, here he was.

He gave me a disarming grin. "Mind if I join you?"

"Milt, you know that's not appropriate. I could get into trouble."

He waved off my concern. "We've been through all that. I'm a big boy. My attorney doesn't have a problem."

"I don't know . . ."

"Hey, you sit down to have dinner, and a defendant comes up and sits down next to you, what can you do?"

He apparently wasn't giving me much choice. I stayed where I was.

47

He returned a few minutes later with his own tray and sat down across from me. By remaining here, I was treading on dangerous ethical ground. I'd have to notify Hammer's attorney and write up another memo of the conversation. But I was exhausted, stressed out, and too irritated to abandon my dinner on his account.

"Looks like you've had a long day," he said.

My first thought was that he had no idea just how long, but then it occurred to me that maybe he did. Hammer was a compact, fit man of medium height, with close-cropped blond hair. Now in his late thirties, he looked like the Army Ranger he once was. He was very handsome in a rugged way, his nose slightly off-center as if broken in a long-ago brawl.

"Yes, it's been a long day," I said. I was famished and started in on my turkey-on-French bread sandwich. Hammer had bought two of them for himself.

"So, did the police give you a hard time?" he asked.

I didn't bother asking how he knew. He seemed to know everything, and more specifically, he seemed to be keeping tabs on me. "They asked a few questions."

"Terrible thing. Did you know Celia Sims?"

"Not well."

"And now Carter has been arrested for the crime."

I was losing my appetite. I had hoped to talk about something else.

"Well, I hope it works out for both of you," he said. "It's not an easy thing, being accused of a crime." He said it in a matter-of-fact way, without resentment, sarcasm, irony, or gloating. For him, defending himself against an indictment seemed just another day at the office. He changed the subject. "Any luck in finding Ms. Darden?"

"I can't talk about that."

"Shame about Rosenthal," he said. "And now they've dumped the case on you. You have to know when it's time to fold 'em, Pen, and this is one of those times." He lowered his voice. "It's best for everybody. You know testifying wouldn't have been fun for Lisa."

I glared at him, knowing Hammer and his fellow defendants were sure to play dirty, putting Lisa through hell on the stand. "I knew I could count on you guys to put the witness on trial," I said.

"That's how it works. Part of the game."

"She has no motive to lie."

"That's where you're wrong."

"Nobody's going to buy your 'woman scorned' story."

"Oh, but they will. It's true. Hell, Shields might have led her on a little bit. He does have a fondness for the ladies. And then she got pissed as hell. What if we introduced incontrovertible evidence that Shields and Lisa actually had an affair?"

I didn't know whether Hammer was bluffing or just trying to rattle me. If Lisa had lied about her relationship with Shields, the case could be in deep trouble. I knew I shouldn't be arguing with Hammer about the case, or talking to him about it at all. I found myself looking around the restaurant, as if someone might spot us. "I'm trying to figure out just what it is you want from me, Milt. You've become my best pal, and it isn't because of my fascinating personality."

"Sure it is," he said. "When you were added to the prosecution team, I Googled you. And after the first couple of references, I just kept reading. You are fascinating."

"Oh, please."

"You've declined all media requests to talk about what happened at North Central Bank, and afterward. But it isn't hard to piece together. You were implicated in a scandal targeting your employer. So was James Carter, who was CEO of the bank. Downfall, they called it. Now, that part of the story alone is fascinating. But that was nothing compared to what happened next—and this was harder to find out. You fought back against the bad guys, virtually alone. And you stopped them."

We stopped them, it was true. But I had to make a deal to do it. I did what I had to do, but I didn't feel good about it.

"Amazing," Hammer continued. "And then the Hollywood ending. You and Carter—your alliance turned into a romance."

"Are we done here, Milt?"

He leaned a little closer to me and lowered his voice. "Hardly anybody knows about the accident," he said.

My hand tightened around my napkin. I didn't want to talk about any of this. But it was safer than talking about the case, I supposed.

"You could read all the articles online," he continued, "and never even find out you're a paraplegic, that you'd been in a car crash in Florida that killed your niece. If you did nothing more in your life than simply cope with the aftermath of that—it would be impressive. But everything else . . ." He spread his hands. "I find you interesting," he said, "because you and I are alike. We're survivors."

After a minute of silence I said, "You have the advantage on me, Milt. You seem to know a lot about me, while I don't have a clue what makes you tick. Why would you get involved with Shields?"

He smiled. "I've got a short attention span. Actual legal work—I'm afraid that bores the crap out of me. I need to stir things up, keep everything interesting."

"You didn't have to be part of this," I said. "You could have rolled on Shields."

"For a nonexistent crime?" He smiled widely. "I like my job. I like PTG. I even like Lopez—he's not bad as bosses go. Shields? Well, how can anybody not like Larry Shields?" Turning serious, he said, "Do you think I'd ever work in the defense industry again? It's a risk, sure. I could be convicted, and then I won't be working anywhere, at least for a while. But risk is not only a necessity—for some people, like me, it's actually fun."

"You're wasting your breath, lobbying me to drop the case," I said. "The decision-makers on that are way above my pay grade."

"They'll listen to you. Think about it. You have to control your own fate here—don't leave it to the big shots."

"None of us controls our own fate."

He responded with a toothy grin. "And, like Lisa, we all have a motive to lie."

Chapter 11

It was after nine when I finally made my way home, to the bottom unit of a duplex on Covina in Long Beach. I parked in the carport, got out, and rolled up the wooden ramp leading to the side door. I went in and had barely gotten my jacket off when I heard a rap at the door. I rolled over to admit Eleanor Tompkins, my landlady.

Eleanor, a heavyset Filipina in her seventies, looked distressed. "Are you okay?"

"Yes, yes. Come in."

She took a timid step across the threshold. "I'm so sorry. I didn't want to let the police in, but they had a warrant, and—"

"It's okay, Eleanor. It's fine."

"I kept telling them you would never do anything wrong, but they wouldn't listen."

"Don't worry about it," I said. "They didn't find anything anyway."

"I saw them take your computer away."

I shot a glance at my desk, which sat in a little alcove off the living room. Sure enough, they'd taken my desktop. Fortunately I still had my laptop, which, for whatever reason, they hadn't searched, perhaps surmising that it might contain privileged work-related material. I turned back to Eleanor. "It's okay. They won't find anything on my computer, either."

I felt bad about Eleanor's involvement, however minor, in this mess. When I'd first gone apartment-hunting, I drove by the places I'd found in the listings so I could identify at a glance those that wouldn't be accessible. I looked for a building with an elevator, but I didn't want to be in a high-rise. The ramp on the side of Eleanor's duplex had caught my eye, so I went up to the door to ask about it. That's when I learned that the ramp had been built for Eleanor's husband, who'd been stricken with Parkinson's and had died three months earlier. Unfortunately, Eleanor lived in the ground-level unit; it was the upper unit that was listed for rent. I thanked her and started to leave, but she stopped me and invited me in for coffee.

Within a week Eleanor, at her insistence, had moved to the upper level and rented the lower unit to me. Every week or so, she'd come downstairs just to chat, and I welcomed the company.

Eleanor could apparently see that I wasn't in the mood for an extended conversation. She started for the door. "I hope I did the right thing," she said.

"No problem at all. It's always okay to let the police in."

Eleanor had just closed the door when my phone buzzed, the screen displaying a call from the US attorney's office. I answered.

"Have you found her yet?" Connie Harper demanded.

"No." I gave her a rundown on my most recent efforts.

"The Bureau got the police to do a welfare check. She's not home."

"Well, at least I know where not to look."

Connie wasn't amused. "Find her. And keep me informed."

I was putting my phone away when it buzzed again; it was Rena Karros.

"You okay?" my friend asked without preamble.

"I guess. What have you heard?"

"I heard Celia was murdered. It was all over the company by late morning. Later I made some calls and found out it happened on James's boat and that they arrested James."

I filled her in on the rest of the story. While it was true, as I'd told the police, that I hadn't seen Celia since the shopping mall encounter, I didn't mention another indirect connection I had with her. Celia had a high-powered job as chief operating officer of Benning, Inc., a technology and defense conglomerate, which sometimes competed with Pacific Technology Group for defense contracts. The general counsel of Benning happened to be none other than Rena Karros, a law school acquaintance I'd reconnected with since moving to Los Angeles a little over a year ago.

Rena had graduated at the top of her class, two years ahead of mine. She had been part of a loose circle of friends I'd hung out with; I'd known her, but not all that well. When I moved out here to the West Coast, I didn't know a soul except for James and impulsively had called her up. We had gotten together, and to the surprise of both of us, hit it off right away —picking up the threads of our friendship where we'd left them years ago.

Rena had occasionally worked with Celia Sims, and the two women seemed to get along well. But Rena soon sensed my discomfort in talking about Celia, so we seldom mentioned her. I tried to avoid even thinking about Celia, because my thoughts were usually jealous, negative, and petty.

"Who on earth would want to kill Celia?" I asked Rena.

"No one has any idea. We're all in shock here. Celia was well-liked. And Dick is demanding answers." Dick was Dick Westcott, Benning's CEO and Rena's mentor.

There was an awkward silence. I couldn't avoid the topic any longer, so I plunged ahead. "Was she dating anyone?" I asked.

"She dated, but there was nobody special, as far as I know."

"Do you know of any reason she might have been at James's boat?"

"No, I don't. But don't jump to conclusions about James, Pen. There's no way he was cheating on you."

"But why was she there?" I whined.

Our conversion lasted for another twenty minutes, with Rena trying to talk me down and help me get a grip. Finally she said, "Are we on for tomorrow night?" Wednesday was our girls' night out.

"Unless something comes up," I said. *Like James somehow getting out of jail,* I thought.

"Be there," she said. "Without fail."

"Thanks, Rena."

"'Night, Pen. Love you."

I next called Alicia Carter, James's daughter.

"Pen," she said, answering on the first ring. "Are you all right?"

She was a remarkable girl, I thought, expressing concern not for herself or even her father, but for me.

"I'm fine," I said.

"Have you talked to Dad?"

"No." I explained how contacting him in jail just wasn't a good option right now.

"I can't believe this is happening to him again."

I didn't have to tell her that it was different this time, that a murder charge was far more serious than the corporate misconduct he had been accused of a year ago. "He'll get through it," I said.

"You're a lawyer. So is Uncle Eric. You can help Dad."

"He'll be hiring a lawyer with a lot more experience in criminal law than Eric or I."

"I just keep thinking about him in jail, and…" I heard sobbing over the line.

I calmed her down, and we talked for another twenty minutes or so. I reminded her that in another couple of months she'd be coming out here for the summer.

"Will he be out of jail by then?" she asked.

"Of course he will," I said, trying to sound confident.

We chatted for a while longer about school, basketball, and a boy who had a crush on her. Eventually the conversation wound down, and we were both silent.

"Are you sure Dad is going to be okay?" she asked.

"Absolutely."

"Okay. Good night, Pen."

"Good night."

I looked at the phone in my hand, reflecting that Alicia was such a resilient girl, surviving her parents' bitter divorce, her father's involvement in a scandal, and now separation from James, who lived half a continent away. James had hesitated before moving back to the area where he'd grown up. But he concluded, after consulting with the attorneys, counselors, and therapists, that thanks to the restrictive visitation rights imposed in Minnesota, he'd be able to see her just about as often if he lived in California and visited regularly. He did a fair amount of business in Minnesota, which made visiting easier. He also hoped that moving away might help to defuse the tension between him and his ex-wife.

I went to bed, exhausted, but was unable to sleep, thinking and praying about James and about the detectives and Adam and Lisa Darden. And I thought about the incredibly foolish thing I'd done that afternoon: I had lied to the police. And it hadn't been a minor fib, but a whopper. I told them I'd had no contact with Celia since we saw her at the mall in mid-January. But in fact I had talked to her again, that same evening.

We'd gone back to James's house—a place I didn't care for to begin with. My mood had been miserable after seeing Celia. James had offered to cook dinner and had run out to pick up a few groceries. I'd sat there in front of the television, thinking about Celia, getting angrier and more jealous by the minute. Finally I had picked up James's landline, scrolled through the stored numbers, and called her.

"Celia," I'd said when she answered, "this is Pen. We need to talk."

"Pen?" She sounded surprised. "Talk about what?"

"Don't play dumb. I saw the way you were looking at him." She let out a short, incredulous laugh. "You're delusional."

"I'm not an idiot. You never accepted it when he broke up with you. I'm telling you to accept it."

"Really? Or what?"

If she was trying to push my buttons, she was succeeding. "Just back off," I said.

"You're sounding a little insecure, Pen."

"Really? I'm not the one who lost out to a cripple in a wheelchair."

"And I'm not the one who feels worried enough to call and make threats. James may have liked the idea of your great sense of humor and feisty attitude, but he's still a man. Sooner or later, he's going to want a complete woman."

I sputtered. "And you're saying I'm . . . you *bitch!*"

"Better watch yourself, Pen."

"You're the one who'd better watch—"

She had hung up. Hung up on me.

It's not unusual for a paraplegic to spend a long time in the bathroom. That's what I had done after the call, hiding out and composing myself until I felt able to go out and face James. But that didn't mean the anger, jealousy, and shame I felt had dissipated. In fact, it had been festering since then.

There really hadn't been any reason to lie. I could have spun the call any way I wanted, with no fear of contradiction. But I didn't want to admit making the call at all, to saying the things I had said, to having the feelings I'd had. I wanted to bury the entire episode. And so I did.

I continued to lie awake, waiting in vain for sleep to rescue me from the shame and the worry. For months I'd marveled at the reversal of fortune I had experienced during the last year. I had left Minnesota unemployed, broke, tainted by scandal, virtually friendless, and seriously questioning my ability to live independently as a paraplegic. Now I had a challenging new career, a relationship with a man who seemed too good to be true, and a close friendship with Rena, who, thank God, was here to support me. Now I began to wonder if any of it was real, if the entire new life I'd built for myself would exist when I woke up.

Outside, a man sat in a nondescript sedan, parked two houses down on Covina. He watched the lights go out in Pen Wilkinson's apartment and pondered his next move.

Chapter 12

My phone was already buzzing when I rolled into my office the next morning. It was Vik. "Connie wants to see you," he said. "Can you come right down?"

When I entered her office, Connie, standing behind her desk as usual, looked up at me over her stylish, severe half-glasses. "What happened yesterday?" she demanded.

It took me a moment to catch on. "You mean with the Newport Beach police?"

"Yes. You didn't tell me when I called last night."

She'd given me no chance to do so during the thirty-second conversation, and it hadn't come up during the meeting with O'Shea. Now I gave her a complete account, and she stopped me several times to ask questions. It was the longest conversation I'd ever had with her. When I finished she said, "You told them all of this, with no counsel?"

"Yes."

She gave me a curious look, perhaps unable to decide whether to be impressed by my confidence or disgusted by my stupidity. "Are they interested in you as a suspect?"

"Potentially, since I might have a motive."

"What do they have on you?"

"I was at the boat that night, at some point before the murder, and no, they apparently don't have any usable surveillance video. They also think they have motive, since Celia used to date Carter. But they won't be able to prove anything substantive on that because there isn't anything."

"The search and forensics came up empty?"

"They're not telling me anything, of course. But you have my word—there was nothing to turn up."

"What about Carter?"

"I honestly don't know what they have on him, other than his being there at some point, owning the boat, and dating her in the past. They must have something more than that, but I don't know what it is."

"I'm not happy at all, Pen. And Dave will not be happy. This is a terrible reflection on our office. It also comes at a critical time."

"What do you want me to do?"

"Continue to cooperate fully—and I mean fully. Under normal circumstances I'd suspend you until you're fully cleared, but I don't have that luxury now. Any progress in talking to Darden?"

"No."

"I've put in a call to Washington and will tell them to get in touch with you for an update. Find Lisa and get her back on board."

I left Connie's office feeling overwhelmed. If I didn't come through, the US attorney would have to go on TV and explain how his office had bungled a major case. The defendants would act all indignant, claiming we never had a case against them. But if we didn't bring Lisa in by Monday, there wouldn't be much point in going before the judge and talking about a trial date. And there might not be much point in my reporting for work on Tuesday.

I had hoped Connie might have some empathy for me, since she'd been a hands-on trial lawyer until recently. In fact, Connie and Vik, before they assumed administrative posts, had been a legendary trial team. Throughout a trial, Vik would do most of the direct examination, coming off as the affable voice of reason. Meanwhile, Connie would play the bad cop, doing most of the cross-examination—ferreting out lies, discrediting defense witnesses, and nailing the scumbag defendant. Then, as the case neared its end, they would switch roles. In the closing statements and rebuttal, Connie's tone would soften as she pleaded for the jury's sympathy for the victims and their families, while Vik would be stirred to indignation, demanding justice and a long sentence for the vile perpetrator. It was powerful stuff.

Back at my desk, I checked the online version of the LA *Times*, which now identified James Carter as the man arrested in Celia's death, although he hadn't yet been charged. The article also disclosed that Celia had been stabbed to death and, infuriatingly, identified James as Celia's "boyfriend."

I nearly exploded. The least they could do was report that James was her former boyfriend. Former. But the little Voice of Reason in the back of my head kept asking a very reasonable question: What was she doing at James's boat?

I picked up the phone and tried Eric Carter. He was in a meeting.

I looked back at the article, which concluded by saying that if he was charged, James would appear before a judge in Santa Ana tomorrow morning.

I took a deep breath, exhaled, and immersed myself in the Shields case. I checked my email, but Adam hadn't replied. I called John Gibson's assistant and scheduled a meeting with the FBI agent to discuss the presentation of financial and accounting testimony at the trial. Then I returned a call from Tim Brinkley, a Justice Department official in Washington who was our contact for the case.

"I hear we have a little problem," said Brinkley—a man I'd never met but had talked to briefly on a couple of occasions. "Tell me about it."

I did.

"Have you asked the FBI to help track her down?" he said.

"Yes. I'm told they're working on it, but they don't seem to have a lot of urgency."

"I see." Brinkley sounded a little irked but not surprised. We talked for another half hour about the case in general, discussing the other witnesses, the order in which they'd be called, the theme of our opening statements, and other matters. When we finished the discussion he paused, then said, "Damnit, this case is doable. Not a slam-dunk, but doable. All we need is our witness. Keep trying."

I hung up, suspecting that something I knew nothing about was happening behind the scenes. I was besieged by strange events, things that simply did not happen. Assistant US attorneys did not leave their jobs with absolutely no notice or cooperation. Junior lawyers were not put in charge, however briefly, of salvaging high-stakes, high-profile political cases. All this was playing out in a way I couldn't begin to understand.

Cassandra waddled in to report on her efforts to find Lisa. "Anything new?" I asked.

"No. I'm basically calling the same people repeatedly. And getting the same non-answers."

"Let's keep the pressure on. Get in touch with the parents and sister. Try to talk them into turning her around."

"All right, but I don't think Lisa is returning their calls, either. You know, if the trial is delayed . . ."

"I know. That takes us into your delivery time frame. And we'd need you more than ever. All I can say is, one crisis at a time. If we don't find Lisa, Junior can arrive anytime he wants."

Her response was testy. "It's a 'she.'"

"Of course. My apologies. Have you met any of these people, Cassandra? Lisa's family or boyfriend?"

"A lowly intern like me? Meeting with actual witnesses? I'm afraid not."

"That may change if we don't get some help soon."

"Really? Scraping the bottom of the barrel, are we? I feel so privileged."

"Damnit, Cassandra, I'm not in the mood. I don't know what I've done to make you feel permanently offended and pissed off, and I'm starting not to care. I need help, not attitude." She looked me over. "I'd say you definitely need help." She left.

I forced myself to calm down. Somehow I had to work with this woman. She was about as warm and cooperative as North Korea, but she was all I had. She obviously resented being at the bottom of the food chain, but I was a long way down myself, low enough that I'd never met Lisa in person, although I'd talked to her on several occasions. I'd also talked very briefly to her sister Stacy. Lisa had stayed with her for a couple of weeks after she moved back to Minneapolis. I wondered if Stacy might be able to convince Lisa to change her mind and testify; she had seemed supportive in the past. But now she wasn't returning our phone calls, either.

My cell phone buzzed, and I pulled up a text message. It was from Rena and said simply: "Thinking of you. Hang in there. Talk tonight."

I texted back: "Thanks."

I decided to call Stacy later. For the moment, I figured I'd try the FBI again. I dialed Gibson and enjoyed yet another intimate chat with his voicemail.

At nine, I went downstairs for two court appearances on other cases, arguing against a defendant's motion to suppress incriminating statements in a campaign finance case, and attending a status hearing on the bribery trial of an IRS agent. Back at the office, I checked my messages and saw that Gibson had called.

I punched in the number.

"Gibson here."

"Tell me something good, John."

"We've already gotten the police up in Minneapolis to do a welfare check. She's not there. I've gotten approval to have a check done on Lisa's cell phone, credit cards, and ATM. We'll also be making some basic calls to family, friends, and colleagues."

"Great. How long will it take?"

"I don't know. A day or two, maybe."

I took a deep breath and exhaled slowly.

"Pen?"

"John, we are running out of time. I've got to go into court Monday for a status hearing, and it would be nice not to look like a complete fool."

"We're working on it." Maybe, I thought. But the prospect of my personal embarrassment obviously wasn't motivating them to speed things up.

"Obviously I'll be interested in the results as soon as you get them."

"Sure. Is there anything else?"

"Nothing whatsoever, John." I hung up, calmed myself down for few minutes, and then spent the rest of the day in serious trial preparation for the Shields case, trying to lose myself in the work and not think about James. At five-thirty my cell phone buzzed, and I checked the caller ID: Eric Carter.

"Yes, Eric?"

"Can you come over?"

"I'll be there in twenty minutes."

I put my blazer on, signed out, and rolled the three blocks to Eric Carter's office on the thirty-fifth floor of an expensive high-rise building. As I waited in the reception area for Eric to come out, I thought about what it might be like to practice law in a place like this. The surroundings were luxurious, and the perks, prestige, and money would be abundant. But I doubted that the actual substance of the job would be much different. There would still be long hours, stress, and internal politics to contend with. And for me, something important would be missing: the feeling that most of the time, I represented the good guys.

Eric came out of the elevator—apparently his office was actually on another floor—and led me to a conference room down a short hallway. He sat down and got right to business. "First of all, have you had any further contact with the police?" he asked.

"No."

He thought about this, and it occurred to me that he didn't know whether to be relieved, for my sake, or concerned, for his brother's.

"It still looks likely that he'll be charged," he said. "We won't know for sure until the hearing tomorrow. If the judge does grant bail, it's certain to be in the seven-figure range. We're working to raise the money now."

"Am I still a suspect, or person of interest, or whatever?"

"I don't know, but we have to assume you are. If anything, your motive is better than James's."

"What is the police's theory of the case?"

"We still don't know."

"Stabbings are messy. They should have found blood on our clothes or in our vehicles and houses."

"If they have anything like that, I think I would have heard about it."

"But they have to have something."

"Agreed. And I'm not sure how we're going to find out. They don't have to reveal their evidence at this stage."

"We can't wait for the preliminary hearing," I said. "We need to know now."

"We don't have a source at the moment."

"Let me see what I can do on that," I said.

He thought about it, exhaled, and nodded. "All right. But be careful. Don't leave any fingerprints on it."

After a moment of silence I said, "Eric, what was Celia doing at the boat? She must have been looking for him."

"It's hard to see any other explanation. But we have no idea why. James says she still has the key to the boat and the combination for the security gate from the old days."

I felt a nauseating wave of jealousy pass through me.

Eric leaned down and put his hands on my shoulders. I looked into his face, which reminded me achingly of James's. He said, "You can be sure of this: James may have run across Celia from time to time, but he was not dating her. He loves you."

I managed to nod.

"Take care, Pen."

I took the elevator down to street level, feeling dazed. Rolling out onto the sidewalk, I heard someone calling my name.

I looked up. I was being hailed by a distinguished-looking crocodile posing as a defense attorney. Brandon Lacey, Congressman Shields's lead counsel, stood next to a limousine parked at the curb. Lacey, a wiry, balding man, walked over to me. "Ms. Wilkinson?"

"Mr. Lacey." As a junior prosecutor, I wasn't on a first-name basis with a high-priced guy like Lacey.

"I hear you're in charge of the case now."

"Just temporarily."

"Right. My client would like to have a word with you, if you have a minute."

"What's it about?"

"I'll let him explain." He started to walk away.

"Uh-uh," I said. "If I talk to him, I want you there." I could easily imagine a guy like Lacey setting me up, complaining to the judge that I was meeting with his client behind his back. I'd already had too much contact with Hammer.

Lacey's expression conveyed discomfort and irritation. Without a word, he turned back and joined me on the sidewalk.

The rear car door opened, and Congressman Latham Shields emerged from the car. Flashing a broad smile, Shields looked the part of a distinguished, successful politician. He was sixty-two years old, with a full head of gray hair, although his midsection was beginning to thicken a bit. He was surprisingly short, but I remembered he was once a fighter pilot.

He extended his hand. "Ms. Wilkinson? Larry Shields. How do you do?"

We shook, and he said, "Are you headed back to the courthouse?"

I nodded, and he said, "I'd offer you a lift, but . . ." He waved vaguely toward my chair and the car and said, "Mind if I walk with you?"

"It's a public sidewalk," I said. We started down the block, with Lacey at his side and two guys—apparently aides or security men—walking in front and behind, but out of earshot.

"What happened to Adam?" he asked.

"Took another job."

He nodded sympathetically. "Hard to keep good help on a government salary."

I didn't reply. Shields was a frequent critic of wasteful government spending and overpaid government employees. The Defense Department was, however, exempt from all such criticism.

"I heard Lisa backed out on you," he said.

"She hasn't told me that," I said, wondering how he knew it.

He looked at Lacey, then gave me a curious glance. "Have you talked to her?"

"I can't comment on that."

"I heard you haven't actually been able to find her."

"Really? And how would you know such a thing?"

He smiled. "I can't comment on that," he said, mocking me. He turned and waved to a passerby who recognized him.

"You know I'm not the ogre Lisa says I am," he continued. "The case is not about your being a good or bad person."

He smiled. "Of course it is. The jurors—they'll be ordinary folks. When they've tried in vain to sift through all the evidence —all the statutes, all the invoices and exhibits, all the legalities— that's exactly what it comes down to. Is this a good guy, or bad?"

His arrogance—his casual contempt for the law—made me seethe. I wanted this guy, badly. "That's what your attorneys tell you?"

"I'm afraid I don't listen much to the lawyers. Right, Brandon?" He chuckled and looked over at Lacey, who smiled dutifully. "I suppose I should, considering the exorbitant amounts I'm paying them. But it's about people, Pen, always. And you have to consider the people involved here."

"What's your point, Congressman?"

"Even if Lisa took the stand, her testimony would be colored by her feelings. You have to consider the personal motivations involved here."

I should have kept my mouth shut, but Shields was pissing me off, and I wasn't in a great mood to begin with. I said, "Lisa wasn't planning on making an issue of your sexual harassment. But if you decide to go after her, using the Slut Defense or the Woman Scorned defense or whatever, then everything will be on the table. We plan to stick to the law, but if you want to get into character and motivations, all I can say is, you dealt it."

"You sound awfully confident for a prosecutor who can't locate her star witness."

And he sounded all too confident about her, I thought. "We'll find her," I said. "And when we do, there will be a full investigation to determine who or what caused her to drop out of contact."

We stopped at a traffic light, and he looked over at me. "This case is a road to nowhere, Pen." He glanced up at the *Don't Walk* sign, then back down at me. "You haven't been in the game that long, from what I hear. Are you sure you're reading the signals from your superiors correctly?"

I didn't respond. I'd been wondering the same thing.

He smiled. "Nice to have met you, Pen." He turned on his heel and walked back toward his car, followed by his attorney and security guys.

I sat at the curb, trying to catch my breath. Had I really just told off a US congressman? What on earth had I been thinking? I always lived with the knowledge that someday, my big mouth was going to get me into trouble. But that realization never seemed to kick in when I needed it most. Shields had to have sensed that all my tough talk had been bluster, with nothing to back it up. I had no witness, no help, and minimal support from my bosses. I glanced across the intersection. The signal now said *Walk*, but I didn't want to move, even if I'd been able to walk. As with Milt Hammer, Shields had been watching me—stalking me, even—and tried to warn me off the case. Why?

Pedestrians were now moving around me, some muttering in irritation, to cross the street. Shields and Hammer knew I had no authority to drop the case. They may have simply wanted to take my measure. But their purpose in confronting me had likely been intimidation, to discourage me from finding Lisa or moving ahead with trial preparation. They wanted me to go to Connie and O'Shea and tell them the trial was not doable. I had little doubt they had had something to do with making Lisa vanish, and for all I knew, they'd made Adam disappear and caused the FBI to drag its feet in cooperating with us. And where were my bosses in all this?

I looked across the street, where the light flashed "Don't Walk" again. It seemed to be my day for mixed signals.

Chapter 13

She woke up with a start. Then she remembered. The horror hit her full force, and she curled up even more tightly.

How long had she been here? Several days—she was pretty certain of that. Beyond that, it was hard to say. At first, she thought about getting up, turning the lights on, and searching the place for a means of taking her own life. But she was too afraid.

She opened her eyes and looked around the darkened room, trying to pull some normal memories from the morass of fright. Tentatively, she sat up. She smelled of sweaty fear. Her eyes were crusted from being tightly shut. Her body ached from being contorted into a fetal position. The man had predicted that she would be able to function within a couple of days, but he'd said that reactions varied.

Probing back further into her memories, she dared to recall the man named Terrence, who had been waiting for her when she returned home. His matter-of-fact, solicitous tone had sounded profoundly creepy as he told her that post-traumatic stress disorder would be a given, but that she should be able to overcome it with time and therapy. He'd spoken with the efficient, detached friendliness of a technician explaining an outpatient medical procedure as he warned her that her muscles would ache for some days from straining against the bonds, and that there was a small chance of damage to her voice box from the screams. He was concerned for her safety and comfort, he claimed, so he had removed her clothing and then provided padded restraints, a soft block to bite on, and padding against the bed's headboard to prevent her from pounding her head. And then he . . .

Her parched mouth contorted into a scream, but no sound came out.

Only when the ordeal was over did he tell her, almost as an afterthought, the reason for inflicting the terror.

No testimony.

Disappear for ten days.

Then Terrence had simply walked away, apparently believing—no, knowing—that his will would be accomplished.

Chapter 14

Rena Karros was one of those people you either loved or loved to hate—or sometimes a little of both. Men wanted her, and women—well, a lot of them wanted to throttle her. Not only was she unnaturally smart, confident, gracious, and beautiful in a way that managed to come off as both exotic and wholesome, but she was also exceedingly—even infuriatingly—nice. I waited for her at a table at our favorite Mexican restaurant in Westwood, where we got together for dinner, in theory, every Wednesday night. In practice, due to travel and work conflicts, it worked out to about every other week.

Rena walked in—no, floated in—promptly at seven. She might cancel appointments from time to time, but she was never late. She was short and slender, with olive skin and short, dark hair, wearing a business suit that probably cost more than anything in my wardrobe, and that was saying something. Rena, three years older than I, had moved out to LA after marrying her husband, also an attorney. Despite a stellar academic record, she wasn't able to land a job with the top firms in LA and ended up at the US attorney's office, not a bad consolation prize. But a few years ago she'd moved on to Benning and last year became its general counsel at the very young age of thirty-nine. She was a Type A posing as a Type B. I was a Type A myself, but I'd never fool anybody.

"Hi," Rena said, giving me a peck on the cheek. "Is Pam coming?"

"She said she would try. I think she could use a margarita or two."

"Why?"

I told her about Adam's abrupt resignation.

She looked genuinely shocked. "Unbelievable," she said. "That's something you just don't do. That's not the Adam I know." Rena knew Adam from her time at the US attorney's office but hadn't worked closely with him.

"Did he quit so he could start running for office?" Rena asked.

"Not right away. Supposedly he's already started his new job."

"Maybe I'll make a couple of calls and see what I can find out," she said. Rena was politically active and had raised money for a number of candidates, including Congressman Latham Shields's opponent.

I looked at my watch. "If Pam makes it, she should be here around eight. Let's hear what she has to say."

We ordered margaritas, and I dug into the basket of chips the waiter placed in front of us. I said, "Well, on to the topic of the day, I guess."

Rena tried to sound encouraging. "You made it through another day."

"I guess I did. But what about James?"

"He's a tough guy—he'll be all right. Just take a deep breath, have a drink, and get a good night's sleep tonight. I know it sounds lame, but things will work out. I believe that."

For no logical reason, I already felt better. "The only way I see to resolve this is for the truth to come out," I said. "They have to find out who really killed Celia."

"It's only been a day. Give the police a chance."

The police had already had their chance, I thought grimly. And they'd arrested James.

I saw Rena look up; Dr. Pam LaRue had arrived. She plopped down in the chair between Rena and me, a tall, athletic figure with her straw-colored hair pulled back. She looked exhausted and a little disheveled. She looked around and saw she was facing toward the wall. "Rena," she said, "will you get the waiter's attention for me? If I don't get a drink fast, I may have to tackle the guy."

Rena executed a slick, eye-contact-only summons of the waiter, and Pam ordered a Corona. Rena and I decided to wait a bit before having another round.

Pam's beer arrived. "Great," Rena said. "Now the staff is safe."

"Right," she said, lifting her bottle to her lips, then setting it down. "Beating up on the waiters would be bad form, since it's Adam's butt I really want to kick."

"Tell us about it," Rena said.

Pam described Adam's announcement the previous week. "I was shocked he would even consider leaving," she said. "As far as I knew, he really liked it at the US attorney's office and his career there was going well. Oh, he'd grumble about Connie and O'Shea once in a while, but he was happy, or so I thought. He liked working with you, Pen. He was looking forward to trying the Shields case."

"What did you say when he told you?" I asked.

"I was dumbfounded. I just said, 'Where the hell is this bullshit coming from, Adam? You've never been interested in making money.'"

"Maybe he wanted to get started on his campaign," Rena said. "He'd be free to run for office if he was with a private law firm."

Pam wrapped long fingers with unpainted, short-cut nails around her Corona bottle. "I asked him about that, but he denied it. He told me he still wanted to run for the Assembly seat and thought he had a good shot at it, but that if anything, it would be harder with the demands of a new law firm." She looked up at me. "He sure as hell put you in a bind."

I nodded slowly. "Especially with Lisa Darden backing out on us."

Rena put her drink down. "You didn't tell me about that."

"I guess I didn't." I brought both her and Pam up to date, swearing them both to secrecy.

Rena listened carefully, saying nothing. Then she leaned forward, lowering her voice almost imperceptibly. "Is something going on here, Pen? Is this just too big a coincidence? Adam leaving and Lisa reneging at the same time?"

I'd been wondering the same thing, especially with my superiors not reacting quite as I'd expected them to. But without proof, I wasn't about to start talking out of school, speculating and trashing people's reputations. "I don't see anything sinister," I said. "Unless we think Adam's part of a conspiracy."

Pam shook her head. "He's behaving like an ass, but I can't see him sabotaging the case. I can't count the number of times he told me how much he was looking forward to nailing Shields. He said he thought the case was winnable."

"Do you suppose he already knew Lisa would refuse to testify?" Rena asked.

"If he knew that, he never mentioned it to anyone."

"And he apparently didn't try to get her back," I added. "I don't think he knew."

"He goes flying off to Singapore and then doesn't even call," Pam said, signaling for another beer. "For the life of me, I just can't figure out what got into him." Rena and I didn't know what to say. "But maybe I shouldn't have been so surprised," she continued. "He's been distant lately—something on his mind. I'd actually been half-expecting the ring for the past few months. Ever since we bought the house together. Hell, we own *dogs* together."

She sat up, accepting the fresh Corona. We ordered dinner, which Rena and I supplemented with another round of margaritas.

"What if he comes back, suitably contrite and promising to make it up to you?" Rena asked.

Pam sighed. "I don't know. I'm just not sure how I'd feel. I thought I knew him so well, and then . . . Then there's the whole political thing. If he runs for the Assembly, he'll be out campaigning all the time, and if he wins, he'll be gone for long stretches, up in Sacramento. We'll just have to see."

Rena stood up to go to the bathroom. "Want an escort?" Pam asked. We knew Rena would be hit on before reaching the back of the restaurant, probably more than once. I'd once attracted similar attention, but that seemed like a long time ago.

Rena didn't smile. "Maybe I should be listening to offers," she said and left without elaborating.

"Uh-oh," Pam said. "Man trouble for her, too?"

"I don't know. She hasn't said anything."

Pam took a long pull from her beer. "So, how are you and James doing these days, Pen?"

I realized I hadn't told her about Celia or James, and Pam prided herself on never watching the news.

She listened intently, incredulous, as I related the events of the past three days. "Good Lord," she said when I finished. "Here I am prattling on, bitching about Adam. That's nothing compared to what you're facing. I'm so sorry, Pen."

Rena returned.

"Any interesting offers?" I asked.

"There's a guy with some really cool tats who wants to take me up the coast on his Harley." A pause. "I'm giving it some thought."

Pam and I looked at each other, trying to interpret the un-Rena-like statement, wondering if she might actually be having marital problems. Rena and I made eye contact, and I understood that we'd talk about it some other time. She didn't seem to feel comfortable discussing it with Pam present.

Despite her seemingly charmed life, I knew she had problems like anyone. Her father was a successful contractor; her controlling, perfectionist mother was a professional pain in the rear. She'd met her husband Steve, a top graduate of Georgetown Law School, while doing a summer clerkship for a law firm in Washington, DC, and they'd moved to LA after they each graduated from law school. She hadn't told me they were having problems, although I knew they were trying unsuccessfully to have a child.

We wrapped it up a little after nine with a group hug and a few tears, and I began the long drive home to Long Beach, my spirits bolstered by my friends' support. I got home and had spread my work out on the dining room table when a knock at the door interrupted me. I rolled over to admit Eleanor Tompkins, who had brought me a plate containing two of her scrumptious homemade cinnamon rolls. "I won't stay," she said. "I can see you're busy. Are you doing okay?"

"I'm hanging in there, Eleanor."

"And James will be out of jail soon?"

"Absolutely."

She smiled. "Good luck." She patted my arm and left.

I found myself wishing she'd stayed longer. I could have used some additional distraction and really didn't want to go back to my work. Which was irrelevant, because my work came to me.

My landline rang, and I checked the ID: US attorney's office. I answered. "Connie?"

"Dave O'Shea," said the intense male voice. I didn't expect him to call me directly. But now, for better or worse, I was the only contact he had for the Shields case.

"I want to know what progress you've made on locating our witness," he said.

As succinctly as I could, I laid out what we had done.

"Keep at it and find her." He hung up.

I replaced the receiver and wondered once again what message I was supposed to be receiving. He went through the motions of telling me it was important to find Lisa, but he didn't seem inclined to aggressively lean on the FBI to make it happen. And now, an even more sinister thought forced its way into the back of my mind: What if he knew I wouldn't find her?

I pulled up my notes of the pivotal meeting at Suite 2416 at the Discovery Hotel in downtown Los Angeles involving Congressman Latham Shields, PTG Assistant General Counsel Milt Hammer, and Hammer's boss, CEO Wilson Lopez. Lopez, incidentally, carried on a bitter rivalry with Benning CEO Dick Westcott, dating from the days when both of them had been in line for the CEO position at defense contractor Horrey Technologies. Neither of them, it turned out, got the job. Since then, Westcott had gone on to be a successful, articulate, politically active spokesman for the business community. Lopez, my defendant, had gone on to be a sleazeball. Even so, the prosecution team considered Hammer the ringleader and driving force behind the scheme.

Lopez had originally denied being at the meeting at the Discovery, saying he couldn't remember attending. He'd changed his story when surveillance cameras in the lobby showed him going up in the elevator, followed by Shields a while later. Milt Hammer had already arrived. No one else from Shields's staff or PTG had attended. But within a week, work had begun on the congressman's vacation home, and Lisa Darden had contacted prosecutors. Lopez and Hammer's company, PTG, had already been awarded a huge Navy contract.

I continued to go over my notes on the meeting, feeling as though I was missing something. But I couldn't figure it out. I picked up the phone and dialed the cell number for Hal Dwyer, who owned the boat two slips down from James's. We had become friendly over the past year, and I knew he had a friend who was well connected with area law enforcement agencies.

"Hey, Pen," Hal said. "How's California?"

"You're not here?"

"No. I've got some business in Minneapolis. How's life?"

"Not so good, Hal." I filled him in on Celia's murder and James's arrest.

"Holy smoke," he said. "Are you okay?"

"So far," I said.

"I keep telling Neil, the marina manager, that he needs better security cameras—better security in general. Who's handling the case for the police?"

"Lieutenant Dan Howard."

"I've met him. He's smart. I think he's fair, too, but you don't want to mess with him."

"Right now he's not telling us what the police have on James. You think you could ask your friend?"

"Yes, I'll give Ted a call and see what he can find out. Should I have him call you?"

"Actually, could you have him call James's brother, Eric?"

"Good thinking."

I gave him the number. "Thanks, Hal."

"No problem. Hang in there, Pen."

Against my better judgment, I watched the eleven o'clock news. The story about Celia came about three minutes into the broadcast. A banner across the bottom of the screen announced: *Breaking News: Murder in Newport Beach.* A picture of Celia, with glossy shoulder-length hair framing her elegant features and smooth, coffee-colored skin, flashed onto the screen. A big-haired reporter, standing in front of Benning's corporate head-quarters near the LA airport, started by showing sound bites from Celia's stunned family members and co-workers, including Benning CEO Dick Westcott. Then the reporter complained that police weren't talking about the investigation, which Lieu-tenant Dan Howard tersely described as ongoing, despite the arrest of James Carter. Pictures from a circling news helicopter zoomed in on the *Alicia C.* Next, there was a shot of a grim-looking Eric Carter, facing an arsenal of microphones, making a one-sentence statement: "James Carter is totally innocent of any crimes or wrongdoing and will cooperate fully with the police in finding Celia Sims's killer." I was surprised; a statement like that normally came from the defendant's counsel. The reporter noted that the police had declined to specify the exact nature of the relationship between Celia and Carter.

I wished somebody would do that, too.

The report went on to describe James as a "controversial" figure in the business world who had implemented large downsizings at three major banks in Los Angeles, Charlotte, and Minneapolis. The report gave a brief and largely accurate account of James's ouster from North Central Bank in Minneapolis in a scandal that later turned out to be the work of corporate saboteurs, noting that he was one of the country's highest-ranking African-American corporate executives. The piece wrapped up by describing James's current position as a venture capitalist and said he was expected to be freed or charged tomorrow.

I wrapped things up at midnight, got into bed, and lay awake for a long time. I found myself wondering over and over again how much contact James'd had with Celia, why he didn't tell me about it, and what it meant.

I wasn't sure I wanted to know the answers.

Chapter 15

Outside, in a nondescript sedan parked down the block, the man named Terrence talked into a cell phone. "I'm doing what you asked," he said. "I'm monitoring the prosecutor."

"How?"

"You don't want to know that." In fact, he was listening to transmissions from a bug he had placed in Pen Wilkinson's apartment.

"Fine," said Rick Stouffer. "There's no sign of the witness?"

"None. Don't worry about it—the Treatment always works."

Terrence heard silence on the line. He knew Stouffer was debating whether to ask what the Treatment was and how it worked.

"Good," Stouffer said at last. "So the prosecutors have stopped working on the case? They've given up looking for her?"

This clever response—demanding results while distancing himself from the methods—surprised Terrence, who began to wonder if Stouffer might not be as big a fool as he appeared. "You don't seem to get it," Terrence said. "I was not hired to make all prosecutors, at all times, give up. I was not hired to guarantee no one would ever look for her. I was hired to neutralize the prosecutor—one specific individual—plus the witness. I did that. Then you came back and asked me to monitor an additional prosecutor, a rookie whom I am assured is not a serious threat. I'm doing that, and I expect to be compensated for it."

"So what do you know about Celia Sims's murder?"

"I was going to ask you the same thing," Terrence said.

"You're telling me you know nothing about it?"

"It has nothing to do with me."

"If you say so," Stouffer replied, sounding skeptical. "But it might have something to do with *us*. She was close to some of the players."

"If I learn anything about it, I will let you know."

"Do that." Stouffer hung up.

Terrence picked up his earphones and took another listen, enough to confirm that Pen Wilkinson had gone to sleep. Her conversations at home had centered not on the Shields case but on James Carter. That was fine as far as it went. But he could see why Pen made Stouffer and his group uneasy. She was capable and had a powerful motivation: she wanted to keep her job. True, she was now tied down with the Celia Sims investigation. But he couldn't count on that. And he wouldn't—his job was to monitor her and, if necessary, neutralize her. And he always did his job.

Terrence considered himself neither sadist nor psychopath. He was simply a professional who enjoyed his job, was good at it, and liked being good at it. There were very few people who did what he did at such a high level, with the same degree of precision, thoroughness, and effectiveness. Even fewer did the specific type of work he did, a job that was hard to describe but that he thought of as behavior modification. His clients paid very well and were justified in demanding results, which he always delivered. But the job had to be clearly defined, and he always had to guard against mission creep.

His latest mission was unique. Stouffer and his group, which they called the Cabal, thought they had hired him. In fact, they had been steered to him by the Partners, who were on the other side of the transaction. The interests of the Partners and the Cabal were mostly aligned. Mostly. Stouffer actually hadn't been terrible to work with. True, he was a preening jackass, and he'd tried to slide in a few extra duties. He'd also been greedy enough to let Milt Hammer work both sides of the same deal. But his money was as green as anyone's. And with Windfall, there would be an awful lot of it.

Chapter 16

I had just rolled out of the shower when my cell phone buzzed. I picked it up off the bathroom counter and glanced at the caller ID: Newport Beach Police Department.

I cursed under my breath and answered the call. It was Detective Kozlowski, asking me to come in for questioning at eight. The timing couldn't have been more inconvenient, and they didn't give me any advance notice. Now was just not a good time to show up late for work. But I was under orders to cooperate fully, and if Eric was correct, I might still be under suspicion. I gritted my teeth and told Kozlowski I'd be there.

I backed my van out of the carport, and half a block down, a beige sedan pulled out, made a U-turn, and drove away. I thought I'd seen the car there when I came home yesterday, but I dismissed the thought as paranoia. I exited the 405 at Jamboree and headed west toward the ocean, noticing the heavy haze that darkened the sky. A metaphor for the situation, I thought.

Back in the interrogation room at police headquarters, the detectives didn't fool around. Howard, dressed immaculately in a charcoal-gray suit, again took the lead. This time, they gave me the Miranda warnings immediately. I was in custody and not free to leave. If they wanted to put the fear in me, they were succeeding. I had to sign another form waiving my rights, and the questioning began.

Howard went over some familiar ground, asking me about my relationship with James and any contacts I'd had with Celia. They asked if I knew where Celia worked and lived, and how I knew. They made me repeat my account of running into her at

Fashion Island, and I lied again, telling them that this encounter had been the last time I'd had any contact with her. I hoped to God they wouldn't ask me to take a polygraph test; I would have made the pointers jump off the scale. Then they went into my knowledge of any contacts between James and Celia. Since my last session with the police, I'd learned from Eric that it was probable the two had met. But I stuck stubbornly to what I knew firsthand. Howard checked his notes, then glanced at Kozlowski, who responded with a nod. She reached under the table, took out an evidence bag, and produced a knife.

It was a paring knife with a black handle. "Do you recognize this?" Howard asked.

"It looks similar to a knife I've seen in James Carter's kitchen."

"What if I told you we recovered this from the bay underneath Carter's boat?"

"I have no knowledge whether that is true or, if it is, how the knife would have gotten there."

"And what if I told you this knife was used to kill Celia Sims?"

"Same answer."

"And what if I told you your fingerprints were found on the knife?"

"Then you would be either grossly mistaken or telling a flat-out lie."

I didn't hesitate in giving the response, but I wondered if it was true. Could I have used the knife at some point? I didn't think so; we didn't do much cooking. And would fingerprints be detectable after the knife had been submerged in the bay? I honestly didn't know; I hadn't worked in criminal law long enough.

Howard sternly reminded me that it was a crime to lie to investigators and asked me if I wanted to reconsider any of my answers. I didn't.

The detectives exchanged glances, and I thought I sensed frustration in their expressions. Kozlowski glanced at her watch. Howard next asked if I knew how Carter had acquired the knife set—I didn't—and whether I knew it was a gift from Celia—I didn't know that, either. Then he got me to admit to having a key to James's house and knowing the security code.

Howard looked up at Kozlowski, who nodded and turned her notepad back a couple of pages. Now she took over the questioning. "Ms. Wilkinson, how long have you been dating James Carter?"

"A little over a year."

"During that time, have you dated anyone else?"

"No."

"Has he?"

"No."

"How do you know?"

"We have an exclusive relationship."

"You have explicitly confirmed that understanding with Mr. Carter?"

"Yes."

"If he were dating someone else, would you know it?"

"That's hypothetical," I said.

She frowned, giving me an expression that said she hated having to question lawyers. "Why don't you answer the question anyway?" she said.

"Why don't you stick to factual questions?" I shot back.

"We'll do the asking," Howard barked.

I smiled. "Of course. Pardon me."

Kozlowski resumed. "You don't know for a fact that he has not seen other women."

"I have no knowledge of his seeing other women."

"So you're not aware that he was seeing Celia Sims."

"I do not accept the premise of your question."

Her follow-up was testy. "If he *was* seeing Celia Sims, you wouldn't have known it."

"Hypotheticals again, Detective."

She looked at Howard with a half-shrug and went on. "Do you have an intimate relationship with Mr. Carter?"

The question made me seethe. They were barging into the most personal, intimate corner of my life like storm troopers. It was none of their damned business. And yet, it was.

"Yes," I said.

This surprised both of them. "You are able to consummate a physical relationship?" Kozlowski asked.

"I believe I've answered the question."

Her follow-up was halting and uncertain. "And you do this . . . regularly?"

"Detective, do you really want to hear the details of my sex life?"

Maybe she did, but they decided not to pursue it. I could see where they were going, of course. In trying to establish that James was seeing Celia on the side, they wanted to show that I couldn't satisfy his physical needs. It was a relevant question, if incredibly offensive. It was no wonder, then, that they looked unhappy with my answer.

Kozlowski looked over her notes and then glanced at Howard, who shook his head. "That will be all for now," she said.

Chapter 17

I drove north to LA, taking deep breaths and trying to talk myself down from the intense, emotional police questioning. On the face of it, the encounter appeared to be a victory for me. They had failed to rattle me, to produce any smoking gun (or bloody knife), or to establish a love triangle between James, Celia, and me. But the knife from James's kitchen helped to explain why he was a suspect. And when it came down to it, the only people with access to James's house, from which the knife was taken, were James, me, and his cleaning lady. And it made me wonder: Assuming the cleaning lady was cleared, and assuming James didn't take the knife, and I didn't take the knife, who did? And how?

If that mystery remained unresolved, questions about timing did not. The detectives had called me in early, conducted the questioning briskly, and glanced at their watches several times. That was because they had a court appearance in Santa Ana, where James Carter, it now seemed certain, would be charged with murder.

I made my way back to the office and stopped by Cassandra's cube. "Anything new?" I asked.

"Nothing," she said. "I keep trying both Lisa and Stacy—no response."

"What about the parents?"

"They say Stacy has assured them everything is okay."

"We need to talk to Stacy."

"I'll keep trying."

"Nothing from Gibson?"

"I'd be the last to hear anything from that tight-ass."

I went into my office, shut the door behind me, and sat behind my desk, trying to collect myself. Then I picked up the phone and called Rena—something I rarely did during the work day.

"What's up?" she said as though she had nothing better to do at the moment than chat with me.

I told her I'd been questioned by the police again.

"What did they ask?"

I managed to pull myself together and haltingly, I described the questioning, finding it hard to talk about the worst parts. "They asked me about our sex life, Rena. They seemed incredulous that James would want me."

"The bastards."

"I suppose they're just doing their job. But it's hard."

"Of course it is. Is there anything I can do?"

"I do have a favor to ask."

"Sure—anything."

"I know you don't think Celia's murder was work-related. But I'd like to talk to somebody at Benning about her. Maybe I could find out something that would give me a clue. Ideally, I'd like to spend a few minutes with Westcott himself."

"Are you sure that's a good idea? I'm sure Dick wouldn't mind at all, but with your job . . ."

"I know it's a little touchy. I'd have to make it clear I'm not wearing my prosecutor hat. I wouldn't tell my bosses about it. I'm just a private citizen with no jurisdiction over the case—an acquaintance of Celia and a friend of James who's trying to help."

"Let me see what I can do and get back to you."

"Thanks."

"No trouble at all."

I was hanging up when I heard the chirp of my cell phone's text alert. I fished the phone out of my purse and accessed the message, which was from Eric Carter:

"J was charged. Bail set at $4m."

I stared at the screen, emotions swirling. I had my work cut out for me.

Chapter 18

The meeting of the Cabal was intended to be a last-minute check on the details, but Rick Stouffer knew it was a gut-check as well. The members needed to support each other, pump each other up, and make sure everybody had the nerve to go through with it. Stouffer walked to a small bar that had been set up against the wall in the airy meeting room overlooking the ocean. He replenished his scotch and turned back to the group.

"Anyone?"

The other two members of the group declined refills, and Stouffer returned to his leather club chair, which had been arranged in a circle with the others. The group had met in person only twice before, each time at this exclusive club in Laguna Beach, of which Stouffer was a member. They jokingly called themselves the Cabal, but Stouffer thought the term fit the group rather well.

The group had been formed less than half a year earlier. Its members were not friends and had little in common other than the similarity of their jobs. But in fact, they did share an important bond. All had been victims of corporate greed and arbitrariness. All had been forced to turn over the fruits of their efforts to greedy CEOs, who appropriated the spoils for themselves and a handful of obsequious cronies. And all were damn sick and tired of it.

"Maybe we should get down to business," Milt Hammer suggested.

"Sure," Stouffer replied. He could see that his other guest, Annette Barnes, was likewise anxious to get started.

"My product is all in place," said Stouffer, who worked for defense contractor Horrey Technologies.

"I've got a couple of loose ends to tie up, but it won't be any problem at all," said Annette Barnes, a tall, rather plain-looking woman. She was vice president for research and development for Benning, the same company that employed Celia Sims and Rena Karros. Milt Hammer, from Pacific Technology Group, simply nodded.

"Looks like we're good for Windfall," said Stouffer. "Just make sure you've got your tracks covered, because there will definitely be an investigation—hopefully not for a while, but it will happen."

More nods around the circle.

"The main reason I wanted to get together is to update everybody on the other conditions set by our partners."

"You mean the trial," Barnes said.

"Essentially, yes. Here's the latest: Our man Terrence is making the case go away. The star prosecution witness has disappeared—not permanently, but for long enough."

"What if she resurfaces?"

"She won't. But if it happens after Windfall, who cares? In addition, we've had a stroke of good luck. The lead prosecutor on the case left to take another job."

"Who's handling the case now?" Barnes asked.

Stouffer was getting seriously pissed at Barnes. "The case is now being handled by a junior attorney," he said. "An inexperienced young lady who really doesn't stand a chance of finding the witness."

"I still don't get it," Barnes said. "What does the Shields bribery trial have to do with us?"

Stouffer shot her an annoyed look. "It doesn't, directly. But our partners are insisting that it go away. They say they're not in a position to proceed with Windfall if it doesn't."

"Why not?"

"I really can't get into that." In fact, Stouffer wasn't entirely sure. He looked at Milt Hammer, who shook his head. He wasn't going to talk about the Partners.

Hammer spoke for the first time. "We don't want to know the details of what Terrence is doing, of course. But he would do well not to underestimate this junior attorney. I've met her, and she's very resourceful and determined."

"Don't underestimate Terrence, either," Stouffer said. "He's the best." He risked a glance at Milt Hammer, whose expression gave away nothing. Hammer was, he thought, the elephant in the room. Nobody really wanted to talk about his flagrant conflict of interest. He definitely wanted Windfall to go ahead, but his interests were also very much aligned with those of the "partners" who wanted the Shields bribery case to go away. Stouffer suspected that Hammer was the real force behind the insistence upon hiring Terrence to deal with the case. And his fellow Cabal members didn't want to know any more than he did how Terrence had eliminated the witness.

It had been surprisingly easy for Stouffer to find Terrence. Stouffer had imagined that such people must exist—professional fixers who operated outside the law, but were more sophisticated than your average leg-breaking thug. Stouffer never imagined it would be easy to find such a person, but all it had taken was a couple of calls before Terrence had called him back. Terrence seemed to fit the bill perfectly: he was intelligent, well-spoken, and called himself a consultant. Truth be told, the guy was creepy, with a nearly constant smile that seemed to combine condescension and contempt, but he was not being paid for his personality. Terrence was also far more expensive than an ordinary criminal.

"What about Celia Sims?" Annette Barnes asked.

"What about her?" Stouffer said. "You knew her, didn't you?"

"Yes. She was capable, even if she wouldn't always listen to reason. We weren't friends."

"I never met her," Stouffer said. "I heard the former boyfriend did it—what's his name . . ."

"Carter," Hammer said. "James Carter."

"You're telling us her murder is a coincidence?" Barnes said. "That it had nothing to do with Windfall or anything else?"

"It doesn't seem to be related, but we'll have to watch it closely." Hammer said. "If they don't establish this Carter as the killer, they'll be looking closely at Benning, where Sims worked, and potentially at you. We don't need anybody doing that right now."

Barnes turned to Stouffer. "You're telling me your buddy Terrence had nothing to do with it?"

"What would be in it for him?" Stouffer asked.

Barnes leaned forward. "Terrence is very motivated to make Windfall happen. Maybe a little too motivated. Maybe he decided to eliminate a highly-placed executive who may have stumbled across something, or just known too much."

"Far-fetched," Stouffer said. "Unless you've been lax in your security precautions."

Barnes's face reddened, but she didn't reply.

"Look," Stouffer continued, "if anything, her murder is going to work to our advantage. The case will be a distraction to this junior prosecutor. She was apparently also dating Carter."

"And that's another coincidence?" Barnes asked, incredulous.

Milt Hammer ignored her. "She's actually been questioned by the police. Extensively."

"You see?" Stouffer said. "That will keep her tied up and distracted. Just chill, people. A few more days and we're home free. Terrence has it under control."

After a moment of silence Barnes said, "Is there any chance this junior prosecutor—what's her name?"

"Pen Wilkinson," Hammer replied.

"Right. Any chance she could have gotten wind of Windfall somehow?"

"I don't see how—" Stouffer began.

"I doubt it, but she would eventually," Hammer said. "Terrence will have to watch her closely over the next few days."

"He's doing just that," Stouffer said.

"So, back to the Celia Sims murder," Barnes said. "Maybe this is the crime of passion it appears to be. But does anybody really believe that? We need to know."

Stouffer turned to Milt Hammer, who shrugged. "I'll read about it in the papers along with the rest of you."

The two guests left, and Rick Stouffer wandered out onto the club's terrace, which was nearly deserted in mid-afternoon. It was a beautiful spring day, with white sailboats dotting the horizon. He hoped the meeting had served its purpose, to hold the Cabal together through Windfall. The group had been formed purely out of self-interest, and after Windfall, there would be no further reason for its existence. In fact, the members had agreed never to see each other again. He knew the Partners were nervous about having to deal with multiple parties, and he kept having to reassure them he had his fellow associates under control.

God, these Cabal members were annoying. Always questioning him, always uneasy, always needing their hands held, always demanding answers about something or other. The winners of the world shouldn't have to deal with people like that. As always, these marginal types were trying to diminish him, to latch onto his success, to take advantage of his idea, to cash in on the deal he'd put together. They would pay the price for messing with him.

He pulled out his phone and called Terrence. "It went fine," he told the consultant. "But after Windfall, I have some people who will need to be dealt with. Parasites and security risks."

"The Cabal wants this done?"

"No, I do, personally. We can talk about the details later, but bottom line: they're gone."

Chapter 19

I sat in front of the television that night, wineglass in hand. I had no idea what program I was actually watching. I'd gotten back to work after the text from Eric but ended up spinning my wheels, preparing for a trial that seemed less and less likely to happen, and trying in vain to find a witness who didn't want to be found.

I'd read an LA *Times* story that aired every piece of dirty laundry it could find, describing "turmoil and disarray" in the US attorney's office. The story reported the apparent change of heart by Lisa Darden, the government's star witness in the Shields case, the abrupt departure of the lead prosecutor, Adam R. Rosenthal, and our motion for a delay of the trial. The article also observed that the "new lead attorney assigned to the case, Doris P. Wilkinson, has been with the US attorney's office for only a year." Thank God they didn't know I had been questioned in a murder investigation. The report then quoted lead defense attorney Brandon Lacey as describing our motion for a trial delay as "an outrageous attempt to subvert the defendants' right to a speedy trial." Finally, the article said that the US attorney's office had declined to comment. O'Shea would be livid about the article, and maybe with me. But the piece was largely accurate.

My phone buzzed. I picked it up from the end table and looked down at the screen: Eric Carter.

"Yes, Eric?"

"I'm outside. May I come in?"

"Of course." I wheeled over to the door to let him in.

Eric looked tired and stressed. He was still wearing a suit, but his tie was loosened. I offered him a glass of wine, but he declined. He took a seat on my couch. "Are you holding up okay?" he asked.

"Barely. The police had me in for more questioning today."

"I know. But obviously they let you go."

I nodded. "And James?"

"He's still in jail. As I said in my text, the judge did set bail, but it's 4 million dollars. We just weren't able to raise that amount today. We're confident we'll have it sometime tomorrow—probably late in the day."

I blinked, trying to hold it together.

Eric said, "Hal's friend Ted called me."

"And?"

"He found out a little of what the police have."

I waited.

"You know James's kitchen knife was the murder weapon?"

"Yes. They showed it to me."

Eric took a breath and exhaled. "Apparently the scene was horrific. Multiple wounds with lots of overkill, the kind of rage that points to a crime of passion."

"And nobody saw anything?"

"There were only a couple of witnesses at the marina. But they weren't much help, apparently. One saw Celia arrive; a different witness saw James leave. They're confused about which happened first. The same two witnesses also saw you leave, but both are fuzzy about when that happened in relation to Celia's arrival and James's departure. Both had been drinking and weren't on deck all the time, or at the same time. About all they can do is place all three of you at the scene at one time or another."

"They didn't see anyone else?"

"No. Of course there must have been someone else, but as I said, the witnesses weren't there all evening, or at the same time, and they were some distance off."

"What do the cell phone location records show?"

"They show that you and James were there at the times you said you were."

"How about Celia?"

Eric grimaced. "Her phone was off for most of the evening. They found it in her purse with a dead battery. So we can't prove she arrived after James left. The phone records do show that Celia and James talked earlier in the day, before you saw James."

"Before . . ."

"I told you, they did communicate from time to time, Pen." I swallowed and nodded.

"Have the police asked you for any DNA samples?" Eric asked.

"No."

"Well, your fingerprints had to be all over the boat, anyway. As I said, nobody knows why Celia went there. And . . ."

"And?"

"It's just not clear why James is the one they charged."

"Instead of me?"

"Instead of you. You had pretty much equal access to the knife, and you were both at the scene. Your motive, if anything, is better than James's."

I couldn't disagree, although I questioned whether I would have the strength or the leverage to stab somebody to death, especially in the vicious way Eric had described.

Eric hesitated, then asked, "Do you have any of that wine left?"

Glad for something to do, I rolled out to the kitchen, then brought back a glass and filled it for him. Eric swirled the wine around, sipped it, and pronounced it excellent.

"James has spoiled me," I said. "I can't drink bad wine anymore, thanks to him." James had an extensive collection at home, and we enjoyed driving out to wineries on weekends.

Eric said, "You need to have some understanding for James, Pen."

"In what sense?"

"He was not sneaking around behind your back with Celia."

"He apparently saw her without telling me."

"Apparently so, yes. He hasn't discussed it with me. But I'm sure it wasn't on any regular basis—and maybe even inadvertent. He probably should have told you. But you have to understand. James and Celia were lovers, yes. But, to an even greater extent, they were friends. They had common interests, many of them business-related. They knew some of the same people. They'd met each other's families. They may have simply enjoyed each other's company, even if they no longer had a romantic relationship."

I didn't say anything. I felt I was the reason James had simply dropped a large, important part of his life.

Eric continued: "James is a straight-ahead guy. He doesn't care what people think, with one exception: He cares what you think. He didn't want to hurt you or give you the wrong idea."

I looked away, then back at my glass. "I feel so small, so jealous. So insecure."

"Have you considered that maybe he feels insecure, too? About you?"

I looked up sharply at him. "James? Insecure? I can't see that, Eric."

"Maybe you should. James, as you well know, is a strong-willed man. He's used to getting what he wants. And you—I won't say you're playing hard to get, but you have been very insistent on maintaining your independence. And, dare I say it, maybe you're having a bit of a trust problem—trouble believing that he's for real. Maybe you've dealt with too many people who aren't."

Eric was right. I'd had a fiancé who abandoned me after the accident, an employer who recruited me for the purpose of setting me up for a scandal, and another employer who had jettisoned me specifically because I was handicapped. More than that, I found it troubling that James hadn't known me before the accident. He only knew what he saw now—what I was now. Maybe I didn't want to admit to myself that the current me was the real one.

"Did he love Celia?" I asked.

"Probably. But not after you came into the picture, and Celia knew it. Remember, she was actually the one who pulled the plug on him, after she saw that she'd lost him to you."

I considered pouring some more wine but thought better of it. I would wake up tomorrow hurt, stressed, and scared. There was no reason to add hung over to the list.

Eric said, "It's a mystery to me, and to everybody, why Celia went to the boat that night. But there's one fact that might make you feel a little better."

"What's that?"

"James wasn't there."

It did make me feel better. But it also deepened the mystery. We sat there for a long moment. I said, "Who killed her, Eric?"

He just shook his head.

After Eric left, I sat there, wondering how I was going to get through tomorrow. I was exhausted, but knew I was too wound up to sleep. What happened next did little to change that.

I remembered that during my conversation with Eric, I'd heard a little chirp from my cell phone, indicating a message. I'd ignored the message then, but now I picked up the phone from where it sat on the end table. The text came from a number I didn't recognize and consisted of a single disturbing, cryptic sentence:

"She didn't mean it."

Chapter 20

Friday, March 8

On my way into the office I called John Gibson and was surprised when the FBI agent answered. Not many people were taking my calls this week. "John, it's Pen. Are you in your office?"

"Yes."

"I'll be there in forty minutes."

I disconnected before he could object. For the next few minutes I waited for the phone to ring and Gibson to tell me he couldn't meet now. But the phone remained silent, so I kept driving, diverting to the west toward the FBI's Los Angeles Field Office on Wilshire Boulevard in Westwood.

As I drove, I wondered about the anonymous text message that had kept me awake for a long time.

She didn't mean it.

The text could refer to just about anything. Except that it didn't. It was directed to me, by somebody who had my phone number. And given the timing of its arrival, it meant only one thing to me: Lisa Darden had not meant what she said in her message to Adam.

I gave up trying to figure out who had sent the message. I had run a backward directory check, but the phone number hadn't been listed. I didn't know whether the text represented an opinion or firsthand knowledge. Either way, it happened to coincide with my own suspicions.

I thought about telling Gibson about the message, maybe even asking him to try to trace its source. But then I asked myself,

Do I have any proof that this is related to any crime or investigation? Actually, none whatsoever.

And then I asked myself, *How would I describe all the help Gibson has given me thus far? Uh, that would be jackshit, Pen.*

It took twenty minutes to park and get through all the security before making my way up to Gibson's office. He met me at the elevator and motioned me down the hall to a conference room.

He pulled a chair aside to make room for me at the table, then sat down across from me. He was of medium height with a smooth face, starting to fill out around the middle, and dressed as always in his FBI uniform—white shirt, dark suit, muted tie. He had short, dark hair, which I had only recently realized was a hairpiece. I'd been to his office once before and seen lined up in a neat row pictures of his attractive wife and four children. I rolled up to the table, which was bare except for a single, neat stack of papers.

As always, he was brusque and to the point. "What can I do for you, Pen?"

"John, the US attorney is calling me at home and demanding to know why I haven't found our star witness for a critically important, politically sensitive case, so I'm a little anxious to know what help you might be able to give me."

"I have some news for you," he said, laying several sheets of paper on the desk in front of me. "We've done the preliminaries—electronic, initial phone calls and a welfare check."

"And?"

"It appears our witness doesn't want to be found. No record of any air travel in the last two weeks. No ATM or bank withdrawals in the last ten days. The last credit card transaction was at a gas station in Minneapolis on Thursday."

"Thursday," I said. "I talked to her on Friday. She sounded fine and was looking forward to coming out on

Sunday and getting started preparing her testimony. What else do you have?"

Gibson picked up one of the sheets from the table and studied it. "We checked her cell phone. First of all, it's been totally inactive—shut off or disabled, depending on the phone —since 2:30 a.m. Saturday. That means we can't locate her using GPS or triangulating with the cell towers. Her last call came at 2:11 a.m. from her sister, Stacy Ellis, and was received at or near her home."

"So what's your take?" I asked.

He ran a hand through his hair. "It's troubling on the face of it. Of course, it's also consistent with what she said she was going to do. She said she was going away for a couple of weeks and didn't want to be in touch."

She didn't mean it.

"Do you really believe that?" I asked.

"We can't take it at face value. We should have picked up some travel activity, and we didn't. We'll have to investigate further."

"So what's the next step?"

"We'll take it to the next level. We've talked to our agents in Minneapolis, and they'll be putting boots on the ground on Monday."

"Monday?" I said, feeling close to despair. "That's when I've got to go into court and tell the judge and the world we've lost our witness."

"We'll find her," Gibson said.

I had no reason to doubt his statement. When the FBI really wanted to find someone, the resources and expertise they could bring to bear on the task could be awesome to behold, and they nearly always succeeded. But, like any big organization, they had their bureaucratic priorities and procedures, and absent an emergency, they might not proceed as quickly as prosecutors wanted. Lisa's announced absence didn't seem to qualify as an emergency, and O'Shea had been unwilling or unable to get them to speed up the search.

"I know you're anxious," Gibson said. "But you're asking for a continuance anyway because of Adam's departure, right?"

I hesitated, wondering whether to share my real concern about Monday. In the darker, more suspicious recesses of my mind, I suspected that Dave O'Shea might be holding off on appointing a new lead attorney because he knew one would not be needed. Maybe he'd already decided, if Lisa couldn't be found and re-recruited by Monday, to pull the plug on the case.

I didn't tell Gibson any of this. I didn't need to.

"You're afraid they're going to give up on the case, aren't you?" he said. "O'Shea may decide he just doesn't need the aggravation anymore."

"So he just lets it go, and a crooked congressman walks."

He gave me a weak smile. "Pen, I know you haven't been with the US attorney for long. But that's Prosecuting 101. It's a lesson you should already have learned, on day one. Crooks walk all the time. You'd better be prepared to let it go or find another line of work."

I wanted to snap back at him. But I knew he was right. It was an unpleasant—even nasty—truth, and I hated it. But it wasn't Gibson's fault.

I thanked him for the astute but thoroughly unsatisfying advice, then drove down to the office. I spent the next couple of hours on non-Shields cases, attending hearings on two motions and then a settlement conference in court, then spending another hour making phone calls, trying to postpone other matters or otherwise prevent them from blowing up due to my neglect.

Then I decided there was another fact I could no longer ignore. I called Pam LaRue, once again finding her at home.

"Pam, it's Pen."

"Hi, Pen." She sounded groggy.

"Sorry to wake you up," I said. I had given up trying to remember her ever-changing work schedule.

"It's okay. What can I do for you?"

"Have you heard from Adam?"

"Just a couple of emails."

"Have you actually talked to him?"

"No."

"Is he still in Singapore?"

"Yes."

"Is there any way you can know that for sure?" I asked.

"Well, he said so."

"An email sent from his account told you so."

There was a pause on the line. "I see where you're going, and I don't see any reason for alarm, Pen. I'm satisfied the email was written by him, based on the language he used, and based on the knowledge it demonstrated."

"You see no signs that it wasn't written voluntarily."

"No. I've seen no reason to fear for his well-being, except from me when he gets home."

"Even though his resignation, his immediate departure, and his sparse communication since then are all unusual and out of character."

"That's correct," she said after a few seconds.

"Okay," I said. "Just checking."

"I'm sure he'll call soon," Pam said.

"If he does call, will you tell him I need to talk to him?"

"Of course."

"Thanks, Pam."

As soon as I hung up, the phone on my desk rang; it was Rena.

"I talked to Dick Westcott," she said. "He can spare you a few minutes this afternoon around four-thirty, if you're available."

I looked at my watch; it was after two. I was heading into the weekend with a missing witness and a mountain of work still on my desk. What the hell, I thought. The mountain would always be there. As long as my job was still there.

"Yes," I said. "I'll be there. And thanks."

I spent ten minutes staring at the seal of the US Justice Department, which served as my screensaver. I had two decisions to make, and they needed to be made now. First of all, could I trust my instincts? My gut told me something was happening here—something bad, that went beyond the normal office politics, legal politics, and political politics. I'd had to make a similar decision the previous year, when faced with a personal crisis of indeterminate origin. Against all experience, advice and common sense, I had concluded that my troubles had been the result of a conspiracy. I'd been right.

If I now concluded that something was seriously wrong with the case of *United States v. Shields, et al.*, question number two was obvious: What should I do about it? The decision wasn't as easy as it had been last year, for an obvious reason: I now had something to lose. I had a new career as an assistant US attorney, a job I'd quickly come to love, one that had gotten me back into the game, and back into a courtroom. To act on my gut feeling now would put that career at serious risk.

I snapped out of my contemplation. I wasn't sure if all the things I'd been through had changed me or simply brought out who I was. For better or worse, as a hero or a damn fool, I was a person who had to act. I went online, and five minutes later I had reserved a flight to Minneapolis.

Chapter 21

Rena met me in the lobby of the main building of Benning's sprawling headquarters, located north of the LA airport. Even with Rena vouching for me, I still had to go through a lengthy security rigmarole, which I supposed was normal for a high-tech defense contractor. As we rode up in the elevator to the eighth floor, I asked Rena, "What was Westcott's reaction when you told him I wanted to see him?"

"I think he's like the rest of us—he's looking for insight as to what might have happened to Celia. He sounded interested in what you might know."

"He'll be disappointed. I don't know squat."

"Put your heads together. See what you come up with."

We made our way along a row of cubicles until Rena came to a stop in front of one of them. I glanced at the nameplate: Dick Westcott.

Rena smiled at my startled expression. "Yes, that's what we all use here. Mine is farther down the row. And there—" she pointed to the next cube down "—is Celia's." The cube was filled with flowers, pictures and other tributes to its former occupant.

Dick Westcott stood up from behind his desk and came out into the hallway to greet me. He cut a striking figure—tanned, erect, six-foot five—with silver hair that was cut a bit longer than standard executive length. He wore black slacks, expensive loafers, and an open-necked blue shirt. He flashed a toothy smile as he gripped my hand.

"Pen? I'm Dick. Pleased to meet you. Rena has described you in glowing terms."

"She's impressively loyal," I said.

Westcott nodded to Rena, and she said, "I'll leave you two —good luck." I was surprised; I'd expected her to sit in on our meeting.

He gestured toward an unmarked door across the hall. "Why don't we go in here?"

The spacious room, decorated in white with a parquet floor, appeared to be a second office for private meetings. The furniture was simple, with a couch, easy chairs, and a desk. One wall was glass, with a nice view. The others were decorated with abstract prints.

"The cubicle is probably more symbolic than practical," Westcott said. "I use this room for sensitive meetings and calls, which is to say, I use it a lot. But I try to be open and accessible, and the cube helps."

I nodded. Westcott was known as a different type of corporate executive—progressive and innovative.

Westcott motioned me over toward the couch and chairs. He took one of the chairs, and I rolled over to face him.

"Tell me about yourself," he said.

I didn't expect that. I briefly described growing up in Florida, followed by law school and jobs in Tampa, Minneapolis, and my current position in LA.

Westcott smiled. "You left out all the good parts. Rena told me about your adventures last year, of being set up and then helping catch the bad guys behind a very nasty scheme. You were a hero."

"I don't know about that. I made it through in one piece— that's about all I can say."

He nodded. "She also said you're unassuming. So, I gather you knew Celia."

"Not well. She helped me with the . . . project you mentioned. But after that, things got sort of awkward."

"Because of James."

"Yes."

"We've done everything we can to help the police," Westcott said. "We brought them in here, gave them access to everything, and encouraged them to talk to anybody they think might be able to help. I very much doubt that her murder is work-related, but we want the killer found."

"So," I said, "you know James?"

He gave me a short, awkward smile. "You don't know about the deal James and I were working on?"

"No."

He crossed his legs and sat back. "Maybe 'worked on' is a little strong. James pitched a deal to me—Sherrod Diagnostics. Have you heard of it?"

"Yes. It's one of the larger projects he's working on."

"It's very promising. A remarkable concept, really—ingestible devices with low-level radio signals that can transmit all kinds of useful information from inside the body."

I nodded. James had been working hard to put together financing for Sherrod, a small company he considered to have great potential.

"I was very interested," Westcott continued. "When that company goes public, it's going to make a killing. Of course, it's still speculative because it needs FDA approval. But that will happen, eventually. Anyway, Celia came to me several months ago and said James had a deal I might be interested in. She offered to introduce us, and I agreed—James was a guy I'd heard about and looked forward to meeting."

I sat in stony silence, upset that James had been in contact with Celia, but immensely relieved that the contact apparently had a business purpose. I was also surprised that Rena hadn't told me. "What happened next?" I asked.

"James came in and we talked about the deal. I realized early on that Sherrod wasn't something Benning would be interested in—just too small and speculative, and outside our core businesses. But I was interested personally. I've invested in a number of startup businesses, mostly in the alternative energy and medical industries."

"Did you invest?" I asked.

"I'm afraid I dithered on it for quite a while. I finally decided last week not to do it."

"Why not?"

"Because it presented a potential conflict for me. It turns out that Benning is developing a product using low-level radio frequencies that might theoretically be a competitor to Sherrod. Sherrod might have wanted to license some technology from Benning, or vice versa. Unlikely, but it would have required disclosures, consents, updates, etc. I'm sure the board would have been fine with it, but it would have been a hassle, and hell, I'm always up on my high horse about corporate ethics, so I just decided to pass."

"You told James this?"

He gave me a sheepish look. "I'm afraid I wasn't very gracious about it. I was sort of busy and really wanted a chance to sit down with James and explain my decision, but he needed an answer, and so I had Celia pass along the news."

"That was Monday?"

He nodded. "The day she was killed."

"Did Celia have any other involvement in the deal?" I asked.

"Not really. She was the one who pointed out the potential conflict. But that was all; she understood from the beginning that this was personal and not for Benning." He smiled. "Another problem was that I would have had to get the deal past Rena. She's a stickler for ethics and conflicts of interest."

"Was Celia involved in anything here at Benning that would have made her unpopular?"

"Sure. Any chief operating officer would have been. Any good one, that is. Those of us who knew Celia well and worked closely with her had nothing but the utmost respect and admiration for her. But in the business world, change is a constant, and in any change, there are winners and losers. To be honest, Celia did some housecleaning when she took over. It was overdue; her predecessor had avoided it. Some people lost their jobs. Some didn't get raises or promotions they expected, or thought they deserved." He uncrossed his legs and leaned forward. "Those types of grievances can be serious. But I told the police, and I'm telling you, that I've racked my brain, and asked around the company, and haven't come up with anyone remotely angry enough to want to kill Celia. That doesn't mean such a person didn't exist, but if he or she did, they've kept it well hidden."

Frustrated, I said, "Are there any special projects or areas of focus she spent a lot of time on recently?"

He smiled, took a brief glance out the window, and looked back at me. "Beginning about six months ago, Celia undertook an extensive review of our bidding processes for defense contracts."

"What prompted the review?" I asked, knowing I had to tread carefully to avoid talking about a pending case.

"We've lost some big ones recently," he said. "On at least a couple of those occasions, we suspected that the process was not entirely kosher. Turns out we were right. Look, I know you're not supposed to talk about this. I'm just telling you what anybody knows. Take that now-famous Navy contract we lost out on. The Navy kept changing the specs over and over, tilting the balance so that PTG looked better qualified to implement the contract. Of course, we know now that Congressman Shields was lobbying behind the scenes to make that happen. We weren't blind; we knew something was going on. But we still thought if we put our best foot forward and turned in a good, competitive set of numbers, we'd have a shot at it. Boy, were we naive."

"How did that story fit in with Celia's review process?"

"She found that our procedures needed some improvement, even with a level playing field. The stakes for these contracts are enormous, and the development process is very lengthy and complex. We have to do better. And on the next one, hopefully we will."

I said nothing. He stole another quick glance out the window, then leaned back, fingers drumming on the arm of the chair. "People have tried to make this into a personality thing, you know. I have a history with Wilson Lopez. We were both in line for the CEO job over at Horrey, and we don't care much for each other. Will was always a little quick and dirty for my taste. Fiddling the Navy contract was all too predictable, I'm afraid. So was hiring a fixer like Hammer to handle it for him."

"Lopez will have his day in court," I ventured.

"Yes, he will, thanks to another guy I have a history with. I confess to being surprised that Dave O'Shea stepped up and did the right thing after all. Maybe his bosses in Washington had to lean on him, but prosecuting a political ally . . . I'm impressed. Dave has never liked me, of course."

"Why not?"

"No single thing, as far as I know. We've just been on the opposite sides of too many political battles."

I wouldn't have minded hearing some more inside gossip about the defendants in the Shields case, or about Dave O'Shea, but I figured I'd better steer the conversation back to matters at hand. "So, about Celia," I began.

"Let me have you talk to someone who might be able to give you additional insight on her," Westcott said. He got up and crossed the room to the desk, where he picked up the phone and punched in a number. "Nick? Could you come down to the conference room for a minute? There's somebody I'd like you to meet."

Westcott stayed behind his desk. I turned my chair around to see a trim man in his mid-forties appear in the doorway.

Westcott said, "Pen Wilkinson, meet Nick Edwards. He's our Group VP for the defense business lines."

Edwards walked over to shake my hand. Westcott said, "Pen is a friend of Rena's who has some questions about Celia. Could you spare her a few minutes?"

"Sure. Just follow me." He gestured toward the door.

I thanked Westcott, who strode over to shake my hand and wish me luck, and I followed Nick Edwards to a similar but smaller conference room three doors down. It took me a moment to realize how smoothly I'd been dismissed and handed off. But I wasn't offended; I'd consumed fifteen minutes of a Fortune 500 CEO's time.

Edwards sat down across from me. He looked distracted but appeared to be doing his best to give me his full attention. "So, you were a friend of Celia's?"

"More like an acquaintance," I said. He waited for further explanation, but I wasn't sure it would help my cause to give it to him. I just said, "I have a very strong personal interest in helping the police find her killer. I'm actually a federal prosecutor, although that has nothing to do with Celia's case."

Edwards studied me for a long moment, trying to figure this out. Eventually, he seemed to decide that he couldn't press further without being rude. He said, "I was probably Celia's closest friend in the company. She was here for about a year and a half, and I reported directly to her. I run our largest business lines."

"How long have you been at Benning?"

"Seven and a half years." He tried to keep his expression neutral, but I was sure he could tell why I'd asked the question —to find out whether he might have been considered for Celia's job himself.

"You knew her well," I said. "She probably told you about James."

"James . . . Carter, right? The fellow they've arrested for killing her."

"Right. What do you think about that?"

"I was surprised, to be honest. I understand they used to be close. And she always spoke highly of him." He paused. "Are you a friend of James?"

"Yes."

Things seemed to click into place for him, and he nodded. His features seemed to soften, and he said, "I wanted Celia's job. Thought I deserved it. Maybe I'll get it now; I don't know. But you know what? She was better than I would have been. She was the best boss I've ever worked for. She really kept this place running. Dick is a brilliant visionary, but as far as sweating the details, motivating people, setting clear expectations—making things work—I've never seen anybody better than Celia."

From my brief work with Celia last year, I wasn't surprised by Edwards's assessment.

Edwards went on: "Not everybody feels the way I do. She was tough on people—occasionally very tough. She moved some people out. But she and I respected each other. I am not only grieved at her death, I am outraged. I want the killer caught."

"Do you have any thoughts as to who the killer might be?" I asked.

He shook his head. "I just can't believe it's work-related. She was highly respected around here, even though, as I said, she had occasional conflicts. I don't know James, but the way she talked about him, I find it hard to believe he was involved. I think the police will have to seriously consider a psycho-type killing or a crime of opportunity."

I didn't know if Edwards really believed what he was saying, but it did have a certain logic to it, and Edwards came off as a highly intelligent guy. "I understand Celia was taking a close look at the company's bidding procedures," I said.

He nodded, and I thought I detected the merest shadow of a doubt cross his face. "It's no secret," he said. "We haven't done well lately. Of course, it appears some of our competitors may have been cheating. But that doesn't mean we don't have to do better."

"What changes have you made?"

"I can't go into detail on that, unfortunately. It's a highly proprietary process. I'll just say that we've tried to streamline things while keeping our eyes on the prize."

"How do you account for the competitors who cheat?"

Edwards shrugged. "That's a wild card. Not much you can do, really. I mostly just let Celia and Rena worry about that. And the authorities. You're a prosecutor, you said?"

"Yes."

"Well, if you do your job, and we do ours, I'm willing to let the chips fall where they may."

It sounded like a canned response. I felt I was losing him, so I decided to wrap it up. "I really appreciate your time, Nick."

He held out his hand. "Good luck. I hope you get to the bottom of it."

Edwards watched Pen disappear around the corner by the elevators and returned to the conference room. He sat down heavily behind the desk and pulled out his cell phone, punching in a local number. When the person answered, Edwards said, "I just met with her . . . Yes, she talked to Dick . . . What do I think?" He paused, scratching his chin. "I think she suspects something . . . no, nothing specific yet. But she's definitely on the right track, or the wrong track, from our standpoint. She asked a lot of questions about the bidding process. Look, I'm leaving this up to you. This is your thing. She has to be watched, and if necessary, taken care of."

"I agree," said Milt Hammer. "And I will take care of it."

Chapter 22

Rick Stouffer was agitated. "You're sure?" he said into the phone. "She'll be in Minneapolis by morning?"

"Yes, she's made a reservation for Minneapolis," Terrence said. "I've been monitoring the airline databases. She'll be there early tomorrow."

"Well, what are you going to do about it?"

"This trip is supposed to be my problem?"

"Don't you get it? She's going up there to look for Darden."

"That's a reasonable conclusion, I suppose."

"And you see no problem with that?" Stouffer asked.

"Theoretically, it could be a problem. But not mine."

"We're paying you to monitor Wilkinson. Hell, you're the one who told us about the trip."

"Yes, that was an extra duty you agreed to pay me for. I take it you now think something additional is required?"

"You have to stop her."

"We made no agreement on that. More than that, I relied on you for an accurate assessment of the job. I didn't sign up for surprises."

"There's no way we could have predicted this. She wasn't given control of the case until Monday. And since then, she turned out to be more persistent than we thought."

"I've done what you hired me to do," Terrence said stubbornly.

"It isn't enough. You need to take care of this Pen, to stop her."

"You sure about that? After I got your message, I checked —her trip is strictly personal. Her boss doesn't even know she's going. She has no resources, no backup—nothing. To top it off, she's in a wheelchair."

"She's . . . what?"

"You didn't know? She's a paraplegic. That will slow her down."

Stouffer was outside his house, pacing around the periphery of his swimming pool. "Hammer says she's pretty smart."

"Maybe. But you're forgetting something. Our witness doesn't want to be found. She doesn't want anything to do with the case."

"So you're saying that even if the attorney finds her, she would refuse to testify?"

Stouffer heard an exasperated sigh over the line. "Yes, that's what I've been telling you from the beginning."

"We can't take any chances. We can't have her finding Lisa. You need to do what it takes to prevent that."

"If that's your judgment, and you're willing to pay."

"Of course we're willing to pay. And yes, that's my judgment. Here's what else I'm thinking: You've got this person flying out to Minneapolis, apparently at her own expense and on her own time, to pursue this. She represents the kind of threat that may not automatically go away after Windfall is completed."

"That's possible."

"And so afterward . . ."

"We can talk about it, yes. And, as you've requested, I'll make sure Pen doesn't find the witness."

Stouffer smiled and clicked off.

And, sitting at a departure gate at LAX Airport, Terrence did the same.

Chapter 23

James Carter rambled around his house, restless, wishing he could *do* something—anything. He found inaction distasteful —offensive, even—but as he got older, he occasionally had to accept that action could be counterproductive. Sometimes, unnatural though it seemed, doing nothing was the best course— occasionally the only course.

Jail had been bad; Carter figured he could handle imprisonment better than most men, but the experience had left him shaken. Not just the potential for physical danger, but the humiliation and disorientation of being hauled out of his bed, arrested, interrogated, and accused of murder. He looked around the neat, tastefully decorated rooms, knowing Pen disliked this place, though she never said anything about it. He always felt bad about bringing her here, so they spent quite a bit of time on the boat, and went out frequently. Celia, on the other hand, loved the house.

Celia. He'd struggled to accept the reality of her death, and he found it even harder to imagine she had been viciously murdered. No one would call Celia a gentle or saintly person, and she'd undoubtedly ruffled feathers in the course of her corporate career. But it seemed unlikely that someone could really feel hatred for her, and he found it totally unbelievable that anyone would kill her. He'd talked to Celia's mother and sister and found them similarly at a loss.

Carter paced some more. He had checked his messages and relayed instructions to his assistant at the office. He'd caught up on bills and email. He'd blown off all the reporters who sought to interview him. He'd had groceries delivered. For weeks prior to his arrest he'd gone on long walks, strengthening the leg that had been pierced by a bullet a year ago. That was out the window now, as was everything frivolous or unnecessary. He was fighting for survival.

He was tempted to fix himself a drink. Sorely tempted. He knew he would have if it wasn't for Pen. In the past, he had sometimes abused alcohol when under stress, and she knew it, had seen it firsthand. He didn't want to disappoint her, or himself.

He felt the need to talk to someone. There was always Eric, of course—thank God for him. But despite his brother's indispensable help, Eric still irritated him, treating him like an irresponsible kid brother. He would have talked to Alicia, but he didn't want to burden his daughter with anything negative. He couldn't, obviously, call Celia. And worst of all, he hadn't yet connected with Pen—her assistant had told him she was on a plane to Minnesota. He knew she was under tremendous pressure—his arrest for murder would be more than sufficient to cause that. But she was also under at least some suspicion for the murder herself and had undergone extensive grilling by the police. Add to that a sudden, improbable turn of events with the Shields case, and the stress level was off the scale. Pen was uncommonly resilient, but how much could one person take?

Despite all of it, he knew her top priority would be trying to exonerate him.

Carter imagined that Pen's feelings about the murder were complicated. He knew she'd felt a lot of jealousy toward Celia, and God knew Celia had the ability to push someone's buttons. Celia's mere existence pushed a couple of big ones for Pen, reminding her of Celia's previous relationship with Carter, and of the fact that she, unlike Pen, was physically whole. Part of him wished he had known Pen before the accident that had crippled her. But he understood that, putting the jealousy aside, she was now a person with more depth, courage, and wisdom than before. He thanked God he knew her now.

His phone rang. He walked into the den, sat behind his desk, and checked the caller ID. "Hello, Eric? Have you talked to Pen?"

"Not since last night," Eric said.

"Her assistant said she's going to Minnesota. Why?"

"She didn't discuss it with me, but I imagine it has something to do with the Shields case. Their star witness, Lisa Darden, lives up there. Did you talk to Tomasky?"

"Yes, this morning." Eric had set him up with Jack Tomasky, one of southern California's leading criminal defense attorneys.

"How did it go?" Eric asked.

"He seemed like a competent guy. Knowledgeable."

"Damnit, James, that's not what I'm asking and you know it. Are you going to hire him or not?"

Carter kept his voice even. "I'm not sure. I'd like some more time to think about it."

Eric exploded. "You do not have *time*. You are in a shitload of trouble, and you don't seem to get it. You need representation and you need it now. What the hell is wrong with you?"

"I'm just weighing my options."

"That's a crock. You're stalling. What was wrong with Alex?"

"Nothing in particular. He's a good guy." Alex Kramer, a partner of Eric's, was a legal heavyweight on a par with Tomasky. Kramer had represented Carter at his initial appearance and a supplemental bail hearing and had been successful in obtaining bail. But Carter hadn't hired him.

"What was the problem with Tomasky?" Eric demanded. "Money?"

"He is expensive. Do you charge a grand an hour, too?"

"No, it wasn't money. One of you must have pissed off the other."

"What did he tell you?"

"He can't tell me anything. You can. But you won't." After a long silence Eric said, "You talked strategy, didn't you?"

"Some."

More silence. Then, "You can't avoid this, James."

"Nothing needs to be decided now. The police might figure it out."

"Relying on the police is not a plan. They're not on your side—they've got their theory and they'll stick with it until a better one comes along. You're relying on Pen to figure it out. That's a mistake. She is involved herself and is overloaded as it is."

"I'm just not prepared to make a move yet."

"I can't stand by and let you do this to yourself."

"Have a little faith," Carter said.

"Faith is good. So is pulling your head out of your ass before it's too late." Eric hung up.

Chapter 24

Saturday, March 9

I woke to hear the flight attendant announce our descent into Minneapolis-St. Paul. I'd ordered a glass of wine after we took off and had managed to catch a couple of hours of sleep. I glanced at my watch: 4:00 a.m. Then I remembered we'd lost two hours changing to Central Time. I changed the time on my watch to 6:00, then glanced out the window: it was still mostly dark outside. I could have caught an earlier flight last night, which would have put me in Minnesota a little past midnight. But then I would have had to hassle with finding an accessible hotel room, then getting myself there, and my rental hand-controlled van wouldn't have been ready for pick-up. It was easier just to get into town and hit the ground rolling.

James had been released in the late afternoon yesterday, according to a text I'd gotten from Eric. I'd tried to call James before getting onto the plane but reached only his voicemail, so I had to be content with leaving him a message. At least he was free—for now.

The trip to Minnesota was a big risk. If I somehow found and re-recruited Lisa Darden, I'd be a hero . . . if my bosses really wanted her found. I had little hope of actually pulling off that feat; at best, I hoped I could just make contact with her sister Stacy, or someone else who could tell me what had actually happened, assure me that Lisa was safe, and confirm that her decision not to testify was genuine and voluntary. If I failed to do any of these things, and my superiors got wind of the trip, would they object? At worst, I could be in serious trouble, but I couldn't forget that anonymous message.

She didn't mean it.

One advantage of the trip was that it took my mind off James, and off Celia's murder. After meeting with Dick Westcott and Nick Edwards, I felt as though I'd imposed on Rena for no good reason. I had learned nothing to indicate that Celia's murder was related to her job. Still, it troubled me that the discussions seemed to keep returning to the subject of bidding on defense contracts, the same subject that, in a different way, had brought me to Minnesota.

We touched down and taxied to a stop. I had to wait until the entire plane emptied before the flight attendant brought the aisle chair. I was able to slide across and transfer by myself. I then asked if someone could pull my bag down and bring it along. The flight attendant, an older woman who'd worked too many red-eye flights, snapped at me to hold on and that she could only do one thing at a time.

"If that," I muttered under my breath.

Finally she told a male flight attendant to grab my bag, and they maneuvered me through the first class cabin to the exit, and then out to the jetway . . . where my wheelchair was nowhere to be seen. The flight attendant seemed inclined to simply leave me and return to the plane.

I've had to learn to be patient with logistical delays and in-convenience. I haven't done quite as well at being patient with people. I asked her to summon help, which she reluctantly did before leaving me there on the jetway. After a five-minute wait, a member of the ground crew arrived and agreed to track down my chair. After another five minutes they wheeled me up to the gate area, where I waited another ten minutes.

In due course my chair arrived, and the gate agent helped me fasten my soft tote bag to the back of it. Then I set off down the long concourse, looking for a bathroom.

It was eight-thirty a.m. by the time I got off the under-ground tram, went up in the elevator, and rolled outside into the ground transportation area, returning a smile from a thirty-ish Asian man who stepped out of the way to let me pass. As I left the building I was hit by a jolt of cold spring air that left me wishing I'd put my jacket on. I spotted my contact about fifty feet down the aisle and rolled over toward him.

"Good morning, Ms. Wilkinson. Welcome back."

"Hello, Stan." We shook, and Stan Katz, a rotund older guy with a bushy mustache, took my bag off the chair and placed it in the front passenger seat of a blue minivan. I'd rented vehicles and other equipment from Stan's company several times when I had lived here.

"Still returning it tonight?" he asked.

"Yes—late afternoon or early evening." I just didn't have time to stay overnight, even though accommodations wouldn't have been a problem. James still owned a condo downtown, which he used when he came up to visit Alicia.

Katz pulled out a clipboard, and we finished up the paperwork. Then he extended the ramp from the side of the van and helped me inside, making sure I was locked into place behind the wheel. I checked out the controls, which were similar to those on my own van. "This van is really nice," I said. "I'm going to need a new vehicle before long." In fact, my van had over 200,000 miles on it. Living in LA did that. I thought that for my next vehicle, I'd buy a regular sedan, since I'd learned to stow my chair.

"Looks like you're good to go," he said. I thanked him and left the airport.

I exited the freeway a couple of miles down Interstate 494 where I knew there was a Caribou Coffee drive-through location. After picking up a double espresso, I set off north toward downtown on I-35W. The sun had risen, and it seemed strange to see Minneapolis with dry roads and bare ground. Though I had actually spent several months here before winter set in, ice and snow featured prominently in most of my memories of the city. I knew it wasn't a bad city, but I found it hard to separate the place from the terrible experiences I'd had here.

My sister Marsha, who still lived in Tampa, provided another connection to Minnesota. Her teenage son, a very bright but troubled kid, had recently moved up here to live with his father, Marsha's ex-husband. I had rarely spoken to Marsha since the accident that had killed her daughter and crippled me. Still, the idea of connecting with my nephew intrigued me. It would happen someday, I hoped.

My mouth felt dry as I approached downtown. The skyscraper housing North Central Bank, my old employer, glared menacingly at me from the skyline. I sipped espresso, tried to shut out the memories, and turned west on I-94 toward north Minneapolis in search of Lisa Darden.

My thoughts turned, as they often had recently, to the meeting in a Los Angeles hotel that had led to the indictment of Congressman Shields and two associates. I supposed that a nice hotel suite was where white collar crimes were perpetrated; deserted alleys and abandoned buildings were for street criminals. The prosecution wasn't sure why the meeting had been held; Shields had been successfully lobbying on behalf of PTG for some time and was apparently receiving at least some money for his efforts. Our best guess was that more specifics of the payments to Shields's building contractor had been discussed.

It had initially been unclear whether the defendants would deny meeting with each other, but the elevator surveillance video had apparently convinced them that denial was futile. We didn't have any details of what their stories would be at trial, since all three men had refused to testify before the grand jury, invoking their Fifth Amendment right not to incriminate themselves. At trial, they'd probably try to sell the meeting as a social gathering, or a discussion of legitimate government business.

But they'd have to explain why such a meeting would have to be held in private and had not appeared on the defendants' schedules, maintained by their staffs.

All of this was clear-cut. So why, I wondered, did my subconscious mind keep bugging me about the mechanics of the fateful meeting? Was I missing something about it? Somewhere in the recesses of my brain, a lonely, critical fact waited patiently to be connected to my consciousness. And somehow, I had to make that connection.

I glanced at my phone's navigation app, which told me I was about a mile from Lisa Darden's house. I followed the directions, which took me over the freeway to the west, into a neighborhood of small single-family homes. The trees and bushes were still bare, the grass a drab brown color.

Lisa's rented house was a single-story stucco and brick structure with a tiny front porch and a driveway consisting of two concrete paths separated by brown, weedy sod. I pulled into the driveway but couldn't see any way to safely get out of the van due to the uneven, sloping grass on the passenger side. I'd have to get out on the street. I put the van in reverse and started to back up when a sudden noise startled me. I squeezed on the brakes and looked to my left, where a woman was rapping on my window.

I put the van in park and rolled down the window. The woman was middle-aged and fleshy, with short reddish hair, a pug nose, and a pug on a leash at her heels. "Hi," she said. "Are you looking for Lisa?"

"Yes."

"She's not there."

"You're sure?"

"I'm sure. I live across the street. She hasn't been here for like a week." The dog looked up at me, then started sniffing around the front tire.

"Did you see her leave?" I asked. "I'm Pen, by the way."

"Georgette. I didn't see her leave," she continued. "I just noticed she wasn't here. I didn't see her leave in the morning, which I usually do, and her newspaper was left out on the step."

"And what day was that?"

"That would have been Saturday. She always goes to a Pilates class that starts at nine. I know because I used to go to the same class before I hurt my ankle. Are you the attorney from California?"

"Yes."

"Barb next door said you've been calling the neighbors, trying to locate her."

"Any idea where she might have gone?"

Georgette shook her head. "It's a little weird. I'm starting to worry about her."

"Did you notice any visitors here on Thursday or Friday?"

She thought about it. "No, I don't remember anything."

"It sounds like she might have left during the night on Friday."

"That's my guess. She could have left earlier, but I think somebody in the neighborhood would have noticed."

"Where are the newspapers from the past week?"

"Barb has been collecting them." The pug was getting restless, straining at the leash.

"Has anybody else been around looking for her?" I asked.

"Well, the police or FBI or somebody official-looking came around early in the week. They knocked at the door and walked around the back and looked in the windows. Then they came over and talked to me." She gave me a sheepish look. "Well, I actually came over and talked to them. They asked basically the same questions you're asking, and I told them just what I've told you."

"Has her sister been around?"

"Stacy? No. I've met her a couple of times, but she hasn't been around in the past week."

"What do you know about Stacy?"

"Not much. Divorced. Between jobs."

"Did you know that Lisa was preparing to go to California?"

"Yes, she mentioned it a couple of times. I got the impression she was looking forward to it. She was supposed to testify at a trial, right?"

"Eventually. She was scheduled to come out and prepare for trial last Sunday."

"She didn't show up?"

"She sent us a video message saying she didn't want to testify anymore. She said she was going away for a couple of weeks and didn't want to be bothered."

She didn't mean it.

"That doesn't sound like Lisa," Georgette said. "She seems direct—maybe a little feisty."

"That's my impression, too, although I've only talked to her a couple of times."

"So what are you going to do? Talk to Stacy?"

"I'm going to try. She hasn't been returning our calls."

Georgette looked down at the dog, then back up at me. "The whole situation sounds sort of weird."

I managed a faint smile. "You don't know the half of it."

Chapter 25

Stacy Ellis lived about four miles north of Lisa, in a suburb called Brooklyn Park. Her house was a forty-year-old split-level featuring a cracked asphalt driveway, a rusted basketball hoop, and faded blue siding. Fortunately, the main entrance was at ground level, with only one short step. I got out of the van, rolled over, and peered through the window beside the entryway. From the corner of my eye, I thought I saw a flicker of movement. I watched some more. Nothing.

I rolled over right against the front step and from my purse produced a telescoping pointer that I carried for situations like this. I extended the pointer and rang the doorbell. No response. I rang again. More nothing. I took out my phone and pulled up Stacy's cell phone number. I entered the number and pressed Send.

I heard the faintest of noises from inside the house, so faint I couldn't identify it. But I was sure it was a ringtone. The call went to voicemail. I hung up, then texted the number: "Stacy, I know you're in there. If you don't come out, I will have the police here in five minutes." It was pure bluff. But I didn't know what else to do.

She came out a minute later, a disheveled but not unattractive young woman with dishwater-blonde hair. Her tone was icy. "I asked to be left alone. This case has nothing to do with me."

"Good morning, Stacy. I'm—"

"I know who you are. You've been leaving ten messages a day on my voicemail."

"If you'd answered even one of them, I might not be here bugging you now."

"I'm entitled to be left alone."

"You're the only person who's had any contact with Lisa since she disappeared."

"She didn't 'disappear.' She decided to take off for a couple of weeks."

"So you say. Prove it."

"I don't have to prove anything to you."

"Yes, you do. Either start talking or I'll have the FBI haul you in for questioning." It was another bluff, but it was the only card I had to play. And ultimately, the FBI would be paying her a visit, perhaps as early as Monday.

She hesitated. "All right, come in." She turned around and started through the door, then turned back, hesitating again. "Oh," she said. "Could we just talk in the garage?"

"Fine."

She went inside, got her keys, and opened up a side door to the garage. Then she raised the main door, and I rolled in. I turned and looked up and down the street. There was no activity—we were, after all, in suburbia. Stacy Ellis had short hair and wore glasses, but bore a strong resemblance to the grainy video of her sister. I suspected that if anyone knew anything about Lisa's disappearance, and why she may not have meant what she said, it would be Stacy.

Stacy got herself a can of Diet Coke but didn't offer me anything. I began the questioning. "Did you know Lisa was having doubts about testifying?"

"Not really. But I knew it was taking a toll on her. She found it hard to concentrate on anything."

"When was the last time you talked to her?"

"Saturday," Stacy said. "She called me late that morning and said she thought it over and just couldn't handle it. She wanted to get away from the pressure, take a couple of weeks off and

make a fresh start when she got back. She said she was embarrassed and didn't want to talk to—what was the attorney's
name?"

"Adam Rosenthal."

"Right—that's who she was dealing with. She didn't want
to have to explain and justify everything to Adam, and didn't
want any pressure—she'd had enough of it. But when she left,
everybody started calling me instead. I didn't want to deal with
it, either. I've got issues I'm coping with in my life, too. So that's
why I haven't been taking your phone calls."

"Have you talked to her since then?" I asked.

"No."

"Do you have any idea where she is?"

"No."

"Did you have the impression she was going out of state?
Or just someplace local?"

"I really have no idea."

"If you called her, would she take the call?"

"I'm not sure. But I don't want to do it. I don't want to bug
her—she needs to be left alone."

I sighed in exasperation, looking around the garage at a
battered Toyota, a decrepit webbed lawn chair, and a rusted
lawnmower. I was reasonably sure she was lying, but what
could I do about it? I pressed on. "Could she be visiting her boyfriend?"

"I suppose it's possible, although I don't think they're that
close anymore. She hasn't seen him in a couple of months."

"He says she hasn't been in touch. Do you suppose he
could be covering for her?"

She let out a short laugh. "I doubt it. Nathan is a Boy Scout
—guileless. He couldn't sell a lie."

"What about your parents?"

"I don't want to worry them," she said quickly.

"Do they know about Lisa's change of heart?"

"I don't know." Stacy squeezed her now-empty soda can, got up, and paced the garage, looking for the recycling bin. After a moment, she found it in front of the Toyota and tossed the can. I wondered if Stacy rather than Lisa was the one buckling from the stress. If she couldn't remember where things were in her own garage, what else was she forgetting? Stacy returned to her lawn chair.

"Do you think Lisa reached this decision on her own?" I asked.

The question appeared to catch her off guard. "I—I assume so. I mean, I don't have any reason to think otherwise."

"For example, did you try to talk her out of testifying?"

Her expression told me she had. "I just told her to do what she had to do."

"You didn't try to influence her one way or the other?"

Her response was frosty and defensive. "Well, what if I did? I have a right to an opinion, don't I? And frankly, what business is it of yours?"

I kept my voice even. "We at the US attorney's office have spent many months out of our lives and a lot of taxpayer money preparing this case. I'm afraid it is our business. We represent the public. It's the public's business whether their elected representatives get away with accepting bribes. And remember, Lisa was the one who came to us."

"All right, I see your point. But she's only human."

"Yes, she is. And human beings are susceptible to pressure. Who was pressuring her, Stacy?"

She didn't answer.

"Was it Shields?"

"I don't know," she said. "But she felt the stress. She knew she'd be trashed and slandered on the witness stand. She knew she'd never work on Capitol Hill again. She could never work for anyone associated with Shields's party. A lot of her old friends and co-workers wouldn't speak to her."

I knew it was all true. And yet, something had happened. I was reaching the end of the line. Stacy didn't want to help. I decided to take one last shot at it. "We could force Lisa to testify," I said. "We could subpoena her. But then she wouldn't be a convincing witness. If she genuinely changed her mind and doesn't want to testify, we'll have to accept that." O'Shea hadn't said that explicitly, but I had little doubt that's what he would decide.

Stacy looked relieved.

"But," I added, "I need to verify that. I have to talk to her myself."

She hesitated, looking anxious.

"Look," I said. "Our concern for her safety and well-being is legitimate. She hasn't been seen or heard from for a week. Her car is in the garage. She's not answering her phone. To top it off, people accused of serious crimes, with a lot of money at stake, have a powerful incentive to keep her from testifying."

Stacy wasn't disagreeing or interrupting, so I went on. "If I could see her and talk to her myself, I wouldn't see any reason to involve the police. And if I'm satisfied that her decision is voluntary, I wouldn't see any reason she'd have to be bothered any further." I knew my ability to deliver on that promise was questionable, but I needed to say something that would induce Stacy to cooperate.

Stacy bit her lower lip, clearly anguished. Finally she said, "I can't promise anything. I'll try calling her and assuring her that you're willing to leave her alone."

"You have my phone number," I said. "I'll be in town until late afternoon. If I don't hear from her, expect to see the FBI on Monday." I thanked her and rolled back to the van.

Stacy walked over to the keypad next to the garage door and pushed a button, closing it. She watched me drive away, as if wanting to make sure I really left.

*   *   *

From his vantage point a block and a half away, Terrence watched Pen through powerful binoculars. He seriously doubted the meeting would lead her to what she sought, but the possibility couldn't be dismissed outright. And if Pen did find the woman she sought, Terrence would have a decision to make. His mandate was to monitor Pen and to keep her from finding the witness. As always, he would do his job.

Chapter 26

I located another Caribou Coffee shop on West River Road and got out of the van and went inside. I was feeling the fatigue from the overnight flight, but I still had a long day ahead. I pulled out my phone, guessing that Cassandra might be in. She was.

"Pen? I thought you'd be in this morning," she said in a disapproving tone.

"Don't worry—I'm working hard," I said truthfully. I wasn't about to tell her where I was working. "Anything new?"

"Nothing. It's strangely quiet. Even Connie isn't in."

That was a bit unusual. Connie was the type who would sleep in the office, if she ever actually slept. "I need a favor," I said.

"All right. I guess I could use a break from these accounting records."

"I'd like to take a look at the hotel security videos again. Could you dig those out for me?"

"Yes, but why? The defendants don't deny the meeting."

"I know. I just need to jog my memory a little."

"Okay. Will you be in this afternoon?"

"More likely tomorrow," I said.

"All right." We ended the call.

My best chance of success by far was Stacy convincing Lisa to meet with me, but I guessed the odds of that happening weren't great. In the meantime, I wasn't about to sit around waiting for something to happen.

On the plane ride, thinking about where Lisa might be hiding, I'd made some assumptions. First, I assumed she'd disappeared out of serious fear. Lisa Darden was a woman who had rebuffed the advances of a powerful US congressman, reported him to the authorities, and agreed to testify against him, at least partially aware of the trauma that would result from those decisions. If she'd later thought better of testifying, I believed she would have had the courage to talk to us directly and frankly about it. I couldn't see her hiding as a strategy to avoid confronting us. Therefore, the source of her fear had to be something more serious. I believed she had to be afraid for her life.

Second, I assumed Lisa was still in Minnesota. She couldn't fly anywhere without the FBI knowing about it, and she apparently hadn't driven herself anywhere because her car was still in her garage. Third, I assumed someone had helped her disappear, if for no other reason than to give her a ride to her hiding place. I was reasonably sure that someone was Stacy—we'd found no other candidates here in Minnesota, no other relatives or close friends. I would have tailed Stacy if I'd had the time and the wherewithal. But since I had neither, a more active approach was called for.

I felt reasonably comfortable in proceeding on these premises, but of course they could be faulty in any number of respects. Lisa could have an accomplice we didn't know about, a shirttail relative or long-lost friend. She could have come completely unglued under the pressure, behaving in some irrational way we wouldn't expect. She could have taken a cab to her hiding place. But a serious investigation might be able to trace the trip. She could—and this was probably the most likely pitfall—have had Stacy use her credit card to check her into a hotel. But they may well have reasoned that it was just as easy for the FBI to check Stacy's credit card activity as Lisa's.

With barely twelve hours to go, I had to act on the highest-probability assumptions. And I did have to act; my urgency was driven by a growing fear that Lisa Darden was dead.

I pulled out my laptop and, methodically going through a list I'd made, called eleven motels, asking if a Lisa Darden or Stacy Ellis was registered there. All, predictably, answered no.

I returned to the van. Then I pulled out my phone and, led by its programmed navigation, set out to visit the same eleven locations. In compiling the list, I'd had to make further assumptions. I doubted Lisa would have been able to check in at a large or chain establishment without an ID or credit card, so I limited my search to independent, mom-and-pop places, where a clerk might be more willing to bend the rules. There weren't many such places left, but they were still numerous enough that I couldn't check them all out, so I decided to concentrate on those in the northwestern suburbs, near where Lisa and Stacy lived and had grown up.

My first stop was a place on Highway 65, a major north-south route, in a suburb called Blaine. The route was lined by modern strip centers, mobile home parks and older businesses. I missed the Econo-North Motel when I first approached it, so I had to make a U-turn and go back. The motel had about twenty units, laid out in two linear segments with the office in the middle. I pulled up and parked, then dialed the office from my cell phone.

"Econo-North," a male voice answered.

"Hi," I said. "I'm parked outside. Could you give me a hand with my luggage?"

A face appeared in the window, and I stuck my arm out the window and waved.

"Okay, sure," the guy said.

A minute later a young man with very short hair and horn-rimmed glasses came out and walked over to the van. "Where is—" he started.

"I'm sorry," I said. "I actually asked you to come out for another reason, since it's kind of a hassle for me to get in and out." I gestured toward the wheelchair and the ramp.

His puzzled look didn't change.

I pulled out a photograph of Lisa Darden. "Was she a guest here in the past week?"

He studied the picture. "What's her name?"

"Lisa Darden, but she's probably using another name."

He looked up at me. "Are you a cop?"

"A lawyer."

He looked back down at the picture. "No, I don't think so."

"You're sure?"

He nodded.

I thanked him, backed out and set off for my next destination.

By one o'clock I'd checked five places, failing to pick up any hint that Lisa was at any of them. In two cases other employees were brought in to look at the pictures, and it was possible, though unlikely, that Lisa could have stayed at one of the motels without being seen by the particular employee I'd questioned. One guy, a kid with an attitude, resented my help-with-the-luggage ruse and refused to talk to me at all, forcing me to pull out my US attorney ID and threaten to send the police. His demeanor changed quickly after that, but he hadn't seen Lisa. I stopped for lunch at a drive-through and then sat in the parking lot, eating my cheeseburger. Time was running out, and I tried not to think about going back to LA in failure.

*   *   *

As he watched Pen pull in at her latest destination, Terrence was impressed. As he tailed her across the northern suburbs of the Twin Cities, he was able to follow her thought processes and could deduce the assumptions she'd made. And now, incredibly, she was getting close. Too close.

Terrence made his decision. He'd intended only to monitor Pen. But now, if he was going to prevent her from finding the target, it was time to take the next step.

*   *   *

Motel number six was in Anoka on US Highway 10, a major route into the Twin Cities from the northwest. The motel was a twelve-unit establishment on the south side of the road, squeezed in between an RV dealership and a church that was housed in a metal building. The person who came out from the office was a middle-aged woman, heavyset, wearing an ill-fitting hoodie.

"Yeah?"

I showed her Lisa's picture. "Have you seen her?"

She squinted at the photo. "Maybe."

"She might have tried to talk you into letting her check in without a credit card," I said.

She snapped her fingers. "You're right. That was her." She tapped the picture with her forefinger.

"What happened?" I asked, feeling my heart rate climb.

"It was last weekend—really late at night on Friday. Actually Saturday morning. Anyway, she comes in and gives me a story about how she's running away from her abusive husband and needs a place to stay but doesn't have her credit card, because she left in a hurry, and doesn't want to use it anyway because he might use it to find her."

"You think she was telling the truth?"

"She might have been. She looked scared. Anyway, I told her I was sorry but I just couldn't do it. Phil and Dot, the owners —they'd fire me. They said no exceptions, not if Bill freakin' Gates walks in here."

"Did she say anything else?"

"No. I mean, I really felt bad. I wanted to help. But I just couldn't. I told her there were shelters she could check out, but she just took off."

"Did you happen to see what kind of vehicle she was driving?"

"No. I was in here with the TV on—half-asleep, if you want to know the truth."

"Was there anybody with her?"

"Not that I could see. There could have been somebody in the car."

I thanked her, and she went back into the office. I just sat there for a long minute, stunned. My assumptions had been correct. I was still in the haystack, but I was closing in on the needle. I pulled out onto the highway and headed west, buoyed by my improved odds of finding Lisa alive, but knowing for certain that she feared for her life.

Chapter 27

Terrence was astonished. Pen had actually done it. He zoomed past the sixth motel and headed for the seventh. When he reached his destination, he circled to the rear. He would have to work quickly.

*   *   *

My next stop was twenty miles further out of town on Highway 10, toward the town of Elk River. The Elk Run Motel was the seediest place yet, its fifteen units sporting peeling white paint, faded shutters on the windows, and an empty, weedy gravel parking lot. With my anticipation building, I pulled up and made the call.

The man who came out was fat and sixtyish, with scraggly, thinning brown hair and a three-day stubble. He didn't stop at my door but headed toward the back of the van, presumably to get the luggage.

"Wait," I said.

He waddled back to my door. "What?" he said, his indifference changing to irritation.

I produced the picture of Lisa. "Have you seen her?"

He tried to remain nonchalant, but his expression gave him away. "I don't know. We get a lot of people going through here."

I glanced out at the deserted building and empty parking lot, seriously doubting it.

"Think hard," I urged. "She probably would have come in sometime last weekend."

I saw him quickly and involuntarily glance toward an end unit, and I knew Lisa had been there.

"Please," I said. "You can tell me."

"Who are you?"

I pulled out my official ID.

He looked at the ID, then skeptically back up at me, trying to figure out why the authorities would send a paraplegic in a van. "I don't want any trouble," he said.

"No trouble," I said. "But I need to know everything you know about her. She's a witness in an important case."

The guy hesitated. "I don't know . . ."

"You tell me and there won't be any reason to involve the police."

He sucked in a breath, then exhaled heavily. "You sure about that?"

"Cross my heart."

"What if she doesn't want to see you?"

My heart slammed against my ribs. She was here *now*. I collected my wits and gave him the same spiel I'd given Stacy. "I need to personally verify that she is safe and is here voluntarily."

He finally nodded, resigned to the inevitable. "Let me talk to her first."

"Has she been here all week?"

"Yeah, but I only talked to her twice. She's been holed up in there—didn't want us to clean the room."

"Has anybody been here to see her?"

"A couple of times, at night. I didn't actually see them, though."

"Get her."

*   *   *

Terrence watched the decrepit motel from across Highway 10, his vehicle shielded from the road by an abandoned trailer, a clump of bushes, and the remains of a long-ago gas station. He assembled his rifle and scope, pulled from a FedEx package, and now expertly wrapped the rifle's strap around his shoulder and wrist, resting the weapon on the hood of his car. He adjusted the scope and watched the door of the motel room, the room he himself had entered only ten minutes ago. No one had seen him scale a fence behind the property and approach the building from behind. While it was true that the Treatment had invariably worked, there was always a first time, and Terrence left nothing to chance. He'd kept track of where his subject had been staying. It had taken him less than thirty seconds to pick the flimsy lock. Inside, the subject had put up very little resistance. Her recovery from the Treatment had been slower than average.

Through the scope, he sighted up the door to the van and waited for Pen to emerge.

*   *   *

The motel guy trudged down to the end unit and knocked. No response. He looked back at me, then knocked again. I gripped the steering wheel with both hands as he produced a key from a ring on his belt, then opened the door. He paused, calling to her through the door, then entered.

He was out ten seconds later, shouting. "Oh, God, I can't believe it!" By then, I'd already slammed the van into gear and shot down to the end unit. I parked sideways, right in front of the door, and shut the engine off. The van's side door was already opening as I unlatched my chair and waited for the ramp to extend directly onto the sidewalk. The man was in front of the door, still shouting. "Hurry, for God's sake! It's— She's—"

I did hurry, although I didn't want to see what was inside. I finally got down and rolled up to the door, nearly running over the fat guy. He paused at the door to let me enter, but ended up hurrying past me toward the bathroom. When I got there, he backed away from the bathroom, biting on his hand. "Oh Jesus, oh Jesus."

Against my better judgment, I looked past him to where the body of a woman swung from the shower head.

*   *   *

Terrence watched the scene in disbelief. Rather than roll across the parking lot, the little cripple had *driven* up to the end unit. More than that, she'd parked sideways, so that she was shielded by the vehicle when she emerged. He stood up and kicked the tire in frustration, a most uncharacteristic display of emotion for him. With emergency vehicles soon to arrive, it was too late to do anything now. He would have to deal with this one in a more subtle manner.

But she would be dealt with.

Chapter 28

I leaned back in my airplane seat, exhausted beyond imagining, but unable to sleep. A gate agent had taken pity on me and upgraded me to first class on the evening flight. But even in a comfortable seat, all I could think about was seeing Lisa Darden's body. As always, I'd sought refuge in activity. After shooing the motel guy out of the room, I'd called the police and then Connie Harper. When the deputies and crime scene personnel from the Sherburne County Sheriff's Department and the Minnesota Bureau of Criminal Apprehension arrived, I gave them a statement, but they had spent most of their time with the motel employees. I had them call Stacy, who came out to the scene, answered questions, and confirmed that the body was her sister's.

Despite my warnings that the victim was an important federal witness and that there might be more to the case than met the eye, the deputies told me when they finally left the scene that they had found no signs of foul play. They had also assured me that despite their initial impressions, the investigation was ongoing and would be thorough. They estimated that Lisa had been dead for only a short time.

As I lay back fitfully in the airline seat, I indulged in a little self-pity. Why me? I wondered. Why did I have to discover this horrible scene? In a couple of days the FBI would have been on the case, and they would have found her. It wouldn't have had to be me.

But it was me. What I had seen today couldn't be unseen, could never be erased from my memory. The decrepit surroundings, the terrible isolation, and the utter despair. The end of a proud, vibrant, courageous life. I would never forget it. And I would not stop until I got to the bottom of it.

When I called Connie, she went through the motions of chewing me out for going to Minnesota and looking for Lisa on my own, but her heart didn't seem to be in it. I thought I detected more than a hint of relief in her voice. She told me there would be an investigation and I would be expected to cooperate, and then asked me if I had any reason to suspect Lisa's death wasn't suicide. I told her no, but that I suspected there was likely more to the story than we knew. She didn't ask why, and I was relieved, because one of my chief reasons for unease was that Lisa's death seemed convenient for everyone, including Connie Harper and Dave O'Shea. Then Connie took me through how I had found Lisa and what I had done at the scene. She closed by telling me not to talk to anybody except the authorities and that she would handle O'Shea, the FBI, and the media. I was grateful for that.

Now, awake on the long flight, I was left to think about what Lisa's death meant for me. It seemed likely that I'd receive at least some blame for not keeping track of her and holding her hand. If I kept my job, I'd move on to other cases, under a new boss, but with a permanent stain on my record. Bottom line: I had failed, in a career sense. But my personal sense of failure went even deeper. Lisa Darden had risked a lot to testify against a powerful man. In a way, she would have been testifying against an entire industry, against the whole military-industrial complex, against the way things worked in Washington. Whether by applying steady pressure, or engaging in something more sinister, the bad guys had won big.

I woke up as we arrived at LAX, having managed a couple of hours of uneasy sleep. I wanted to stop on the concourse for coffee or an energy drink, but I couldn't find anything open. I made my way through the terminal, retrieved my van from the garage, and set off in search of caffeine. There were convenience stores open on Century Boulevard, but by now I thought I could make it home, so I skipped the hassle of stopping.

At last, I pulled into my carport, got out, and rolled up the ramp to my door. I let myself in and was on my way to the bedroom when I realized I hadn't checked my messages. I glanced over at the clock on my kitchen stove: 1:43 a.m. I was inclined to wait until morning but then decided I'd better get it over with now.

I pulled out my phone, accessed voicemail, and discarded a couple of work-related messages. The next one was a keeper. It was from James.

"Hey, Pen, it's me. I'm home. I know you went on a trip. Call me when you get a chance, day or night. I don't care what time it is."

Trembling, I hit the speed dial for his number. He answered, sounding fully awake. "Honey, is that you?"

"James."

"Ah, man, it's so good to hear your voice."

"And I . . . I . . ." I couldn't go on. I sobbed for a long minute while he waited patiently for me.

"Are you okay?" he asked. "Silly question."

"I'm all right," I sniffed. "I just had a rough day. And a really long one."

"I just hope you're not worrying about me."

"Are you kidding? Of course I'm worried about you."

"Don't be. I'm doing fine."

"Yeah, give me the tough guy routine."

He didn't answer right away, and I said, "Seriously. I need to know how you're doing."

Another pause. "It wasn't easy, of course. They show up at the house at six in the morning to arrest me. Not a fun experience. Then they hauled me down to the station and read me my rights."

"What did you do?"

"Something I'm not great at. I kept my mouth shut."

"You asked for a lawyer, I hope."

"Sure. Keep in mind, at this point I didn't even know Celia was dead. So I called Eric, and he sent one of his partners down. The guy let me answer a few basic questions, but then they started asking me all about Celia, and about you, so I shut up again."

"What happened next?" I asked.

"You know the rest, basically. After forty-eight hours they had to charge me or let me go. They decided to charge me. So I went into court for an initial appearance and bail hearing, while Eric and my financial people were working to get me released. Since they got me out, I've just been chilling."

"Not at home, I hope."

"Actually, yes."

"But there must be reporters camped out in front of your house."

"I just ignore them. They've pretty much gone away." After a short pause he said, "Pen, listen to me: Before we go any further, you need to know a couple of things."

I waited.

"First of all, I did not kill Celia."

"Of course not. Why would you say such a thing?"

"You're a prosecutor. You know anybody is capable under the right conditions. But I didn't, and I want you to hear me say it."

"Okay."

"Second, the things they're saying about Celia and me are not true. I was not dating her. I was not 'seeing' her. Over the past year, I've run into her a grand total of four times. In each and every case, it was either a business meeting or at a function with mutual friends. I never saw her alone, ever."

"A business meeting—you mean the Sherrod deal with Dick Westcott?"

"Right. I had her introduce me to Westcott—he makes personal investments in venture capital companies, and I pitched him on the Sherrod deal."

"Yes, I know."

"He was pretty interested," James continued. "But he seemed to cool on it. On the day she was killed, Celia left me a message telling me he wasn't going to do it."

"Yes." It was all consistent with what Westcott had told me.

"I know I should have mentioned it to you," James said, "but I didn't want to risk giving you the wrong idea. I should have had more faith in you, and in us. I recognize that now, and for that, I'm sorry beyond words."

"Why was she at the boat, James? And how did the killer get your knife?"

"We find out those two things, and the case is solved. But right now, I don't have a clue."

"Do you have a good attorney?"

"I'm working on that. But let's not talk about the case anymore."

"All right."

"Tell me what's been happening with you."

I told him about my questioning by the police, but I didn't want to dwell on it. Then I told him about the Shields case and my trip to Minnesota. He stopped me at the point where I found the motel and said, "Good grief, Pen. I shouldn't have been surprised that you took it upon yourself to go out to Minnesota. But you found her, by yourself, with nothing more than *that?*"

"I wish I hadn't. I wish it hadn't been me."

"Finish telling me."

I wrapped up the story, and he said, "Good God, are you okay?"

"I guess so. It was horrible. I just—let's talk about something else."

"Of course."

"I talked to Alicia," I said and described my conversation with her.

"I talked to her, too," James said. "She seems to be doing okay, everything considered. When this is over, I'll have to see if I can sweet-talk Anita into a special visit."

"Yes—both you and Alicia will need it."

He hesitated. "I wish I could see you right now. I don't know . . ."

"It just won't work," I said, feeling hollow and disappointed. "It's so late. And I've got to go into the office tomorrow. I'll be over tomorrow night, without fail."

"Yes, of course. I just feel so helpless."

"I know. So do I. But know this: We will find out who killed Celia. And we'll do it soon, to end this nightmare."

"I believe you," he said quietly.

We continued to talk, about everything except Celia's murder. After a while I glanced at the clock again: It was 2:37.

"Do you have to go in on a Sunday?" James said. "For God's sake, honey, give it a rest."

"I can't. I'm dangerously behind on my other cases."

"Just go in late and take it easy."

"I will," I promised.

We were both silent.

"I don't want to go," he said.

"Neither do I."

"I'll see you tomorrow night. I promise."

"That's a promise I will definitely hold you to."

"I love you."

"You too, James."

" 'Night, babe."

"Goodnight."

I hung up and looked at the phone for a long time. I ached to see him, to hold him. But despite his absence, I felt hopeful again. The horror of Lisa's death receded a little, as did the uncertainty over my career. It was enough to get me through one more day.

Chapter 29

Sunday, March 10

Connie Harper, feeling weak and anxious, drove into the deserted parking garage at 9:00 a.m., toward a space near the elevator. The nightmare that was the Shields case was at last nearing a disastrous end. At first she had hoped to get through it with her career still intact. Now she hoped to simply escape with her life. But the case had refused to resolve smoothly. It had ended abruptly, with the embarrassing death of the government's star witness in a seedy motel in Minnesota. Worse, the suicide had been uncovered by one of her own people, by Pen.

She shook her head, wondering what had possessed Pen to go out to Minnesota on her own. But she knew; it was the same prosecutorial zeal, and the same hunger for answers, that had driven Connie herself in younger years. Despite Connie's doubts, Pen had turned out to be the real deal—too much so. After the case was officially dismissed, Pen would have to go. She knew too much, undoubtedly suspected even more. And she wouldn't let it go. Connie felt bad about that; Pen was becoming a fine prosecutor, could probably step into Adam's job without undue difficulty. It wasn't fair. But then, none of it was. Not to Pen, not to Connie—not to anybody.

She got out of her Lexus, looked up, and gave a little yelp as she saw the man standing between the cars, blocking her exit. Then, seeing who the man was, she staggered, braced one hand against the car, and vomited onto the floor. She backed away from the man, trembling.

"What do you want?" she said in a near-whisper. "The case is going to end. It's over. It's what you wanted."

Terrence nodded. "That's good, yes. Unfortunately, things have changed a little bit."

"How? What could you possibly want now?"

"A couple of things. First of all, there has to be an announcement tomorrow."

"Yes. That will happen."

"Second, this case has to end cleanly. Pen has to stop work on it."

"I'll make sure she does," Connie promised.

"Will you?" Terrence stepped closer. "I need to make sure of that, Connie. Because the last time you promised to help me with the Shields case, you let me down."

"I told you," she pleaded. "I didn't have the power to just drop the case. Not even O'Shea could have done that, not without consulting Washington."

"There are other ways to get rid of a case."

"I did the best I could. You know that. There were certain avenues we didn't investigate. I put an inexperienced attorney in charge of the case. I got the FBI to go slow on finding Lisa. I—I . . ."

"Bottom line, none of it worked. I had to make your witness go away. And now I'm telling you there's a very remote chance it could still blow up if things aren't done properly. I want this Wilkinson chick out of it, permanently."

Connie nodded.

"If not, I'll be back. And this time your son will receive the Treatment, too."

Connie nearly lost control again. She slid down to the floor next to the pool of vomit. "Oh, God, no. Please, no."

But Terrence was gone.

Chapter 30

I was in the office by noon, hoping to spend a quiet day catching up on non-Shields matters. I listened to the radio driving in and concluded that the media hadn't yet picked up on Lisa's suicide. My phone buzzed within five minutes after I got situated at my desk. I answered.

"Come down right away," Connie said.

I turned in my office and looked around. How did she know I was here? Eyes in the back of her head?

I made my way to Connie's office, knocked, pushed open the door, and rolled in. Then I saw something I'd never seen before: Connie was seated at her sit-down desk. She looked terrible—pale and haggard. I imagined I probably didn't look too hot, either. The stress was getting to all of us.

"I'm not happy with you," she said without preamble. "Going out to Minneapolis without authorization was not the kind of stunt to endear yourself to me or anybody around here."

"I went on my own time and—"

"—at your own expense. I know. I don't care. We don't tolerate cowboys here. If you're not a team player, you'd better start looking for another job."

I said nothing.

"In fact, if I were you I'd expect some disciplinary action. I'll have to talk to Dave, and we'll let you know in the next day or two."

I waited.

"The case is over," she said. "You will cease work on it immediately. Vik will attend the status hearing tomorrow and

155

present our motion for voluntary dismissal. At some point the FBI may be in touch—they'll be helping the local police investigate Lisa's suicide."

She turned her attention to papers on her desk, and I realized I was dismissed.

I turned around and began to roll out of the room when I heard her voice behind me. "You can return those disks, whatever they were, that you had Cassandra pull from Evidence. Do it today."

I turned back and studied her. Her head was still buried in a brief. I resumed my exit.

I went back to my desk, trying to fathom what Connie could be up to now. There was nothing suspicious per se about her general admonition to move on from the Shields case to other matters. But the last bit, about the surveillance disks, was really too much. She tried to sell it as an afterthought, a housekeeping matter. But it was, I was sure, the entire point of our meeting. She pretended not even to know exactly what the disks were, but of course she knew. How did she even know about my request to retrieve them if she wasn't keeping track of those items specifically?

But Connie Harper didn't know me very well. I went first to Cassandra's cubicle. She wasn't in. I found the disks on my desk but decided I couldn't risk playing them while Connie was still around. So I plunged into other work, trying to prioritize neglected matters that would be coming up this week. I took a break at one and ate the sandwich I'd brought from home. Then I called down to Connie's office. No response.

I rolled down the hallway and confirmed that her office was dark. Another attorney walked by, and I asked whether Connie was in.

"No, I saw her go home," the guy said. "She didn't look too hot."

"She was using her sit-down-desk," I said.

The attorney looked stunned.

I returned to my desk, popped the first disk into my computer, and began watching. My right foot began doing its phantom fidget as the screen flickered to life. The feed I viewed came from a camera showing the main guest elevator bank at the Discovery Hotel. The date and time displayed in the corner. I pulled up my notes containing the timeline of departures and arrival—the first of the defendants had arrived at 8:20 p.m. I began watching at 8:00. A number of people had arrived and departed during the next twenty minutes. Then it dawned on me that I shouldn't be looking for the departure or arrival of the defendants—I should be looking for someone else, someone I wasn't supposed to know was there. What else could there be that Connie didn't want me to see? But how could he or she be there in plain sight? This footage had already been viewed by the FBI and the prosecution.

I stopped the disk and pulled up our notes for the case. For twenty minutes I hunted through the system for a list of people compiled by the FBI—ones who'd been seen entering or leaving the hotel that night. I couldn't find it. I knew I didn't have a paper copy, so I went to Adam's office and started looking through his paper files. I found a working file containing the notes he'd used to compile our timeline. But there was no list of people. I spent another twenty minutes looking in his office, then a further fifteen minutes doing the same in Cassandra's cubicle. No luck.

I went back to my desk with a growing curiosity, combined with a nagging sense of unease. I replayed the disk. This time I stopped the feed, zoomed in as best I could on the face of each person arriving or leaving, and clipped and saved the image for later study. At 8:20, Congressman Latham Shields arrived. He glanced nervously around and headed directly for the elevator button, pushing it quickly. He didn't want to be exposed any longer than necessary. No one else waited with him, although two people came off an elevator, not appearing to recognize him. Shields got onto the car the couple had vacated. The rear wall of the elevator was, fortuitously, covered with a mirror. With enhancement, the video showed a reflection of Shields pressing the button for the twenty-fourth floor.

The next arrival, at 8:29, was Milt Hammer. He made an attempt to hide his face but didn't seem to have calculated the camera angle correctly, and I could see his face clearly from the side. In any event, when questioned by the FBI, he'd admitted to being there that night. That was all he'd said before he'd abruptly stopped answering questions and lawyered up. But the damage, from his standpoint, had been done, and the video likewise showed him pressing the button for the twenty-fourth floor. I studied the footage laboriously for the next ten minutes until the arrival of Wilson Lopez, the CEO of Pacific Technology Group. Of the three men, he was the only one who looked fearless and unself-conscious. Like the other two men, he went to the twenty-fourth floor.

The departures were staggered, beginning at 9:25 with Shields. Maybe it was my imagination, but I thought I detected a little more spring to his step on the way out. And why not? He was now a much richer man. Lopez and Hammer did not leave until 10:25, a full hour later. They came down five minutes apart. We had speculated many times as to what Lopez and Hammer might have talked about during the hour after Shields left. They could have just stayed to drink and shot the breeze. But now a different possibility presented itself: They may have been meeting with someone else. I took a bathroom break, then returned and plowed through another hour of video, seeing nothing unexpected. I glanced at my watch; it was now after 3:00 p.m.

I wondered again what—or who—it was that I wasn't supposed to see. The disks showed what we as prosecutors wanted them to show, that all three of the defendants were there at the same time. More than that, they showed the three men, except for Lopez, to be ill at ease—to look guilty. I knew there had to be additional footage, from the elevator lobbies on different floors, but we didn't have them. The disks we had were all we needed to make our case. But did they show all that had really happened? In particular, did they show everyone who was really there?

I saved the image files containing the faces to my laptop, then packed up the disks and went down to the Ice Box to put them on Cassandra's desk for return to Evidence.

To my surprise, Cassandra was sitting at her desk.

"Oh, hi," I said. "I didn't know you were in."

She didn't look up.

Her computer was on and she was looking at the screen but didn't appear to actually be doing anything.

"You heard about Lisa?" I said.

"Yeah."

A normal person might want to hear some details of what had happened, but Cassandra wasn't acting normally.

"Are you all right?" I asked.

"Fine."

I put the disks on her credenza. "Well, thanks for getting these for me. They can go back to Evidence now."

She didn't say anything.

I started to leave, then on impulse, I turned back. "I'm going to get some coffee. You want to come along?"

She turned and looked at me for the first time, her face expressionless. "All right."

I was surprised; she'd spurned so many similar invitations that I had pretty much given up extending them.

We went past the darkened, empty offices to the vending and coffee alcove. Cassandra rinsed out the carafe and made us a fresh pot, then sat down across the little table from me while we waited.

I said, "Connie didn't want me to see those disks. Do you have any idea why?"

"No."

"There has to be a list somewhere of the people who went up the elevator at the Discovery that night. It's not in Adam's office. Do you know where it is?"

"No."

"We should get together tomorrow morning, go over our to-do lists, and make a plan to catch up on everything else now that *Shields* is over."

"Yeah, whatever."

My patience gave way. "Damnit, Cassandra, I've had it. You're treating me like crap, and I want to know, once and for all, what the problem is."

"I don't have a problem with you."

"Do you resent me because I've got an attorney position and you don't?"

She shrugged. "No."

I nearly exploded with frustration. "Then what the hell is it?"

She didn't answer.

Then a thought flashed through my brain, a thought that didn't seem to make much sense, but I found myself voicing it anyway. "Is it about James, somehow?"

She gave me a startled look, and I saw I'd guessed correctly. "Do you resent me because I'm dating a wealthy man?"

She stared at me, wide-eyed, then her face crumpled into a mask of tears and despair. She shook her head, sobbing. "I resent you because you're dating a good man."

Shocked, I said, "Something happened with Anthony?"

"He left. He took off. We were having problems, ever since the pregnancy. I wanted to get married but he didn't. We argued. Finally, he didn't show up for the doctor's appointment. He said he needed time to think about it—about us, and the baby. What a coward. The *bastard!*"

I reached across the little table and took her hand. "I'm so sorry, Cassandra."

She just shook her head, looking down at the floor, and I knew she thought I was being patronizing and phony.

"I had a fiancé leave me," I said.

This got her attention. She looked up at me, glanced at the wheelchair, and then she understood. "The accident."

I nodded.

I rolled around to the other side of the table, leaned over, and embraced her. She sobbed for several minutes, with me joining in. Eventually both of us calmed down, and I got Cassandra back to her cube. She thanked me and said she just wanted to sit for a while.

"Sure," I said.

She looked up. "I'm sorry for how I treated you. I mean, I guess none of this is your fault. You're just so polished, and professional, and you've got this boyfriend who's a good guy and successful and adores you, and I'm just this . . . mess."

"You're not a mess. We need you. *I* need you."

I started to leave, then I turned back. "On Wednesday nights I get together with a couple of friends for a girls' night out. Maybe you'd like to join us."

She thought about it. "Might be fun."

"Think about it. And hang in there."

She nodded.

I didn't know if the ice had been broken completely, but I felt like we'd begun to establish a bond, and I dared to hope things might be different going forward.

On my way to the elevator my cell phone rang. I glanced at the screen: Eric Carter.

"Yes, Eric?"

"Can you meet?"

"When and where?"

"Long Beach in an hour."

161

Chapter 31

I hadn't eaten, so we agreed to meet at the same French bakery-restaurant where I'd had the weird dinner with Milt Hammer. I was surprised when Eric arrived wearing jeans and a golf shirt; I'd always imagined him as having been born in a dark lawyer's suit. He leaned down and kissed my cheek. "Have you ordered?"

"Not yet."

"What do you want?"

I asked for a Caesar salad. Eric returned a few minutes later with the salad and with a sandwich for himself. We spread everything out and began eating.

"I'll be seeing James later tonight," I said. "How's he doing?"

"About how you'd expect, I guess. You be the judge."

"So what's the latest?"

Eric spread mustard on his sandwich. "I got another call from your friend Ted. At this point, he thinks we know pretty much what the police know—the evidence and their theory of the case. There are only a couple of points that are really new, but I thought I'd lay it all out for you so you can see where we stand."

I nodded, not wanting to eat yet.

"The police believe that James and Celia were dating—that they never really stopped. Then, they theorize, Celia dumped him. There isn't a ton of evidence showing contact between them, but there is some. There's a witness who saw them at a party once, plus records of a few phone calls." One of those calls, I realized, had been placed by me, from James's landline.

"These contacts," Eric continued, "are spaced out enough to give an impression of an ongoing relationship."

I seethed with anger at the police and, truth be told, a little bit at James and Celia, too. "Go on," I said through gritted teeth.

"The police recovered James's knife from the water underneath the boat."

"A stupid way to dispose of a murder weapon."

"No more stupid than murdering a supposed estranged girlfriend on your own boat and leaving her there to be discovered. It's not about astuteness, Pen. It's about emotion."

"I suppose."

"The crime scene reconstruction strongly suggests—and this is new—that even though the body was discovered on deck, the stabbing took place belowdecks, which you can't reach by yourself. Somehow, Celia managed to get herself topside before she died. That explains why they concluded it was James, not you."

I actually thought it was possible that in a pinch, I could get belowdecks by myself, but it would be pretty much impossible to get back up. I also doubted that Howard and Kozlowski had really thought through the mechanics of stabbing somebody from a sitting position. If they'd really analyzed the direction and angles of the stab wounds, I thought I'd be in the clear. For the time being, I decided to keep those thoughts to myself. That decision came from a basic rule of courtroom practice: When you're winning, shut up.

"So, here's the case," Eric continued. "First, James was at the murder scene on the night of the murder. No dispute there. Second, you've got history of a romantic relationship and circumstantial evidence suggesting an ongoing relationship." He ticked off the points, using his fingers. "Third, Celia had a key to the boat. Fourth, you've got the boat and the murder weapon belonging to James. Fifth, the weapon was found under his boat. Sixth . . ." He had to switch hands for additional fingers. ". . . you have evidence that the crime was of a personal nature, with overkill that indicates a crime of passion." He put his hands down. "There's one additional item," he said.

I waited.

"Celia left a message on James's voicemail that afternoon. It said . . ." He pulled a card from his pocket and read from it. "'James, I'm sorry, but it's just not going to work. We can talk later.'"

I knew now that Celia was almost certainly referring to James's proposed venture capital deal with Dick Westcott.

I waited. Eric replaced the card in his pocket.

"That's it?" I said.

"Yes, as far as we can tell."

"That's full of holes. I can see reasonable doubt in half a dozen places."

Eric was careful in answering. "The internal logic is sound," he said, "even if the evidence supporting some of its elements is shaky. There may not be any smoking gun, but there's a bloody knife. Means and opportunity are a given. That leaves only motive, and for that, they tell a story of a lovers' quarrel. It happens to be a story that's false. But there is substantial evidence to support it, and it hangs together. This is not a frivolous case, Pen. It's deadly serious."

"But what about the transaction they talked about?" I asked. "The small tech company that Dick Westcott was interesting in financing? That's what Celia's voicemail had to be referring to."

"True," he admitted. "But they could turn the deal against us, too. James and Celia could have had a falling-out over the transaction, which could have provided additional motive for the killing."

Depressed, we both began eating. Eric was tactful enough not to point out that there was no evidence pointing to any other suspect, except perhaps to me. I had a potential motive, and the means, but no opportunity. Neither of us spoke for several minutes. Finally I said, "I assume you've laid all this out for James."

"Yes, I have."

"Has he settled on an attorney yet?"

"We're still working on that."

I put my fork down. "Eric, what the hell is going on here? He needs a lawyer. He can afford one. There are lots of good ones around."

"It's complicated. He . . . didn't hit it off with the partner from my firm. He's talked to a couple of others, but nothing's been finalized yet."

"But—"

Eric held up his hand. "I really shouldn't say any more. As I said, it's complicated and probably privileged, too."

I stabbed at a lettuce leaf with my fork. Add another frustrating mystery to the long list, I thought.

Eric pushed his chair back. "I need to get going. I'm sorry about how all this is working out, Pen. I'm just . . . sorry."

I reached out, trying to maintain my composure. He walked around and hugged me awkwardly. I said, "I don't know what I'd do without you, Eric."

He patted my shoulder. "Call me if you need anything."

*   *   *

Later that night, at James's house, in the bedroom, we held each other under the covers. I looked up at the digital clock on the nightstand; it was close to midnight. We'd said very little about the murder. I didn't mention my conversation with Eric at all. We just wanted to be with each other, and we didn't want anything to spoil it. I buried my head in his broad chest while he stroked my hair.

"Is this it?" he wondered aloud. "The end of our fairy tale?"

"I don't think fairy tales exist," I said. "There are good times and bad times. The last year has been good."

My hand touched his face, and I could feel his smile. "Not good," he said. "Amazing. So are we paying the piper now?"

165

"I don't think that's how it works. There are just ups and downs. They're inevitable."

"To call our current situation a 'down' doesn't really do it justice."

"I guess not. But you could have said the same thing about Downfall, James. Those saboteurs had us on the ropes. Or about my accident. Or your divorce. We survived it all. We'll survive this, too."

I felt his smile again. "We do have some experience with this survival stuff, don't we?"

I didn't respond.

"We'll get through it," he said. "The government's case is weak. There's all kinds of reasonable doubt. If we have to go to trial, we'll win."

Once again, I was silent. I knew very well that a defendant never really won a murder trial. Given the stress, the expense, the loss of privacy, and the damage to his reputation and relationships, the best a defendant could do was survive, and hope a reasonable chunk of his life survived with him.

"There's just one problem," James continued. "I've felt like we could survive anything because we have each other. If somehow things go wrong, if I do get sent to prison . . ."

"Don't talk like that," I said. "That is not going to happen, period. I won't let it happen."

He pulled me closer. "I know you won't."

Chapter 32

It took a massive amount of willpower to get going the next morning. This was the day my failure would be announced to the world. The media had reported Lisa's death last night. I watched the brief reports on TV while I sat in James's kitchen with my laptop. I was looking at the pictures I'd captured from the elevator lobby cameras. I still didn't recognize anybody, and I had no idea what Connie and O'Shea might be hiding.

I drove to the office, did a quick email and voicemail check, and called John Gibson.

"Welcome home," he said. "Did you have a nice vacation?" His voice was infused with something unfamiliar—mischief, maybe. I was surprised; the straight-laced agent wasn't exactly the King of Levity.

"Everybody knows?" I groaned.

"Oh, yes. Your trip is destined to become the stuff of legend."

"John, I didn't do it because—"

"I know, I know," he said. We talked for a few minutes about the events in Minnesota.

"Impressive," he said when I finished. "You missed your calling, Pen. You should be working over here."

"I'll be happy to be working anywhere." In truth, I was pleased by the compliment. All the times I'd worked with Gibson, he'd always seemed to have an attitude of condescension, as if everything he told me was something I should already know. "What about the investigation into Lisa's death?" I asked.

"I talked last night to one of our guys up in Minneapolis—they're looking over the shoulder of the local authorities. He tells me that so far, they see no evidence the suicide wasn't genuine. Lisa went over to that motel and hid out a week ago Friday night. The people there checked her in off the grid."

"How did she get there?"

"Stacy. She said she got a call from Lisa that night. Lisa wanted to hide out for a couple of weeks to avoid testifying. She picked Lisa up, took her over to the motel, and got the car back to Lisa's house. She also checked in on her during the week. She's sticking to her story that Lisa just got cold feet about testifying."

"Connie says I'll have to give a statement, too."

"You already gave one to the police up there. They may have some follow-up questions, but it won't be any big deal."

"So we just close the books on it."

"We have to. We have to move on."

"Moving on," I repeated. "Everybody seems anxious to do that."

"Let's face it—this was an awkward case and an awkward ending for everybody. We'd all just as soon forget about it."

"Okay, John. I get it. But there's one item I'd like to discuss before I just file the entire thing away."

"Sure. What is it?"

"A couple of days ago, I went through the surveillance disks from the Discovery hotel elevator bank."

"Yes?"

I could tell he was listening closely. "It occurred to me that there must have been other ways of getting up to Shields's room."

"Yes," he said. "People could have caught the elevator on one of two other floors, where there are meeting rooms and ballrooms. They could access those levels by escalator. There's also the freight elevator, but that's not open to the public."

"So, I'm assuming the footage from cameras on those levels was also checked."

"Of course."

"We only have the footage from the main elevator bank."

"Then I assume the rest was not needed and returned to the hotel." For the first time, Gibson sounded wary. "What's going on, Pen? You think someone else was at that meeting?"

"I don't have any specific reason to think so. I'm just asking whether it was checked."

"Sure, it was checked. Not by me, but I know it was."

"In fact, I'm assuming that every person who was seen going up in those elevators during the relevant time period was checked out."

"To the extent we could, yes. We showed the pictures around, matched them up with rooms, and even ran some through the face recognition databases. There were a few faces we just couldn't track down."

"Then there must be a list of all the people you were able to identify."

"Yes. Adam would have had a copy."

"What if I told you Adam didn't have a copy? That no one over here does?"

A pause. "Are you sure?"

"Yes."

"That's the kind of document that shouldn't get lost, Pen. Let's hope it's just been misfiled or mislaid, and that it will turn up soon."

"Sure," I said. "I hope it will turn up, too. In the meantime, though, maybe you could help me out by looking up the document number in the system. Or just send me a copy if that's easier."

A longer pause. "Why do you need this?"

"It's a loose end. I want to make sure all our paperwork is in order before I put the case to bed and close the files."

I don't know, Pen. Let me quietly check and see if I can find it. Then we'll talk."

"Fine. Thanks, John."

I spent another hour working on other matters, then went downstairs to a hearing at which a defendant entered a guilty plea, which I had previously negotiated. That finished, I turned around to leave the courtroom but spotted a familiar face in the back. The crocodile.

Brandon Lacey, Esq., lead attorney for Congressman Latham Shields, looked as though he had all the time in the world, even though his time probably billed at a thousand dollars an hour. He saw me approach and stood up. "Pen," he said. "What a pleasant surprise."

I said nothing, and he smiled. There was, as we both knew, nothing random about his presence here. Lacey followed me out into the hallway. I stopped next to a bench, and Lacey sat down. The corridor was deserted for the moment.

"We thought we would give this one more try," he said. He spoke softly so that I had to strain to hear him. There was nothing random about that, either.

"Give what one more try?" I asked.

"You're an enterprising young lady," he said. "Full of pluck and initiative." He lowered his voice even further. "You shouldn't have gone to Minnesota."

I waited.

"We have tried to handle this situation with subtlety, to produce a good outcome for everyone. But you ..." He shook his head sadly. "You and your ideas. You and your pluck and initiative." He paused in exasperation. "What on earth were you thinking, Pen? Your naiveté would be amusing if it wasn't creating so many problems, not the least for yourself."

"Let me worry about my own problems," I snapped.

"You're right," he said. "I really don't care about your difficulties. So let me lay it out for you plainly." He looked around.

Only a couple of people had walked past us during our conversation, and there was no one within earshot now.

"You're finished," he said. "You seem to be the only one not to recognize that. Your career, if it continues at all, won't be worth pursuing. The only question is where we go from here. Most people would draw the obvious conclusion and let go of the case. I'm afraid you may not."

"I'm just an underling, Mr. Lacey. I do what I'm told."

His features tightened. "But not *only* what you're told. You're so far out of your league, so divorced from reality, that you may have ideas about trying to press on somehow. I'm telling you not to do it, Pen. You won't be just out of a job. You will be destroyed. Your life will not be worth living." He stood up, began to leave, and then turned back. "If it continues at all."

I sat there, stunned and disbelieving, as he walked away. I'd been up against other defense attorneys who played hardball. But this one had just threatened to have me killed. And why? He had to know the case against his client was finished — what threat could further investigation present to Shields and his cronies?

With shaky, sweaty hands, I managed to roll myself back to the office.

Vik was waiting for me. He sat in my visitors' chair, a somber look on his face.

"I guess you know why I'm here," he said.

I tried to mentally shift gears. "A suspension or the axe?"

"Suspension. For just a week." He laid the letter on my desk. "I'm sorry, Pen. Connie talked to Dave, and they agreed this was necessary."

"Somebody has to take the fall for the Shields case tanking?"

"Don't look at it that way. There's plenty of blame to go around. I'm the one who has to go in front of Judge Cooley this afternoon and ask for voluntary dismissal. And O'Shea's statement will take responsibility. You won't be mentioned."

"Gee, thanks."

"It will only be a week," he said. "Believe me, you'll be welcomed back. I'm not sure who will be running the section, but there will be a ton of work to do."

"Do I go right away?"

"I'm afraid so."

Vik left. I sat for a long time, staring into the Justice Department seal on my screen. Was I really finished? What should I believe, Brandon Lacey's threats or Vikram Tandon's reassurances? If they actually let me resume my career, I'd have to count myself incredibly lucky—doubly lucky, since my foolish lie to the police about the call to Celia, apparently undiscovered, would have been enough by itself to get me fired. But even if everything blew over at the office, my gut told me that Vik, Connie, and O'Shea wouldn't save me from the dire consequences predicted by Lacey if I pressed on.

I started to gather up my items to take home, then stopped myself. I couldn't take any work with me. I hooked my backpack/briefcase, now unusually light, on the back of my chair, put my purse on the little shelf underneath, and made the long trek to the elevator. Nobody seemed to take any notice of my departure. I rode down in the elevator, but I didn't go to the van. Instead, I went to the Discovery Hotel.

Chapter 33

The hotel was only four blocks away, and I figured I could use the exercise. I found myself looking up and down the street, half-expecting to see Brandon Lacey or another of Shields's henchmen. The day was damp and smoggy, and a truck almost ran me down as I crossed the street in front of the courthouse.

My part in the drama—*United States v. Shields*—was over. Vik would go into court and announce that the US attorney was dropping the case. Lisa's suicide had made our need to drop the case obvious, which worked out well for Dave O'Shea. If the reason hadn't been obvious, Judge Cooley may well have required O'Shea to appear personally in court to explain the dismissal. While it was usually true that anyone brave enough to stand between O'Shea and a television camera was well advised to purchase additional insurance, it wasn't the type of publicity he wanted.

And me? I'd serve my week's suspension, and we would all move on. For me, moving on was an urgent priority—James needed help, and he needed it now.

Why, then, I wondered, was I unable to let go of the mystery of the forbidden surveillance footage? The fact that it was forbidden stimulated my curiosity, of course, but I knew it went deeper than that. I had known from the beginning that one part of the Shields case was playing itself out, unseen, at a level far above mine. John Gibson may have been able to simply dismiss such machinations as "politics" and to stay out of it. I couldn't.

I realized that Lisa Darden had given her life for the case, and I needed to make sure she had not given it for a lie. And I remained profoundly suspicious of how nicely everything had worked out for the powers that be. Shields, Hammer, and Lopez would walk. The machinery of Pentagon procurement, riddled with influence and politics, and lubricated by gobs of money, would grind on without interference. Dave O'Shea and the attorney general in Washington could claim that they had tried in good faith to prosecute a politician from their own party, but gosh darn, they'd been thwarted by the tragic suicide of an essential witness. Win—win—win. But, rightly or wrongly, I felt compelled to take up the cause of the losers.

I rolled past the hotel's front desk to a narrow hallway off the lobby. Halfway down the hall I knocked on the door for the security office, and five minutes later I was talking to the head of security, a chunky, bald guy named Dale. He inspected my ID, which Vik had thankfully not confiscated. "That case with Congressman Shields? We gave copies of everything we had to the FBI—that would have been . . . maybe a year ago."

"I know. There's just a little follow-up we need to do for our trial preparation." I hoped he hadn't heard about Lisa Darden's suicide. Vik's announcement of the end of the case wouldn't occur until this afternoon.

Dale scratched the back of his head. "You mean you need something we haven't already given you?"

"No, no." I lowered my voice. "We've got it—just not downtown. I really need to take a look at some footage this morning, and the FBI is telling me I've got to go all the way out to Westwood to look at it, which would pretty much shoot my day."

He gestured toward a computer terminal. "Your people sat right here and went through all kinds of stuff before even deciding what to subpoena."

"I understand."

"I don't know. We need to do things legally. Maybe I should call our attorney."

I gave him my best smile. "Like you said, Dale—you've already produced it, so the attorneys have already signed off. It's covered by an ongoing subpoena. All I'm asking for is a few minutes to look at them right here—then I'll be out of your hair." I touched his arm. "There aren't too many situations that are improved by bringing in even more lawyers, are there?" I smiled again.

He gave in. I felt mildly guilty for flirting with the guy but glad I could still pull it off. A few minutes later I was sitting in a small adjacent room with a computer terminal. Dale brought up the main menu and showed me how to access what I needed from the hotel's server. Then he left me alone.

I'd already viewed the footage from the elevator alcove on the main floor; now I needed to examine other access points to the elevators. I decided to skip the footage from the freight elevator for now. Guests weren't supposed to use it, and it required a key card. I started with the footage from the first meeting-room level, above the main level where the defendants had gotten on. I decided to focus on the departures rather than the arrivals, figuring that maybe less attention had been paid to that footage.

I began at 10:15, after Shields left, but ten minutes before the departures of Hammer and Lopez. There was virtually no one getting on or off on this level, so I was able to speed through the footage. Soon I passed 10:31, the time Hammer had left. I kept watching for another five minutes and was about to move on to the arrival times when I saw the elevator door open and a person get out. I stopped the playback and zoomed in.

And then I got close enough to see who it was, the person I was not supposed to see, who couldn't possibly be there, but was. I nearly fell out of my wheelchair.

Chapter 34

Rick Stouffer sat at his desk, dealing with annoyances. Annoyances from annoying people—bosses, employees, customers, suppliers—who couldn't make their own decisions, couldn't do their own work—people who kept making demands on his time and energy. Soon it would be over. Soon he'd be able to tell these parasites to take a hike.

The door to his spacious office opened, catching him off guard. Damnit, couldn't anybody knock? But the familiar figure who walked in was not one of the everyday parasites.

"Good morning," Terrence said, smiling and confident.

Stouffer was flustered and appalled. "What are you doing here? We didn't schedule anything. And to meet here . . ."

Terrence, immaculately groomed and dressed in an expensive dark suit, strode around behind the desk, right up to Stouffer. "We have a few things to discuss," he said.

Stouffer started to get up but felt Terrence's hand on his shoulder. And then he was in agony, writhing in pain. He opened his mouth, but Terrence quickly jammed a handkerchief into it, muffling his screams.

"I'm going to let you go," Terrence said after a few seconds. "And I'd like you to be quiet. Are we agreed?"

Stouffer nodded vigorously.

Terrence removed his hand, which had been applying a nerve grip he called the "Mr. Spock Pinch," from Stouffer's neck. Satisfied that Stouffer was done screaming, he removed the handkerchief from his employer's mouth, moved around to the front of the desk, and took an armchair.

Stouffer sat, slack and stunned, for a long minute before sitting up and rubbing his shoulder. "What the hell," he gasped. "What was that all about? Who do you think you—?"

"Let's deal with your questions," Terrence said, leaning back and crossing his legs. "First of all, how did I get in here? I used this." He produced a badge wallet from his pocket. "I flashed a set of FBI credentials. They're very good, very convincing. But let's move on to the more important question: *Why* did I come? I came in order to convey to you some very important facts. Three of them, to be exact."

Stouffer waited, ignoring the flashing lights on his phone, wishing that he could go back to dealing with ordinary annoying people.

"Fact number one," Terrence said. "I am a serious person. Very, very serious. I am not some flunky or employee or customer that you can issue orders to, blow off, or jerk around."

Stouffer said nothing.

"Fact number two: You not only misrepresented the scope of this project to me, but you then attempted to unilaterally expand that scope. You did that in contravention of our agreement and my advice, and it was an implicit rebuke to my competence. Among other things, you failed to disclose that one of your principals is part of a bid-rigging scheme. I am very unhappy about that."

"Things come up," Stouffer said. "Shit happens. Conditions change."

"The standard excuse of every fuckup who fails to plan and anticipate. You're right, of course. Conditions do change. That brings us to fact number three: Our agreement has now changed. The scope of my duties has expanded. You yourself have agreed that my compensation needs to be adjusted. And so here's my new compensation: Five percent of Windfall."

Stouffer was flabbergasted. "Are you insane?"

"An interesting question, but irrelevant right now. Five percent, payable at the closing."

"Impossible."

"No, no. Very possible. There's plenty of money to go around, and I'm taking more risk than anybody. I deserve to be compensated, and I will be, with five percent."

"Look, I can't just decide this on my own. I'd have to consult the others."

"Sure."

"Then I'll give you our answer—"

"I don't need an answer. This is not a negotiation. You can consult all you want, but on the date of closing I will receive five percent of Windfall. If not, there will be no Windfall. I guarantee it. If the others don't agree, you can pay it out of your share."

"You can't do this."

Terrence stood up. "I just did. And you will not attempt to undo it. I'm very sure of that."

Stouffer drew himself up, tried to look tough, and succeeded in looking pathetic. "How can you be so sure?"

Terrence smiled. "Because if things proceed in any manner other than what I've just described, you will be dead within twenty-four hours of closing."

Chapter 35

US Attorney Dave O'Shea was bitching about the food. He lifted up a soggy triangle of toast from his sandwich and pulled out an anemic strip of bacon, holding it up for his dining companion to see. "They call this a club sandwich?" He sighed. "The price we pay for a confidential lunch."

Across the small table from him sat the FBI's assistant director in charge of the Los Angeles field office. The LA office, one of the Bureau's largest and most important, rated an assistant director rather than a special agent as its head. Kirk Hendricks was a pale, fair-haired six-foot-three, a point guard to the squat, dark-haired O'Shea's middle linebacker. "You could have come out to Westwood," Hendricks said. "Our dining room is very reliable."

"I'm staying close to home today. We make the announcement in court at two, and we're issuing the media statement at two-thirty. Melissa wanted to clear the language." He nodded toward a picture of a gray-haired, bespectacled woman on the vanity wall of his office, next to the portrait of the President. She was attorney general of the United States.

"How bad is the fallout going to be?" Hendricks asked.

"Bad for a couple of days—the liberals and watchdog groups will give us hell. But when we make the announcement on the sting—that will drown it all out and everything will be quickly forgotten. This is the best way it could have worked out. Of course, they'll demand a thorough investigation of Lisa's death."

"Which we'll give them."

O'Shea lifted his sandwich to his mouth, then put it back down. "So what is the investigation going to show?"

Hendricks chewed carefully on a mouthful of cheeseburger before answering. "We're on it up in Minneapolis—it's potentially a federal witness-tampering case, after all. The local authorities say it looks like a legitimate suicide. But our people are looking over their shoulders, and they've seen a couple of troubling things that need to be cleared up."

"It would be nice to get it cleared up quickly."

"But we can't get it wrong."

"For Christ's sake, stay on it. We don't need a bunch of local gomers screwing it up or going off-script."

"Our SAC up there tells me the locals are good. But we'll make sure everything is airtight."

O'Shea chewed grimly on his inadequate sandwich. "I just keep thinking about Westcott. Any way he could have been behind this?"

Hendricks rolled his eyes. "You've got Dick Westcott on the brain."

"The guy's scum, Kirk. But he has to be handled carefully. He's got the *Times* in his pocket and one hell of a fundraising network."

Hendricks nodded. O'Shea, formerly a senior partner at a large LA law firm and an assistant minority leader in the state senate, had crossed political swords with the politically active Benning CEO repeatedly. "I'll say this about Larry Shields," O'Shea said. "He's a cunning son of a bitch, and he knows you're dealing with a snake when you get involved with Westcott."

"Shields wiggled out of this one," Hendricks pointed out.

"As usual. But Westcott won't. We've got him this time. Hell, everybody knows Larry is a sleaze. But Westcott and that Boy Scout image—it makes me want to puke."

They ate silently for a few minutes. Hendricks said, "Quite an adventure up in Minnesota for your young attorney."

O'Shea shook his head and chuckled. "Connie is losing her touch."

"How so?"

"Her management style is to scare the hell out of her people, and then they pretty much manage themselves. It's usually very effective." He shook his head again. "I'm just glad things worked out with this case—otherwise they'd be calling me out for all the screw-ups. I mean, you've got the section chief bailing on us, right before the trial—no notice or anything. Then Connie just leaves this paraplegic chick in charge—doesn't even appoint a replacement right away. Then our witness vanishes—nobody babysitting her. So then our young lady takes it upon herself to go up there and find her—and does."

"Gutsy," Hendricks said. "And we weren't giving her a lot of help."

"We weren't, either. Connie wasn't minding the store. I'm serious when I said she's losing it. I don't know where her head was at with this case. If she doesn't get back on track, I might have to do a little housecleaning." He shoved some French fries into his mouth. "Well, on to the other big topic of the day."

"Celia Sims, the Benning COO."

"She had some involvement," O'Shea said.

"Such as it was, yes. And then she turns up dead."

"Well, how stinky is that?"

"It looks like hell," Hendricks agreed.

"Who caught it?"

"Newport Beach PD."

"They're good."

"Yes. Our people in the resident agency down in Orange County are monitoring the investigation. Their best judgment is that the boyfriend did it."

"James Carter. He's been a supporter—I've met him a few times over the years. He's a heavyweight guy—a good guy, from what I could tell. Are they sure about him?"

"They charged him, but it doesn't sound like a slam-dunk. They waited the full forty-eight hours."

"What's their theory of the case?"

Hendricks gave him an enigmatic smile. "Here's where it gets interesting. The vic, Celia Sims, apparently dumped him because for the past year he's been officially dating another woman."

"So he was seeing Celia on the sly."

"Right. But guess who Carter's 'official' girlfriend is."

O'Shea gave him a questioning look.

"She is none other than your young, paraplegic, go-getter attorney."

O'Shea nearly spit out his Diet Coke. "Pen? Are you shitting me?"

Hendricks grinned. "No shit."

O'Shea thought about it for a moment, then said, "Oh, crap. Any chance—"

"No, they're pretty sure Pen didn't do it."

"That would be all I need," O'Shea groaned. "How did they clear her?"

"They put her through the wringer, and it turns out she was there at some point that night and had access to the murder weapon. But the cops think the murder occurred belowdecks, even though they found the body topside. They don't think Pen could have gotten down there and back up by herself. And her vehicle and apartment checked out clean."

"Good Lord," O'Shea muttered in astonishment. "Who the hell is this chick?" He shook his head, then looked back at the FBI man. "Any chance Westcott could have sniffed something out? Maybe Celia was going to blow the whistle, and then—"

Hendricks was shaking his head. "Give it up, Dave. We have no indication that she was going to turn, or that Westcott had anything to do with this."

"So you're sure nothing has leaked? That this is just coincidence? Because her murder looks fishy as hell."

"Our guy on the inside tells us we're clear. I'd say the biggest risk is from your end. What if Pen has gotten wind of this somehow?"

"From handling the Shields case? There's really only one point of connection."

"Yes—our guy on the inside. But now, with the Sims murder, there's a second one: Pen herself."

"We've pulled the plug on her for now. After Friday we can sort it all out, decide on her long-term future. But we've got to get through Friday. That will be a nice announcement."

"Nice, indeed." Hendricks glanced toward the photograph on the vanity wall. "Will Melissa try to get in on that?"

O'Shea smiled. "No way. I'm keeping that all for myself."

Chapter 36

Rena invited me over to her house for dinner. Or maybe I invited myself—I don't really remember whose idea it was. But it worked out; she wanted to cheer me up, and I wanted to ask her some questions. I parked in the driveway of her lovely Spanish-style house, built in the 1920s, on Lincoln Boulevard in Santa Monica. I called from the van to say I'd arrived, and by the time I made it up to the front entrance, Rena was there to help me up the three short steps and through the door.

Rena looked, as always, fresh and perky, even after what had to have been an exhausting day. We settled in near the fireplace in the open living room, which sported the original wooden beams. It was a large room, but charming—perfect for entertaining and political fundraisers. A bottle of wine and two glasses already sat on the coffee table.

"Thanks for doing this," I said.

She waved it off. "I can't tell you how much I look forward to these get-togethers. You sit and listen to all my career and personal problems without any eye-rolling, God bless you. So, how was your day?"

"It would have to improve a lot just to suck."

Her eyes narrowed. "What happened?"

"I'm suspended."

Her mouth opened, then closed. "Why?"

I managed a small smile. "They had their pick of reasons, I guess. The one they chose was my involvement in the Celia Sims murder investigation. But I'm sure they could have figured out some other grounds, too—unprofessional conduct for my trip to Minnesota; insubordination—whatever."

"What happens now?"

"I wait a week and then see if they're serious about taking me back. Maybe they're telling the truth; they are short-handed."

"Why now?"

"Isn't it obvious? The Shields case is over—I'm not needed for that. And because of the timing, it's an implicit way of sticking me with some blame for how the case turned out."

"I suppose." She shook her head. "Let's eat."

Rena took the wine bottle and glasses, and we proceeded through the house to the dining room. The table had been set for two; Steve had a business dinner with clients. Rena brought out the salmon salad and fresh rolls, prepared by their part-time maid before she'd left for the day. We dug in.

"So, out with it," I said after a few bites. "What's the story with you and Steve?"

She sighed and put her fork down. "It's the same old thing."

"Kids."

"Right. We met with the doctor last Thursday. She told us it's hopeless."

I took her hand as her eyes turned watery. "Rena, I'm so sorry."

"She told us I'm too old. But we've actually been trying since I was younger. We've tried all the artificial boosts. Now she's telling us it's time to officially give up. I want to adopt. He doesn't. I'm not sure we can work it out."

I was shocked. Rena and Steve had been married so long, and they seemed to be such a great couple. We talked, haltingly, for a while longer about her marital difficulties before returning to my career problems.

"I know Connie," Rena said. "She's tough on her people, but she's pretty loyal to them, too. It's not like her to scapegoat anybody."

"What if it's coming from higher up than Connie?"

She gave me a grim nod before taking a sip from her glass. "O'Shea is a political animal—it would be in character for him."

"Connie's been behaving strangely anyway," I said. "She looks stressed out and exhausted."

"Maybe she's sick."

I hadn't considered that. "Could be," I said. In fact, a couple of weeks ago Connie had taken two sick days, which nobody could remember her ever doing before.

I reached for the roll basket, stopped myself, and then decided what the hell. I tore open and buttered another delicious fresh popover.

Rena said, "What on earth possessed you to go up to Minnesota?"

"Mainly, I was worried about Lisa. She might have gotten cold feet about testifying, but she didn't seem like the type to hide from a difficult situation. I didn't think she would have broken off all contact."

"But you never even met her. And nobody else seemed worried about her."

"I guess I just trusted my instincts."

"And you were right. Tell me about the rest of the trip."

I did. I faltered when I reached the part about finding Lisa's body. Rena reached over and took my hand as I brushed away a few tears. Then she said, "What's your take on the suicide?"

I collected myself and phrased my answer carefully. "I see no evidence that she didn't kill herself."

"But why would she commit suicide? You said yourself that you'd talked to her just a couple of days before she was scheduled to come out here. That she was fired up and looking forward to it."

"It looks like she killed herself, and the evidence supports that, according to the police. But I don't believe there was no outside interference. Somebody got to her, or threatened her, or influenced her somehow."

She didn't mean it, I kept thinking.

I paused, buttered the rest of my popover, and ate it.

"More wine?" Rena asked.

"I think I'll pass. I'm pretty tired, and I still have to drive home."

Rena decided to pass, too. She leaned forward and said, "Tell me the rest."

I led her, step-by-step, through the process that ended with my examining the surveillance disks. "So," she said, "you looked at the footage pretty much because Connie didn't want you to?"

"Not just that. She did pique my curiosity, but I had the idea before that. Remember, I ordered the disks from Evidence before I left for Minnesota."

"Why?"

"I didn't really know at the time. Something was nagging at me, in the back of my mind, but I didn't know what it was until I actually started looking at them. It was then that I realized I'd never seen any list of other people—the non-defendants— who went up in the elevator, nor had I seen footage of other floors where the elevators might be accessed. I knew somebody had to have viewed the footage, but I'd never seen it."

Rena nodded, and I went on to explain how the list of people going and coming that night had apparently disappeared. "Do you think Adam took it?" she said.

"It's possible, but I don't know why."

"So why don't you think Connie wanted you to look at the disks?"

"Because of who I saw coming down in the elevator after the others had left."

Rena made a circular hurry-up motion with her left hand. "Come on, out with it."

"Celia Sims."

She gasped, looked away, then back at me. "My God. Are you sure?"

I nodded.

"But why? Why would she be there?"

"I've racked my brain, trying to figure that one out. Think through it with me."

"Okay."

"Celia came down right after Hammer and Lopez left, but an hour after Shields left."

"When did she go up?"

"I don't know. I couldn't find any footage of her going up— only down. But I'm assuming she probably went up after Shields left and that she wouldn't have been involved in the meeting with the three defendants."

"That makes sense," Rena said. "PTG and Benning wouldn't have both been involved in trying to bribe Shields. They were actually competing against each other for the Navy contract."

"Exactly," I said. "So then, assuming her presence there was not the wildest coincidence in the world, you've got her meeting with the PTG people in a separate meeting not involving Shields. Why would she be doing that? Would PTG be trying to hire her?"

"That would be a nice explanation—an innocent one. But I can't see it. Celia had just started with us a few months earlier. And by all accounts, she was happy and doing very well. In fact, she was heard to talk disparagingly about Lopez."

"What if they just wanted to talk over industry issues?"

"I never would have approved of that," Rena said. "There is some interaction between competitors at industry conventions or Washington receptions. But it's best to avoid the appearance of collusion. In addition to that, Celia was new. She didn't really know these people. And this was a secret meeting." She reached absently for her long-empty wine glass, then put it down. "I'm arguing against myself," she said.

"How so?"

"I'm thinking there's no way Celia could have been involved in some sort of conspiracy with PTG. I'm thinking there's no way she would have done anything wrong at all. And now here I am, eliminating all the other possibilities."

I was inclined to agree with Rena. To the extent I was able to look objectively at Celia at all, I knew that that she had a strong sense of right and wrong and had little time for people who cut corners.

"I guess we have to consider some non-innocent explanations," I said.

She gave me a reluctant nod, then held up the wine bottle. Once again, I declined.

"We might as well say it out loud," I said. "PTG and Benning were both bidders on that big Navy contract. PTG had Shields lobbying for its bid, and it won."

"Yes. But PTG also had the low bid."

"So they didn't need Shields?"

"It's more complicated than that," Rena said. "If the military wants to, it can write the specifications so that they favor one bidder over the others. The Pentagon actually works with the contractors to develop the bid documents, and many drafts and proposals are exchanged informally before the bidding actually takes place."

"That's where the lobbying comes in."

"Yes. You can write it so that one of the parties has a clear economic advantage—maybe you're specifying technology they already have, or can produce more cheaply. They can try to steer things, in the way they write the bid documents, to enable the company they want to come in with the low bid."

"So what could have happened with the Navy contract?"

"PTG and Benning were the only two serious bidders. Shields was pushing hard for PTG, which has large facilities in his district, and of course, was paying him for his services."

"So could they have colluded in submitting their bids?"

"I don't know. As I recall, the dollar figures were close. But you don't just collude on one contract—the other bidder has to get its chance to win. And there are often more than two bidders. I just don't know . . ."

"How can we find out?" I asked.

She ignored me. "There has to be some other explanation. I absolutely cannot see Celia doing this. And just as troubling . . ."

"Yes?"

"As unlikely as it is that Celia was involved, it's just as farfetched to imagine Dick Westcott being involved in or condoning anything like this. He has a reputation for being squeaky clean, and that's been my experience with him. And I'd like to think it wouldn't be happening on my watch, under my nose."

I pressed on. "We have to find out, Rena. Even if it seems impossible. We have to figure out what Celia was doing there that night, and what's going on in general."

"I know. I'll see what I can find out."

"Be careful. You don't want to tip anybody off."

"I'll be a model of discretion. Give me a day or two."

"Thanks," I said. Despite my jealousy, I didn't really want to believe the worst about Celia, either. But the evidence against her was mounting, including the most damning item of all: She was dead.

Chapter 37

I drove home, drained. One part of the ordeal was over for me. The Shields case was no more. Now, at least, I had more time to focus on the second massive problem: Finding out who had killed Celia. However, thanks to the security camera footage, these two challenges looked like they might be different parts of the same conundrum.

I noticed as I put my key in the lock that the main overhead light was on in the living room. Normally only a table light would be on, triggered by a timer. I tried to remember if I could have left it on.

I rolled into the house and gave a little yelp, startled by the sight of two people sitting on my sofa. One was my landlady, Eleanor. The other was a youngish man with Asian features who looked vaguely familiar. Two teacups sat on the coffee table.

Eleanor stood up. "Hi, Pen. I hope you don't mind my letting this gentleman in to wait for you."

I looked at the man, who smiled at me. I stared at him for a moment, trying to place the face, before recognizing him as a bystander on the curb at the Minneapolis airport. I opened my mouth to shout at Eleanor to run, but the words stuck in my throat.

"Agent Terrence offered to come back later, but I told him I was sure you'd be home before long." She walked past me to the door and began to let herself out. "I'm glad you told me it was okay to let the police in—Agent Terrence is such a nice man." She left. When I turned back to Terrence, or whatever his name was, he had a gun out.

He smiled at me. "Let's establish some ground rules, Pen. No screaming, no fleeing, full cooperation. I would hate to see any harm come to Mrs. Tompkins. Now, take the bag off the back of your chair and put it by the table." I complied.

He walked slowly across the room, pointing the gun at me. I grasped the wheels on my chair, trying to breathe.

He crouched down beside me. I could feel his hot breath as he slowly moved the pistol up to my face. "Open up," he commanded.

Trembling, I opened my mouth, and he slowly pushed the gun into it. I tasted metal and oil.

"Are you prepared to die?" he asked quietly.

I managed to give my head a little shake.

"You should be. Nearly everyone who gets in my way dies." I closed my eyes and prayed.

Then the gun was gone. I opened my eyes. Terrence was standing up, stashing the weapon in a holster. "But not right now," he said. "I'd really, really like to kill you, after what you did in Minnesota."

I caught my breath. "I saw you in Minneapolis," I said. "At the airport. Did you kill Lisa?"

"I had to, yes. You're to blame, really. If you hadn't tracked her down, there would have been no need to act."

"You did something to her before that," I said. "A week ago Friday night."

"Yes."

"Why didn't you kill her then?"

"My client asked me not to."

"Who's your client?"

He just smiled.

"And you're going to kill me?" I asked, trying to keep my breathing under control.

"As I said, I'd like to, but no, I'm not. Not right now, anyway."

"Why should I believe that? You're letting me see your face. I can identify you."

He laughed. "Believe me, when we're finished, you will have no interest whatsoever in identifying me to anyone, least of all the authorities. In fact, you'd probably rather die than give me up. No, I'm not going to kill you. But you are going to have an unpleasant experience."

I tried to imagine what that might be.

He said, "Wheel in here closer." I obeyed. "Now," he said, "transfer over to the armchair."

I did so. He came over, took my wheelchair, and kicked it off into a corner. I was trapped. I noticed for the first time that he wore an earpiece, which was connected to some kind of radio unit on his belt. Was he communicating with a lookout or other accomplice?

He said, "In a few minutes we'll be moving to the bedroom to get things started. I always put my subjects on the bed—it's the most comfortable place for our business. And I'll ask you to remove your clothes, too."

"What if I refuse?"

"Then I'll remove them for you. It's for your own comfort— nothing prurient about it."

"What's your real name?" I asked.

"Believe it or not, Terrence is the name I was given at birth."

"You convinced Eleanor you were an FBI agent."

He nodded. "My creds are very good. They convinced Lisa, too."

"Did you kill Celia?"

"Celia Sims? I'd rather not comment on that."

"So what did you do to Lisa?"

"The same thing I'm going to do to you," he said. He returned to the couch, where for the first time I saw an attaché case on the floor next to where he'd been sitting. He opened the case, which was mostly felt padding. In the center, I could see, in specially cut openings, a vial, syringe, duct tape, some leather cuffs or restraints, and what looked like a rubber chewing block. I began to tremble again.

"The nice thing about the Treatment," he said, "is that there's no coercion involved after it's done. You'll be free to go. I will, however, be making a couple of suggestions for you on behalf of my client. That's all they are—suggestions. But if you're like previous subjects, you would rather die than fail to implement them. For a time, you'll want to die anyway."

He sat down on the couch across from me and leaned forward. "The Treatment was developed in a Soviet psychiatric hospital, the kind where they used to send dissidents during the Communist era. It's been on the black market ever since, but it's expensive—more than $10,000 for a single dose. Fortunately, you never need more than a single dose. The beauty of the Treatment —what makes it so unique and so expensive—is that people do recover. In fact, they're usually able to function again after a couple of days, give or take. There are plenty of psychosis-inducing drugs out there, but they'll mess you up permanently. Now, it's true that with the Treatment, the immediate urge to commit suicide is very strong. I will sit with you for an hour after it wears off to make sure you're okay. There will be some permanent damage—post-traumatic stress disorder is a given. But with time and therapy, you can recover."

"My God," I croaked. "What does this stuff do?"

"It's hard to describe. Subjects have told me it gives them a sense of their entire self disappearing. Apparently that is more terrifying than any monster or sensation of fear our minds can produce. It is an experience people will do literally anything not to replicate. The CIA supposedly offered several million dollars for it—for interrogations, you know. But my Russian contact rejected the offer. He figures they'd analyze and replicate it and —well, there goes his monopoly."

"You don't have to do this," I said. "Tell me what you want."

"Don't worry—I'll tell you exactly what I want. I want you to cease and desist all inquiries into the Shields case and into the Sims murder. Period. That's easy, isn't it? In a couple of days my client's business will be completed. You can begin your recovery, and life will go on."

"I'm suspended," I said. "I can't do anything, anyway."

Terrence shook his head. "I've done a little research on you," he said. "And I followed you around up in Minnesota. You don't seem like the type to let a little thing like a suspension stop you."

"I'll do what you want," I said, trying to get my breathing under control.

He stood up. "I know you will. But I'm going to give you a little incentive. Now, time to get things underway." He pulled the duct tape out of the attaché case.

I opened my mouth to scream, and he moved forward, drew the gun, and pointed it directly in my face. "Uh, uh. Now, let's keep things civilized here." I was hyperventilating, trying to keep from screaming.

"I'm going to take the gun away now," he said. "If you make any sound, I will have to hurt your landlady—rather horribly, I'm afraid."

He took the gun away, then stood upright, his attention elsewhere. His hand went to his ear—like those creepy agents in *The Matrix*—as he listened.

Then he looked up, his features contorted with rage. "I knew I should have killed you in Minnesota." With that, he took the duct tape and went to work.

*   *   *

Outside, the man in the Range Rover wondered if he'd done the right thing. Was he going soft in his old age? He'd seen Pen meeting with Rena Karros—definitely not a good thing. And then she'd come home . . .

For a moment he wondered whether he should have simply gone in there and stopped Terrence. But that would have risked blowing everything up, and he would have had a ton of explaining to do. The sirens were growing louder now, and he hoped Terrence wouldn't do anything rash. He also hoped the "consultant" wouldn't figure out who had intervened—Terrence was not a guy to mess with.

The sirens were very loud now, and at last he saw a figure dart out of Pen's door, run down an alley, and disappear.

Chapter 38

I had all good intentions of telling the police everything, but I could see they felt out of their depth. How could a couple of young Long Beach patrolmen fathom the connection between a sophisticated extortion/intimidation attempt designed to thwart a federal investigation and a seemingly unrelated murder case —both outside their jurisdiction? After they'd removed the gag and duct tape, I ended up telling them almost everything, including a description of Terrence. But I left out the part about the psychosis-inducing drug Terrence had called the Treatment, figuring that part of it was strange enough to make them question my credibility, if not my sanity.

"And he said he was an FBI agent?" one of the cops said.

"He admitted he used phony FBI credentials," I corrected. "I didn't see the creds, but Mrs. Tompkins did."

The officers consulted their sergeant, a tall, frazzled woman who looked like she'd been up for three days. Probably a lot like me, I imagined. When she'd arrived, I'd repeated the story for her, somehow managing to hold it together and sound coherent. The sergeant disappeared, muttering that she'd have to consult her captain. In the meantime, the patrol officers had canvassed the neighborhood, looking for a vehicle and for the anonymous person who had called 911 to report a home invasion at my address. Neither effort was successful. Eleanor Tompkins sobbed uncontrollably, apologizing over and over again for admitting the intruder. In reassuring her that it was all right, I felt a little better myself.

Finally the sergeant returned. "We'll have to bring in the Bureau," she announced. *Good luck with that,* I thought. She said the FBI would be around to interview me, probably in the next day or two, and asked if I had a place to stay in the meantime. I said I'd find one. It was a little after ten when the police left, warning me to keep the door locked and not to admit anyone.

When they finally left, I must have felt as though I had permission to fall apart. I barely managed to pick up my phone and punch in the speed dial number for James.

He answered after one ring. "Pen? Is that you?"

"James, I need help. A man broke in—got in, and he was going to . . . oh, God . . ." I began to lose it.

"Is he still there?" James said.

"No. He was scared off. The police came, and, and . . ." Going, going, gone. I couldn't talk.

I heard James say, "Hold on. Don't go anyplace. Don't open the door for anyone. I'll be right there."

It seemed to take James forever to get there, but when I looked at the actual time elapsed on the clock, I realized he must have averaged about a hundred miles an hour on the road. When I heard his BMW screech to a halt in the driveway, I wheeled over to the window, confirmed it was him, and let him in. He rushed in through the door, leaned down, and embraced me tightly. "Oh, Pen, oh baby. What did they do to you?"

He disengaged, held me at arm's length, and inspected me. "What did they do?" he whispered.

"He put a gun in my face. In my mouth."

I looked into James's face. His eyes burned with rage. "Then what?"

"Then he scared me to death," I said. "That's all. But he was going to—oh, God . . ."

"It's all right. It's okay. Come over and sit with me." He pushed me over to the couch, lifted me onto it, and sat down next to me. We sat there for a long time while he held me, soothed me, and patted my back.

At last he let me go, got up, and returned a minute later with a glass of water and a box of tissues. I drank the water, wiped my eyes, and blew my nose. He looked at me expectantly. "Ready?"

"I think so." I stopped myself. "This is partly about Celia," I warned.

He gave me a look that combined puzzlement and astonishment. "I've got to hear this."

I told him about seeing Celia on the surveillance disks. Then I described Brandon Lacey's threats and my suspension by the US attorney's office.

"Good Lord," he said. "After you found Lisa, they suspended you? After you showed initiative like that? Why?"

"I'm not sure. To begin with, they may not have wanted me to find Lisa. And they definitely didn't want me to find out Celia was at the hotel that night."

"I don't get it," he said. "What was Celia doing there?"

"That's what we need to know. But I'm afraid of what we'll find out, James. It looks like she might have been mixed up in something bad."

James shook his head doubtfully.

"It's a good bet that whatever she was doing there got her killed," I said.

He nodded. "Go on."

With difficulty, I pressed on, telling him about the thug named Terrence, how he had talked his way into my apartment, then tried to give me a terror-inducing drug.

"Who called the cops?" he asked.

"A really interesting question, which I can't answer. I'm just awfully glad they did."

"Go on."

"Terrence was listening to a radio of some kind," I said. "I thought at first that maybe he had a lookout, but I think now that it was probably a police scanner. He taped me up and put a gag in my mouth—I think that was just to scare me some more, since there was nothing I could do to him and the police were already on the way. Then he said things were changing, that there wasn't time for the Treatment anymore. He said if I didn't cooperate he was going to kill me, and that I could count on it."

"Cooperate?"

"He told me to back off the Shields case and the investigation into Celia's murder."

"Both of those things," James observed, realizing the significance instantly.

"Yes. That means they're connected somehow, probably through that meeting at the hotel. It means that his client, whoever it is, has a stake in stopping both investigations."

"Celia was involved in trying to bribe Shields?"

"I don't see how. Shields was actually working for Benning's arch-competitor, PTG. And she left an hour after Shields did."

"Then," he said, voicing the thoughts I'd had all along, "Shields was involved in Celia's murder?"

"I don't have a clue why he'd want Celia dead. I don't think he actually met with Celia that night—based on the departure times, it looks like only the PTG people did. But at this point, anything is possible."

There was a knock at the door.

I was still sitting on the couch, so James got up, went to the window, and looked outside.

"Who is it?" I asked.

"The police."

"I wonder what they—"

"The Newport Beach police. They're here for me."

"For you?"

"I called and told them I'd be here." He came back, rolled my chair over, and lifted me into it. "I have to go," he said.

"What?" I was thoroughly confused.

He handed me a slip of paper. "You can stay at this address for as long as you want. It belongs to Glenn Helton—he and his family are in Europe."

Helton, I knew, was a wealthy friend from James's banking days. The pounding on the door grew more insistent.

"Glenn's place is very accessible," James continued, "and has a household staff, including an armed security guard."

"James, what the hell—"

He put a finger over my lips. "When they set bail and let me out of jail, there were strings attached." He lifted the cuff of his pants to reveal an electronic ankle bracelet.

My stomach lurched. "Oh, no."

"I wasn't supposed to leave the house. I'll be going back inside now. I'm counting on you to be your usual tough, resourceful self."

I recoiled at the thought. At the moment I felt about as courageous as Scooby-Doo.

He hugged me tightly. "I'm sorry, hon."

The knock sounded again. James kissed me, then went over and admitted two officers, submitting to a frisk and cuffing. They took him away, and the smile he gave me as he left, while sad, seemed to be hopeful, too.

Knowing I had a man like this, willing to go to jail for me, how could I not be hopeful? I knew I had to suck it up, to avoid disappointing him and myself.

I also knew I had to get out of the apartment. I packed a few things and left the house. Outside, I could see that James's car was gone; he'd probably had someone retrieve it. As always, he was calm and focused in an emergency. I followed James's directions on the long drive to the home of Glenn Helton. I made a number of turns on side streets but didn't see anybody tailing me, so I headed north on the I-405, hoping nobody had bugged the van with a tracking device.

My destination proved to be a mansion located in the hills above Malibu, which was surrounded by a high fence and protected by a gate. Feeling somewhat reassured, I pulled up and identified myself, and a male voice said I was expected and welcomed me. The gate slid open, and I drove up to the main house.

A uniformed maid, a short, rotund Latina named Isabella, came out to help me out of the van and welcomed me into the house, a large Mediterranean-style villa. She took me around the back of a huge open staircase and onto an elevator, which took me up to the second floor. We proceeded down a long hallway to a guest room that was bigger than my entire apartment. Isabella helped me get unpacked and settled, then told me just to give the staff a call if I needed anything.

After the maid left, I rolled over to a set of French doors, opened them up, and went outside to a balcony. I could see, far below, streams of headlights and taillights from the traffic on Pacific Coast Highway, and beyond PCH the dark vastness of the ocean. I tried to keep from flashing back to the terror of my encounter with Terrence, knowing I had to get beyond the fear and come up with a plan. The biggest problem now, other than staying alive, was determining whom I could trust, knowing instinctively that sharing what I knew with the wrong person could be fatal. I found it profoundly troubling that the two people who wanted me to stop investigating Celia were a psycho killer and my boss. I wasn't sure what, if anything, that told me, but it seemed clear that Connie and O'Shea couldn't be trusted.

I reluctantly concluded that the confrontation with Terrence was not a matter for the Newport Beach police. Even if they had the capacity to investigate a professional thug like Terrence, they saw Celia's murder as a crime of passion and seemed disinclined to believe that anyone other than James was involved. They also had no real ability to determine the significance of Celia's presence at the Discovery Hotel that night. In any event,

I didn't want to share crucial information with a police department that had its own agenda, and for whom protecting my best interests was, to put it mildly, not a priority.

All signs seemed to point to the FBI as the entity best equipped to deal with this complex, multi-jurisdictional puzzle. But the Bureau had behaved a bit strangely thus far, taking a cautious approach similar to that of my bosses at the US attorney's office. And now that I was suspended and out in the cold, was the Bureau likely to listen? Apparently they would be contacted by the Long Beach police, but I'd sound out Gibson myself in the morning.

I closed the doors to the chilly night, pulling the curtains on the spectacular lawn with tall, commanding palm trees and the ocean. I couldn't stop thinking about Terrence, whose cocky condescension had changed to fury when the sirens interrupted him. He professed to be "civilized," but there was nothing civil about his pointing a gun in my face, duct-taping me, and threatening to kill me. I wondered—not that I was complaining—why he didn't just shoot me. But next time, he'd promised, that was exactly what he'd do.

I looked around the huge, luxurious guest room, then out the window again. This would be a nice place to hide. I could just stay here and wait for everything to blow over.

But I wouldn't. Not with James sitting in a jail cell, facing trial for murder—potentially facing the death penalty. As long as I had any power to act, he would not be there a minute longer than necessary.

Chapter 39

I was up early, having slept little. It took a large breakfast, fixed by the Heltons' cook, plus an extra cup of coffee to get me going. Breakfast was a luxury for me; I was always in a hurry in the morning, requiring so much time to fiddle in the bathroom and get myself ready to go, then facing a typical LA commute. I enjoyed the fresh fruit, freshly baked croissants, and an omelet, knowing that if I ate this way every day, my weight would balloon.

Back upstairs, I called John Gibson and, predictably, reached his voicemail. I left a message telling him there were new developments and he would want to talk to me. He called back fifteen minutes later.

"Pen. What's up?" Abrupt and to the point, as always.

"Good morning to you, too. I was thinking you might like to know that a thug forced his way into my apartment last night and threatened to kill me unless I backed off the Shields case."

"Wait, wait. Whoa." He paused. "I'm sorry, Pen. Things are a little hectic today, and . . ." His voice trailed off. Then he said, "Tell me from the beginning."

I did, starting with my identification of Celia on the hotel surveillance system and ending with my encounter with Terrence. He let me talk without interruption, and I told him everything. When I'd finished he said, "Are you all right?"

"No, John, I'm not. I'm actually pretty scared."

"Of course. Well, I just couldn't be sorrier about all of it."

I said nothing.

He said nothing.

Finally he said, "The Bureau is going to be contacting you, right?"

"Supposedly."

"I don't know which agents are going to catch that one. I'm sure they'll do everything they can."

"The new agents will be starting from scratch. They don't know anything about the Shields case or the Sims murder."

"I suppose that's true," he said. "If they ask me to bring them up to speed, I'll be glad to help out. But I wouldn't want to stick my nose in."

"Then let me tell you something else. You and your fellow agents may want to take a look at the statement I gave the Long Beach police. I pointed out that Terrence admitted killing Lisa Darden. Any chance you might actually care about that?"

Silence.

"The Shields case is your case, John. Yours. There's a psycho out there who used fake FBI creds to threaten, disappear, and finally kill a witness in your case. Then he used the same creds to threaten the former prosecutor on your case—me. You could at least act like you give a rat's ass."

"It's just not that simple. Of course, there will now have to be a full investigation, which includes Lisa's death. But as for my involvement—well, the Shields case has been dismissed."

"Terrence didn't get the memo," I said. "And what about his admission that he killed Lisa?"

"That hasn't been independently verified, although of course it will be investigated. But the murder is a local matter. And there are other FBI agents involved, and it's complicated. Then, unfortunately, you've got that suspension, and—well . . ."

"And you've been told not to help me in any way. You might want to ask yourself why that is."

He didn't say anything.

"The suspension is total bullshit, John, meant to cover some-body's political tracks, or maybe even something worse. In the meantime I've got a professional hood putting a gun in my face and threatening to kill me, James is in jail for a murder he didn't commit, and I'm suspended. Forgive me if I don't give a damn about your internal politics or procedures, or your bureaucratic caution. If I have to figure this out by myself, I will. In the meantime, you know where you can go."

I hung up, shaking with rage. He called back immediately. I ignored the call. He could be the one to eat some voicemail for a change.

After a minute I moved to the balcony, letting the spectacular ocean view calm me down. The phone buzzed in my hand again. I glanced at the screen: Rena.

"Hi," I said.

"Can you meet?"

"When?"

"Right now. The sooner the better."

Half an hour later we sat at a Starbucks in Santa Monica. I couldn't imagine what Rena had learned that would cause her to take off in the middle of a work day. She sipped a decaf latte while I worked on a grande cup of hot, black coffee. I realized Rena didn't know about my encounter with Terrence.

When I told her, she stared at me in disbelief. "Are you serious? Are you all right?"

"I'm still pretty shaken up, but he didn't hurt me. I need to tell you this, because if what you know has anything to do with Celia, this could put you in the bullseye, too."

She looked down into her cup, more shaken than I'd ever seen her. "This is madness," she said quietly. "You need to turn this over to the police, or the FBI."

"Been there and done that. They're not picking up the ball. Meanwhile, I've got to move. James is in jail again." I explained.

Rena looked appalled, but impressed at the same time. "If you had any doubts about James . . ." she began.

"I didn't," I said. It was the truth. Mostly.

She took a deep breath, nodded, and exhaled. "Here's what I learned. I did a quick analysis of major bids Benning has done recently. I started out with the Navy contract Shields was lobbying for."

"You lost that one," I said. "PTG won, thanks in part to Shields."

"Yes. What I found was that our bid was quite high. But PTG's bid was almost as high. In fact, the bids were high enough that the Navy talked about throwing them out and starting the bidding process over. But they ended up going with PTG."

"Benning and PTG were the only two bidders?"

"There was a third bidder, a British company, but their bid wasn't considered serious."

"Why not?"

"They were a foreign company, and no one believed their technology was up to snuff."

"So what does all this tell us?"

"I'll get to that in a minute," she said. "But let me interject one other thing: I asked around and confirmed that Celia was acquainted with Milt Hammer."

"Acquainted?"

"In a business context only, I'm told."

"Why would she be meeting him and Lopez that night at the hotel?"

"I'm not sure—it just adds another twist to the case. I've met Hammer myself. He's a sleaze."

"But a charming one," I said.

"No argument there. Anyway, in looking into the recent bids, it's not always easy to sort out. Some contracts involved multiple bidders. Still, it's possible to pick out a number of contracts where Benning and PTG were basically the only serious bidders. In the past few years there was a rough but discernable back-and-forth pattern in these head-to-head bids. In many cases both bids were unexpectedly high. And they were always very close—unexpectedly so."

"It smells," I said. "Is the Pentagon investigating?"

"They're thinking about it, according to a call I made to Washington this morning. The pattern has—shall we say—not gone unnoticed."

"If the pattern holds," I said, "then Benning would probably be allowed to win the next bid."

She made a wry face. "Funny you should mention that. There's a major, multi-service contract for retrofitting the F-35 fighter coming up for bid in a couple of weeks. Both Benning and Pacific are bidding. So is Horrey Technologies, another local company. DMB—that's an American subsidiary of a British company—is considered to be a more serious competitor on this one, but most observers believe one of the American companies will end up with the contract, for political reasons if nothing else. You remember how the government bent over backwards to award that huge tanker contract to Boeing rather than a foreign company. And most people think Benning and PTG are in the best position to win."

"If the bidding has been fixed for years, why did PTG need to pay Shields?"

"That's easy. There are plenty of things a congressman can do for a defense contractor. Lobbying for more funds, encouraging modernization and new weapons systems. During the last bid, for example, he lobbied the Navy to add all kinds of expensive features to the specifications. And when embarrassing questions are raised about anything, it's nice to have some clout on your payroll. What did they pay him—half a million? That's petty cash to Pacific Technology Group."

"You think this new F-35 contract may have triggered Celia's murder somehow?"

Rena shook her head. "I don't know what to think, Pen. Tying any of this to Celia's death is several big leaps beyond what we know now. And I still have a major problem believing Celia would be in on it, if it fact there was a scheme."

"If she was in on it, would she have told you?"

Rena considered the question. "I'd probably be the last person she'd tell," she said. "I didn't know her that long, and of course, I'm the damned general counsel."

"What about Westcott?" I asked. "Would he know about it?"

"No."

"You sound very certain."

"No objective reason for the certainty, I guess. I just know the man, that's all. He's considered a leader in corporate ethics and responsibility. When he hired me he said, 'Keep us out of trouble, Rena. That's your only real job. If there is ever any pressure on you to do anything other than the right thing, you let me know. You will never have to worry about me backing you up.' And in my experience, he meant it. But obviously I've got to talk to him about this, and soon."

I took a sip from my now-cold coffee. "A bid-rigging scheme sounds far-fetched, but facts are facts. We have to assume it really exists."

"For now," Rena agreed. "Are you going to tell your bosses?"

"They already know."

Rena looked up, stared at me, then nodded slowly. "That's why they've been behaving strangely. That's why they don't want you involved. They have something going, and they don't want it messed up."

"Yes, and it infuriates me that they don't trust me enough to tell me what's going on. It fits with what Terrence told me—that his client's business will be completed in a couple of days, or something like that. The principals will be meeting to fix the bids, and the FBI will be there to trap them."

"That has to be it," she said.

"But some things are still not right," I continued. "There are some rogue actors here. Who does Terrence work for? What does the Shields case have to do with any of it?"

"So what are you going to do?"

"I'll have to step around the bid-rigging carefully; I don't want to mess up their sting. But I can't stop investigating—something else is going on, something related to Celia's murder."

"Do you suppose—" She stopped herself. "Maybe Celia is the one who blew the whistle. And that's why they killed her."

"It makes sense," I agreed. "Presumably the FBI and US attorney are investigating that, too."

"The Newport Beach police have to be told," she said. "They think James killed her."

I blew out a breath. "I need to wait, at least a couple of days. If I tell them Celia may have been killed because she was involved in a bid-rigging scheme, they might go blundering into Benning and PTG and spook the bid-riggers. They might blow the government sting."

"Unfortunately, that's true."

"If I thought it would clear James any quicker, I'd do it anyway. But the police aren't going to let him go until they're sure they've got a better suspect. We don't have one yet." I glanced into my empty cup. "I wonder if they know what Terrence was doing the night Celia was killed. But assuming he was the killer, who hired him?"

"One of the parties trying to protect the bid-rigging scheme," Rena suggested.

"That fits, too."

"The FBI must know all of this," she pointed out.

"In an organizational sense, yes. But they don't seem to have put it together. They're not involved in investigating Celia's murder. I doubt if Gibson or any other single person has the entire picture."

"So you're pressing ahead." It was a statement, not a question.

"As long as James is in jail, I'm pressing ahead."

"What are you going to do next?"

"I don't know."

"But knowing you, you're kicking around some ideas."

"I think I'm the one being kicked around."

"Be careful."

I managed a thin smile. "I've gotten good at that."

I thanked Rena profusely, and we hugged, agreeing that girls' night out tomorrow would probably have to wait. She left, and I sat at the table, watching the busy comings and goings, listening to the loud hiss of the espresso machines. Finally I figured I'd better get going. I took my empty cup and looked around for the trash bin.

Then it hit me.

I sat for perhaps five minutes, thinking it all through. Then I pulled out my cell phone, found the number for Stacy Ellis, and entered it.

"Hello?"

"It's Pen," I said. "Are you in California?"

A pause. "Yes."

"I thought you might be. We need to talk."

*   *   *

Terrence put his binoculars down. Pen was meeting with Rena Karros again, which couldn't be good. He was long past the point of scaring her; Windfall was too close, with too much at stake. He'd have to take care of her. He'd look for his chance, and it would come. Until then, he had plenty of time to think about a most interesting question: Who had called the police when he was in Pen's apartment?

Chapter 40

We agreed to meet at the Westfield Mall in Century City. I threaded my way east through the heavy traffic on Santa Monica Boulevard, turned south on Avenue of the Americas, and then into the mall. She was waiting at the curb when I pulled over. She peered inside, hesitated, and then got in.

We left the mall and turned south before she spoke. "I'm not going to testify," said Lisa Darden.

Lisa, not Stacy.

"We can talk about that later. Right now, I'd just like to know what happened."

"Before that, you can tell me how you figured it out."

"I only talked to you twice," I said. "But I probably had some memory of the voice. And of course I'd seen that video of you—it wasn't a good one, and you'd changed your appearance, cut your hair and put on glasses—but the resemblance was very strong."

"I fooled you in Minnesota."

"Yes, you did. But your ecological awareness did you in."

She gave me a quizzical look.

"The Diet Coke can," I said. "You had to look around the garage for the recycling container. You didn't know where it was. It wasn't your garage."

"You figured it out from that?"

"Not immediately, but that started my thought process. I realized that you didn't know the code for the garage door opener. When you opened the door, you had to go inside, get your keys, and enter through the side door, even though the door had an automatic door opener. You were able to *close* the door using the keypad, but you didn't need the code for that. All you had to do was push one button—probably the Enter button."

She shook her head. "Such a little thing."

"You checked her in at the motel, didn't you?"

She nodded. "Stacy was in no shape to do it herself."

"I thought so. The motel guy recognized your picture."

I turned west on Olympic, then made several other turns. I didn't notice anybody following me, but I was all too aware that such precautions aren't foolproof. Lisa was also looking behind us from time to time. "I might as well ask the obvious question," I said. "Did Terrence intend to threaten Stacy, or did he do it by mistake?"

"No, Stacy was the target. They used her to get at me. It was a message that they would do it to me if I testified."

"Do you know what Terrence did to her?"

"It was a drug. It was horrible. It made her kill herself."

"No, Terrence killed her. He admitted it. He followed me to Minnesota, got to the motel ahead of me, and hanged her."

She gave a little shriek. "My God."

"Actually, he admitted killing you. He didn't want me to know you'd switched identities."

She stared straight ahead, trembling. I needed to keep her on track. "What happened that night?" I asked.

She took a breath, pulled herself together, and said, "After the guy left, she got out of the house—just started driving around. She was hysterical—crazy with fear. Finally she pulled over and managed to call me. She said I was supposed to not testify and to disappear for ten days."

"Why didn't you just do that?"

She glanced in the rearview mirror again. "At the time, I was focused on Stacy. She refused to go back to her house, and I wasn't about to argue with that. I told her to come to my place, but she was afraid they'd find her there. She wanted to hide out somewhere, so I went and picked her up, and we looked for a place that would take her off the books. Eventually we found that God-awful motel. We got her settled, and then I had to start thinking about disappearing—that's what I was supposed to do. So I sent that message to Adam."

"But we didn't stop calling."

"No. I expected that, I guess, but I figured it would be Adam calling, not you. Anyway, I realized I needed a plan in case somebody showed up looking for me. If I really disappeared, there might be a serious search, and I'd be found. That's when I got the idea of posing as Stacy."

"So you cut your hair short, put on some glasses, and went and stayed at her house."

"Yes. That way I could disappear and not testify, but I wouldn't have to hide like Stacy, and I'd have a place to stay, at Stacy's house. I could just hide in plain sight. I really didn't have any problem until you showed up. But I hadn't met you, and I'd changed my appearance a little, and it worked. I figured I was home free after that."

"Did you stay in touch with Stacy?"

She nodded. "I got us a couple of disposable cells so we could talk without leaving a trail. I talked to her every day, and I thought she was recovering from the experience, doing better. But . . ." Her voice broke, and the tears flowed freely.

"Terrence says the suicidal urges subside," I said. "She probably wasn't going to kill herself."

She sniffled, then gave me a sharp look. "How do you know he said that? And how do you know his name?"

"I had a little chat with him."

"You—are you all right?"

"Pretty much. He was scared off before he could give me the Treatment. Have you told anybody Stacy is dead and you're alive?"

"Just my parents."

After half a block of silence she said, "How much trouble am I in?"

"Technically, you could be charged with mis-identifying the body—maybe failing to report a crime. And depending on what you've done since, maybe obstruction of justice."

"I was scared to death," she said.

"I guess that would factor into any decision by the prosecutors. Tell me, why did he target Stacy? Why not just do it to you?"

"I just don't know," she said.

I didn't believe her.

"Why didn't you call the police?" I said.

"If you'd gotten the Treatment, or seen somebody who has, you'd know why."

I guessed I probably understood. I forced myself to keep on driving. Somehow I was back on Santa Monica Boulevard, and I turned back toward Century City.

After a couple of minutes I said, "So you went down and identified Stacy's body as yourself."

She nodded. "I knew I couldn't pull it off much longer, but I thought it would get me through the ten days." She turned to me. "Are you going to tell anyone I'm alive?"

"I don't know. I haven't had a chance to think about it."

"Please don't. Let me handle it."

"I don't want to put you in danger," I said.

"That's very thoughtful of you," she snapped. "But isn't it a little late for that? And if you hadn't looked for Stacy, she'd be alive now. Terrence wouldn't have killed her."

That may have been true in the short run, I thought, but the FBI would have been looking for Lisa in another day or two and would have found Stacy fairly quickly.

We pulled up at a stoplight. I said, "That brings us to the reason you're here in California, and the real reason you were not given the Treatment."

"I told you."

"I'm afraid I'm not buying it. I—"

Before I had time to react, Lisa opened the passenger door and bolted from the van.

I just watched her, frozen in astonishment, as she crossed a busy sidewalk and ran between two office buildings. Horns honked behind me. I jerked forward, then made a right turn, trying to spot Lisa. I continued down the block, looking for her, unsuccessfully. I caught a green light at the next cross street and started through the intersection.

And then the world exploded.

It took me a moment to realize I'd been hit by a vehicle, somewhere on my side of the van. My airbag deployed; I couldn't hear anything. Fighting through a mental haze, it took me another moment to realize that I should probably get out.

That's when I smelled smoke.

There isn't much that strikes fear in a paraplegic like fire does. And here I was, dazed and trapped in my vehicle. I stabbed frantically at the button to open the side door and extend the ramp. Nothing happened. I reached down to release my chair, but I couldn't reach the lever. The crash had pushed something into the way.

My memory of what happened next was fuzzy. I smelled more smoke. I blacked out and then drifted in and out of hazy consciousness. I had a vague awareness of being rescued from the van, then a gurney, and being loaded into an ambulance. I was in the ambulance for a while, and then I felt the ambulance moving. I jolted awake as the ambulance swerved to an abrupt stop; were we at the hospital?

There was commotion and doors slamming. And after a couple of minutes the back door opened, revealing an attendant.

But not an attendant.

It was Terrence.

Chapter 41

US Attorney Dave O'Shea, looking into the video monitor at his friend, FBI Assistant Director in Charge Kirk Hendricks, didn't waste time on pleasantries. "What can you tell me about the Long Beach incident?"

Hendricks's response was calm and measured. "We've been called in by Long Beach PD. We've seen their reports. First off, we don't know who reported the incident. All the neighbors deny it, and the call was from an untraceable cell. What does that tell you?"

"Somebody was watching Pen's place," O'Shea said.

"A-plus, Sherlock, and we need to know who it was. Second, she says this guy threatened to kill her unless she stayed away from both the Shields case and the Celia Sims murder."

"Who is this guy, anyway?"

"He calls himself Terrence. Professional hitter, but they also hire him to terrify people."

"You're familiar with him?"

"We've heard of him. Our file on him is pretty thin."

"What do we know?"

"We think he was born in Korea but lived here most of his life. Works internationally, with multiple passports and identities. Well connected, especially in Russia and Eastern Europe."

"Presumably Terrence is a phony name."

"Maybe, maybe not. We don't even know if it's a first name or a last name. But Pen said he confessed to threatening, then killing, Lisa Darden."

"Killing." He paused to take it in. "That would explain a lot of things. So now we have a murder on our hands. I guess the Shields case isn't over after all."

"This changes everything," Hendricks said. "We'll now have a full-blown investigation into the murder of a federal witness and an assault on a federal prosecutor."

"Damnit, I want whoever is behind this, Kirk. The case may have worked out well, but you don't terrify into hiding and then kill a federal witness. And if Larry Shields is behind this somehow, I'll get him on witness tampering and then turn his ass over to the locals on a murder rap."

"Absolutely. But again, what's the connection between Pen and Celia?"

"They were dating the same guy."

"That connects Pen and Celia. But how does Shields fit in? What links his bribery case with the bid-rigging?"

O'Shea's response was cautious. "Well, we've got a guy involved in both."

"It's not Hammer."

O'Shea thought about it. "No, it's not Hammer."

"And keep in mind: The Shields case had already been dismissed when he went after Pen. I think maybe we need to look for another connection."

"Should Terrence be a suspect in Celia Sims's murder?" O'Shea asked.

"He'll have to be considered, of course, since he warned Pen off the Sims investigation. But the murder still looks like a crime of passion—lots of overkill."

"Ironically, Terrence sort of did us a favor. We needed Pen out of the way. I suspended her, but I'm not sure how much good it did. Maybe Terrence got through to her."

"I've got some good people on the Long Beach thing," Hendricks said. "If there's a link, we'll find it."

"It damn well better be fast," O'Shea said. "If there's any threat to the bust, we've got to put it to bed, pronto. You'd better start by picking up Pen. We can't have her out there freelancing —who knows what the hell she'll do?"

"I doubt if she's in much shape to do anything after the encounter with Terrence. But to be on the safe side, we're trying to find her right now."

"You don't know where she is?"

"Not at the moment."

"Kirk, you're the freakin' FBI. You know what terrorist leaders in South Waziristan eat for breakfast. For Christ's sake, find her." Then, more quietly: "What a cock-up. And we're so damn close."

Chapter 42

Rick Stouffer was in his office, working with an interior designer on plans for redecorating his vacation home on Maui, when Milt Hammer called. Stouffer dismissed the decorator and sat behind his mammoth desk to take the call.

Hammer was irate. "Dammit, Rick, what the hell were you thinking, sending Terrence after Pen?"

"Settle down, Milt. I didn't send Terrence. He sent himself."

"He's supposed to be working for us."

"He is, but don't forget, he's got a stake in this, too."

"I know he does. He shouldn't. Giving him a percentage of Windfall was a mistake."

"I didn't want to do it, either. You know that. But it was necessary to bring the others on board."

"Percentage or no, Terrence does not have carte blanche to go around terrorizing people. He went too far. Nobody should be hurt."

Stouffer leaned back in his chair, cradling the phone under his neck. "You actually know this woman, don't you, Milt?"

"A bit, yes."

"You seem awfully concerned for her welfare, especially considering that until yesterday she was trying to put you in jail."

"Her welfare has nothing to do with it. Making Windfall work is the only thing I care about."

"That's all Terrence wants, too. You can be sure of that."

"That's just swell that he wants the same thing we do. But we've got to be smart about it. Now, thanks to him, Long Beach is swarming with cops and feds. Another murder will flat-out sink Windfall."

"That will never happen. They're all way too late. Windfall can't be stopped, Milt."

A long pause. "I just hope to hell you're right."

"I am. But you know, I still have a question—something that's really bugging me."

"Which is?"

"Who called the cops to Pen's apartment?"

Hammer clicked off the throwaway cell and looked around his office. Had he let everything get too complicated? Was he playing too many angles, juggling too many subplots? Did Stouffer, who thought he was running Windfall, know he was being played? If Hammer was honest with himself, he'd admit that this was what he lived for—manipulating, conning, charming. But in this case there was a purpose that went far beyond mere enjoyment: He would not, under any circumstances, go to jail.

It could still work out, he thought.

Phase One was complete. The Shields case had been dismissed. Shields was obviously happy. Down the hall, Hammer's boss, Wilson Lopez, was happy. Adam Rosenthal, enjoying a lucrative new job, had to be happy. After the sting/meeting Friday night, Dave O'Shea and Kirk Hendricks would be happy. And when Windfall happened, Hammer, Rick Stouffer, and a handful of others would be not only very happy, but very rich.

Not everybody would be pleased when all the shoes dropped, of course. Several people, including Nick Edwards, would have to pay for the bid-rigging scheme. O'Shea would be very perturbed when his arch-foe Dick Westcott did not, as Hammer had promised, appear for the bid-rigging meeting. James Carter was stuck in jail until somebody figured out who'd killed Celia Sims. And of course, a lot of people were unhappy about Celia being killed.

And then there was Pen.

He admitted to himself that he was a little smitten with Pen. And he'd let that get in the way of his better judgment when he called the authorities to rescue her from Terrence. But he couldn't help it. From the time she came onto the prosecution team, he'd felt that Pen alone had his number, that she alone was not buying his BS, and he was impressed by that, loved her attitude. Maybe even loved her, a little bit. She would be okay, he thought, if he could just keep her clear of Windfall for the next forty-eight hours. But could he?

Maybe, maybe not. In the end, it didn't matter. If he had to unleash Terrence again, he would. He'd do whatever it took. Windfall would happen. And he would not, under any circumstances, go to jail.

Chapter 43

Jail could break the toughest of men. And James Carter thought of himself as tough. He sat back on his bunk, staring at the white cinder block wall in front of him, trying to ignore the din of television and background noise, along with the unpleasant smell of incarceration. He'd had a cellmate last night, but the guy had been sprung this morning, leaving Carter with the tiny cell all to himself. He was relieved—felt safer to be alone. But now he found himself craving conversation, even with a tattooed robbery suspect with meth-rotted teeth.

He'd never had a moment of doubt about going to help Pen. She'd been through a terrifying experience, and the least he could do was to settle her down, comfort her, and guide her to a place of safety. He wondered what she was doing now. Actually, he didn't. He knew she was trying to find out who had killed Celia. She was trying to clear him. He felt guilty about maintaining contact with Celia, a foolish mistake that had not only jeopardized his relationship with Pen, but allowed the police to theorize that he was still dating Celia. More than that, he felt vaguely guilty in a more general sense, knowing that if it wasn't for his prior relationship with Celia, she wouldn't have been murdered on his boat. And Pen wouldn't have come under suspicion.

He stood up and walked over to the Plexiglas window in the door of his cell. He'd be in here twenty-two hours a day, except for the three hours per week of outdoor exercise he was permitted. He tried to imagine being here a long time. It might happen, he thought. A high-profile murder case could take months to come to trial.

And what if he was convicted?

Carter listened to the human sounds around him, the sounds of violent men—tough men. He had risen rapidly in the business world by being aggressive, taking risks, making difficult decisions—by being tough. But he knew, ever since Minnesota, that while his ability to endure was better than average, Pen's was off the scale. He thought he had been through it all. He had been fired from his job twice, divorced, publicly criticized and humiliated. He'd been set up for ruin by corporate saboteurs, received hateful letters, emails, and calls—many of them racially bigoted—after implementing layoffs in companies he ran. He had even been shot.

But nothing compared to being hauled out of bed in the middle of the night, frisked, cuffed, Mirandized, led off to jail, strip-searched, processed, yelled at, and thrown into a cell with violent men. Nothing compared to the stories in the media, his mugshot on television, the reactions of friends, colleagues, and business associates, of having to tell his daughter of his arrest for murder. And then, having to face Pen. He couldn't imagine seeing her here, in the little visitor's booth, separated by glass, talking through an intercom that cut off automatically after the allotted time. And yet, all these trials and indignities were positively trivial in light of what he faced now—life in a maximum-security prison. Maybe even life on death row.

Carter slid off his bunk and spent the next ten minutes doing pushups, sit-ups and knee bends, going faster and faster, punishing himself. He needed to stay active. He could lift weights, he supposed, but he instinctively stayed away from the tattooed, bulked-up cons who hung out in the weight area.

Sweating and breathing heavily, he plopped back down on his bunk. His presence here was as bewildering as it was frightening. Why on earth had Celia visited his boat that night? He'd once loved Celia, and he grieved for her now. She had been strong, confident, proud, and intensely driven. A lot, in other words, like James Carter. And when he'd fallen out of love with her, it was less a case of his not liking Celia anymore than of not liking himself. He hadn't known what to make of all the adversity, hadn't known who he was after his corporate career was destroyed. Then he'd met someone who knew a thing or two about being strong and driven, but also knew who she was despite overwhelming adversity. He'd craved that kind of grounding, found himself drawn irresistibly to it, and to Pen. Somehow, she knew who he was, and amazingly, still loved him.

As he'd fallen in love with Pen, he realized they had become partners in healing. For Pen, the need seemed obvious, but the damage to her psyche went far beyond the physical injury. With time, therapy, and his love, she might someday get over the hurt and rejection she'd experienced in trying to resume her life after the accident and the trials she had undergone in battling the corporate saboteurs. But he knew she would never completely recover from the guilt resulting from the accident that had killed her six-year-old niece.

And what about his own guilt from the thousands of lives he'd messed up, sometimes irretrievably, in implementing massive layoffs? Or the shame he felt from his failed marriage, leaving his daughter with a broken home? Or the trauma of a control freak waking up one day to realize he controlled nothing? The past year had been a quiet, day-by-day miracle, doing good work and living a good life with the extraordinary woman he loved. He would do anything to preserve that miracle.

Make that *almost* anything.

Eric was seriously pissed at him for rejecting his trusted partner, Alex Kramer, and Jack Tomasky after that. Carter had put them off, didn't hire either of them. It had nothing to do with any lack of trust in Eric, or in the attorneys, for that matter. But they were leading him down a path he couldn't follow.

He wouldn't do it.

Chapter 44

I woke up. I half-expected not to, but my existence was apparently destined to continue, at least for the time being. I didn't recognize the room, but it appeared to be a living room, not a basement, or a hospital. I was lying on a couch.

I remembered the ambulance and Terrence. I struggled, seized with fear, trying to sit up, looking for my chair.

"Pen." The soothing voice belonged to a man, but not Terrence. I looked up into the familiar face of a man who wasn't even supposed to be in this country. But here he was.

Adam Rosenthal.

"Good God, Adam, is that you?"

"None other. Everything's fine." He went to the doorway leading to another room and said, "She's awake."

Dr. Pam LaRue came in, carrying a flashlight. She didn't look happy as she strode over to the couch. "How do you feel, Pen?"

"Tired. A little mixed up. My chest and arms are sore. Where am I?"

"You're safe," Adam said. "This is a rental apartment in Culver City, owned by my uncle. Nobody knows you're here, or can trace you."

"What time is it?"

"Seven-thirty a.m."

"What day is it?"

"Wednesday."

I gasped. I had been out for nearly seventeen hours.

"First things first," Pam said. "Let's get you to the bathroom."

"I don't have my stuff," I said.

Adam smiled. "No problem. We got you some new stuff." He and Pam carried me to the bathroom. A half-hour later I called for them to come and get me. They appeared a minute later with a rolling desk chair, which they used to get me to the kitchen. They rolled me up to the table, where a glass of juice and a slice of toast waited for me.

"I'll get you some coffee," Adam said. "I know you need it."

"I'm not really hungry," I said.

"Then let's take a look at you," Pam said. "You can eat afterward." She spent the next ten minutes examining me. I had some nasty bruises on my chest and arm, and a cut on my left ear. Pam shined a flashlight into my eyes, asked me questions, and performed some other simple mental acuity tests. Finally she stood up. "You're not real sharp, Pen, but I don't see any classic concussion symptoms. You'll just need to rest, and we'll need to keep an eye on you." She looked toward the kitchen, where Adam had disappeared. "I'm sorry about how this happened, Pen, and sorry I can't stay. Believe me, Adam and I are not finished discussing this, or any number of other things. I hate it when he's right."

Before I could ask what Adam had been right about, he reappeared. Pam clasped my hand. "I have to get going. I'll check you out again in a day or two. If you have any problems, call me. And take care of yourself." Then she left.

"What were you right about?" I asked Adam.

Adam flashed a sheepish grin. "She was furious at me for bringing you here instead of to the hospital. But I argued that you needed to be in a secure place and that you didn't seem to be hurt that badly."

"Where's my chair?"

"I'm afraid it's wrecked."

"Damn." I had a backup chair, but it was at home.

"Eat," he said.

I did. I took a couple of bites and discovered that not only was I hungry after all, I was ravenous. He made me a second piece of toast, and I ate it all.

"I guess you have some questions," he said.

"Yes, I do," I said. "You were following me. Lisa kept looking in the rearview mirror."

Adam lifted an eyebrow. "Not quite as dazed and confused as Pam thought, are you?"

"Had Lisa been in touch with you?"

"We'd been in touch ever since Stacy's death. Yesterday she called and said she was out here and that you had figured out the switch in identity and were demanding to see her. She didn't know you and wasn't sure she could trust you, and she was also afraid Terrence might be watching you."

"I guess she was right," I said.

"It appears so. Anyway, she asked me to cover your meeting. I saw you pick her up and followed you from there."

"Looks like my conversation with her didn't increase the trust level," I said. "She took off on me."

He gave me a troubled look. "I totally did not expect her to run off like that, and I have no idea why she did it."

"First tell me how I got here," I said.

"I was following you and Lisa. I'd assured her that she was perfectly safe with you, but she knew she'd done some things that were wrong and maybe illegal, and that you were a prosecutor and knew about them. Anyway, I was cruising along Santa Monica and saw you had stopped, and then I caught a glimpse of Lisa running between those two buildings. Then I saw you turn. I didn't know what the hell was going on. I didn't make the same turn. Instead, I cut off a block early to see if I could catch Lisa."

"Did you?"

"No. And I still don't know where she went. But I drove around for a while and finally came back to that street you'd turned on. And then I saw your van in the middle of an intersection, with an old sedan plowed into the side of it. The paramedics were just arriving, so I watched them get you out of the van and load you up. Then I thought I'd just follow you to the hospital to see if you were okay. That's when things got interesting."

My breathing grew shallow as I recalled the crash, the smoke, and then Terrence.

"The ambulance had only gone a few blocks," Adam continued, "when a big SUV came along, cut in front of it, and ran it up onto a sidewalk. A guy got out of the SUV and went over to the ambulance."

"Terrence," I said.

"Based on Lisa's description, it must have been. Anyway, he ran over to the driver, who had his window down, and punched him through the window. The guy went out like a light. Terrence ran around to the passenger side. The other attendant had locked his door, but Terrence pulled out a gun and smashed the window. He hit the attendant over the head and knocked him out. It all happened so fast; I was just sitting there in the car, watching it happen."

"Didn't anybody do anything?" I asked.

"There were a couple of people watching from the sidewalk, but they were as stunned as I was. So then Terrence yanks the attendant's body out onto the sidewalk and rips off his coat and cap and puts them on. After that, he runs around to the back and opens up the door. He was shutting it again when I ran up behind him."

"What did you do?"

"I yelled at him, asked what he was doing, and told him I'd called the police."

"Had you actually called?"

"No, so it wasn't too smart to confront him, I guess."

"Good Lord, Adam, what were you thinking?"

"I wasn't, I guess. But then other people who'd seen what happened started to gather around. So he points the gun at me and shoots. He missed, and I realized later that he must not have actually been trying to hit me. He just wanted to scare me, I suppose."

"Why would he want to scare you?"

Adam shrugged. "Hey, it all happened in a blur, and I know not all of it makes a lot of sense. Anyway, I hit the deck, and so did the crowd, and he ran back to the SUV and took off. I'm still kicking myself for not getting the tag on it, but it was probably stolen."

"What happened next?" I asked.

"I pulled you out of the ambulance, carried you to my car, and brought you here. You don't remember any of that?"

"No."

"Not surprising—you didn't seem too coherent."

I tried to take it all in. "Adam, that's amazing." *Maybe a little too amazing,* I thought. "It was incredibly brave," I continued. "And foolish."

"Not one of my smarter moments," he admitted.

"So this was all . . . yesterday afternoon."

"Right. I called Pam, and she came over and examined you. She thought you might have a concussion, but she said you didn't seem too bad and thought the best thing to do was just let you sleep. I'm betting you haven't been sleeping much lately, anyway."

"That's true." He walked over to the coffeemaker, poured two cups, and brought one over for me.

I sipped the brew, which was excellent. I felt a hundred percent better than when I'd woken up but was still a little woozy. "I need some more answers," I said. "Why did you quit, and what are you doing back here in LA?"

Adam set down his cup. "The first contact came three weeks ago, from a high-powered recruiter. She didn't even say who

230

her client was at first. I've been approached from time to time, of course—I'm sure you probably have, too."

Actually I hadn't, but I'd only started the job a year ago.

"They came on strong," Adam continued. "Dangled an obscene amount of money in front of me, wined and dined me, flattered the hell out of me. I didn't pay much attention at first, but they really weren't going to take no for an answer. Finally I started to show some interest, and when they thought they had the hook set, they dropped it on me: We need you right away."

"Why?"

"They had a training class starting, and they had this seminar in Singapore starting last week, blah, blah, blah."

I was starting to feel an intense desire to leave the apartment but figured my best bet was to play along and to try to get some answers. "Who were these people?" I asked.

"I'd heard of the firm," he said. "Maybe you have, too. Isaacson and Brandt. Based in London, but with offices in most major cities around the world. The LA office is one of their biggest. They needed bodies for white-collar criminal defense work and made a strong play for me. I told them that within the next year I planned to make a run for political office, and they were actually supportive of that."

He paused, and I asked the obvious question. "Why, Adam? I thought you liked it at the US attorney's office. More than that, I thought you were dedicated to public service. Almost all of us could make more money in the private sector; you never talked about leaving. And then to leave us high and dry in the middle of the Shields case—I was damned disappointed in you."

He sat up straighter and put his cup down. "Of course it was a shitty thing to do, bailing on you like that. And yes, I look like a hypocritical phony, snapping up a job offer from a bunch of sharks like Isaacson and Brandt. I took the risk of looking that way because I thought it was important."

"What was important?"

He gave me a sad smile, then took a long, thoughtful sip from his cup. "I've tried to be as discerning as I can about my strengths and weaknesses. I know I'm a good leader. Pretty good at seeing the big picture and relating to people. As an attorney, I'm pretty good, too. But not as good as you. And not as good as Connie or Vik. Not as good as Cassandra is going to be." He smiled and shook his head. "We as prosecutors acquire a pretty jaded view of the world, of course. But sometimes it comes in handy. And it's especially useful when somebody offers you something that seems too good to be true."

"So you—"

"I decided to play along. I just wasn't buying their offer. I'm good, but not that good. I'd be a nice catch, maybe, but not the prize catch. It was all just too much. What sealed it for me was the insistence that I leave just before the Shields trial. The timing was just a little too coincidental for me."

"Did you tell anybody?"

"Nope. Nobody. These guys at Isaacson are connected, Pen. Word might have gotten back. If I was going to play them, it had to be convincing. So I burned all my bridges and took the plunge. Accepted their offer and turned in my notice, effective immediately."

"And what did you find out when you started work?"

"Basically nothing. I had to be careful, of course, so I acted like just another thrilled but entitled recruit. But I started asking questions right away, expecting that when I reached the end of the trail and found out who was really behind my hiring, Larry Shields would be there. But he wasn't."

"Who was?"

"Nobody, as far as I could tell."

"Who were your clients?"

"They never actually assigned me clients. I wasn't there long enough. I just went to these conference sessions in Singapore.

They told me that when I got back, they wanted me to work with a guy named Eugene Wen."

"Who's he?"

Adam shrugged. "Chinese businessman with an office in LA. I don't know a thing about him. But I'm out of there—they'll have to find somebody else to represent him."

"So you're back at square one."

"Technically, yes. But I'm more convinced than ever that my hiring was a put-up job. I can't give you any solid evidence for it, but I can feel it in my bones." He got up, walked over to the coffeemaker, and poured himself another cup. He held up the cup to me, but I waved him off.

Adam sat down again. "Your turn," he said. For the next half hour I filled him in, telling him about Lisa's defection, the strange behavior of Connie, Gibson, and O'Shea, and my trip to Minnesota. He grinned broadly when I told him of tracking Lisa down in Minnesota.

"Now that had to throw a monkey wrench into somebody's plans." He quickly turned serious. "When you found Stacy in that room, was it . . . bad?"

I nodded. "Of course, at the time I thought it was Lisa."

"She surprised both of us. I heard about her 'death'; it was quite a shock to get a call from her. So who hired Terrence? Shields?"

"That was my first thought," I said. "But now it looks like Terrence has to be involved from another angle." I went on to tell him about Celia's murder, James's arrest, my suspension, and the visit from Terrence.

He picked up immediately on the link made by Terrence between the now-dismissed Shields case and Celia's murder. "What on earth could connect those two things?" he said.

I told him about the security footage showing Celia apparently meeting with Hammer and Lopez. Then I launched into Rena's theory about a bid-rigging scheme and how Celia might have found out about it and then been killed to prevent her from blowing the whistle.

Adam thought about it for a full five minutes. "That's a hell of a theory, Pen. As far as I can tell, it fits all the known facts. Of course, there's very little evidence supporting it."

"I know."

"How is Rena doing?" he asked.

"Pretty well, I guess."

He smiled. "Yes, her life and career are fabulous as always, and she's probably embarrassed about it."

I returned the smile but realized I knew Rena a lot better than he did, and she was probably a little more candid with me about the frustrations in her life. She had achieved extraordinary career success, but she was starting to wonder if it was worth the price.

"So," Adam said, getting back to matters at hand, "it looks like O'Shea, Connie, and the FBI kept you in the dark."

"Yes, and I'm not happy about it. It makes me look like an idiot. I don't think I've given them any reason to distrust me."

"I'm sure you haven't," he said. "But you have to understand: O'Shea and Dick Westcott have a history, and it's not a happy one. I don't know all the details, but there's genuine animosity there. O'Shea would love to nail him—if not personally, then his company. He'd like to put a few kinks in Westcott's halo. That means they're playing this sting very close to the vest. I doubt if they were afraid you would leak anything; they just wanted you to act convincingly, to proceed with business as usual."

"Maybe," I said, still fuming.

"So when do you think they're going to drop the hammer?" he asked.

"Soon. Rena says the F-35 contract will be coming up for bid in a couple of weeks, and so they'll have to be meeting soon if they're going to fix the bids."

"So what are you going to do?"

"About the bid-rigging? Nothing, I guess. The higher-ups seem to have it in hand, and I'm not going to screw it up for them. But I've got to figure out Celia's murder; James is in real trouble." He nodded. "It sounds that way. You need to do what you have to do."

"So what are *you* going to do?"

He let out a long breath. "Good question. I played cowboy and it didn't work out. I can find a job somewhere, of course, but I'm AWOL from Isaacson, and I never wanted that job anyway. I guess I'll just try to patch things up at the office and play it by ear."

"Sure," I said, trying not to betray my disbelief at the entire story. "What do we do with Lisa?"

He shrugged. "That'll be up to Connie and O'Shea. If they want to try to re-recruit her, they can do their best, I guess. But the FBI is going to have some questions. They'll be questioning her about the witness intimidation, and of course Stacy's death, and her experience with Terrence will go to the heart of it. She hasn't returned my calls since I agreed to follow her, and she disappeared on you. Not big on gratitude, I guess."

"Or just scared. Why do you think they went after Stacy instead of her?"

"I don't know, but bottom line is, it worked." His features tightened. "They've got to stop this guy. I'm just glad he didn't get you."

"Amen."

"Look, I've got to go out for a few hours." He glanced at his watch. "I should be back by dinner time. Meanwhile, do you think you can get by here?"

"I'm sure I can." I glanced around; the place was small enough, with enough furniture that in a pinch, I'd be able to get myself around by grabbing onto door jambs, chairs, bookcases, or whatever.

"Oh, I forgot to give you some details," he said. "I had your van towed to a body shop—you need to call them with your insurance information. You'll find an email with the details. Then tonight we can head over to your place and pick up your other chair. I talked to the police. They'll want you to give a statement on both the accident and the attack on the two ambulance drivers, although I told them you really didn't know anything about that. The car that rammed you was stolen, by the way, and its driver fits the description of Terrence."

I was impressed but not surprised. Adam did have a way of taking charge.

He put his jacket on. "Remember, Dr. Pam sternly prescribed rest, and since you can't go anyplace anyway, you might as well follow doctor's orders."

I forced a smile. "Sure. Adam, I don't know how to thank—"

He held up his hand. "No trouble at all, especially after what I put you through on the Shields case. See you tonight—let's have a relaxing dinner. Don't worry, we'll keep you safe until we figure out Celia's murder and put Terrence out of business."

"Where are you going?"

He smiled. "To mend some fences."

Chapter 45

After Adam left, I sat for a long moment, thinking about everything he'd said. Some parts of his story made sense, but many others seemed unlikely or even absurd. I didn't have time to sort it all out now. I needed to get myself out of the apartment and back to the work of getting James out of jail. My first order of business was to check my messages. My phone's battery was dead, so I plugged it in and accessed voicemail. There were three messages from an FBI agent I didn't know, asking me to get in touch to talk about the Long Beach attack by Terrence. I couldn't afford to be sidetracked by questioning, so I didn't return the calls. I doubted the FBI wanted to find me that badly, but in case they did, I shut my phone off.

Next on my to-do list was getting myself mobile again. That was not a priority for Adam, who expected me to stay here and rest for a few days. I couldn't do that. I felt terrible, but there was work to do. In a city the size of LA all it takes is an Internet connection and a credit card to get just about anything. I fired up my laptop and picked up the apartment's landline. First I checked on my van, which the shop said wouldn't be fixed for at least a week. Within twenty minutes, I arranged for a replacement rental van and a new wheelchair to be delivered to the apartment.

Still in the rolling desk chair, I propelled myself out to the kitchen, where I poured myself half a cup of reheated coffee and waited for my new wheels to arrive.

Adam claimed to have admitted defeat in finding out why he'd been lured for a lucrative job in the private sector, but I thought it was worth a look. In particular, there was a name that had seemed to mean something.

I went back to my laptop and Googled Eugene Wen, the client Adam's new employer wanted him to represent.

Mr. Wen proved to be a shadowy figure. I found very little information on him, and it took a while to sort out other Eugene Wens. A Los Angeles *Times* article made brief mention of him, describing him as a Chinese-American businessman with extensive interests in the West, but with rumored ties to the Chinese government and military. He was described in a *Forbes* article as an international business consultant and dealmaker, with offices in Hong Kong and Beverly Hills. He specialized in transactions involving mergers, acquisitions, and technology licensing deals, mostly for high-tech companies.

Beyond these two articles, it was tough to find anything further. Most of the hits were second-hand references to the items I'd already read. It wasn't until the sixth page of results that I found something that stopped me cold. A technology deal put together by Wen's firm, Sino-American Capital Acquisitions (SACA), had been shot down by the US government on national security grounds. The Pentagon, it seemed, didn't want the Chinese to have access to the technology developed by a small company SACA had tried to acquire.

I sat back and thought about it, considering another pot of coffee but deciding against it. For the past couple of days, I'd ignored the small warning bells in the back of my brain, which had been telling me that something more was happening, something beyond even the bid-rigging scheme. The bells were now deafening.

I couldn't find anything more about Wen or SACA, which had no website. I then searched for images rather than web pages. I found only one image of Wen, showing a distinguished-looking Chinese man in his fifties, with ramrod posture and salt-and pepper hair, shaking hands with somebody at a social occasion.

I clicked on the link for the web page the image had been taken from, and multiple tumblers clicked into place. The occasion for the picture was a fundraising event for a politician.

Congressman Latham Shields.

With only a few minutes to go before my new wheelchair and rental van were due to arrive, I had a decision to make about John Gibson. Was the FBI agent a driving force behind the scheme to keep me in the dark, or was he, as I wanted to believe, a decent man who was constrained by his job? I turned my cell phone on and called him.

"Pen," he said. "Everybody's been—"

"Looking for me, I'm sure."

"More than that—worried about you. We got reports saying you were in an accident, involved in an assault . . ."

"I'm okay," I said. "Listen, I need to tell you something."

He waited.

"I know about the bid-rigging scheme."

Silence.

"I understand that I wasn't supposed to know and that you weren't supposed to tell me. Now I'm suspended, so there isn't much I can do to gum up the bust. But my problem is this: Somebody tried to either kill me or snatch me. That was the accident and assault in Century City you heard about."

"You need to come in so we can protect you," he said.

"That's the company line, I'm sure. And of course I heard from your colleagues about the Long Beach assault. Call me cranky and uncooperative, but I have no interest in being taken into custody or questioned for any reason. I think you're a good man, John. But is there any reason on this earth I should trust either O'Shea or the FBI bureaucracy?"

He had no response for that.

I said, "I put my personal safety on the line in order to make this little charade work. I think I'm entitled to know a few basic details about what's going on. So here's my proposal: You meet with me and give me a few of those basics. In return, I promise to tell you anything you want to know. I also promise to do and say nothing to foul up the arrest, nor will I ever reveal how the FBI and the US attorney's office put my life in danger by keeping me in the dark about this operation."

"I don't know, Pen . . ."

"Suspension or no, I'm continuing to look for Celia Sims's killer. I wouldn't want to stumble upon anything sensitive."

"You're blackmailing me."

"Spoken like a jaded FBI agent."

He hesitated. "All right. Check your texts."

He hung up. A minute later my phone chimed. Gibson had left me a text with the address of a Starbucks near the Burbank Airport.

Chapter 46

My new chair and van arrived. I took care of the paperwork, gathered my belongings, and headed off to meet Gibson. I found him already seated at the Starbucks. I rolled up to the table, facing him.

"Thank you for coming," I said.

"Let's make this quick, Pen. I can't believe I'm doing this."

"I went through hell to pull off a charade. O'Shea never wanted to prosecute Shields."

"There might be a charade here, but not the Shields case," Gibson said. "It was for real, as far as I could see. I spent a lot of time and effort on it. O'Shea may not have been wild about it, and he may have jumped at the chance to dump the case, but the investigation was for real, and I believe the prosecution was, too."

"How long have you known about the bid-rigging case?"

"Four months."

"When is the meeting about the F-35 bid going to be held?"

"Friday night."

"Is Hammer involved?"

Hesitation. "Yes."

"Is he your source?"

"I can't comment on that."

"What other companies are involved? Horrey Technologies?" I guessed.

"Yes. An Executive VP named Maxwell."

"Who is involved from Benning? Westcott himself?"

"No. A guy named Edwards."

My brain hurt as I tried to take that in. Nick Edwards. Celia's friend. Then, unbidden, a terrifying thought came to mind. I didn't want to ask the question, but I couldn't stop myself. "Is Rena Karros involved?"

"Who's Rena Karros?" he asked.

"The Benning general counsel."

"No."

I was relieved, and ashamed of myself for asking the question. I said, "Moment of truth: Was Celia Sims involved?"

"We don't think so," he said.

"She was at the Shields meeting, after Shields left."

"We know, but we never saw a trace of any involvement by her after that. We have no other evidence. She was not our source."

"Why was she killed?"

"We don't know."

I looked at Gibson and exhaled. My theory had been blown out of the water. The Shields case, the bid-rigging scheme, and Celia's murder looked once more like three unrelated matters. Except that Terrence didn't think so.

"Pen?"

"Yes, John. Sorry. It's my turn. If there's anything you genuinely want to know, I'll tell you."

He said nothing.

"You're not really interested in anything I have to say, are you? You're just supposed to bring me in and keep me out of sight and out of the way. Let me ask this: If I could tell you where Terrence was, would you be interested?"

"Of course we would."

"All right, stay tuned on that. I'll get out of your hair now. Thank you for doing this."

He took a breath, steeling himself. "You haven't been treated right, Pen. And I . . . I'm sorry."

I shook his hand, acutely aware of how much it had cost him to say it. He got up and left quickly.

Still seated at the table, I pulled out my phone and called Lisa Darden at Stacy's cell number. Predictably, the call was routed to voicemail. I left her a message: "Lisa, it's Pen. I'm very disappointed that you took off on me. Here's the deal: I need you to answer a few questions. If you don't, the case is back on. I will do everything in my power, including going to the media, to revive the case against Shields, and I will have you served with a subpoena and force you to testify or be cited for contempt of court. If I don't hear from you in the next ten minutes or so, the game is on."

As I waited at the table, I felt a headache coming on. Almost instantly, my skull felt like it was ready to come apart. I popped two Advils from the supply I kept in my purse and sat with my head in my hands.

Lisa called back a minute later, fuming. "How dare you threaten me? Who do you think you are?"

"Sorry, Lisa. I just needed to get your attention so you'd return my call. I need some questions answered, and we can talk about whether or not I keep the answers a secret."

"Why should I trust you?"

"Why shouldn't you? I've never lied to you. I've kept your secret so far. I'm sworn to uphold the law and subject to sanctions if I don't. Can you say that about all the other people you've dealt with?"

Her response was weary, defeated. "All right."

I took a deep breath, trying to fight through the headache and concentrate. "I'll pick you up at the same mall in Century City at four. But there's one question I need you to answer now. I won't be angry, no matter what you answer. But it's really, really important for you to give me a truthful response. Did you have someone follow us when I picked you up last time?"

"Yes. I had Adam follow us."

"Thank you. See you at four."

I hung up and just sat for a moment, trying to absorb all that Gibson had told me. I already knew a lot of it, but it was still jarring to hear him matter-of-factly confirm my suspicions. One thing I hadn't known was that Nick Edwards, Celia's close friend, who considered her the best boss he ever had, was a crook. Did Celia figure him out, and so Edwards killed her? Rena would not be at all happy that she'd missed an illegal conspiracy going on right under her nose at Benning. And what about Celia? She'd shown signs of being involved, but the FBI didn't think she was. Had she withdrawn from the scheme? Or had she remained involved, maybe using Edwards as the front man?

I pushed aside feelings of frustration, hopelessness, and fear that I'd never figure it out and forced myself to move on to the next task. My head still pounded, but the Advil had taken the edge off the pain. I pulled out my laptop and accessed Google Earth. After a couple of minutes I was looking at an aerial image of the home of Glenn Helton in Malibu, where I'd stayed night before last. I spent the next half hour moving the image around and back and forth, enlarging and examining, with a single question in mind: What was the best vantage point from which to watch the gate and driveway?

I soon realized that the only clear lines of visibility came from a ridge across a small canyon. Looking up and down the road that snaked along the top of the ridge, I found two potential spots where there were gaps between the houses and openings in the foliage, where a vehicle could be parked. I marked those points, then set about finding a location from which *those* spots could be watched. The place I found was back on Helton's side of the canyon, down the road from the banker's mansion. I switched to the map view and found myself a route to the observation point, then set off in the van. On the way, I stopped at a big-box sporting goods store in Glendale, went in, and emerged ten minutes later with a new pair of powerful binoculars.

It took me close to an hour to reach the point on the road where I could see across the canyon. I assumed that Terrence hadn't given up trying to find me and take me out. I also assumed that he was able to track me to the rendezvous with Lisa yesterday by following me from Helton's house, that he did that by bugging my van with a GPS tracking device, and that from there he had followed me to the rendezvous with Lisa. I knew now that it wasn't he who had been following Lisa—it was Adam. But Terrence had unwittingly trashed his means of tracking me by ramming my van, forcing me to rent a clean vehicle. And now, the logical thing for him to do was pick me up again at the last place I had stayed.

I drove carefully up the winding road to my observation post, passing it once, then turning around and locating the spot. I scanned the ridge across the canyon, searching in vain for the two potential lookout sites. After opening my laptop and consulting the Google Earth image again for familiar landmarks, I finally located the two gaps in the houses and the foliage. I didn't see anything at the first one. But on the second, further south, I spotted a parked vehicle.

I zoomed in, using the new binoculars. The vehicle was a blue SUV. A single figure sat in the front seat. I adjusted the focus and saw something in front of the figure's face. Binoculars. I watched for a long minute, trying to hold the binoculars steady, until the figure put its own binoculars down and I could see the face, albeit from the side.

Terrence.

My blood flash-froze in its veins. I started the van and headed back up the ridge for a couple of blocks, taking no chances that he might swing his binoculars my way. Searching between the houses, I saw another gap from which I could observe Terrence. I pulled over, lifted the glasses, and found him again, once more peering through binoculars. I was nearly behind him now; he'd have to do a very thorough search to spot me. I pulled out my phone and sent a text. Then I called John Gibson.

"You said you wanted to know where Terrence is," I said. "I'm looking at him right now."

He was quiet for a moment; I didn't think he believed me. "Are you serious?"

"Yes."

"You're positive?"

"Yes."

"Where is he?" he said at last.

"On a ridge overlooking a canyon in Malibu. I just sent you a text with a link to a Google Earth page, along with the GPS coordinates."

He was quiet again, only this time I could sense him accessing his messages. Then, "I have your word this is for real?"

"Yes. He has a scanner, so use a secure channel or keep it off the air."

"Are you in a safe spot?"

"I think so."

"Can you stay and keep this line open?"

"Yes. But this is not me calling. This is a tip from a reliable informant."

"Come on, Pen."

"I'll answer questions afterward and testify if necessary. But I've got things to do later this afternoon."

He muttered something in disgust and then told me he'd call back soon. I hung up, glanced at my screen, and saw three messages from Adam. I ignored them and looked at my phone for a long minute. My next call was absolutely critical. I needed to know something that was not public information. It was not a closely guarded secret, but I had no ready way to find it out, and I really needed to know. I took a deep breath and called Cassandra on her cell.

"Hi, it's me," I said. "How are things going?"

"It's quiet. Very quiet. Something is going on, but of course they're not going to tell an underling like me."

I hesitated. We were on better terms now after our little crying session in the break room. But how much better? I was about to ask her to do something that could get her into trouble if anyone found out. Of course, it would get me into even worse trouble.

"I need a favor," I said.

"Sure," she replied without hesitation. Her response gave me an emotional boost; it was really nice not to be treated like a pariah.

"I need Milt Hammer's home address." He had managed to keep it off the Internet.

"I don't suppose I should ask why."

"Not much point, since the request is coming in a phone call that never happened."

She had it for me in less than a minute. I wrote it down, thanked her profusely, and hung up.

I waited. Gibson called me back ten minutes later.

"We see the vehicle," he said. "Blue SUV?"

"That's it."

"Where are you?"

I described my location and vehicle, and a minute later he said, "Okay, I see you. I'm looking at a live feed from the chopper." I looked up in the air and could see the helicopter a long way up, almost directly over the SUV, where Terrence wouldn't be able to see it. I swung my binoculars down the road to where it descended to meet Pacific Coast Highway. Two squad cars, probably from the sheriff's department, already blocked the road, down where Terrence couldn't see them.

Gibson asked, "Why is he there, Pen? Is he going to shoot somebody?"

"He's waiting for me. I stayed at a house across the canyon the other night. It's four or five blocks from me, down toward the ocean. What he wants to do when he finds me—I'll leave that up to your imagination."

"Can you see the tags on the car?"

"No."

"Neither can we. Be nice if we knew it was stolen—we'd have independent probable cause. I hope you're damn sure, Pen. We're going to have to pull the chopper for a few minutes now —we diverted it in a hurry and it's low on fuel. The sheriff's cars can't see him, so your visual is all we've got."

"Don't worry—I'm sure it's him."

"All right. It'll take another thirty minutes or so before we're ready to move. Just stay there. Don't move."

"I won't."

I continued to watch Terrence, who peered through his binoculars with infinite patience. And then he seemed to sense something. He sat up straight, put the glasses down, and looked around. And then he put the binoculars back up to his eyes and began to slowly, systematically sweep the landscape, turning ever so gradually in my direction. He got closer. Then closer yet. I couldn't duck down in the van. I knew he was going to see me.

There was no time to drive away. I put the binoculars down, grabbed a newspaper and put it up in front of my face. While I did so, I called Gibson.

"I think he's made me," I said. "He might be moving soon."

"Okay. Just stay there. We've got the canyon blocked."

I made myself wait a full five minutes before I put the newspaper down. When I looked, Terrence was gone.

I jerked the binoculars quickly to the right and saw that he was headed down the slope toward PCH. As he approached the roadblock, I saw that the officers had stopped a minivan. One deputy stood next to the van, talking to the driver and glancing into the back, while the other stood behind the cruiser. A second cruiser, containing a single officer, was parked next to the first one, blocking the road.

Within seconds I was back on the phone to Gibson. "John, he's headed toward the roadblock. Tell them to look out!"

"Roger that," Gibson replied.

The officer standing away from the van pointed up the slope as he saw Terrence approaching. The first officer turned around. The single deputy in the other car got out and assumed a firing position behind his car. The deputy next to the van now realized how close Terrence was. He reached through the driver's window, pushed the driver over on her side, and then reached for his gun.

He was too late.

Terrence screeched to a halt, and his hand appeared at the driver's window, holding a gun. He shot the deputy next to the minivan, who went down, holding his leg. A second later, the sound of the shot reached me. A couple of seconds later I heard multiple shots. I couldn't tell who had fired them.

I gave a little shriek. "Officer down, at the roadblock!" I yelled into the phone.

The remaining two deputies appeared to have Terrence pinned down. He was now crouched behind the opened door of the SUV. I couldn't see the minivan driver; I hoped she was safe.

What happened next defied belief. Terrence appeared to throw something from behind his door. An instant later, one of the squad cars was engulfed in flames. A second after that, I heard a *whoosh* sound. It must have been a Molotov cocktail.

The shooting stopped. Terrence got out from behind his door and walked calmly to the non-flaming cop car. I couldn't see the officer who had been crouching behind it, but Terrence fired at something behind the squad, and I assumed it was the officer. Terrence calmly got into the squad car, executed a Y-turn, and took off down PCH.

"More officers down!" I screamed into the phone. "He's stolen a squad and is headed south on PCH!"

Thirty seconds later Gibson came back on the line. "Can you see him?"

"No, he went out of my line of sight right away."

"Stand by." In truth, I was relieved that Terrence had driven south. That meant he couldn't come after me.

I waited a minute. Five minutes. Squad cars, ambulances, and a fire truck arrived at the roadblock. I speed-dialed Gibson. No answer. I imagined he was a little busy at the moment.

I waited ten more minutes. The fire in the squad car was extinguished. Paramedics attended to a shaken but apparently unhurt minivan driver. Two ambulances sped off with lights and sirens. Half a dozen additional emergency vehicles arrived. Then my phone buzzed.

"John?"

"Where are you?" he asked.

"I haven't moved."

"Don't. Stand by."

It was another fifteen minutes later when he called back. "He got away, Pen. He ditched the squad and jacked a car at a strip mall."

"What about the officers?"

"One dead, burned to death. Two others shot, one critically."

"My God!" I said. After a few seconds I pulled myself together. "So what happens now?" I asked.

"I've been doing some quick negotiating, and here's the deal: You go to the sheriff's station to answer some questions. You can keep it simple—just what you saw. You don't have to talk to us—yet. But as we agreed, there will have to be a lot more questioning by us, and soon."

"All right."

"You sure you're okay?"

I took a breath. "I think so." Which was total bull.

Chapter 47

It was late afternoon when I picked up Lisa at the Westfield Mall. My statement at the sheriff's station in Malibu had been uneventful. Terrence was, as far as I knew, still on the loose. I hadn't seen any television reports, but I imagined the images of the shootout scene taken from circling news helicopters.

Lisa got into the van, looking sullen and resentful. She fastened her seatbelt and glanced over at me. "What happened to you?" she asked. I didn't realize I looked as bad as I felt, although Lisa couldn't see the worst bruises on my shoulder and chest from the car crash. My headache continued unabated, and I was having trouble concentrating. I shouldn't have been driving. I looked over at Lisa. "No big deal," I said.

"You've made a lot of threats," she said. "I've told you, I just want to be left alone."

"That would be a nice world, if we could all just leave each other alone," I said. "Unfortunately, it doesn't work that way. It would have been nice if Terrence had left Stacy alone, and me, too."

She searched my face. "Why did you have to bring him up? Are you trying to scare me?"

"If you're not scared, you should be." I told her about the shootout in Malibu, watching her face gradually lose color. "And," I added, "if you want to know why I look like hell, he's the reason."

"So he's still out there," Lisa said.

"He's still out there."

She was silent.

"I'm going to give you a name," I said as we turned on a side street, south toward Olympic. "The name is Eugene Wen."

Her face showed nothing. If she was trying to keep a straight face, she was good.

"Tell me if you've heard the name. And give me the truth, please. If you don't, the US attorney's office will not be pleased."

A flash of anger shot across her face. "Yes, I've heard the name."

"Have you ever met him?"

"No."

"But Shields has."

"Yes."

I could feel my heartbeat ramping up. It was time to take the shot. "A deal is going down with Wen in the next day or two," I said.

Again, she didn't respond.

"If you tell me, Shields won't know it came from you. You have my word."

"All right. I've heard something like that, yes."

"How did you hear about it?"

"I overheard it."

"Would you like to elaborate on that?"

"No, I wouldn't."

"Who else is involved?"

"I don't know," she said. "Business people. I don't know their names."

"I'm going to give you another name. The name is Milt Hammer."

This time her impassive expression gave way.

"Is he involved?" I asked.

"Yes." No hedging or equivocation.

"Do you know what the deal is about?"

She shook her head. "Just that it's a really big deal."

"When is it going down?"

"I think tomorrow."

I circled back to the north, then east toward the mall. "I don't suppose you'd want to tell me what you're doing in LA, or why Terrence targeted Stacy instead of you."

"No, I wouldn't."

I nodded. I was pretty sure I knew the answers anyway, and most of them involved Congressman Latham Shields.

"You wouldn't have to tell Shields that we met," I said. "In fact, it might save my life if you didn't."

"I'll think about it."

I stopped in front of the mall. "You may think you're powerless against Shields," I said.

She didn't reply.

"You may not have cared about disappointing Adam, or me, or the government. But don't disappoint yourself."

"Don't lecture me," she snapped.

"Is this who you really are? Or are you the person who bravely blew the whistle on a corrupt phony?"

"I don't have a choice."

"We always have a choice," I said. "It's not too late. If you change your mind, call my office. Talk to my assistant." I handed her a card with Cassandra's number.

She took the card, stuffed it in her pocket, and got out of the car. "Don't hold your breath," she said and walked away.

I watched her enter the mall, grateful for the information I had gotten, but trying to absorb yet another piece of bad news: Lisa had inexplicably gone over to Shields. Worse, she was probably going *back* to Shields, which meant she hadn't been forthcoming about their previous relationship. At least we wouldn't discover the truth unexpectedly on the witness stand.

I put the van in gear and headed for Milt Hammer's house.

Chapter 48

I'd had nothing to eat since breakfast at Adam's uncle's apartment, so I stopped at a McDonald's drive-through for a hamburger and a shake. I was starting to feel seriously tired and a little woozy. I forced myself to concentrate on the road as I crawled through rush-hour traffic on the 405 toward Redondo Beach. I found Hammer's house, a single-story stone-and-redwood structure, on a quiet side street just off Torrance Boulevard. I drove by; the house looked empty. I circled the block, looking for a vantage point, and settled on a parking space half a block down the street, away from Torrance Boulevard, in front of another house that looked empty.

My phone trilled, and I glanced at the screen: Pam LaRue. "Yes, Pam?"

"How are you feeling?" she asked.

"Not too bad," I lied. She asked me a series of more specific questions and accepted the answers reluctantly. She apparently thought I was still at the apartment.

"I'm so mad at Adam I could shoot him," she said. "He just comes waltzing back home like nothing happened." She paused. "I just don't know. About our future, I mean. I have to think about it."

"Good luck," I said. "I hope everything works out for you."

We disconnected. I relaxed, shifted a bit in my seat, and settled in to wait. While I waited, I tried to put together a number of disjointed facts. I'd stumbled upon a bid-rigging scheme—Gibson had confirmed that. Hammer was involved on behalf of PTG, and so was Nick Edwards from Benning. O'Shea and the

FBI knew about the scheme. How did they know? Because, it seemed obvious, Milt Hammer had told them. He'd flipped on his fellow bid-riggers, making a deal for leniency in the Shields case. I sipped sparingly from a bottle of water. A few people on the street came home from work, but nobody paid any attention to me as far as I could tell.

Two nights from now, the conspirators would meet to fix the bidding for the F-35 contract, and the FBI would get it all on video before arresting everybody. O'Shea and Connie had kept me in the dark about the sting, wanting me to behave "naturally" and eliminate any possibility of the operation leaking. O'Shea was taking no chances in his quest to nail Westcott and Benning.

Now it seemed clear why O'Shea, Connie, and the FBI had discouraged me from doing much additional investigating on the Shields case. They didn't want me to learn that Milt Hammer was up to more than just bribing a congressman. And in fact, O'Shea's fears that I might figure it out were justified; here I was, with what seemed a pretty complete knowledge of the bid-rigging scheme and accompanying sting. So there was the story.

Except that it wasn't. Not by a long stretch.

I woke up with a start. It was dark. I glanced at my watch; I'd been asleep for about half an hour. I'd needed the sleep desperately, but it had caused me to miss Milt Hammer's return. His garage door was open, and the lights were on inside.

As I waited for Hammer to make his next move, I sat and chewed on the facts some more. Something else was going on, something other than the bid-rigging scheme, and according to Lisa, my double-dealing pal Hammer was in on that, too. And why not? Bribing congressmen and rigging defense contracts wouldn't begin to exhaust his vast, cheerful venality. And then there was Eugene Wen, the shadowy guy Adam had heard about. Lisa had learned these facts from Shields, with whom she'd apparently had a rapprochement. His indictment had now been dismissed, and he had no reason to be involved in a bid-rigging scheme, which meant something more was afoot. But what?

Eugene Wen might be the key, I thought. He was a player in the defense high-tech business, as was Hammer. A law firm associated with Wen seemed to have engineered Adam's timely departure from the Shields case. So the known players were Wen, Hammer, and Shields. What were they up to? I wasn't sure. But thanks to Terrence, who had warned me off both the Shields case and Celia's murder, I had faith that the answer would somehow lead to an explanation of that murder—and would thereby help to clear James.

I sat up. Hammer's car was pulling out of his driveway. I started the van, waiting to turn the lights on. Then I followed him out onto Torrance Boulevard. A few miles later he turned south on the 405 Freeway. It was easy to stay with him until we got to Laguna Canyon Road; then I had to hang back a long way in order to avoid being spotted. When we got into downtown Laguna Beach, I lost him. Guessing that he had gone south, I made a left on PCH and threaded my way through the traffic as quickly as possible. I pulled up at a red light, glanced over at the car stopped beside me in the right lane, and saw that it was the Jaguar. I quickly turned my head, hoping he hadn't seen me.

The light turned. I let Hammer pull out first, then moved over into the right lane behind him. He drove only a couple of blocks further before making a right turn down a short side street leading to the beach. I kept going and took the next right, which turned out to be a driveway between two buildings, with a small parking deck behind them. Behind the lot was a larger building, a private club of some kind, overlooking the ocean.

I saw Hammer pulling into the lot from the other end. He handed the keys to the valet, and then turned around to greet another man. I couldn't see the other guy well, but there was no mistaking the make of the car he got out of: a Bentley. The two men walked into the club together.

I made a Y-turn and went back out onto Pacific Coast Highway. After several turns I ended up back on the little side street Hammer had used to access the club. Right across the street from the club I parked in a handicapped spot from which I could see the little parking deck. Then I settled in to wait.

Chapter 49

The atmosphere tonight was more relaxed than at the Cabal's previous meeting, Stouffer thought. They were in the home stretch now; Windfall would be complete within twenty-four hours, and the obstacles had been removed. Even the uptight Annette Barnes seemed to have chilled a bit, accepting his invitation to have a drink. Milt Hammer, who'd walked in with Stouffer, poured himself a drink and joined his partners.

Stouffer listened to the conversation without really joining in. Barnes and Hammer were talking about the finer points of overseas bank accounts and tax havens, and lamenting the hefty shares being demanded by fellow employees who'd helped with Windfall. Stouffer himself engaged in imaginary conversations with his boss, the CEO who'd hosed him again and again, limiting the size of Stouffer's bonuses and stock options, falsely blaming his own stinginess on the board of directors' compensation committee, and even proposing caps on amounts that could be spent on country club memberships. There seemed no limit to the man's petty tightfistedness, no expenditure too trivial for scrutiny and cutbacks. And now, the CEO would be the one forced to swallow *his* rage and eat shit.

Windfall had not originated with Stouffer, and in fact the individuals who'd proposed it and brought the parties together would be well compensated for their lucrative idea. Stouffer, who considered himself the driving force behind the project, resented having to pay people for nothing more than an idea. Still, there was no denying that when all the dust settled and all the parties were paid off, Rick Stouffer would be richer to the tune of a cool twenty million dollars.

Finally, Stouffer called the meeting to order, and the trio assembled around a conference table in an adjacent meeting room. Stouffer welcomed the group. "I know how hard you've worked, and how much attention you've paid to every detail," he said, "but I still think it would be valuable to spend some time going over everyone's product, along with the shares and the security issues."

One by one, the participants described in detail the nature of the defense-related technology they'd stolen from each of their respective companies and how they'd covered their tracks in doing so. There were performance specifications for torpedoes. There was stealth technology for fighter aircraft. There were encryption codes for missile defense systems. There was cruise missile guidance technology.

And much, much more, all of which would be sold to Mr. Eugene Wen for a cool $100 million. The value to Wen's Chinese clients was incalculable. Since the Pentagon and its contractors had recently hardened their computer systems against intrusion, the Chinese could no longer rely on hacking as their preferred method of obtaining American secrets. Although the Windfall technology could not be accurately valued, due to its unavailability on the open market, it had cost the United States untold billions to develop. The Chinese, even if they were willing and able to spend what it cost to try to keep pace, would find themselves chronically behind if they relied on homegrown efforts.

Chinese intelligence agents had thoughtfully supplied Wen with a wish list of technologies they coveted from each company, and the Windfall participants had provided samples. After some back-and-forth, the parties agreed upon the specific items to be sold. Stouffer imagined that there might be some damage to national security as a result of the transfers, at which point Washington would feel the need for additional spending to regain

American superiority. The beneficiaries of that spending would, of course, be the defense contractor employers of the Windfall participants, which might mute some of their indignation over the thefts. But Stouffer, despite warning his associates of investigations to follow, doubted that some of the thefts would ever be discovered. They'd planned too carefully.

The Windfall participants would all be obligated to compensate accomplices at their respective companies, especially computer experts, for their help in stealing the relevant documents without raising suspicion. Terrence would also have to be paid off. Still, the deal would make them all unimaginably rich. All would be able to thumb their noses at the employers who'd treated them so shabbily. All would leave behind the humiliating years they'd spent in futility, trying to play by the rules, only to be used, abused, and kicked around. All would be able to upgrade their lifestyles, to have the things and the experiences they deserved. Their days of being looked upon—and looking upon themselves—as losers would be over. Windfall would catapult them far up into the ranks of life's winners.

When Hammer and Barnes finished detailing their respective portions of the plan, Stouffer dutifully recounted his own experience of recruiting Horrey Technologies' assistant chief technology officer and their director of security to evaluate the Chinese requests and covertly fulfill them. They'd agreed to do it for a total of less than $300,000.

Losers.

When they'd all finished, Annette Barnes, the professional pain in the ass, said, "I think you're underestimating the risks of discovery here. These people who helped us would probably give us up with very little hesitation."

Stouffer managed to avoid sighing. "That's why I insisted that all of us develop an exit strategy, Annette." With help from Milt Hammer, they all now possessed extra identities and passports, along with connections, bank accounts, and properties in friendly, non-extraditable countries.

"But," Stouffer continued, "all this is based on a worst-case outcome. Now, as you all know, we have taken care of our partners' main concern about proceeding with the deal. The Shields bribery proceedings have been dropped, and we are good to go."

"Yes," said Barnes. "I see that the chief witness against Shields mysteriously committed suicide up in Minnesota. I sincerely hope that never comes back to us."

"Not a chance," Stouffer replied, "because it was a legitimate suicide."

"You're telling me Terrence had no involvement whatsoever?"

"I wouldn't go quite that far," Stouffer admitted. "But there is no way it could be linked to Terrence, much less to us."

"What about that young hot-shot prosecutor? I heard she actually went up to Minnesota to track down the witness."

"Sure. But what did she find? A body."

"But—"

"Look, we're going belt-and-suspenders on this thing, leaving nothing to chance. Just for good measure, this young prosecutor was suspended by her bosses when she got back. Not only that, but Terrence has been keeping an eye on her."

There were nods of satisfaction around the table.

"I'm a bit concerned about security for the exchange," said Barnes. "Why, again, does it need to occur out in the open?"

Stouffer was grateful when Hammer responded. "It's simple, Annette. Everybody will be out of range of any listening or video recording devices. Nobody will be trapped in an enclosed area, which eliminates the possibility of any hanky-panky. I would refuse to participate if we did it any other way."

"Actually my question is a little more basic. Why do we need a physical exchange of media? Why not do everything electronically?"

"We considered that," Stouffer said. "But in the end, our judgment was that we simply couldn't guarantee secure, simultaneous transmission. So we'll bring our hard drives and memory sticks and do it the old-fashioned way."

"Just like a drug deal," Hammer added.

Everyone laughed, but the laughter, Stouffer noted, seemed a little uneasy.

"And the money will be transmitted on the spot, right?" Barnes said.

"Not only that," Stouffer replied, "but each of us will get a call from our bank while we're still at the scene. Everything will be confirmed and concluded on the spot."

Several other details of the transaction were discussed before Stouffer asked if there were any further questions. There were none, and Stouffer adjourned the meeting, saying, "Get a good night's sleep, people. Tomorrow we will receive—well, you know what's coming."

Everyone laughed. Early on, they'd begun referring to the culmination of the project as a windfall, and eventually the term caught on as the name of the project itself. Stouffer hoisted his glass, as did his compatriots around the table.

"To Windfall," he said.

Chapter 50

Milt Hammer left first, but I decided not to follow him when he left the club. I was concerned about his noticing a tail, and I had no expertise in following people surreptitiously. I decided to follow Hammer's buddy in the Bentley instead. I was lucky—I'd dozed again but woke up just in time to see the two men leaving. Now my headache was worse than ever. I pulled out my little Advil bottle and dry-swallowed three pills. The Bentley pulled out of the little parking deck and swung south on PCH.

Hammer had been inside the club a little under an hour and a half. I'd Googled the club while I waited in the van and learned that its yearly dues would have consumed more than a third of my prosecutor's salary. Hammer could have been meeting with other people in addition to the Bentley's driver, but there was no way to know for sure. I tried calling Cassandra, hoping to ask her to run the guy's license plate and find out who he was, but got only voicemail. I'd have to improvise.

The Bentley's destination proved to be an exclusive oceanfront gated community in San Clemente. The driver pulled up at a gate, talked to a guard at a booth, and was admitted. I couldn't follow the car in, so I maneuvered along a service drive on the opposite side of the fence from the short street that ran parallel to the ocean. I stopped when I saw the Bentley turn down a driveway and disappear.

I used my binoculars to zoom in on a stone post, which bore the house number. I pulled out my phone and Googled the address. Within a minute I knew that the property belonged to a

Richard Stouffer, Senior Vice President at Horrey Technologies, that the Spanish-style house contained 10,416 square feet, and that it had last sold two years earlier for $6.2 million. I still didn't know what Hammer's latest scheme was about, but it seemed to involve the usual: a rich man who wanted to get richer. Richard Stouffer worked for a tech company, which fit with my thought that some kind of illegal technology transfer involving Eugene Wen was in the works. According to Gibson, Horrey Technologies' participant in the bid-rigging scheme was a guy named Maxwell, which seemed to confirm that Stouffer, from the same company, was up to something different.

I put my phone away and headed north on PCH, not sure of my destination. Going home was out of the question; I couldn't imagine returning until Terrence was caught. I didn't want to go all the way back to Helton's. Even though it was probably the last place Terrence would go now, the fact remained that he knew about it and had waited for me there. When I reached downtown Laguna Beach, I paused at a light, took a deep breath, and took a right on Skyline Drive. I climbed up toward the top of the hill, trying to calm myself, knowing that James Carter's house was the logical place to stay, and that I'd be safe here—James had guarded his privacy by thoroughly hiding his ownership with layers of shell corporations. It was also the last place I wanted to be. But I didn't know where else to go.

I pulled up to the house and realized I would have to leave my van in the driveway. My garage door opener had been in my van, which was at a body shop somewhere. Getting out of the van was a little more complicated than usual. Unlike my wrecked vehicle, this one didn't have a dock for securing my chair in front of the steering wheel, and in any event, my rented wheelchair didn't have a bar welded into place that would allow me to secure it. So I had to swivel back in the captain's-type chair, unlatch my new wheelchair, set it up, maneuver it around, and transfer to it.

I rolled up to the front door and did a wheelie up the short step at the entrance. The next part was trickier. I'd spent many weekends here, and visited many other times, but on each occasion, James was with me to open the door and pull me up over the threshold. I had to unlock the door, give it a hard push, then wheelie up into the house, reaching up to catch the door as it swung closed again. It took a couple of tries and a good whack from the door, but I finally made it. I disabled the security system and reset it, then rolled slowly into the living room.

This had been a place of horror for me. A little over a year ago a psychopathic killer had tried to drown me in the swimming pool—and nearly succeeded. I inched slowly toward the large glass doors leading out to the patio and pool, then turned away. I knew that after a year of therapy I should be able to deal with the memories, but I just didn't feel like it right now. James's house was beautiful, decorated in a nautical theme, with a spectacular hilltop view overlooking Laguna Beach and the now-dark ocean. I found I didn't care for the nautical style, maybe because it reminded me vaguely of Florida and therefore of events I wanted to forget. In my time living out here, I'd fallen in love with Spanish-style architecture.

I found I was trembling, gripping the wheels of my chair tightly. I took a deep breath, practicing one of the desensitization exercises I'd learned in therapy. Then I rolled over to the refrigerator and found a bottle of water, avoiding the glass doors leading to the swimming pool. When I felt calm enough, I reached for my phone and called Alicia, James's daughter.

"Hi, it's me," I said when she picked up.

"Pen! Mom says Dad is back in jail again. What happened? Did he do something wrong?"

"No, he did something right." I explained.

"A man threatened you?" she said. "Are you all right?"

"I'll be okay. But I was pretty scared at the time. And your dad was there for me right away."

"Even though he knew they'd send him back to jail?"

"Yes."

"That's awesome," she said.

"Your dad is an awesome guy."

We talked for a few more minutes; then I ended the call so we could both get some sleep. I sat back and drank from my water bottle. My thoughts turned to James, sitting in a jail cell, and I knew that however bad things seemed for me at the moment, he had it worse. I ached to have him back—here, or anywhere.

I allowed myself to think about my job. I was supposed to go back in a week. But what if I wasn't really welcome? What if my career was at a dead end? I was sickened by the thought of starting over, trying to revive my career yet again. But I knew that if I had James I could cope with it, that things would work out somehow.

I found myself wondering about James, and about our future. Despite his communications with Celia, I told myself there was no reason to doubt his commitment to me, considering all he'd done so far, everything from installing a lift on his dock to subjecting himself to jail in order to comfort me. But mostly, I thought his commitment was genuine because I felt it. It just felt right. *We* felt right. I just needed to hold him tonight. But I couldn't. And if I didn't find Celia's killer, none of it mattered. I'd never hold him again.

My phone buzzed, startling me from my musings. It was Rena, sounding uncharacteristically tense and agitated. "Pen, you need to be careful," she said without preamble.

"Rena, what is it?"

"This bid-rigging thing is serious. I don't know who's involved or where it leads."

"What do you mean? What happened?"

"I finally got a chance to talk to Dick Westcott about my suspicions."

"And?"

"And it was the strangest conversation I'd ever had with him. He asked all these questions about what I knew and who I'd learned it from. Then he said I had to be really careful about making accusations—that the reputations of the company and its employees were at stake. And then—it got really strange. He said he was really disappointed in me for behaving so rashly and unprofessionally. He said he might have made a mistake by promoting me to general counsel at such a young age. He said—and I quote—that I 'might want to start considering other career opportunities outside the company.' I just—I couldn't believe it." She sounded near tears.

"Rena, I'm so sorry I got you into this. So what's going on? Is Westcott in on the scheme?"

"I don't know what to think. I really don't. But I'm scared and confused." The admission was unprecedented—downright incredible—coming from her.

"It should all be clarified soon," I said. "In the meantime, you'd better pull back until we know what's going on and who's involved."

"I guess I have to."

We were silent for a long moment.

"Well, hang in there," I said, knowing the words sounded lame and inadequate.

"You be careful, too," she said. We disconnected.

I sat and looked at the phone, my feelings of guilt threatening to overwhelm me. I had asked Rena to help, to make a few simple inquiries, and now it looked as though helping me might have crippled her career.

The phone chirped in my hand. The notification screen indicated an incoming text. I didn't recognize the number, and there was no name on it. But the number was different from the one that had sent me the anonymous text about Lisa. It said:

"Saw you following me tonight. I saved you from Terrence once, but I won't do it again. Stay away or I'll be forced to have him kill you."

Chapter 51

I woke up the next morning and realized with a start that it was past nine o'clock. I felt woozy and achy, my head throbbing. Was it really only yesterday morning that I'd woken up at Adam's uncle's apartment? I went to the bathroom and got dressed as quickly as I could, then found some corn flakes and made some coffee.

Normally, a message like the one from Milt Hammer the night before would have kept me awake. If nothing else, the text had confirmed that Hammer was involved—in it all the way up to his brush-cut scalp. It also left me with the amazing assertion that it was Hammer who had called the police, chasing Terrence away from my apartment. I couldn't imagine why he'd done that. But now I was left to wonder who Terrence was working for and who was really behind the large deal that would be going down soon—maybe today.

I finished my breakfast and called Adam.

"Pen—are you all right?"

"Just peachy, Adam."

"You just took off—we didn't know where you were, or—"

"I'm fine. We need to talk."

"About what?"

"About this guy you heard about at Isaacson & Brandt— Eugene Wen. I found out some disturbing things about him."

"Like what?"

"Let's talk in person."

He agreed to come to Long Beach. I picked him up in front of the Hilton on Ocean Boulevard, and we drove down to Palm

Beach Park. I took a slot in the parking lot and shut the engine off. Gray, threatening clouds loomed overhead. Adam didn't say anything during the short ride. He seemed to be studying me the entire time.

Finally he said, "You shouldn't have run off, Pen. You're not looking too hot."

"I've had better days."

"You said you found out something about Wen?"

"Yes, and about you, too."

"What do you mean?"

"We can cut the crap, Adam. I'm tired and feeling a little sick and a little punchy and not really in the mood right now." I reached into the side pocket of my bag, fingering the knife I'd put there to replace the one confiscated by the police. I hoped to God I was judging him correctly.

He tried a smile. "Come on, Pen. This is me you're talking to. What's wrong?"

"That crash may have knocked me around a little bit, but I still have most of my wits about me. You asked me swallow too much, Adam. Maybe I could have believed one or two things, but not all the BS you piled on me."

"What do you—?"

"Maybe I could have accepted that you had tossed away a stellar career as an assistant US attorney, leaving your employer and friends high and dry, to go off as a self-appointed spy on a secret undercover investigation. And maybe—just maybe—I could accept that you had failed, come to your senses, and returned within a week to try to resume your old life."

He let out a heavy sigh. "Come on, Pen."

"But then there was your story about the encounter with Terrence on the street. You forget that I actually met the guy. And I can tell you he didn't seem to me to be in any mood for niceties. He was run off by police sirens at my apartment, but he made it pretty clear that he wouldn't be deterred again. You're telling me that after ramming my van, forcing an ambulance off the road, assaulting the two drivers, and abducting me, he simply gives up and runs away after an unarmed challenge by you? If there were actually shots fired, there would have been serious police interest, not the type you'd be able to bury with a couple of phone calls. Oh, and you'd be dead."

He said nothing. Across the choppy harbor a massive cruise ship moved into the channel.

"Whatever your motives were, I suppose I should be grateful to you for saving me from Terrence," I said. "But the thought of you being in cahoots with a psychopath like that makes me sick. I thought I knew you, Adam."

"Pen, I never—"

"Don't lie to me! I'm sick of all the lies. There's only one possible explanation: Terrence turned me over to you voluntarily, as the result of a deal. Was it prearranged? Or did you negotiate it on the spot?"

He didn't answer. His shoulders slumped, and his eyes followed a lone jogger who made her way along the beach.

"So then," I continued, "you whisked me away and left me in the apartment—stranded, shaken up, unable to do anything —without even my wheelchair. None of that was accidental."

I studied him carefully. He was tensing up. My hand tightened around the knife.

"I offered you a way out," he said. "I protected you. What is it you want, Pen? Are you just trying to show how clever you are? I already know that. I just can't figure out what your agenda is."

"You mean what my price is? What it will take to hold my nose and look the other way?"

Again, he didn't answer. I relaxed slightly. "Why did you send me the text telling me Lisa didn't mean it?"

"You knew it was me?"

"It didn't make much sense, but I'd pretty much run out of other candidates."

"I'd accessed Lisa's video message, then left it in my box, showing it as unread, knowing Connie would pick it up eventually. Even though I'd communicated with Lisa after that, I couldn't stop thinking about that message. I wanted you to know it wasn't for real."

"Why? Wasn't that the idea? Weren't we all supposed to believe Lisa's message and stop looking for her?"

He shrugged. "Yes, I guess so. I guess I went off-script. Sort of impulsive. I realized it was a mistake afterward, but it was too late."

"Tell me about Wen, Adam."

"What about him?"

"Eugene Wen. The mysterious businessman. You really took pains to be nonchalant and dismissive when you mentioned him. But mentioning him—that's what the whole charade was about, wasn't it? It was the entire reason you 'rescued' me and brought me to the apartment. You wanted to see if the name meant anything to me. It didn't. But it does now."

He said nothing. He was giving me the silent treatment, and it was making me angry. "Do you think I don't know how to use a search engine?" I demanded. "That I'm a complete fool? What's the deal with Wen? What is he buying—military technology? And who is he buying it from? Hammer?"

His stony expression gave way to exasperation. "For God's sake, Pen. What does any of this have to do with you? What possible interest could you have in any of it?"

"It became my business when you bailed on me right before trial and then disappeared my witness."

"It had nothing to do with Lisa," he said.

It was the first allegation he had actually denied, I noted.

He continued, "O'Shea didn't want the Shields case anyway. Neither did Washington. Hell, neither did Connie—I never figured out what her problem was."

I'd pretty much figured out what Connie's problem had to be, but I wasn't about to tell Adam. "So what's going to happen to Lisa now?"

"All I know is that she won't testify," he said.

He apparently wasn't going to tell me about Wen's scheme, so I decided to try another angle. "What was Celia Sims doing at the hotel that night?"

He shook his head. "You just don't quit, do you?"

"And who wanted her dead? Did she find out about your scheme with Wen somehow? Was she involved in it?"

After a moment he said, "Terrence would have killed you if I hadn't worked things out with him."

"I've already said I'm grateful to you for saving me from that. But why do I get the feeling that Terrence wouldn't have been on my case at all if it wasn't for you?"

"Blame me all you want, but as far as I'm concerned, you brought it on yourself. You're undeniably smart, but you're either incredibly naive or incredibly egotistical to think you can just walk into a situation like this."

I paused, looked out the window, and shook my head. "Why, Adam? Why did you need any of this? You're tall and handsome and charismatic. You had a successful legal career. You were looking at a successful political career. You've got Pam. I looked up to you. Everybody did. For heaven's sake, what was lacking in your life that would motivate you to get involved in all this?" I studied him, looking in vain for any hint of an answer.

He didn't respond.

"Get out of the car," I muttered.

He looked over toward me.

"Get out of the damn car!" I screamed. "Get out of my life!"

His expression changed from shocked, to bewildered, to pitying. He opened the door, got out, and began walking across the parking lot.

Chapter 52

Almost immediately after blowing off Adam, I started to regret it. There were things I hadn't asked him, important things. But he hadn't been giving me much in the way of answers anyway. I called the corporate headquarters of Horrey Technologies, the company that employed Hammer's buddy Richard Stouffer, and learned that the executive was currently in the office. I drove down to Horrey's corporate headquarters in Orange County, located along the I-5 freeway near the Lake Forest exit. From a gas station down the street I could see the main entrance to the two-building campus. Stouffer seemed my best bet; Hammer had spotted me. My biggest fear was that Hammer might have warned Stouffer to look out for me. I tried to park in an open area and adjusted my rearview mirrors so I could see anybody trying to sneak up behind me. I kept my knife handy and my phone out and ready to call for help.

While I consumed my drive-through lunch, I tried to absorb all the implications of the bid-rigging scheme. I wasn't sure whether Dick Westcott was involved. After his strange reaction to Rena's inquiries, it had to be a possibility. But at least one of his underlings—Nick Edwards—clearly was. I turned over and over in my mind the mystery of Celia's presence at the Discovery Hotel meeting, presumably for the purpose of bid-rigging. I tried and utterly failed to reconcile that presence with John Gibson's assurance that Celia wasn't involved in the scheme.

The appearance of Richard Stouffer's Bentley interrupted my musings. He was driving fast—places to go; people to see . . . Technology to sell?

He turned south on the I-5, and I tried my best to stay back. Hammer could have warned him to look out for me, although Hammer may not necessarily have known that I had seen Stouffer at the club in Laguna Beach, identified him, and traced him to his workplace. I was just glad he hadn't switched cars. Stouffer seemed to drive as if traffic laws didn't apply to him. He weaved in and out of the carpool lane, driving over ninety for one stretch, and blew through two stop lights. Somehow, I managed to stay with him. He didn't necessarily seem rushed—just indifferent to the law.

I was breathing hard, a sweaty wreck, by the time Stouffer took the Beach Cities exit and headed toward the ocean. I moved up closer—I couldn't risk losing him now. His destination proved to be the huge marina at Dana Point. Stouffer pulled into a parking lot near a dock at the north end, flanked by a restaurant and a couple of shops. I turned around and drove back up the hill, looking for a vantage point. I climbed for a couple of minutes, considered a couple of spots, and settled on the parking lot of an inn and restaurant. It was a long way away, and I could barely see the parking lot and dock through the trees.

I pulled out my binoculars and scanned the area for Stouffer, wondering if he was about to engage in the big transaction that Lisa thought was imminent and that Adam had not denied. Would Eugene Wen make an appearance? And why a marina? Would a meeting take place aboard a boat?

Stouffer stood next to his car in the parking lot, talking on a cell phone. Then another car, an Acura, pulled up and parked next to Stouffer's Bentley. A tall woman wearing a business suit got out and greeted him. Their greetings seemed muted, unenthusiastic.

The next person to arrive was a young man with Asian features who drove up in a nondescript sedan and got out, carrying a briefcase. He approached Stouffer and the woman, and the three people conferred briefly. Then the Asian guy walked over with Stouffer to one of the marina's two long docks. They went past a small building with a little store to an alcove with a table and chairs. The Asian man sat down at the table, opened his briefcase, and produced a laptop, which he set up at the table. Stouffer left him and returned to the parking lot.

Back at the Bentley, Stouffer made two brief calls on his cell phone while the woman stood nearby, fidgeting. After about ten minutes the tardy party finally arrived, and of course it was the only person I was absolutely sure would be there: Milt Hammer.

Hammer was in an expansive mood, greeting Stouffer with a handshake and backslap, with a peck on the cheek for the woman. After the greetings, the three returned to their vehicles and all returned with briefcases, except for the woman, who brought a cloth tote bag. The goods, I thought. I now found myself wishing I had a camera or camcorder; my cell phone wasn't going to be much good at this range. I took a few still photos with the phone anyway, hoping that with enhancement they might be of some use.

The three people admitted to the marina by Stouffer joined the Asian man at the table. There weren't enough chairs, but none of them seemed interested in sitting down anyway. The four people looked at one another. Finally, Stouffer put his briefcase on the table next to the Asian guy's laptop. The executive took a small plastic box out of the briefcase, and I strained to see it. But I could tell, even at long range, what the box was by the motions the Asian man went through. He was plugging a disk drive into his laptop.

I could feel my pulse pounding as I put the binoculars down. They had to be exchanging information, probably selling it, and probably to a representative of Eugene Wen. Why, I wondered, were they doing this out in the open? Why not in a back room or on a boat, where they couldn't be seen by prying eyes or the police?

It didn't take long to puzzle out the answer. They weren't worried about privacy—they were clearly visible by anyone who happened to walk or drive past. They weren't worried about the authorities, who didn't expect any action from Hammer until a bid-rigging meeting to be held tomorrow night. Instead, they were worried about their partners; they didn't trust each other. They wanted to be out in the open. I pulled out my phone and dialed Gibson on his cell.

I got his voicemail. I left a message. "John, it's Pen. I'm at Dana Point marina. Hammer and two execs from other companies are doing a huge illegal sale of defense technology to Eugene Wen, out on the dock at the north end. This is not the bid-rigging scheme—it's separate and bigger. We need some troops, John."

I called Gibson's office and got voicemail again. I pressed zero and was connected to another agent, whose name I didn't recognize.

"Agent Gibson is out in the field—I'm not sure where. You could call his cell." I left an urgent message with the agent and hung up, my hands shaking.

The Asian man continued to inspect material from the disk drive while I pondered what to do next. Even if Gibson got my message, he wouldn't be here soon—his office was more than an hour north in LA. And when he called back, he'd need to know what probable cause I had for a crime being committed, but what I had was thin. There was no proof that the transaction was not innocent, or even that there was in fact a transaction. I couldn't prove that tech secrets were involved, or that Eugene Wen was a party. All I had was Lisa's assertion, source unknown, that a major deal involving Wen and Hammer was going down.

Big deal, I thought. To do anything, the FBI would need to open a file and conduct an investigation, issuing subpoenas and warrants based on sworn probable cause. That could take weeks. By then the information, and maybe Wen himself, could be long gone. Some or all of the tech-company representatives might flee the country, too. And Gibson could easily dismiss what I had seen as part of the bid-rigging scheme, even though the guilty parties weren't supposed to meet until tomorrow night. I just hoped he'd trust me enough to act.

The man with the laptop finished his inspection of Stouffer's drive, nodding his approval. The woman was next, producing a small bag containing half a dozen flash drives. The Asian guy plugged the first one in. This time the inspection went more quickly. I pondered my options and couldn't think of any good ones.

I couldn't just storm down there and confront them. If they were in a good mood, they'd just ignore me. If not, they'd shoot me, or stuff me into the hold of a boat for future disposal. It would be the latter, I guessed. Hammer had already warned me, and he apparently had Terrence at his disposal. I racked my brain; there had to be *something* I could do. I looked at my phone, willing Gibson to call.

The inspection of the woman's materials wrapped up, and Milt Hammer brought out his disk drive. The Asian guy took a break and made a call on a cell phone. Then he began the inspection of Hammer's goods.

Now I noticed a large cabin cruiser begin to make its way out of the harbor and into the marina. I figured it had probably been summoned by the phone call.

Decision time. I still had a shot at going back to my career. Did I really want to do anything to jeopardize that? My right foot was doing its phantom fidget again.

The big boat cruised up to a slip about twenty yards down from the shady dealers.

I pulled out my cell phone and called 911.

"Nine-one-one," the female voice answered. "What is the nature of your emergency?"

"A massive drug deal, going down right now, on the dock at the north end of the marina at Dana Point." I figured "illegal technology sales," or even "espionage"—more difficult to explain—might not get as quick a response.

"You're witnessing this?"

"Yes, as we speak. But you'd better hurry. They're preparing to leave by boat."

"What is your name, ma'am?"

I swallowed hard, knowing that for this to work, I'd have to make the call credible. Anonymity was not an option. "I'm Pen Wilkinson. I'm a federal prosecutor. There are currently four participants, dressed in business attire."

"Have you personally witnessed the drugs?"

"Yes, I have." As long as I was lying, I thought I might as well make it good. "They're all carrying briefcases, and I saw stacks of money in them. I believe they're armed, too."

"Where are you?"

"I drove away from the scene. I'm now at the parking lot of the inn up on the hill overlooking the harbor."

"Very well. Will you stay on the line, please?"

The line was silent. I'd done it. They might send some deputies, who might or might not get there on time. And if they did?

If the participants were smart, they would simply pack everything up, give the deputies a friendly greeting, and deny everything. The deputies would probably ask everyone for identification and ask them what they were doing. But as long as the officers didn't see anything themselves, it was unlikely they would demand that the briefcases be opened. If they did, all they would see were disk drives—no drugs, no money, and no guns. And what they found wouldn't have been admissible in court without a warrant. All the plotters had to do was remain calm.

Two guys jumped off the boat and tied up at the dock. Even from this distance I thought I could see telltale bulges under their light sport jackets. They looked up and down the docks. Then an older Asian man wearing a dark suit got off the boat and walked toward the meeting. The two guys from the boat walked over and stood at a discreet distance, keeping watch. The guy with the laptop finished up with Hammer's hard drive.

The 911 operator came back on the line. "Are the people still there, ma'am?"

"Yes, they are, but they're preparing to leave."

"Stand by. Stay away from the area. Would you provide me with your address and phone number, please?"

I did. The man with the laptop stood up and greeted the older man. Introductions were made, and the three plotters all shook hands with the man I assumed to be Eugene Wen, although I couldn't see his face well enough to tell for sure.

One of the two guards took a cell phone call. He shouted to the group, and there was a general stir. The man with the laptop quickly closed the computer up. He started gathering up the disk drives, but Milt Hammer put out a hand to stop him. The group apparently hadn't been paid yet.

An argument ensued. One of the guards stepped forward. Hammer didn't back down. Stouffer seemed to slink toward the back of the group. The woman moved forward to support Hammer. I looked around for Wen, who was gone. I moved the binoculars and spotted him walking at a brisk pace back toward the boat. I swung the field glasses back to the group and saw one of the guards pull a gun.

But so had Milt Hammer.

Nobody fired. It looked like a standoff.

That's when the cops showed up.

Two squad cars from the Orange County Sheriff's Department wound their way down the hill toward the marina. There were more words exchanged. I saw Richard Stouffer hiding behind a pillar. The guy with the laptop made another attempt to gather up the drives. This time Hammer fired, up into the air. He was not about to let Wen get away with the materials, not without paying.

The gunshot was a huge mistake. It caused the deputies to come in hard. The guards now ran for the boat. The laptop guy stumbled.

Three deputies emerged from the cars, guns drawn, and sprinted toward the meeting. Hands were raised all around. The guards on the boat didn't stop. They were making a run for it. What was the use? I wondered. They would be stopped by sheriff's department watercraft, or the Coast Guard, and tracked by helicopter. They were cooked.

Fascinated and appalled, I continued to follow the proceedings down below. The 911 operator was no longer on the line. But I would be called upon for questioning, sooner rather than later.

I put the binoculars down, resting my arms for a moment. Then it hit me. The guards had gotten a call warning them about the police *before* the squad cars had been visible. That meant there must be a lookout somewhere. For a transaction like this, there almost had to be someone keeping watch. How could I have been so stupid? I started the van and turned around to look out the back window.

But it was too late.

Two big SUVs with tinted windows pulled up behind me. I was trapped.

A man sprang from one of the vehicles, gun drawn, yelling at me to put my hands up. I looked back; it was Terrence. I raised my hands.

No time was wasted on formalities. Before I could react, Terrence had yanked open my door and grabbed my phone, tossing it into the back seat. I wouldn't be tracked. Terrence grabbed me and hauled me out of the van, dragging me across the parking lot. A second guy with a gun had joined him, covering me, as if I posed any threat.

They were about to put me into the back of the closest SUV but were stopped by a voice from the second vehicle. "We'll take her," the male voice said.

Terrence changed course and dragged me to the other identical black GMC Yukon. He opened the door and, holding me around the waist, swung me up into the vehicle. He was incredibly strong.

I found myself on a jump seat, facing toward the rear. On a seat facing me sat two people, one I was surprised to see, and the other I was not. The surprise was presented by Eugene Wen, whom I recognized from his picture on the Internet. The man on the boat must have been a decoy. I was not surprised to see the second person, but I was profoundly, crushingly sad.

Rena Karros.

Chapter 53

"You don't look surprised," Rena said.

"Not surprised," I agreed. "I just feel like an idiot. A fool, for trusting you, for being your friend."

Her eyes flashed. "If you had really trusted me, if you had acted like my friend instead of a selfish cowboy, none of this would have happened."

"Was our friendship ever real?" I asked.

"Yes. I liked you. I could talk about my problems with you, without having to think I was competing with you."

The words stung and enraged me. She felt comfortable with me because I was too much of a nobody to be a competitor to her. "Sooner or later, I would have found out what you really are," I said.

"I saved your life. Terrence was going to kill you."

"So you interceded and told him to give me the Treatment instead? Gee, thanks."

"It was better than you deserved. You just couldn't leave it alone."

"You wanted me to close my eyes? To see no evil?"

"Evil," she scoffed.

"What else do you want to call it? You used Celia. You used her friendship. What was that, if not evil?"

She let out a short laugh.

"What's so funny?" I demanded.

"You and Celia," she said. "You hated each other so much. But you're so very much alike. Both naive to the bone. Both wanting to uphold some abstract idea of goodness, even if it hurts you and the people around you."

I glanced over at Wen, who wore earphones and was viewing something on a tablet or iPad, seemingly paying no attention to us.

"Why bid-rigging?" I said. "Why did you cross the line?"

"Self-defense. PTG had Shields in their hip pocket, and it was killing us. We kept losing out. Dick was demanding results. So were the board and shareholders. We had to do something."

"And that conversation you had yesterday with Westcott, where he accused you of slandering the company and told you to start looking for another job?"

"It never happened," she confirmed. "I made it up. One last attempt to throw you off track."

"You tried to get too cute," I said. "You should have had Adam bury all the footage of Celia, coming and going, and you should have removed it from the hotel's system, too. You just wanted to have something in reserve to hold over her—am I right?"

She didn't respond.

"The FBI told me Celia was not in on the bid-rigging scheme," I said, "but there she was at the hotel. So I'm guessing she was tricked into going to that one meeting by someone she trusted. A friend. Maybe a new friend at a new company. You."

She wouldn't look me in the eye. "Were you there that night?" I demanded.

She looked up, exhaled, and spoke. "Yes, I was there. I went up in the freight elevator—talked a nice maintenance man into taking me up. When the serious discussion about setting the next bid started, Celia just clammed up and wouldn't commit to anything. She didn't want any part of it. Afterward she read me the riot act and asked if I'd lost my mind."

"She had to be tempted to go to the Feds right away," I said. "She probably agreed not to, but only after you promised you would drop the idea of bid-rigging. But you weren't about to be stopped. You just passed along the plot to somebody else at your company, to Nick Edwards. And then you found a bigger idea, a technology theft scheme. You and Hammer, and probably Shields. Who had the connection with him?" I gestured toward Wen, and the old man looked up for the first time. He was listening after all, and the message from his expression was clear: Rena wasn't supposed to answer.

We rode in silence. We turned south on the I-5. I assumed we were going to an airport. "Where are we going?" I asked at last.

"I'm going to a new life," Rena said. "To hell with this company, with these people. To hell with this country."

"You're skipping," I said. "You're a crook, leaving your husband and fleeing the country one step ahead of the cops."

"Thanks to you," she said sourly.

She was right. Five minutes later and the transaction would have been completed. Nobody would have been able to prove anything. If the parties trusted each other, it still could have happened. And now, my chances of escaping this ordeal alive shrank to just about zero.

"How did Celia find out about your tech scheme?" I asked.

"I don't know," she admitted. "We kept the security very tight. A couple of months ago she told me she thought Nick Edwards was into something dirty. She asked if the bid-rigging scheme had been revived, and I assured her it hadn't been. Last week, she asked if Annette Barnes was into something. That's when I knew she'd stumbled onto our project. It was a $100 million deal, Pen."

I gasped, and she gave me a sour smile.

"Yes, it was huge. We called it Windfall."

"What was Stouffer's role?" I asked.

"He thought he was running the venture. What a fool."

"Terrence was working for you. And Wen. And Hammer. Not Stouffer."

She nodded.

"You took a chance, putting me onto the bid-rigging scheme," I said.

"Not really. It was a way to divert you. And of course it kept O'Shea and Hendricks busy. What connection was there between the bid-rigging and Windfall? None, except me. And Adam erased any proof of that."

"Wrong. Hammer was the other connection. That's how I found out about Windfall, by following him."

She shook her head. "He's such a sleaze." I thought I saw the faintest of smiles on her face, and I knew what she was thinking: *But a really likable sleaze.*

"Hammer called the police when Terrence was in my apartment," I said. "Why did he do that?"

"He did it because he likes you, and for no other reason."

I found that pretty much impossible to believe, and my face must have showed my skepticism.

"It's true," she said. "No accounting for taste. But it probably didn't make much difference. If there was ever a person stubborn enough to resist the Treatment, it would be you."

"So what happened with Celia?" I said.

"She was on to Annette Barnes, who was involved in Windfall. That's when I knew it was over. That's when I knew . . ." She hesitated, sighed.

"That you were going to kill her," I finished.

Rena shook her head sadly. "She was going to blow it all up. I couldn't threaten her with the surveillance footage from the hotel. She was willing to implicate herself. I still had hopes of talking her out of it. But I was kidding myself. I knew something had to be done."

"How did you get James's knife?"

"I didn't. She did."

"She—" Of course.

"I didn't know when she was going to act, to turn herself and us in," Rena said. "So last week I started following her."

"Why didn't you have Terrence do it?"

"He was in Minnesota."

"Ah, right. He was busy terrorizing and killing Stacy Ellis."

Rena ignored that. "After a couple of days, Celia began to get suspicious and took precautions against being followed, but I'd put a GPS tracker on her car."

"What happened the night of the murder?"

"She went up to James's house. She was probably looking for advice or support before going to the authorities. But James wasn't there."

"He was down at the boat with me."

"Yes. And she probably didn't call him ahead of time. She didn't want to call when you might be around."

"What happened then?" I asked.

"Celia let herself into the house." I felt a wave of jealousy sweep through me at the thought of her still having a key to James's house. "She came out a few minutes later. That's when I saw her put the knife in her purse."

"She was creeped out," I said. "Sensed somebody following her. Impulsively grabbed a weapon for self-defense."

"Probably something like that."

"So then she went to the boat."

"She was still looking for James. She probably didn't miss you two by much."

I looked out the car windows. We were still traveling south on the I-5. I glanced over my left shoulder and saw that Terrence occupied the shotgun seat up front. There couldn't be any doubt now that they were going to kill me—Rena seemed willing to tell me anything. But as long as she was telling, I figured I might as well keep asking. "What happened at the marina?" I asked.

"I followed her down there, and she went onto the boat. She knew the combination to the gate. Why she went there, I'm not sure. She must have known what kind of car James was driving and known he wasn't there."

I almost smiled. James had turned in his Lexus for a new BMW only a couple of weeks earlier. Celia didn't know what he was driving.

"Then," Rena continued, "I did an incredibly foolish thing. I parked on the street and then followed her onto the boat. It was idiotic; I might have been spotted by a witness, or a surveillance camera, although it was foggy and drizzly. Or James might have been there; I didn't know what he drove. It was stupid, but I did it anyway. The gate was ajar, almost like it was meant to happen. I couldn't help myself. By then I was beyond any thoughts about Windfall; it was just hatred for Celia. My blood was boiling."

"I'll bite," I said. "Why did you hate Celia? What was your blood boiling about?"

She looked at me with genuine puzzlement. "Why was I upset? *Why?* My God, girl, you are clueless." She shook her head. "How many hours have we spent talking over the past year, Pen? Haven't you gotten to know me at all?"

I was stumped. For the life of me I couldn't understand what she would have against Celia, whom she'd described as a friend and colleague. "Why?" I asked. "Why did you kill her?"

"It was about unfairness, pure and simple. I should have gotten the job of chief operating officer. I earned it. Celia took it instead. Dick simply handed it to her, undeserved, out of the blue."

I was stunned. Rena was general counsel of a Fortune 500 company at thirty-nine. And it wasn't enough.

"Let's be honest," Rena said. "Celia was competent. But she got the job at least in part because she was a minority. And meanwhile I was ignored, passed over, just as I'd been by the big law firms when I moved out here, who all thought I was a hick from Florida or a Southern sorority queen. It was a travesty."

"And for that Celia deserved to die?"

"Maybe. Maybe not. But I couldn't help myself. Westcott was blind to everything. He all but promised me the job, but guilty liberal that he is, he became enamored with Celia."

"That is a complete crock, Rena. You're rationalizing murder."

Her eyes flashed. "I was better than Celia. Westcott had lost any sense of actual ability and merit. He ruined me. I saw Celia, smug and undeserving and entitled and self-righteous, and I lost it. My rage got the best of me. On the boat we had it out. She admitted she was going to the authorities and coming clean about everything she knew. And she was going to warn off Barnes. That would have sunk Windfall. I couldn't let any of that happen. She wasn't going to screw me again."

She was lost in the retelling, transported back to the scene. "I pulled a gun and made her hand over the knife. Then I made her go below decks. And then I took my rage out on her. Over and over again. It was white-hot rage—I couldn't stop. I heard later that she crawled up to the deck—I don't know how she did that. Afterward, I just wiped down the knife, tossed it overboard, and went home. I had no thought that you or James might be blamed. I just kept waiting to be identified, by a witness or from a surveillance video. But it never happened."

"You'd let James go to prison?" I asked. "Or even be executed?"

"He seems like a nice man," she said. "Maybe even a good man. But I don't know him well."

"How about me? Would you let me take the fall?"

She shook her head in disgust. "I am the only reason you're still alive. Terrence could have killed you half a dozen times in the last week, and he wanted to do it."

My chest tightened. I knew it was true; Terrence had told me himself. "And so—what? You got him to back off?"

"Yes," she said. "I told him to go ahead and give you the Treatment, but nothing more. I don't know why I intervened. I guess I thought there was still hope for you, that you could still be my friend somehow. But that's all out the window now, Pen. You've ruined all of my plans. Because of you, I now have to leave the country."

"So when you kill me, you won't exactly be consumed by guilt."

This strange woman looked me in the eye—not Rena, not my friend—no one I'd ever seen before. "I won't feel the slightest guilt," she said. "When it comes down to my life versus yours, sorry, but mine comes first. And I have a lot more to contribute to this world than you do."

I sat back, stunned. How do you respond to something like that?

We turned off the freeway, and I tensed up. We were a long way south, and I didn't pay much attention to our destination, but I figured we were probably at Palomar Airport, near Carlsbad. We stopped at a gate, where the driver swiped a card through a reader to admit us to the airfield. We drove along a fence to a hangar, followed by the other SUV. I looked over at Rena; I thought I sensed her tense up, too. Only Wen seemed unperturbed, continuing to read his iPad.

I said, "Whose idea was Windfall, Rena? Yours? Hammer's?"

Wen glanced up from his tablet, his look disapproving.

"Is that subject a no-no?" I said.

Rena didn't say anything, but she gave me a withering look.

"They're going to get rid of me," I told Rena. "Is there any reason they shouldn't get rid of you, too?"

"Shut up," she said without conviction.

"I mean, you may have a lot to contribute to the world and all, but really, what can you contribute to Mr. Wen?"

She didn't answer, and I said, "You can contribute testimony against him, that's what. I don't know where you're going, but it could get pretty lonely, sitting in Paraguay or wherever, and you might just be tempted to make a deal, and—"

"Shut up!" she cried, serious about it this time.

"You're right," I said. "It will never happen. You're loyal to Wen and he knows it. True, you did turn against me, and Celia, and your husband, and Benning, and Westcott, and the other participants in Windfall, but Mr. Wen knows you'll never turn against him. You're close personal friends, obviously."

She leaned over and slapped me, hard across the face. I held my face, trying to clear the ringing in my head, and glanced at Wen. He didn't move, didn't change expression, and still read from his screen. I'd hate to play poker against the guy.

I began to wonder what they'd do with me. They obviously needed to leave right away; they might not have time to drive me to a remote area to dispose of me. Would they just leave my body in the hangar?

Suddenly I felt eyes on my back. I turned around and looked at Terrence.

"You're wondering, aren't you?" he said, smiling his weird smile. "You'll be coming with us on the plane, but you won't be landing with us."

I felt cold all over. "So you're going to . . ."

"Yes, we're going to throw you out of the plane."

I gave a little shriek. "My God. Can't you shoot me first, at least?"

"And mess up Mr. Wen's plane? Not a chance."

I looked over at Rena, whose expression was noncommittal. She had no problem with my being dropped into the ocean. Good God, who *was* this woman?

I started to hyperventilate. I pressed three fingers together, triggering the relaxation response my therapist had taught me. Within a few seconds I could breathe again, but beyond that, I was a mess.

Our SUV stopped momentarily. Then we proceeded into a hangar, followed by the other vehicle.

"You can't do this," I said. "Another cold-blooded—"

"Shut up!" thundered Eugene Wen, looking up from his tablet, red-faced. "Shut the hell up, you little pipsqueak. You've cost me millions." He looked around the vehicle in disgust. "I don't know what I pay these clowns for. They couldn't handle a cripple in a goddamned wheelchair."

I glared at him. The only thing I despised more than being called a cripple was being referred to as a "little" anything. How I'd love to put this guy in a supermax.

The vehicle stopped. The driver and Terrence each jumped out and opened a rear door. Wen and Rena got out first. Then Terrence grabbed me by the waist and pulled me out of the vehicle. He dragged me across the concrete floor and dumped me ten feet away, like a sack of garbage, next to a workbench. I looked across the hangar, which was empty. Another man had gotten out of the second vehicle and was pulling luggage out of the trunk. Wen and Rena stood a short distance away, conferring with Terrence and the guy who'd driven our SUV. A sleek corporate jet sat outside the hangar, visible through the partially open door. I pulled myself up into a sitting position, propping myself up with my hands.

The conversation broke up. Wen and Rena started toward the plane, then stopped cold.

Their path was blocked by Adam Rosenthal, who pointed a gun at them.

Terrence and the guy who was handling the luggage both went for their guns.

"Don't," said Adam. "Or I'll blow Wen's head off."

Wen slowly turned around and nodded at Terrence and the luggage guy, who reluctantly stashed their guns. Our driver didn't pull a gun; it wasn't clear whether he was armed. Meanwhile, nobody paid any attention to me, so I reached up to the workbench and began feeling around on top of it. I grabbed a screwdriver, then looked back toward the others. I still wasn't being observed, so I continued feeling for a better weapon.

Adam's expression was grim and determined as he held the pistol. "So this is the thanks I get, Rena? You skip the country and leave me behind after I've done your dirty work?"

So *that* was it, I realized. That was why Rena was having problems with Steve. That was why Pam thought Adam seemed distant lately. Adam had fallen for Rena and had done her bidding. And the revelation seemed to suck the last small bit of authenticity—the last morsel of humanity—out of the friend I'd known as Rena Karros.

"Nice try," Adam continued, "but you weren't answering your cell, and I just had a bad feeling about the setup for Windfall. So I made some calls and found out where Wen's jet was."

"You can come with us," Rena said to Adam, sounding to me as though she was improvising.

She must have sounded that way to Adam, too, because he rolled his eyes. "Now I'm supposed to trust you? It's a little late for that. I've burned all my bridges for you, thrown away my job, my political career, destroyed evidence. I did it for you."

I felt something heavy and metallic on top of the bench and pulled it toward me, inching it toward the edge. And then it fell off. I gave a little gasp as a heavy wrench landed, not on the concrete floor, but on my leg. No one noticed—my leg, and not the concrete floor, had absorbed the impact. I'd have a bruise, but of course it didn't hurt. And the cushioning—the silencing—of the fall had saved my life. I slowly propelled myself across the concrete floor to get closer to the action, periodically reaching back to drag the wrench behind me. I didn't see much chance of surviving this mess, but I didn't want to spend my last minutes cowering in a corner.

"Adam," Rena said, her gaze locking in on him. She gestured around the hangar. "You thought I was just going to leave you? We didn't have time to find you, that's all. Windfall blew up, and we have to get out of here. I still want you. And Mr. Wen knows he's obligated to you. We would have sent for you. You have to believe that."

"Give me a break. You've turned on everybody else."

"That's not fair, Adam. You're different. I . . . love you. You know that."

I listened to her and could almost believe it. Damn, she was good. Outside, the plane's engines fired up with a deafening whine. I dragged myself closer until I was at the back corner of the SUV. I could barely see the guy from the other vehicle, nor could I see Rena, Adam, Wen, Terrence, or our driver.

Our driver was standing right in front of me, but I could see between his legs. I glanced back at the guy from the other car. He was slowly reaching inside his coat.

"Adam!" I yelled, jerking my head around the front tire. "Look out!"

Adam noticed the gunman and fired. The guy went down. Terrence pulled his gun and shot Adam in the chest. Before Adam hit the floor, Terrence wheeled and shot Rena. I screamed. Now Terrence and the driver noticed me. Terrence aimed the gun, but I ducked back behind the tire.

I waited for Terrence to walk around the car. There was nowhere to hide. I could see Wen and the driver sprinting for the jet.

Terrence appeared, holding the gun, and slowly aimed it at me. "This is long overdue, you miserable little cripple. You trashed Windfall and cost me millions."

Lying on the concrete floor, I glanced underneath the vehicle and noticed a pair of feet, about twenty feet away. Terrence, following my eyes, looked over the hood of the vehicle and quickly swung the gun up in the direction of the feet. I lashed out with the wrench, hitting his leg as he fired. The person across the hangar fired twice, and Terrence went down beside me. I rolled away from him, screaming.

I fought off nausea as a figure came around the front of the car—John Gibson. He kicked the assassin's gun away, but Terrence, lying motionless with blood pouring from the side of his head, posed no threat. Gibson moved over to me, crouching behind the SUV as he helped me to a sitting position.

"I'm okay," I said.

"Any other hostiles?"

"Just Wen and his driver. They're both on the plane."

The hangar exploded with activity. Uniformed officers fanned out and secured the scene, followed by paramedics who attended to the four shooting victims. Rena was lying lifeless in a pool of blood. But I thought I saw Adam move. The driver Adam had shot was wounded in the leg but still conscious. Someone shut the plane's engines off, and the hangar's noise level now receded to a background buzz of shouted commands and crackling radios.

Gibson found a rolling chair next to the workbench and lifted me up into it. "I'll be right back," he said. He walked to the hangar door, stepped outside, and made a couple of brief calls. Then he began talking to a deputy. After a minute the conversation deteriorated into a shouting match. I couldn't make out much of what they were saying, but there were plenty of accusations and threats. After a couple of minutes the deputy stalked away. Wen and two other men were exiting the plane with their hands up when Gibson returned. "The deputies need to ask some questions now," he said. "Are you sure you're okay?"

I nodded. A detective in plain clothes appeared a minute later and asked a series of basic questions, mostly aimed at identifying the shooters and victims, and briefly reconstructing how everything had played out at the scene. I confirmed that Wen and his thugs had kidnapped me from my vehicle, but when the deputy began to ask for more detail on what had happened at the marina, Gibson gave him a sharp look, shaking his head.

"That's for Orange County sheriff and FBI," he said. The deputy reluctantly wrapped up the questioning and walked away.

"We're setting up a command post at the FBI office in Santa Ana to coordinate all these situations," Gibson said. "There will be more meetings and questions up there. You can come with me."

"I need to make a call first," I said. I borrowed his phone and called Lieutenant Dan Howard, reporting on Rena's confession that she had killed Celia. I'd hoped for an encouraging reaction, but Howard listened without comment, told me he would look into it, and said we should talk again that evening. I returned Gibson's phone. The hangar was still busy. Adam and the driver who'd been conscious were gone. The bodies of Rena and Terrence still lay on the floor, surrounded by crime scene personnel. I saw Rena and felt tears flooding down my face.

Gibson supplied me with a tissue and waited patiently while I composed myself.

"Are you ready?" he asked after a few minutes.

I nodded. "I need to leave now."

Chapter 54

"Is Adam going to make it?" I asked Gibson as we pulled onto the I-5 freeway.

"No."

I began to choke up but managed to pull myself together. "What was that argument you were having with the other deputy?"

"Just a little jurisdictional dispute." We rode in silence for about five minutes. "Are you up to filling me in?"

"I think so." I told him about following Stouffer to the marina, the transaction there with Eugene Wen, the intervention by the deputies, and our trip to Palomar Airport. He had already heard my description of what had happened at the hangar.

"Your turn," I said when I'd finished. "I left you a voicemail, and then you showed up with a posse at Palomar. What happened?"

"What happened is that I was stupid," he said. "I was at a meeting in Santa Ana, making plans for the bid-rigging sting, when your call came in. I didn't answer. I figured I'd call you back after the meeting."

"What was wrong with that?"

"What was *wrong?*" He turned toward me, a look of genuine distress on his face. "We almost lost you, Pen. Terrence was ready to shoot you. I barely made it. If I'd waited any longer, I'd have been too late."

"But you did make it—how did you get there so fast?"

"You didn't answer when I called you back, so I called the sheriff's department to see if they'd gotten any word of something going on down at the marina. Turns out they were on top of the situation. One of Wen's guys at the marina gave him up right away—even told them Wen and his accomplices were heading for the plane at Palomar. The deputies called their counterparts in San Diego County and alerted them. I asked where you were, and they said they'd found a handicapped van up on the hill but hadn't had a chance to check the rental records on it. They said that there was still a wheelchair in the back, so I figured Wen had gotten you." He took a long breath and exhaled. "It didn't sound good."

"What did you do?"

"I was driving south by then and put on the lights and siren. I blew past Dana Point and down to Palomar as fast as I could. When I got there, the deputies were already on the scene and setting up a perimeter, so I joined forces with them. The noise of the plane apparently covered our arrival and—well, you know how it ended."

"Not quite," I said. "You had a loud argument with that deputy at the hangar. It wasn't just a little jurisdictional spat, was it? The situation called for a SWAT team, not one FBI agent with a handgun. I saw your feet in the middle of the hangar. You had no cover—you just came in on your own."

He managed a weak smile. "Yeah, the sheriff's people weren't too happy with my cowboy act. But we heard the shots, and the SWAT team wasn't yet ready to storm the building, and I knew you were in there, so . . ."

"John, I don't know what to say. Except thank you for saving my life."

He waved off the thanks. "I was trying to make up for my stupidity. If I'd answered your call right away, I might not have had to cut it that close. And speaking of saving a life, I was standing out there in the middle of the hangar without a great line of sight or knowledge of the situation. Terrence came up firing. But he seemed to flinch just a bit as he fired.

And he missed. You hit him, didn't you? Probably with that wrench."

I nodded.

After a long moment of silence he said, "So we're even, right?"

I managed a smile through the tears. "And we're stuck with each other."

*   *   *

When we arrived at the FBI's resident agency in Santa Ana, two pleasant surprises awaited me: my rented wheelchair and my cell phone. "They need a little longer with your van," Gibson said, "but it should be here soon."

Gibson and I joined a group of agents and deputies for another round of questioning. I was excused from the meeting after half an hour. I had rolled down the hallway, looking for something to drink, when my cell phone rang. I answered.

"Howdy," said the voice at the other end. "Heard you had a hell of a day."

"Congressman Shields."

"You and I have some things to talk over, and I bet you haven't eaten yet."

I sighed, dreading the conversation and wondering what on earth he could want from me. "When and where?" I asked. He invited me to his club for eight o'clock that night. I accepted and hung up.

I found some bad coffee in the break room and drank it by myself for a few minutes before Gibson walked in and sat down across the plastic table from me.

"How are the interviews with the Windfall suspects going?"

"We haven't gotten much so far, except from the low-level guy who told us where Wen was," he said. "They've mostly lawyered up. Wen is demanding to talk to the Chinese consulate."

"Some of them will talk," I said. "They'll give up the others."

"I think so, too," Gibson said. "The people from the companies are pretty high-level, but they've had help from other people to access the technology and cover their tracks. Those are the people we need to find. They'll talk. The partners in the scheme were caught with tons of classified material, meeting with a foreign agent. So what are your plans?"

"Shields wants to meet with me."

"Why? Just to gloat?"

"Maybe. I just don't know. The meeting won't take long; I've got to go over to Newport as soon as I'm finished with him." I looked at my watch; it was a little before six. I was waiting for my lengthy statement to be transcribed, but I knew there would be a lot more questioning in the days and weeks ahead. I was anxious to get going, not only to move things along in Newport Beach, but to keep moving in general. I knew that as soon as I stopped moving, the horror of that afternoon would start to take hold in my brain.

We made small talk for several minutes before Connie Harper walked in. Gibson greeted her, then excused himself and left. Connie took a chair across from me. She just sat there for a couple of minutes, apparently trying to work up the courage to say something.

"I'm sorry," she said at last. I was impressed; this was a person not used to apologizing. "I'm sorry for the way I treated you. But Terrence . . ."

"He gave you the Treatment, didn't he?" Her haggard appearance and unprecedented sick days now made sense to me.

She nodded.

I reached over and took her hand. "I'm so sorry, Connie."

"I should have reported it immediately, but he . . ." She forced herself to go on. "He threatened to give it to my son." She gave a great, heaving sob, and tears streamed down her face. It was a full five minutes before she was able to compose herself.

Finally she said, "I always thought of myself as strong. I never, ever thought I could be just . . . broken like that."

"Everybody has a breaking point."

She nodded, then sat up, collecting herself. "I talked to Dave. He's pleased about the Windfall case, of course. It will be a while before we'll have enough information to make much of a public statement about it. In the meantime, you'll be coming back."

I was pleasantly surprised, if a little wary.

"Dave agreed to bring you back on board," she said, "but things may still be a little difficult."

"I understand." It may have looked like O'Shea had come out of today's proceedings smelling like a rose, able to trumpet the huge Windfall bust. But he'd apparently planned on either arresting or embarrassing his arch-foe Westcott as part of the bid-rigging scheme. That wouldn't be happening.

"I don't know whether I'll be back," Connie said. "I'll be taking a medical leave—then we'll just see what happens."

"Come back," I said. "Don't let Terrence win."

I thought she was going to break down again, but she just squeezed my hand and nodded. She said, "Sooner or later we'll have to decide what to do with Lisa."

I'd told Gibson Lisa was alive. "She went over to Shields."

Connie sighed. "Just as well." She started to get up, then sat back down. We sat there, looking at each other awkwardly for a few moments. Finally Connie nodded to me, got up, and left.

I wheeled back down the hall and found Gibson at the command post. We spent a few more minutes finishing the paperwork, and I left. My van was parked outside. I was waiting for the ramp on the van to extend when I had an intriguing thought.

I pulled out my phone and stared at it. What the hell, I thought. It was worth a try. I dialed the number.

"Hello?"

"Lisa, this is Pen," I said. "I have a proposition for you."

Chapter 55

When I had staked out the exclusive private club in Laguna Beach, I'd never imagined I'd be returning, only twenty-four hours later, as a guest. But here I was, courtesy of Congressman Latham Shields. On the way over, I'd called Lieutenant Howard, who told me he was still working on the information I'd given him and that he would have further questions, but not until tomorrow. He didn't anticipate any further developments tonight, which I found disappointing but not surprising. I thought I might stop over there anyway when I was done here at the club. And now I was about to have dinner with the person who probably had a more complete knowledge than anyone of all that had happened. The call I'd made before coming here had created the prospect of a most intriguing development, but for now I had to focus all my thoughts on the meeting with Shields.

I was in a small lounge in the rear of the club, sipping an excellent Chardonnay, when an efficient-looking young man walked in. I recognized him as one of Shields's security guys. He apologetically asked for my cell phone, which I surrendered. He then scanned me, my purse, and my wheelchair for recording or transmitting devices. Satisfied, he escorted me to an elegant but windowless private dining room where Shields sat, drink in hand, next to a person whose presence was depressing but predictable: Lisa Darden.

The congressman, looking expansive and relaxed, rose to greet me. He offered me his hand, which I reluctantly shook. Lisa didn't stand up, wouldn't look me in the eye.

"Lisa, you didn't have to do this," I said.

"Just butt out, okay?"

Shields put a soothing hand on her back. "Give us a little time here, would you, dear? We won't be long."

She stood up, gave me a resentful look, and left the room. She wouldn't be going far, I knew, since she'd left her purse on her chair.

Shields moved Lisa's chair away from the table to make room for me, then sat down. "Heck of a day," he said. "You doing okay?"

"I'm fine." I was anything but fine, of course. I'd had a clean shirt in a bag in the van, but Adam's blood was still visible on my trusty black Misook pants.

Menus sat in front of us on the table, and Shields picked his up. "I recommend the lamb chops," he said.

"I won't be eating anything," I said.

"It's been a long day. You must be hungry."

"I watched three people die today, including two good friends. I'm not in the mood. You asked to see me, Congressman. Why don't you tell me whatever it is you want to say?"

He slowly put his menu down, studied his glass, and took a sip. "Fine," he said. "We can play it any way you want."

I waited.

"I'd like to put this thing to bed as soon as possible," he said.

"If you're asking for an assurance that the bribery charges won't be reinstated, you know I can't give you that."

He waved away my statement. "Of course. I'm more concerned with the larger situation."

"It does keep getting bigger," I said. "A bid-rigging scheme. And now a technology theft ring. But I'm afraid the investigation is only getting started on those things."

"I thought maybe I could help your investigation."

"Why would you want to do that?"

He smiled. "You know I'm a law and order kind of guy."

I shook my head. "You're a one-man crime spree, Congressman. First the bribery, then witness intimidation and murder. And now Windfall. I should have known from the start it wasn't a Eugene Wen project, a Milt Hammer project, or even a Rena Karros project. The mastermind was you."

He smiled again.

"You know we're clean in here," I said. "No bugs, no wires. Keep it hypothetical if you want. But tell me why a US congressman would take money for running interference for a defense contractor."

He gave me a condescending smile, indulging my hopeless naiveté. But his expression quickly turned dark, brooding. "What it comes down to is this, Pen: I refused to be made a fool of. I refused to have people laughing behind my back."

I just looked at him, uncomprehending.

He said, "I saw all the money floating around the defense establishment—hell, government in general. The massive contracts. The lobbying fees. The perks. The junkets. The consulting fees. The board of directors positions. There's just so damn much money, there for the taking."

"So you succumbed to the temptation?"

He shook his head impatiently. "Don't you understand? *I will not be made a fool of.* I will not have everybody I see at parties getting rich, raking it in, being smart—while I fly coach, wear cheap clothes, and fill out a reporting form if a lobbyist wants to buy me a cup of coffee. I will not have these people laughing at the poor dumb schmuck Boy Scout." He pounded his palm on the table, his face getting red.

"It sounds as though in those circles, there's no greater crime than earnestness," I said.

He glared at me. But he didn't disagree. Larry Shields would never be convicted of a lack of worldliness or sophistication or savvy. He would never be a chump or a schnook. He would rather be seen as crooked.

"That attitude doesn't seem to have worked out too well for you," I said. "There was that small matter of the indictment."

He shrugged, as if a criminal indictment was merely a hassle, an unavoidable cost of doing business.

"So," I said, "you seem to have moved on to bigger and better things. Such as a bid-rigging scheme."

"Things like that do happen," he said. "And I knew some of the people who were involved. But I can tell you I was never a part of any such scheme."

"Your co-defendant, Milt Hammer, was."

Shields studied his glass. A waiter appeared with another drink for him and a refill for my wineglass.

"I tried to make things up to Milt," Shields said when the waiter had left.

"You felt responsible for Lisa going to the authorities."

He nodded. "I hired her. And—hell, I shot my mouth off in front of her when I'd had one drink too many. So when Milt and Lopez and I got into trouble, it was mostly my fault, even though I'd carried a lot of water for them over the years." He took a sip. "Yeah, I knew Milt was up to something with Westcott's company on the bids."

"And they cut you out."

He shot me an ugly glance. I'd scored, and he knew it. His expression changed to a sheepish smile. "Being made a fool of again. After all I'd done for these people. But I had nothing to add to that whole process, anyway. I was just looking out for their interests in general, trying to get the best specs I could, for whoever was in line to win the bid."

"So you decided to think bigger."

"It wasn't my idea."

"Did you approach Wen?"

"No, I was approached first."

"By Rena Karros," I said.

He took a long, thoughtful pull from his glass. "Rena wasn't a supporter of mine, of course. She worked for the other party. But I knew her—ran across her from time to time. She raised a fair amount of money from the same types of people I knew, mostly from the defense industry and big law firms. I ran into her after the indictment, and we talked about how much money was out there, and how she'd missed out on the big money when Westcott passed her over, and I'd missed out when I screwed up and got indicted. One thing led to another, and pretty soon we were talking about ways to cash in. It made a lot of sense. We tried to think big, to put together product from multiple sources and sell it as a package. She had the contacts among the defense contractors, and I knew Wen. We took it from there."

"But you both managed to keep your fingerprints off it," I said.

"I had to cut Milt in. Like I said, I sort of felt responsible for the trouble we got in, and I wanted to make it up to him."

"And make sure he didn't give you up and make a deal for himself on the bribery charges."

Shields didn't answer.

"I'm sure Milt appreciated it when you cut him in on Windfall," I said. "But he wasn't exactly counting on you. He turned against his fellow bid-riggers and gave them to O'Shea. He wasn't planning on going down for the bribery. And you had a backup plan, too. You managed to get the Windfall people to take care of Lisa."

"Rena knew a guy named Stouffer, from Horrey. She explained the idea to him, and he got the fever. I mean, he wanted in, bad. So did the other people he found. He sort of took over the project and ran with it."

"And provided you with an additional layer of insulation."

"True."

"So what about Lisa?"

"We did sort of dump the Lisa problem in their laps. We told Stouffer and the others the case needed to be taken care of if they wanted to do business with us. Milt had a conflict of interest on the deal, but the rest didn't care. They saw serious dollar signs. So the group took care of it "

"Not quite that simple," I said. "You steered them toward Terrence. Wen was connected to him."

"Terrence seemed like the kind of guy we needed. No violence unless it was necessary. And that Treatment of his—well, he said it worked every time."

"You didn't take any chances," I said. "You had Rena and Wen work on Adam, getting him to erase the evidence from the bid-rigging meeting, and then to leave his job right before trial. And then you had Terrence give Connie Harper the Treatment."

Shields nodded. "And things worked out pretty well."

"Just peachy, except for the innocent sister being terrorized and then murdered."

"That was a shame. We never intended that. Nobody was supposed to get hurt. That was the whole idea."

"It might have worked, if you hadn't used Terrence to try to give me the Treatment to solve Rena's problem with Celia. That's what linked the two cases and got me involved."

"I knew nothing about it. I never met Celia Sims. I didn't know Rena had any exposure on the bid-rigging plan. She told me she and Celia pulled out of it and Adam covered their tracks."

I took a long sip from my wineglass, scarcely able to believe that this congressman was confessing one crime after another to a federal prosecutor. But, as always, he felt smug and untouchable. "You had Terrence give the Treatment to Lisa's sister rather than Lisa herself. And afterward Lisa turns up here in California. Obviously something is going on."

"Really?" he said with a little smile. "And what do you think that might be?"

"Add to that the fact that Lisa steadfastly refuses to testify in any retrial. Why did you do it to Stacy and not Lisa, Congressman?"

"I think you know."

"Let's see," I said. "Killing Lisa wouldn't have been a good idea, even though you probably thought about it. The investigation would have been intense. It would have been risky—it's pretty hard to insulate yourself totally from a murder-for-hire. So then you settled on intimidating her. You had a guy who was very good at it. And you didn't want Lisa turning up in a really messed-up state, traumatized and scared to death, like Connie Harper did. Questions would be asked. So you decided to go at her indirectly."

He gave the slightest of nods.

"So Terrence went at Stacy. Seeing the effect on her was probably more than enough to convince Lisa not to testify. But why would she be back on your side again? Why wouldn't she be furious with you for getting her sister killed and trying to intimidate her?"

"Lisa had sort of a love-hate thing going with her sister. Stacy was a loser. She was a whiner and a parasite, with a taste for booze and bad taste in men. Don't get me wrong—Lisa was horrified when Stacy was killed. Frankly, so were we—it wasn't what we wanted at all. But she was tired of propping Stacy up."

I'd suspected something like that. "But there's more," I said.

He held his glass up to the light and studied it. "Yes, there's more."

I waited.

"As you may have guessed, things between Lisa and me are a little more complicated than she has let on. It wasn't just a case of her pig of a boss hitting on her. We have feelings for each other."

"You're married."

"My wife and I lived separate lives for a lot of years. We pretty much go our own way when it comes to relationships. At any rate, Lisa always knew she was welcome to return to me. She was very upset by Stacy's death, but she got over it. She decided to come home."

I tried to get my brain around what had happened. When Lisa left the message for Adam, stating her refusal to testify, she apparently had done it under duress, to prevent further harm to Stacy and herself. In Adam's words, she didn't mean it. But upon further reflection, with her sister dead and Shields apparently holding all the cards, she'd decided to cast her lot with him. "So where does all this leave you and Lisa now?"

"I suppose if you asked her, she would tell you she fully expects to become the next Mrs. Latham Shields."

Suddenly the windowless room seemed suffocating. I needed to get out.

"What if I asked you?" I said.

"I guess I'd be a little more cautious in my answer."

"I'll bet."

"Look, I'm not as big a cold-hearted bastard as you think I am. I didn't keep Terrence off of Lisa solely for selfish reasons. I'm genuinely fond of her. And down the line—who knows? We'll just see how things develop."

We were silent. Shields seemed, if not smug, at least content despite the collapse of Windfall. He'd shed his legal troubles and emerged with a loyal, un-traumatized mistress. And his profession still abounded with money-making opportunities. I had an overpowering desire to leave. But I needed to know something first. "Why are you telling me all this?" I asked.

"Because I need to know if I can expect any more trouble from you."

I found it hard to believe that this man actually saw me as a threat. There were ongoing investigations, and maybe some of them would be able to implicate Shields. But on my own, there was nothing I could do. "What do you want me to say, Congress-man? As far as I'm concerned, you're guilty of a lot of offenses. But I haven't been assigned to prosecute you for anything. And it's not like I have the wherewithal to work nights and week-ends on my own in a personal vendetta against you. Not that it wouldn't be a worthwhile endeavor."

He laughed, long and loud. "I'm glad you see it that way." He sat up and leaned forward, turning serious. "It's too bad you didn't adopt that attitude sooner."

I said nothing. What was he getting at?

"It's not as though you weren't warned," he said. "Terrence warned you. Lacey warned you. Hell, your own bosses tried to get you to back off. But you thought you were smarter than all of them. Smarter than me."

I stared at him, stunned. The jovial congressman had adopted a menacing tone, his face reddening. Jekyll had turned to Hyde.

He stood up, walked slowly around the table, and stood in front of me. "Who the *fuck* do you think you are?" he hissed. "You are nobody, a clueless little twerp, trying to act like a big shot. Screwing up my deal, trashing my financial security." He leaned forward. "Let me tell you how it's going to be: You are not going back to your job. Not now, not ever. And don't bother looking for a new job. Nobody will touch you—I'll see to that." He walked around behind me, leaning down, continuing to talk into my ear from behind.

"And that rich boyfriend of yours? You'd better not count on him. Rena confessed to killing Celia Sims, right?"

I nodded.

"Who witnessed the confession besides you? Terrence? Wen?"

I didn't respond.

"I know a lot of people in this town, Pen. The district attor-ney. Reporters and TV station owners. Judges. And I'm here to tell you, I'm calling in all my markers. All of them. Believe me, James Carter will never see the light of day. He's going down for murder, and I won't rest until it happens."

He grabbed the arm of my wheelchair and yanked it around violently. Now I was facing him. He grabbed both chair arms and leaned down, putting his face next to mine. "I told you, I . . . will . . . not . . . be . . . made . . . a . . . fool . . . of."

Whap. His hand came flying across my face. I gasped at the stinging blow. The congressman had *hit* me.

"How dare you—" I began.

Whap. He hit me again, his face contorted in fury. My head snapped backward and my vision blurred.

And then it was over. Hyde stood up and morphed back into Jekyll. His expression returned to normal. He straightened his tie, looking smug, invincible. He buttoned his suit jacket, paused briefly, and smiled. "Have a nice life, Pen." He turned and started for the door.

But when he opened the door, a man stood in the doorway: Special Agent John Gibson.

Shields gave him a puzzled look, then looked back at me. I said nothing.

He looked back. Two other men, obviously FBI agents, appeared beside Gibson, who said, "Congressman Shields, you are under arrest for bribery, espionage, theft, conspiracy, and accessory to murder."

"What the hell," Shields sputtered. Then he looked at Lisa's purse, still sitting on her chair, and he understood. "That *bitch.*"

One of the agents walked over and slipped the transmitter, disguised as a lipstick tube, from the outside pocket of the purse.

"And," Gibson added, spinning Shields around to face the wall, "let's not forget assaulting a federal prosecutor, you son of a bitch." He shoved the congressman hard against the wall, cuffed him, and read him his rights.

When they finished, Shields turned around and glared at me. "You just made a big mistake," he said.

"That sounds an awful lot like bluster, Congressman. You know, you shouldn't have called me a little twerp. Not a 'little' anything. I'm four inches taller than you are, anyway."

"We'll see you in the courtroom," he said. Despite the defiant words, his look spelled defeat.

I didn't respond, but I knew I'd never get the chance to prosecute Shields. If the case ever went to trial, I'd be a witness, not a prosecutor. But there would be no trial. Shields would plead guilty and make the best deal he could. This time there would be no hearsay testimony; no ambiguous motives; no complex accounting schemes. This time, we had his own plain words, admitting to many crimes and planning many more.

This time, we had him cold.

I followed the agents and Shields out of the dining room to the hallway, where Lisa Darden waited. When Shields stopped in front of her, she returned his gaze, looking him squarely in the eye. Neither said anything, and they took him away.

Lisa looked at me for a long moment, her face a complex mixture of sadness, anger, satisfaction, and fear.

"That was good acting when I came into the room," I said. "When you told me to butt out, I almost believed you."

"On some level, I did mean it. I was convinced that Larry was untouchable, that I'd never be safe if I left him. But when you called, you told me what I needed to hear: that we could put him away, once and for all. I thought of Stacy, dying alone in that horrible place, and I knew he had to pay." She leaned down and embraced me. "Thank you," she whispered.

"No, thank *you.*"

We disengaged, and she smiled, looking right at me. She was looking everybody in the eye now, including the person in the mirror.

Chapter 56

I sat alone in a conference room at Newport Beach police headquarters a little before midnight. Somehow I was still functioning at the end of Windfall, on the longest day of my life. Finally Detective Mary Kozlowski came in, and I spent the next half hour answering questions about Rena. Twice, Lieutenant Dan Howard stuck his head in the doorway, motioning Kozlowski out into the hallway for brief consultations. Finally Kozlowski completed her questioning.

"Can you wait here for a bit?" she asked.

I nodded. Waiting gave me time to worry about whether the police would take Rena seriously as a suspect. There were several reasons they might not.

To begin with, Shields had been right: Rena's confession to me had been hearsay; the police had only my word that the conversation had happened at all. More than that, it would be awkward and difficult for Howard and his department to admit they had arrested, and for the district attorney to admit he had charged, the wrong man. To top it off, identifying the real killer as a person already dead would be a most unsatisfying conclusion for both Celia's family and the public. It was like Oswald being killed by Ruby: no trial, no conviction, no punishment, no closure. The police had every motivation to dig in their heels, or at least to drag them, in looking into an alternative suspect after they had already filed charges.

I'd been alone in the room about half an hour when a grim-looking Howard walked in. My breathing grew shallow as I waited. The detective looked uncharacteristically disheveled, his shirtsleeves rolled up, his face stubbly. Without a word, he sat down across from me, exhaled, and looked me in the eye. "We got it wrong," he said. "Karros did it."

I felt tears well up in my eyes but managed to keep my composure.

Howard forced himself to continue. "The way she described it to you was consistent with all the evidence. We found traces of Celia's blood in her car. We did a cell phone check and can place her at the marina during the relevant time frame. But the clincher was a piece of evidence we held back from public disclosure."

I waited.

"There was a shoe print," he said. "A bloody partial print on the deck of the boat. It was badly smudged. It could have fit Celia's shoe, but we weren't sure. Theoretically it could also have been yours, but it was hard to imagine you leaving a shoe print, even one that unclear. It was a loose end, and it bugged us, but there was no other evidence pointing to anyone else, so we assumed it must have been Celia's. After you came to us with the tip about Karros, we executed a warrant on her house and found the shoe in her closet. The blood had dried on the bottom of the shoe, and she obviously hadn't realized she'd left a print. She had apparently gotten rid of the other clothes she was wearing that night."

He paused, stared down at his hands, then back up at me. "What can I say? We're human, we make mistakes, and we got it wrong. I knew it wasn't airtight, but all the evidence we had pointed to Carter, and the DA decided it was a go. I will extend my deepest apologies to Mr. Carter, as will the district attorney. We thought we had the right man."

I was relieved and also impressed. Even though the ultimate decision to file charges had been made by the DA, Howard's part in this high-profile mistake could be fatal to his career, forcing him into early retirement or worse. But he'd forthrightly assumed responsibility and acted promptly to rectify the error. Even though he was the man who had arrested James for murder, I found myself feeling sorry for him.

"We won't be able to complete everything tomorrow," Howard said. "There will have to be a lot of paperwork and meetings with the DA. We're looking at Saturday morning."

I nodded.

As I drove home to Long Beach, I reflected that plenty of follow-up remained. I needed to give a more detailed statement. Further searches—of Rena's house, office, and vehicles—needed to be done. More witnesses needed to be questioned. The blood found on Rena's shoe and in her car needed to be identified. The detectives would need to coordinate with the FBI, as well as the sheriff's departments in Orange and San Diego counties, in their investigations of the Windfall scheme, the bid-rigging scheme, and the shootings at Dana Point and Palomar Airport. But the end was in sight.

I let myself into my apartment, relishing the silence. My face and head throbbed. I was shaken up and exhausted beyond imagining. But the sun would be up in a few hours, and the new day would bring me closer to my reunion with James, and a life without fear. I sobbed uncontrollably.

Chapter 57

Saturday, March 14

I was up early, taking a long shower and fussing over my clothes. After a full day of rest, I felt a hundred percent better than I had on Thursday, even though I was making liberal use of Advil, makeup, and ice to treat my bruised, swollen face. At the kitchen table, I pulled up the news on my laptop and saw headlines on two sites, reporting that a major development in the Celia Sims murder case was imminent and a press conference was scheduled for noon at Newport Beach police headquarters. I was on my way out the door when my cell phone rang.

"Hello?"

"Pen? Dave O'Shea."

"Oh, hi."

"How are you feeling?"

"I'm fine, thanks." In truth, I didn't know how long it would take to recover from the exhaustion and the trauma of being slapped around and having guns stuck in my face. But now, less than an hour from seeing James, I was definitely fine.

"You did some gutsy things," O'Shea said. "Good job. We'll look forward to having you back, as soon as you're ready."

"Thank you."

The morning was overcast, the skies threatening, as I drove to the Orange County Central Jail Complex's Intake Release Center in Santa Ana. I found a handicapped spot on the street, got out, and rolled toward the entrance. My view was blocked by two television crews and by several other people who looked like reporters.

Eric Carter came out of the building first. "Thank you for coming," I heard him say to the little gathering. "We'll have only a brief statement here; the main event will be at Newport Beach at noon."

There were a couple of groans from the reporters. They crowded in even tighter and began firing questions.

I heard James's voice answering them. "I'll just say that I'm glad this mistake has been rectified, and I'm grateful that Celia Sims's killer has been identified—"

"Who? Who?" the reporters demanded.

Eric interjected, "We'll let the police and DA tell you about that."

James said, "I'm grateful for the support of so many friends and family, and I'm looking forward to going home."

"Mr. Carter—"

"James—"

Eric stepped forward to cut off further questioning. The reporters moved to the side as James made his way down the sidewalk, but they continued to shove cameras in his face and shout questions.

James didn't seem to care. He emerged from the group, spotted me, and began to walk purposefully toward me. Halfway to his destination, he broke into a trot.

And then we were together, smothering each other with embraces and kisses. I wanted the moment to last forever, but when I looked up, Eric was motioning for me to turn around, which I did to hide from the cameras. The reporters were asking me my name and my relationship to James, but I dodged the questions. By the time we reached my van, I had the door open and the ramp extended. Eric stepped between me and the cameras, shielding me as I transferred to the driver's seat. James stowed the wheelchair and took the passenger seat while the ramp retracted and the door closed. We drove away.

We went out for breakfast at a diner on PCH. James was amped up during the ride, relating rapid-fire anecdotes about his time in jail. We insisted that Eric join us, and the three of us took a corner booth. James and I ordered large meals, while Eric asked only for coffee.

James stared at me from across the table. "Nasty bruise," he said.

"I'll be okay."

"I wish I'd been there to shoot Terrence myself, the bastard."

Eric took a noisy sip from his steaming mug. "So," he said to me, "are you a hero or a goat at the US Attorney's office?"

"Officially, I'm fine. O'Shea called me this morning to check on me. But hero or goat? I guess a little of both."

"Are you kidding?" James said. "They should be giving you a medal or a citation or something."

"That's not how it works."

"No, it's not," Eric agreed. "Dave O'Shea has been telling reporters privately that the Dana Point bust is going to be huge, and he's promising a press conference in Washington within the week. Then, of course, there's the Shields arrest. However, O'Shea is reported to be very displeased about something, and no one is quite sure what."

I nodded, digging into a Belgian waffle with strawberry glaze. Eric didn't know about the bid-rigging scheme and the collapse of the sting, and I wasn't really at liberty to tell him.

"I saw you avoiding those reporters—why are you so publicity-shy on this?" Eric asked me.

"It's a long story."

"A story that might have something to do with O'Shea's mysterious displeasure?"

I nodded.

"I'll continue to do my best to keep your name out of this. But we'll have to make James available in the next day or two."

"No problem," James said.

Eric reached into his inside jacket pocket and produced an envelope, which he handed to James.

"What's this?" James asked.

"A little something to celebrate your freedom."

With a quizzical look, James took a single sheet from the envelope. I tried to look over his shoulder; it looked like an itinerary from a travel agency.

James's mouth opened in shock as he read from the sheet. "Alicia."

"She'll be arriving at one," Eric said. "For the rest of the weekend."

James looked up in astonishment. "How on earth—"

"—did I get Anita to agree to this? It was her idea."

"No way."

Eric nodded. "Way. I told you, although it seemed counterintuitive at the time, that it was smart to move out here. It gave everybody some distance and breathing room. Anita doesn't feel cornered and threatened. You let her feel as though she won."

James stared at the travel folder, fighting to stay composed.

Eric finished his coffee and stood up. "I have to get going."

"Not so fast, big brother." James stood, and the two of them embraced. "Thanks," James said. "For everything."

Eric leaned down and hugged me. He looked up at James. "She's the one you should be thanking."

Eric left. James and I ate silently for a while, feeling an awkwardness settle over us. I put my fork down. "Maybe we should talk someplace else," I said.

"No," he replied. "I can't wait. I need to say something."

"So do I." We looked around. It was now mid-morning, and the restaurant wasn't crowded.

"All I could think of while I was sitting in jail was how big a fool I'd been for seeing Celia without telling you. I kept wondering whether I'd totally blown it. Can you trust me again?" James asked.

"I never stopped trusting you."

He looked relieved but a little skeptical.

"All right," I admitted, "so I did want to sort of throttle you a little, but I still trusted you."

James laughed. After a few seconds I joined in, and the tension was broken.

He took my hand. "I just . . . well, I explained it to you before. I just didn't want to take any chance of giving you the wrong idea."

"Do you have any idea why she came looking for you that night, at your house and then the boat?" I asked.

"She wasn't looking for me."

"What?"

"She was looking for you, or at least for both of us."

"Me? But why?"

"Celia called that morning. We talked about the Sherrod deal with Westcott. The deal wasn't looking good, but I was pressing for a final answer. I'd been communicating through Celia about the deal. So we talked about Sherrod for a while, and then she drops the bomb on me. She told me that last year she'd been tricked into getting involved in some kind of scheme that was probably illegal and that she hadn't reported it. She was ready to blow the whistle on it and accept the consequences. She didn't give me the specifics, but I could tell she was scared. She wanted to make the approach to you about it."

I couldn't speak.

"I encouraged her to do it," James continued. "But I said you were having a serious problem at work and to give you a couple of days. Apparently she decided during the day that she didn't want to wait."

"Why on earth would Celia pick me to handle something so sensitive?"

"She'd seen you in action—knew she could trust you."

"I'm so embarrassed about pressuring you to cut off Celia and her whole world. I should have trusted you. And the way I acted toward Celia—the things I said . . . I feel about two inches tall, especially now, after finding out she wanted to come to me when she needed help."

"She told me the same thing about her feelings toward you," he said.

"I wish we'd had the chance to say it to each other."

James looked at me. "Celia's funeral is Monday. Will you go with me?"

"Of course," I said.

"Thank you."

We left the restaurant, pulled out onto PCH, and headed down the coast toward Laguna. "Why don't we stop here?" James said. We were passing Crystal Cove State Park.

I pulled in, and we drove over to the parking lot and got out. The morning fog had cleared, and a hazy sun warmed us as James pushed me along the gravel path above the ocean. We paused in a particularly scenic spot, watching the waves and the gulls and a few surfers.

We said nothing for perhaps five minutes.

"You've always held back a part of yourself from me," he said at last.

I opened my mouth to protest, but he held up his hand to stop me. "I understand," he said. "You had a fiancé dump you and an employer fire you because you were handicapped. Then you had a boss hire you in order to set you up for a corporate scandal. And now Rena, one of your closest friends, betrayed you. Why the hell should you believe I'm for real?"

"I've found it hard to accept that you'd want me," I admitted. "The past year hasn't seemed real. I keep waiting for you to wake up and realize who I am."

"I know who you are," he said. "I know you're the woman I love. You're in a wheelchair. I don't care."

"I know you don't. I get that now."

He gave me a curious look. "You do?"

"I know," I continued. "I know why you never managed to hire any of those high-powered defense attorneys Eric set you up with. These guys have a lot of ego. They charge a ton of money, but they insist on calling the shots, and they're in it to win. Every one of them told you that your only realistic trial strategy—your best chance of creating reasonable doubt—was to point the finger at me, the other leading suspect in Celia's murder. They could have easily found some so-called expert to claim the stabbing actually took place up on deck, or that I could somehow get myself up and down those steps on the boat. And of course, I had a motive."

He crouched down next to my chair and looked into my eyes.

"But you wouldn't do it," I said. "You told every one of them no. You were willing to risk a murder conviction for me. My God . . ." I couldn't go on.

He reached over and embraced me tightly as the tears flooded down my face. "There was no risk," he whispered. "I knew you'd figure out who killed Celia."

Eventually I calmed down. James produced a couple of tissues, which I used to wipe my face. He started to pull his hand away, but I hung onto it tightly. "It's been a roller coaster," I said. "We did things to hurt each other, then we did things to make up for it. Maybe we just need to catch our breath."

He nodded. Then he stood up, looked around, and glanced at his watch. "Okay," he said. "I've caught my breath. You?"

"Totally." He leaned down and kissed me.

"Reconciliation for Type A's," he said.

"It's the only way," I said. "Our way."

AN INVITATION TO READING GROUPS/BOOK CLUBS

I would like to extend an invitation to reading groups/book clubs across the country. Invite me to your group and I'll be happy to participate in your discussion. I'm available to join your discussion either in person or via the telephone. (Reading groups should have a speakerphone.) You can arrange a date and time by e-mailing me at brian@brianlutterman.com. I look forward to hearing from you.

Not Sure What to Read Next?
Try these authors from Conquill Press

Jenifer LeClair
The Windjammer Mystery Series
Rigged for Murder
Danger Sector
Cold Coast
Apparition Island
www.windjammermysteries.com

Chuck Logan
Fallen Angel
www.chucklogan.org

Brian Lutterman
The Pen Wilkinson Mystery Series
Downfall
www.brianlutterman.com

Steve Thayer
Ithaca Falls
www.stevethayer.com

Christopher Valen
The John Santana Mystery Series
White Tombs
The Black Minute
Bad Weeds Never Die
Bone Shadows
Death's Way
www.christophervalen.com

Coming Soon
The Darkness Hunter by Christopher Valen
Broker by Chuck Logan
For more information on these titles go to:
www.conquillpress.com